THE HEART OF WAR
MISADVENTURES IN THE PENTAGON

D1357914

A NOVEL BY
KATHLEEN J. McINNIS

Post Hill
PRESS

A POST HILL PRESS BOOK
ISBN: 978-1-68261-651-2
ISBN (eBook): 978-1-68261-652-9

The Heart of War:
Misadventures in the Pentagon
© 2018 by Kathleen J. McInnis
All Rights Reserved

Cover Design by Cody Corcoran

Post Hill Press
posthillpress.com

Published in the United States of America

For Krysten
and
the Action Officers in the Pentagon,
working every day to keep us safe

CHAPTER ONE

"ARE YOU SURE THIS IS SAFE?" I screamed over the noise of
the whirling blades to the sergeant to my left. His machine gun
pointed outward into the dusty, blue beyond, looking for anyone—
or anything—that might use our helicopter for target practice. It
was a stark reminder of the precariousness of our situation. Then
again, war zones aren't exactly garden spots.

The sergeant shrugged and tapped his helmet. *Can't hear you.*

Great. I briefly flirted with the idea of trying to communicate
my question through crude gestures and pantomime. But then I
realized that doing so would involve prying my white-knuckled
hand off the side of the Chinook—an even dumber move than
sitting there in the first place.

This is not what I signed up for when I joined the Pentagon. Hell, if
you'd told me a couple years ago that I would be hanging onto the
side of a helicopter for dear life while flying over Afghanistan, of
all places, I would have called you certifiably insane. Professors
of International Relations with pacifist streaks usually tend to
avoid battlefields. Not to mention organizations that kill people
and break things.

Careful to keep my grip on the helicopter, I peered down between my boots at the brown baked mountains of the Hindu Kush which were peppered with dried scrub brush and the occasional cluster of homes. The villages grew more frequent, eventually merging together as we flew and forming the outskirts of the city of Kabul. And although the mountains themselves looked like they were made of dust as fine as powdered sugar, somehow the houses clung halfway up the slopes and squeezed themselves into narrow valleys before spreading open into the city itself.

I couldn't help but reflect on the fact that hundreds of feet of air were all that was separating me from the streets below. Or that hunks of metal weighing forty tons shouldn't be airborne.

My helmet—which would have suited a Neanderthal—slid over my eyes. I didn't want to release my death grip on the helicopter, but there was a decent shot it would fall off my head if I didn't adjust it. A flash of horror crossed my mind as I thought of the Afghans below—shopping, attending mosque—suddenly having their daily lives interrupted by a helmet plummeting from the sky. Or, for that matter, the crash landing of a certain young American woman who was stupid enough to sit off the back of a Chinook.

I jerked my head up and backwards to slide the helmet back into place and felt it whack the back of my neck. Able to see again, I looked off into the distance and saw a black speck floating behind us. I could just make out another helicopter's long barrel shape and dual rotors. Looking from the city below to the hills in the distance, now partially shrouded in late afternoon haze, I remembered my brother Jon's interpreter talking about his homeland in his lightly-broken English. *We could make it beautiful again,* he said, *if only there were peace.*

If only. How many more people would give their lives for a dream of peace that warlords and terrorists were constantly shattering? Was it really worth it? Or would the consequences—leaving the Afghans to themselves—be even more terrible? All I knew was that after my brother Jon died, I swore I'd never risk life and limb for near-hopeless causes in countries on the other side of the world. But now I was doing exactly that, in exactly the place Jon lost his life.

A hand waved to my left. The sergeant was shouting something, but between the wind and the earplugs I was wearing, I couldn't make out a word. So he opted for a different form of communication: pointing emphatically to something, or someone, behind me.

I noticed my hands were cramped as I turned around. Another soldier was beckoning me to move off the edge of the ramp and back into the bright orange jump seats in the body of the aircraft. I was simultaneously awash with relief and panic; relief at the prospect of getting off the ledge and into relative safety, panic because I had no idea how to do so without falling out of the damned thing. My body armor was enormous—presumably designed to match the Neanderthal-sized helmet—which meant that my center of gravity was hopelessly thrown off. This wasn't going to be pretty.

I closed my eyes and grimaced as I realized what I had to do. All shreds of my carefully crafted dignity, bravado, and poise evaporated as I allowed the soldier to drag me by my armpits back into the craft. I could feel the soldiers snickering as I crawled on my hands and knees like a baby while making my way to the jump seats, finally clambering ass-first into my seat. If I'd managed to cultivate an air of authority, it was dead and gone by now.

Whatever. I doubted any of these soldiers would be in my meetings at our embassy in Afghanistan. And besides, I'd never been so grateful to sit in such a desperately uncomfortable seat in all my life.

The rear door, on which I had previously been perched, closed as we descended into Kabul International Airport. Without seeing where we were out of the back, and without any real windows in the fuselage, it was suddenly dark and claustrophobic. As we descended, I could feel everyone in the helicopter tensing as reality hit home: we were all trapped in a massive metal box that was about to touch down in a war zone.

I felt the Chinook land and then move along the runway. After several minutes of darkness, my eyes were shocked by the sudden brightness of the Kabul sun peeking in through the reopening cargo door. One by one, we jumped out the back and made our way to the meeting point—a quaint yet dusty little rose garden near the side of the Kabul airport.

I squared my shoulders as I walked across the tarmac. Diesel and dust and jet noise and an unbearably sticky heat emanated from the airplane engines and the black, cracked pavement. Despite my earlier humiliation, with the rotors turning, military planes landing, surveillance drones taking off…it was hard not to feel like a badass. I was reminded of Sunday afternoons watching *Top Gun* with Jon. It was a genuine, Tom-Cruise-walking-down-the-flight-line, "Highway to the Danger Zone" kind of moment as the U.S. military's finest— and heaviest—machinery whirred around me.

That is, until I happened to catch a glimpse of myself in the airport's mirrored window. My curly blonde hair—the parts that were sticking out from underneath the helmet—were so blown out that I resembled a metal rocker circa 1985. My mascara was streaked, my eyes were bloodshot from sleep deprivation, and my suit jacket was hopelessly wrinkled by the body armor. My pants were streaked with oil stains.

As I contemplated the unfortunate fact that I looked like a blonde Gene Simmons, I heard a familiar voice to my right.

"Heather?" It was my colleague Royle.

His voice—his presence—sent a shiver of nervousness through me.

It was the first time I'd seen him in his army combat uniform instead of the dress blues he wore around the Pentagon. But it wasn't his attire that made him seem different. Rather, his shoulders were less tense, his gait more relaxed. And despite the fact that he seemed to be turning a bit red in the face, he looked more comfortable at that moment—on the ground in an urban war zone—than at any time I'd seen him in Washington, D.C.

He opened and closed his mouth a couple times before finally saying, "Leopard print?"

"Leopard print?" I asked, wracking my brain to figure out what he was talking about.

"You might want to…" Royle said, pointing downwards, blushing. "Nevermind." He turned around, abruptly ending our conversation and walking to meet an Afghan in a grey-green uniform carrying a Kalashnikov.

I looked down toward my shoes as I entered the rose garden. Nothing out of the ordinary there. *Maybe he's referring to the oil spots on my pants?* It was only when I removed my body armor that I realized that my fly was down, a button was open, and my panties were now on display for the whole world to see. *Fantastic.*

Why am I here again? I asked myself, not for the first time.

Oh, right. Because I was the one who recommended to the Secretary of Defense that we go back to war.

CHAPTER TWO

Three months prior...

IT DAWNED ON ME THAT SOMETHING WAS AMISS WHEN I CLIMBED THE ESCALATOR OF THE PENTAGON METRO STOP FOR THE FIRST TIME. It was a cloudy day, and the muggy June heat had turned the metropolitan D.C. area into the steam room of a particularly musty men's locker room. Unfortunately, as I felt the blast of oppressively humid air while rising to ground level, it occurred to me that I'd forgotten my deodorant that morning. I was wearing my new outfit—a black pantsuit with a white button-up shirt—which was both a blessing and a curse. A curse because I was wearing several layers, making me sweat even more; a blessing because my jacket would hopefully keep the stink from escaping. Gross, but probably manageable once I got back into the air conditioning—as long as my new colleagues gave me plenty of personal space. And as long as I didn't lift my arms.

Even more nagging than the smell: an unknown number had left a voicemail for me while I was underground in the metro. Somehow, I just knew it wasn't going to be good news.

*"Heather, it's Robin from DASD Townfield's office. There's been, well…
how do I put this? There's been a change of plans. Look out for an Air Force
colonel named Tom Voight. He'll be picking you up."*

Uh-oh, I thought. *Why would a colonel be escorting me?* A feeling
that was not unlike being called to the principal's office nestled in
my stomach. I tried calling back. No answer. *Is it possible to be fired
before I even start?*

Although anxious, a very small part of me felt relieved. Maybe
this was the universe telling me that working in the Pentagon wasn't
in the cards?

Figuring the colonel must be waiting for me inside, I took a
deep breath and found my way to the end of the visitor's line,
which snaked through stainless steel barriers across the pristine,
white pavement. Despite the tented white awnings intended to
shield us from the sun and heat, the temperature was at least eighty-
five degrees and I felt sweat dripping down my back.

I looked around to orient myself. I was standing at a visitor's
entrance, but I still had no idea where the actual Pentagon was. It
took me a minute of staring before I realized that the massive wall
in front of me *was* the Pentagon. It was long, at least the length of
a city block, but it was also squat, only five or so stories tall. Yellow-
tinted windows punctured the grey granite wall, as if the building
itself was some sort of ghastly jack-o'-lantern, sitting in the gloom
of the muggy morning.

A wave of somber commuters climbed the escalators and
shuffled past me to enter the building. The ones that were not in
military uniforms all wore dark-colored suits, the men with either
red or blue ties. They shuffled their way through the station's exit
in a sort of strange, disturbing unison. Almost all of them were

men in their mid- to late-forties, looking a little paler than what's normally thought of as healthy, and clinging tightly to their travel coffee mugs and faux leather "executive portfolios" that my best friend Amanda called the "old man's Trapper-Keeper."

At least if I'm fired, Amanda will get her apartment back to herself again, I thought.

The line crept forward and I fiddled with my engagement ring. Despite the thick haze of humidity blanketing the area, the small diamond managed to sparkle. I fished my phone out of my purse and dialed Ryan.

"Babe," he answered, groggily. "What time is it?"

I looked at my watch. "It's eight fifteen here. So, five fifteen where you are? I'm sorry to wake you, but I just needed to hear your voice."

I could hear Ryan stretching beneath the sheets as he flirted with consciousness. "What's the matter?"

"I don't know. I just, I think something's wrong."

"It's probably just first-day jitters, right?"

"Sure." I shuffled forward, inching closer to the visitor's entrance.

Ryan's voice became more alert. "You know, you don't have to do this. You can turn around now and be on a plane back by noon."

"Right." I stifled a heavy sigh, wary of a repeat of the same conversation we'd had over and over again.

As tempting as it was to walk away, it really was too late. It was difficult enough to make ends meet in San Diego on an academic salary, but with my student loans, it would mean running off a financial cliff. But Ryan knew that already. He just didn't want to accept it. Part of me didn't want to, either. I was about to spend a year in the U.S. government's war headquarters, and the only reason

I could sleep at night was because I was going to be working on a peace plan for Afghanistan.

Ryan let out a small laugh.

"What's so funny?"

"I was just thinking about when I met you. Back in college."

I smiled. "My younger self would be having conniptions if she saw me now."

"Undoubtedly. But you always manage to figure out the right thing to do. You always have. That's why I love you so much."

"And you always manage to make me feel better. Stronger. That's why I love *you* so much." The line lurched promisingly. "I'd better go. I'm just about to the entrance."

"About to cross the Rubicon, eh?"

"Guess so."

"Well, good luck bringing peace to the war machine. And just remember: I'd be thrilled if you came home tomorrow."

I hung up the phone and stepped into the visitor's entrance. My heart skipped a beat as a thought washed over me with the intensity of a tsunami: I was entering the most powerful building on earth. The headquarters of the United States Department of Defense. Home to the leadership of the most powerful military in the history of the world.

The Pentagon.

Everything I'd heard about the building flashed across my mind. Within the walls directly ahead, the United States government formulated strategies, directed operations, purchased tanks and aircraft, and made decisions that affected people all over the world. It was where military advice to President Callahan was formulated. It served as home to the military services of the United States—the Air Force, Army, Navy, and Marine Corps.

The place that ordered my brother to go to Afghanistan. Where he took his last breaths.

The deluge of nervous energy suddenly broke and gave way to pangs of sadness, with a twist of anger. *Ryan was right*, I thought. *I am crossing the Rubicon.*

I squared my shoulders and braced myself as I passed through the heavy, honey-colored doors of the Pentagon. This was, after all, where the world's most sophisticated technology was married to the world's most powerful military forces. I prepared myself to see the world maps depicting where U.S. troops, seamen, and airmen were stationed. Sleek, bright, white computer terminals running the most high-tech software on the planet. Retina scanners and body sensors and touch screens that could link everyone in the Pentagon to any location in the world. Telltale signs that I was entering the nerve center of the U.S. government's very own Death Star.

Instead, it looked like a regular office building. I blinked and furrowed my brow. Polished, grey concrete floors and sterile, white walls were cast with a nauseating, slightly greenish hue by the fluorescent lighting. As I watched more zombie-like Pentagon workers shuffle through the next set of security barriers and off to their offices in the great governmental beyond, I realized that I was standing in the center of bureaucratic purgatory. The only difference between this place and any other office building was the disproportionate number of people wearing military uniforms wandering in and out.

I was underwhelmed.

I looked around. A busy reception area with rows of black seats was just off to the left. A group of reasonably well-behaved school children took over the back, while the seats were dotted by small clusters of office drones, most of which were leaning in conspiratorially and speaking in hushed tones.

I was just fishing out that week's edition of *The Economist* from my purse when I saw a man who looked a bit like my brother Jon out of the corner of my eye. The man—who was now looking in my direction—had roughly the same height, lean build, and close-cropped, dusty dark blonde hair as Jon. But this man was older, with more ruddy cheeks and deeper-set wrinkles. And instead of an Army uniform, his was Air Force blue. My heart skipped a beat before I realized, just like every other time, it wasn't Jon. The inevitable sharpness of disappointment settled in, a needle that stabbed my heart.

He walked up to me, close enough that I could see his forearms were covered with thick, light blonde hair and the freckles and moles that follow age and plenty of sunshine. The lapels on his shirt announced his rank: full-bird colonel. "Dr. Reilly?"

"Yes," I said. "How did you know?"

The man chuckled as his eyes scanned the rest of the room. While there were two or three other women in the waiting area, I was the only one not a part of a group. "Ah," I said. "Gotcha. I take it you're Colonel Voight?"

"That's what the name tag says. But please, call me Tom. Or Voight. Or Marsh. Whichever you prefer. Just not 'sir,'" he said.

"Marsh?"

"My call sign. I hate formalities."

I raised my eyebrows in surprise. Jon spoke about the colonel he served under in Afghanistan with the distanced reverence most people normally reserved for talking about the good Lord himself. I always figured colonels were supposed to be serious, straight-laced people that announced their rank as often as possible.

Kind of like academics.

"How about I call you Voight, if you drop the 'doctor'?" I said.

"Sounds like a deal. Now, let's get you badged up," he said, turning to lead me to yet another security desk. I noticed a large, slightly off-kilter American flag as we walked.

"What's with that flag? Something about it doesn't look right," I said.

"It's a quilt. The faces of the fallen," Voight said. "Each square has a picture of a person that died here on September 11th."

"Oh," I said, surprised that a place like the Pentagon—that treated money as no object and people as cogs in a machine—would have such a visible reminder of human loss and suffering in its entryway.

"My buddy is on one of those squares," Voight said, his voice laced with that hushed restraint that goes along with painful memories. "Went to flight school together."

"I'm sorry." I was unsure of what else to say. Especially after Jon's funeral, condolences always felt artificial to me. Constrained. Losing someone you love leaves a painful and profound void, and saying, "I'm sorry for your loss," is like a Band-Aid after open-heart surgery.

"Yeah, well," Voight said, clearing his throat as we stepped onto a set of escalators. "Life goes on. Or at least, that's what they tell me."

"Know the feeling," I said.

Voight raised his eyebrows and nodded but said nothing as he briefly lost himself in thought. "You'll need to give the good gentleman behind the desk your ID so you can get your visitor's badge," Voight said, snapping back into the moment as we joined yet another line.

Visitor's badge? Not an employee's badge?

"Look, is there some kind of problem with my contract that I'm not aware of?" I asked while handing my ID to the man behind the counter.

Voight looked at me with a strange combination of apprehension and curiosity, and I could feel the blood drain from my face.

"I take it you weren't informed of the reorg?" Voight finally said.

"Reorg?"

"I take it that's a no," he said, frowning.

I collected my bright yellow badge from the attendant and we started walking. Voight swiped through the waist-high security barriers while a guard let me through, and then we stepped onto a set of escalators.

"Where do I start?" Voight continued, rubbing his chin and moving out of the way of the escalator traffic. "That's one of the many frustrating things about this place—they're always reorganizing. This is the third one I've gone through in two years. I'm beginning to think that all of these reorgs are part of an elaborate counter-espionage strategy. How can any foreign intelligence agents know what we're doing when *we* barely know where we're reporting to work every day?"

"Okay, but I'm not following. What does all this have to do with me?"

"I really have no idea how to put this to you, Heather." We stepped onto an escalator taking us up to the next floor. "But the bottom line is that your position got shuffled in the reorg."

"Shuffled?" I asked, feeling the early stirrings of acid reflux.

"So, one of the things you should know about this place is that it's actually easier to deploy the Fifth Fleet to the Pacific than it is to hire someone."

"But the Fifth Fleet is based in the Middle East," I said.

"Exactly. It either takes an act of Congress or divine intervention—or both—to become a gainful employee of the Office of the Secretary of Defense," Voight said.

"Why? Are there budget cuts or something?"

"Sort of. There's *always* budget cuts. But I'd say this is more like the unholy marriage of budget cuts and bureaucratic dysfunction. What matters to *you* is that when they did the reorg, they looked at your billet and decided that it was one too many in Central Asia."

"What? Why?" I could feel myself on the verge of a panic attack, my mind racing, brainstorming escape options. But the facts hadn't changed in the ten minutes since I'd spoken to Ryan. It was simply too late to go back to San Diego.

"Because the war's over. We've withdrawn our troops—or most of them, anyway. They don't need as many people in that office anymore."

"Has anybody bothered to tell the Taliban the war's over?" I said. "Or the Islamic State? There's a *civil war* going on over there."

"Hey, don't shoot the messenger."

"Let me get this straight. You're telling me I don't have a job here anymore?"

"Well, you see, I have good news and bad news on that front. The good news is that your paperwork was *way* too far along to cancel. So you have a job."

I breathed an audible sigh of relief as the prospect of bankruptcy faded.

"Don't get too excited. The bad news is that you're now working in Deputy Assistant Secretary of Defense Ariane Fletcher's office. Pronounced 'ari-AHN.' Or, more precisely for our purposes, 'Ma'am.'"

"Ari-AHN Fletcher?"

"You've never heard of her?" Voight asked, stopping in his tracks.

"Should I have?"

Voight chuckled. "That's okay. You'll find out what she's like soon enough. Anyway, Fletcher's in charge of the newly re-established office for Coalition Affairs."

"Re-established?"

"It was disestablished three or four reorgs ago, apparently."

"Why didn't Mr. Townfield tell me what was going on?"

"He probably figured someone else had told you."

"And the admin people?"

"Probably figured Mr. Townfield told you."

"So what *is* my job supposed to be?"

"Beats me. I think DASD Fletcher is figuring that out now."

I paused while massaging the bridge of my nose. "Am I the last person on earth to know that my job has been fundamentally changed?"

"Seems like it," Voight nodded. "But don't worry. That seems to be par for the course around here. The last person to know what's going on is usually the only person who is directly affected."

"Who can I contact to fix this?"

"Good luck with that."

"But I was going to spend my fellowship helping develop a long-term peace plan for Afghanistan. Aren't coalitions totally different?"

"Well, yeah," Voight mused. "Military coalitions tend to kill people and break things. Peace plans—at least in theory—stop people from killing each other and breaking things."

"Great," I said. My sense of horror at my situation was becoming overwhelming.

"Hell, four weeks ago I did space policy, which, as near as I can tell, has zero relevance to coalitions. But the bosses around here seem to be more concerned with warm bodies in seats than actual expertise. Does it make sense? Not really. Welcome to the puzzle palace, Dr. Reilly."

"Thanks?"

"We should probably get upstairs. Lucky you, there's a staff meeting at nine that you're just in time for. Shall we?"

I sighed and nodded. *Might as well.*

Voight escorted me across another lobby and then through a pair of grey steel doors that demarcated the beginning of what appeared to be the main corridor into the Pentagon. We walked in silence; I was grateful for the opportunity to process everything I'd just been told. I could just manage to keep my posture straight and my face mostly blank, but I was plagued by millions of doubts about whether I could do this new job, whatever it would be, giving me a strange lightheaded sense of vertigo.

Yet despite the bad news, as we walked through the corridor I couldn't help but entertain the idea that the scene from the not-too-distant future—the one I'd envisioned upon entering the building—was just ahead.

I stepped through the doorway and saw a bunch of RedBox kiosks instead.

"Not what you expected?" asked Voight.

"No, not really," I responded, feeling bewildered. "Not at all, actually."

"Yeah, well, the Powers That Be want to make it as easy as possible for us worker bees to slave away around the clock. You can find just about all the basics here." Voight pointed toward a hallway on the right. "Over there's the florist, the gift shop, and the chocolate shop—I think the idea is to help us appease our irritated spouses for working late all the time. The chocolate place has a sale every Thursday night, and I highly recommend the 'sweetheart' bouquet at the florist's."

"What's over there?" I asked, pointing to my left.

"A barber, a drycleaners, and a bank. And down over there," Voight said, pointing to another corridor, "is the Virginia Department of Motor Vehicles. It's kind of impressive when you think about it: two spectacularly incompetent bureaucracies housed in one massive building. Poetic, actually. Anyway. You can do most of your errands without ever leaving."

"At least it's convenient?"

"Maybe. Or a trap. I can't tell which."

"You've been here a while, haven't you?"

"Yes, and more than once. I was here for three years in the early 2000s. But this time, two years. And, if things go the way I hope, I'll be out of here in a year."

We rounded an atrium about two stories deep. I looked over the glass railing to see tables and chairs…and a Popeye's? A Dunkin' Donuts, too? It looked like a mall food court rather than the ground floor of the headquarters of the world's mightiest military. We stepped onto another set of escalators and I watched the people below become slightly smaller as we ascended. People in uniforms and suits sat chatting over bagels and coffee and whatever else they needed to wake themselves up and face the day. The utter banality of the view—in the heart of the Pentagon—was striking.

"Huh," Voight said, suddenly distracted as he looked across the atrium. "That's probably not too good."

"What's going on?"

"See that guy rushing down the hallway over there?"

I looked in the direction Voight was pointing. A man wearing an Army officer's uniform with a chest full of medals was walking twice as fast as everyone else around him. Almost as if on cue, he looked back toward us. I caught a flash of his bright blue eyes before he stepped onto a set of escalators. Voight waved.

"That poor bastard is Lieutenant Colonel Adam Royle—or, I guess Colonel now? He was frocked."

"Frocked?"

"It's complicated, but it basically means he was promoted early. Whatever. He's our office's chief of staff now. Great guy. Pretty much keeps to himself. Apparently, the senior poo-bahs around here see him going places."

"Wow—that's kind of cool."

"He's definitely a high flyer. Which is why it's a total mystery how Fletcher got her mitts on him for our office. In any case, the bottom line is that if he's rushing around right now—that's probably not good news for us." Voight sighed. "Man, the hits around this place just keep on coming."

"I take it this isn't your favorite place in the world," I said.

"You could say that."

"Then why do you stay here?" I asked.

"Two reasons," Voight said. "One, I'm in uniform, so I was ordered to be here and therefore don't really have a choice. And two, someone's gotta support the guys and gals downrange. Especially in this new coalitions shop—putting people in harm's way is a very real possibility. So I figure it might as well be me that helps get them what they need. Speaking of, what's your excuse?"

"You mean, why would a *woman* be doing this stuff?" I asked, expecting to have the same tired conversation—again—about why people with feminine anatomical parts might be interested in the same things as the menfolk.

"No. I mean, why would someone who hasn't sworn an oath to uphold and defend the Constitution—or wear a fancy uniform— choose this field? Or—more to the point—choose to work *here?* I mean, I have to at least feign interest because it comes with the territory of being in the military. But you *chose* to be here. Why?"

"Oh," I said, surprised. "I've mostly studied conflict resolution and peace-building. So when this academic fellowship came up, I thought I'd see if I could apply what I've learned here."

I decided I'd leave out the bit about my crippling debt. And the fact that I was ambivalent, at best, about working in the Pentagon. It seemed like these were details that were better left unsaid.

"So you have a PhD, and you're here to change the world," Voight said as we climbed another set of escalators. From my point of view, this is an excellent combination."

"Why's that?"

"Because I can punt all the hard stuff to you," Voight said with a wink as we stepped off the top escalator and into a wide, brightly lit corridor.

The wall to my right was punctuated with a window every ten feet or so. To my left, the white walls were interrupted every so often by grey metal doors—all identical but for the differing signs with unintelligible acronyms and alphanumeric characters next to each door. The hallways were suddenly even busier with people scrambling, presumably to get to their first, or next, meeting. I checked my watch; it was five minutes before our nine o'clock staff meeting.

"What's behind these grey doors?"

"They appear to be offices," Voight said.

"They're not?"

"How do I explain this? What are those calendars you get at Christmas? My kids love 'em, but not as much as I do. Every year my wife has to get me my own, or I'll swipe theirs. I keep telling her that with working in this place, I need the sugar high more than they do. Anyway, each day you open up a box and get some sort of surprise goodie, and you never know what's behind each little door. You know what I'm talking about?"

"An advent calendar?" I offered.

"That's it. That's what these offices are like. An advent calendar. You never really know what's behind each door unless you go in. There's one around here that the fighter pilots turned into a man cave. Complete with a keg and an Xbox."

I laughed. "Where is it?"

"Beats me. Fighter pilots don't tend to associate with us lowly C-17 guys." Voight grinned. "And besides, if they're going to be inviting anybody into their lair, it's going to be someone who looks a lot more like you, and a lot less like me."

"Gotcha," I said, and fiddled with my engagement ring. "You know, I've seen pictures of the Pentagon a bunch of times before, but it never really occurred to me that there's a courtyard in the center," I said, looking out one of the windows as we walked. Below, at ground level, I could see lush green grass, tall trees, and the odd nervous-looking smoker. A building shaped like a gazebo was situated in the middle.

"Me neither, until I got here. That building in the center? It's called the 'Ground Zero Café.'"

"Why? Because of September 11th?"

"Naah. It's a Cold War thing. When the Soviets were spying on us, they looked at their satellite imagery of the Pentagon and saw loads of people wandering in and out of there. They naturally concluded that it was a nuclear missile silo. Makes you wonder what other stuff they got wrong. And for that matter, what we got wrong. What we continue to get wrong. Not that it really matters. In the nuclear apocalypse, this place will probably still be the first to go."

"That's a cheery thought," I said. The conversation I had with my mom when I decided to take the job flashed across my mind.

She suggested a number of reasons why it wasn't a good idea for me to take the gig, including her most emphatic argument that I'd be working in what she called a "terrorist's bull's-eye."

"Don't think about it too much. If it happens, we'll all be vaporized. So we, at least, won't feel a thing," Voight said.

"You're not helping."

"What? It'll all be over before we know it!"

"Still not helping."

"Fine. Speaking of hard stuff, I've got one for you. What do you know about Moldova?"

"Why do you ask?" I said, startled by the sudden change in conversational direction.

"From what I can tell, our boss, Ms. Fletcher, seems to be of the opinion that we should do something about Moldova. Or with Moldova. I'm not quite sure which. Frankly, I'd forgotten Moldova was a country until I got to this desk."

I paused for a moment, trying to recall everything I'd ever heard about Moldova, which, in the grand scheme of things, wasn't very much.

"It's a small country—stuck between Romania and Ukraine. There was a civil war there in the early 1990s, but it doesn't seem like there's much going on there now," I said. "Unless I'm wrong?"

"I doubt that," Voight said.

"So then why does Ms. Fletcher care about Moldova, of all places?"

"Not a clue. She was in charge of the Eastern Europe and Russia shop before moving to coalitions. I get the sense she's having difficulty letting go of her old job."

"Ah."

"And, here we are, at nine o'clock exactly," Voight announced as we reached yet another nondescript steel door. "Strap on your helmet and buckle your seat belt. Your wild ride at the Pentagon officially begins *now*."

CHAPTER THREE

"WHO DO I HAVE TO BLOW TO GET THIS MEMO MOVING?!"
shrieked a dainty-figured woman as she charged into the office that
fifteen of my new colleagues and I were stuffed into. The crowd
instinctively parted, as if she were Moses and we were the Red
Sea. She approached the massive oak desk at the far end of the
room and set a file down before removing her tortoiseshell reading
glasses and sweeping them onto her head, her bright red nails vivid
against her olive skin. Her auburn hair was wrapped into a bun on
the nape of her neck.

We'd been crammed into that office for nearly twenty minutes
waiting for this woman to arrive, who I presumed was Deputy
Assistant Secretary of Defense Ariane Fletcher. I'd spent the
time surveying the room and stealing quick glances at my new
colleagues—a crowd of men and women in suits, peppered with
the occasional military colonel, whose faces were rapidly turning
different shades of white, grey, or green (or, in Voight's case, all
three). I noticed Royle—the man we'd seen rushing around just
moments earlier—standing in the back of the room, stone-faced.
A small television screen sat off to the side with MSNBC on
mute, and the white walls of the room were adorned with framed

photographs of my new boss smiling alongside various Washington luminaries. I recognized the faces in some of them: President Callahan, Secretary of Defense Sidwell, Secretary of State Rivera, Wolf Blitzer, Senator McCain. Aside from Fletcher, I was the only woman in the room.

"We've been dicking around on the Moldova issue for far too long," Fletcher said, leaning forward on her desk, her blouse unbuttoned just low enough that just about everyone in the room could see the black lace trim of her bra. I blushed with embarrassment for her.

No one spoke. It would have been amusing: a room full of military and national security professionals, many distinguished by their ranks and ribbons on their uniforms, most of whom had undoubtedly seen combat in either Iraq or Afghanistan, all thoroughly intimidated by the woman with red lipstick sitting behind the heavy oak desk. But it wasn't. Rather, a thick fog of collective cringe blanketed the room, stifling all coherent thought and raising everyone's fear that they might misspeak, thereby unleashing another torrent of Fletcher's chastising.

"Well?" Fletcher said, her voice louder.

The silence that followed went from deafening to excruciating—or maybe it was the other way around. An almost primordial need to fill the conversational void bubbled up within me.

"I don't understand," I said, raising my hand.

I could feel quiet, stunned stares coming from my colleagues. Their shock made me feel incredulous. Weren't staff meetings supposed to be the time when employees got things cleared up for them by their bosses?

"Excuse me?" Fletcher asked, cocking an eyebrow, ice in her voice.

I caught a glimpse of Voight. His expression was somewhere between amused and horrified.

"It's just—what I mean is, uh, ma'am—is why, do we care about Moldova?" I said. "Don't we care more about Asia and the Islamic State?"

"Heather, is it?" Fletcher asked, her voice softening ever so slightly, reminding me of a panther coaxing its prey into the open terrain. I nodded.

"Heather, the Islamic State doesn't possess thousands of nuclear warheads. The Islamic State hasn't illegally annexed parts of Ukraine. The Islamic State isn't threatening the very existence of our allies in Central and Eastern Europe. *Russia is.* And Moldova—in Russia's neighborhood—presents a unique opportunity to start checking Moscow's aggression. The Moldovan Minister of Defense asked me to help him make his country less susceptible to Russian influence." Fletcher's voice began to crescendo, the icy calm falling away.

"We *have* to draw a line somewhere. This is a key opportunity for the United States, but the window on this is going to close if we keep *dicking around.* The Moldova issue is my top priority. I want solutions on how to get this unfucked, ASAP." Fletcher slammed her portfolio on her desk.

"Now, clear the room. Heather, you stay. Royle, you too."

Voight looked back at me, his eyes full of condolences, and then left with the rest of the group.

Fletcher sat down at the head of a heavy wooden table on the side of the room and motioned for me to sit at the opposite end. Royle sat next to her, his tall, lean body angled away, his uniform cluttered with badges and ribbons and a patch that read "Special

Forces" on it. Perhaps it was the intelligence in his eyes? Or the air of confidence he projected? Regardless, it occurred to me that he was attractive, in an unconventional sort of way. His nose was a little big, his chin was a little small, and his chestnut-with-a-twinge-of-cherry hair was cropped short. Although his face was mostly blank, his blue eyes stared at me for a moment and it almost seemed as if a flicker of recognition flashed across his features. Despite my growing unease with my situation, I forced a small smile toward him, which evidently shook him out of his thoughts; he immediately turned his gaze to a green notebook on his lap.

"So, Heather," Fletcher began. "With this reorganization, we've found ourselves in quite unusual circumstances. When we decided to undertake this restructuring, we had to reallocate a number of positions. And frankly, against my better judgment, we took your billet from the Central Asia desk. And you along with it. The only reason I decided *against* terminating your contract—and it was a close call—was because it would take way too long to hire someone else. And we're already quite short-staffed as it is. So, here we are."

I decided to stay quiet, despite my offense. Fletcher was clearly in "transmit" rather than "receive" mode.

"The thing that gives me pause about you is your utter lack of experience."

No experience? After busting my butt for a decade to get my degree and a teaching job? *Really?*

"But, ma'am, I have a doctorate in—"

"Exactly," Fletcher said. "You have a doctorate. I've seen any number of you people over the years. You have a PhD and a couple years of teaching under your belt. Which generally means that you're adept at misapplying obscure theories and philosophies to real-world problems. You all deliberately misunderstand situations, criticize what those of us who actually work in the real world are doing, and utterly fail to propose actual solutions to problems. All this while calling yourselves 'experts.'"

I hid my hands under the table so that Fletcher wouldn't see them tremble. I could tell she wasn't done yet.

"So why don't we use this big brain of yours and tell me how to stop Russia from threatening us and our allies."

"But I've studied Afgh—"

"Right. You've studied peace-building in Afghanistan, and written lengthy articles in obscure journals. Your arguments, by the way, about how we've screwed everything up over there were particularly unhelpful."

"But the analysis—"

"Have you ever been to Afghanistan, *Dr.* Reilly?" Fletcher's voice oozed with patronizing sarcasm.

Shit. I took a deep breath.

"My research used quantitative data gathered by people in the country—"

"Exactly, Dr. Reilly. You haven't even been there, yet you say you're an expert? All this, in conjunction with your little outburst during the staff meeting, leads me to believe you are singularly unprepared for working in a complex bureaucracy like the Pentagon."

My ears started ringing. *I moved across the country for this?*

"But all I did was ask a question."

"Royle and I were just talking about how neither of us thinks you're going to be a good fit for the office, given the priority we'll be placing on Moldova," Fletcher said, ignoring me completely.

"He thinks we should give you a nothing-burger account. Make it easy for you. I'm inclined to agree with him."

I looked at Royle in shock. *He couldn't even wait for me to start before throwing me under the bus?*

Royle opened his mouth to say something, eyes wide, but after looking from me to Fletcher, he closed it. Instead, he returned to scribbling in his notebook, as if by doing so he could somehow vanish from the room.

"Or maybe you should go home to academia now, and save us all the trouble of getting you up to speed," Fletcher said.

I'd never felt so disrespected in my whole life. *Screw the money. Nothing is worth this,* I thought. *Ryan, looks like you're getting your wish.*

I scooted my chair back from the table and took a deep breath to steady my nerves so that I could tell them—with an unwavering voice—exactly where the two of them could stick this position. But just as I was about to open my mouth, Royle turned so his right shoulder faced me. I froze as I saw a white wing with a red sword on a blue background: the patch of the 173rd Airborne Brigade, Jon's brigade, on the jacket of his uniform.

I remembered what Voight had said earlier that morning. *"Someone's gotta support the guys and gals downrange…. So I figure it might as well be me that helps get them what they need."*

Would Jon have died if someone like me had been in the Pentagon, working to make sure he got everything he needed?

I exhaled, swallowed my pride, and then looked up at Fletcher. "Ma'am, I want to help."

"Excuse me?" Fletcher said, surprised.

Royle put down his pen and stared at me intently, pursing his lips. I took another deep breath.

"I realize my academic work isn't applicable to what you are doing here. But this office is new. Nobody here has experience working on Moldova."

Fletcher slowly tapped her forefinger against the table.

"Go on."

"You said earlier that you were frustrated that you couldn't get things moving forward on Moldova. Maybe that's because your team doesn't know the place like you do. I know how to do research. I can help the team get up to speed. And that's got to be helpful as your team develops options, right?"

Fletcher raised an eyebrow and closed the leather portfolio in front of her, signaling that the meeting was over.

"If I do let you stay, you will need to consider the next couple months a probationary period."

I nodded.

"I do not tolerate laziness, sloppiness, or being interrupted. And if you don't pull your weight, you *will* be off my team. Is that acceptable to you?"

"Yes, ma'am."

"Then close the door behind you and get to work," she said, dismissing me. I stood up.

"And Heather?"

"Yes?"

"Don't fuck up."

CHAPTER FOUR

HALF AN HOUR LATER, I'D BEEN HANDED A STACK OF PAPERWORK AND SHOWN TO MY DESK—A CUBICLE NEXT TO VOIGHT'S—AND DISCOVERED THAT, AT LEAST TECHNICALLY SPEAKING, I HAD A FUNCTIONING COMPUTER WAITING FOR ME. Unfortunately, although it turned on and off, actually *doing* something on it was another matter entirely. And, according to Voight, it could take upwards of a week for the IT folks to "do their thing" and set me up in the system.

"Well, that stack of in-processing paperwork will take you a while," Voight said. "At least a couple hours."

"But Fletcher wants me to start researching Moldova now," I said.

"Fletcher wants a *lot* of things," Voight said. "But the IT guys work on their own schedule. You can thank Bradley—Chelsea?—whoever-he-is-these-days Manning and Wikileaks for that. Asshole."

"Asshole? Manning? But she's kind of a hero, isn't she?" I asked. "Making government more transparent?"

"Hero? Seriously? The only thing that bastard did was make it even harder for us to get our allies to talk to us. Oh, and make it much easier for the bad guys to figure out exactly how dysfunctional we are. Wikileaks is pretty much a front for Russian intelligence. And don't even get me started on Edward Snowden. Class-A douchebag Kremlin agent."

"But you've been talking about how dysfunctional we are all morning."

"Sure. But that's for us to know. Not them. Regardless, you're not going to have your computer fixed up for at least a couple days."

"Great. Is there a library I could go to?" I asked. "I need to get started on this Moldova research."

"Sure. I'll take you there after my next meeting. I should be back in an hour and a half."

Voight left and I turned to face my desk: my nonfunctioning computer, the grey burlap fabric of my cubicle walls, the light grey desk, and a bookshelf above me. And then I got to work.

Forty-five minutes and a hand cramp later, I'd finished half of the paperwork, and I had to go to the bathroom. I looked down at my bright yellow badge that said "VISITOR: ESCORT REQUIRED" across the top—all too true, especially since I had no idea where the bathroom actually was. I got up and started wandering the office in the hopes of finding someone who could escort me.

It was an odd-shaped space overall, long and narrow. The Pentagon's architects definitely cut some corners and got creative in order to stuff an office of twenty or so people in there. The room was bisected, each half holding a narrow corridor lined with about five or so cubicles. Fletcher's office—the only one with a door and a modicum of privacy—was situated near the entryway and the currently empty receptionist's desk. The low-rent, industrial version of Berber carpets covered the floor; the clean, orderly scents of paper reams and weeks-old paint permeated the office. A small red leather couch, a coffee table with magazines neatly organized on top, and a fake ficus tree were all crammed together into the tiny receiving area.

It was a fairly typical office space. Except that it had no people in it.

I was alone. And nature was calling. Urgently.

I sat down on the red leather couch, crossed my legs, and tried to read the *Financial Times*—a below-the-fold story on how the Islamic State was infiltrating Southern Afghanistan caught my attention for a precious couple of seconds.

Nature's call was turning into a cacophony of alarm bells.

If I didn't go soon, I was going to pee my pants.

I did not want to pee my pants.

And I especially did not want to pee my pants in Fletcher's office on my first day at work.

I left the office and stepped into the narrow, empty corridor. It looked just about the same in either direction. I tried recalling how Voight got me there earlier that morning, but I just couldn't remember. So, I turned right and started walking as quickly as I could.

And kept walking. And walking.

This isn't the right way, I thought as I turned a corner and entered another long hallway. But it was too late to turn back. I was committed. I just had to pray that I would find a bathroom before I exploded.

I broke into a run when I turned another corner and saw a sign for the women's bathroom.

"Hey!" someone shouted. "Stop!"

It was a Pentagon policeman.

"I'm sorry, officer, I can't!"

I ran into the ladies room. I burst into the stall, only just avoiding an utter catastrophe.

"Ma'am?" I heard a deep booming voice echo across the bathroom's tile.

"Yes?" I squeaked, still relieving myself while heavy footsteps stopped in front of my stall.

"I'm going to have to ask you to step out of the stall," the officer said.

"Can you give me a minute?" I asked, still mid-flow.

"Yes," the officer said in a deliberately calm tone. "But I'm going to have to ask you to step out, leave the door open, and *do not* flush."

I finished my business and then did what I was told. After I stepped out of the stall, the officer, a large black man with closely trimmed hair and a barrel-shaped chest, dutifully inspected my remains. I was beginning to wonder if it was possible to be permanently red in the face from embarrassment.

"Okay, you can, uh, finish your business now. I'll be waiting for you outside," he said, then left.

I took an extra-long time washing my hands before exiting the bathroom.

The police officer was waiting in the hall, speaking into his shoulder microphone. Somehow his chest looked even larger than it did when I was running into the bathroom.

"Yes, situation is under control. No hazardous material was inserted into the plumbing. No further assistance necessary. I have her in custody."

Oh god, he thinks I'm a terrorist.

"I'm sorry, officer," I interrupted. "But there's been a mistake. I work here."

"Then why are you wearing a visitor badge?" he asked.

"It's my first day. I haven't gotten a permanent badge yet."

"Okay. Then why are you walking the halls without an escort? Your badge says quite clearly that an escort is required for you."

"I really, really had to go, and there wasn't anybody to walk me."

"I'm going to have to take you to the metro entrance so we can file a report," he said, his expression utterly devoid of any sense of humor.

"A report? I just had to go to the bathroom!"

"Protocol," he said. "Let's go."

Back in college, after Jon passed away but before I'd met Ryan, I'd dated a fraternity guy for a hot second. My life was kind of a blur for a while, and both my mom and Amanda were getting pretty concerned that I'd flunk out. But, at the time, I just didn't care. One day I woke up late in his room, just in time to stumble out while students were making their way to their ten-o'clock seminars. It wasn't long before I learned the true meaning of the "walk of shame." People were staring at me, which felt bad enough. But it wasn't until I caught a glimpse of myself in a mirrored window that it really hit home. I looked like a mess. A little on the emaciated side from too much booze and not enough food for weeks at a time, topped off with streaked makeup and a bird's nest for hair. I felt humiliated.

Walking down the Pentagon corridors with the policeman, people staring at me as if I were somehow linked to Osama bin Laden himself, I was reminded of that walk of shame. It occurred to me that, both times, I wasn't wearing deodorant.

We arrived at the Pentagon Force Protection Agency's offices. Several stern lectures by the policeman and a set of fingerprints later, Voight collected me for the second time that day. His lips were pursed and his features were stony, giving me the distinct feeling that I'd *really* screwed up this time.

"Voight, I'm so sorry about this—"

"You should be," Voight said, his voice tight. "This is very..." He took a short breath. "Very..." He coughed.

Does he think Fletcher is right? That I'm a bad fit in the office? I'd felt stupid during the fingerprinting, but now I felt a mixture of guilt and embarrassment over having done something so dumb.

"I can't take it anymore," he said, and then burst into howls of laughter, tears streaming down his face. I watched him in shock as he bent over, his hands on his knees, and sat down to continue his belly laughter.

"I just figured out your call sign!" he said, bursting into snickering laughter again. "Whiz Kid!"

CHAPTER FIVE

"THERE YOU ARE! Finally! Drinks are on me," Amanda said as I walked up to the bar of the 18th Street Lounge.

"This wasn't the easiest place to find," I said, which was a bit of an understatement. The entrance to the bar was tucked away beside a mattress store with bright red "50% Off!" signs in its window. Only a small, business card-sized brass plaque gave passersby any inkling that the wood-framed mirrored door to the left was a cocktail lounge. The place was dark, lit with the occasional small crystal chandelier, and dotted with twenty- and thirty-somethings sitting on antique, crushed-velvet sofas.

"Sure. That's part of its charm," Amanda said. "What are you having?"

She pulled her wallet out of her classic, black Kate Spade bag. Amanda always had a sense of quiet refinement about her. Although she wore a lapis blue dress suit—a bold choice in a conservative town that preferred its dark grey attire—her red hair was swept back into a tidy bun that, along with her matching pearls, emanated an elegance that I knew I'd never be able to pull off. It was one of the things I loved about her.

"Something stiff. And I'm paying," I said, looking over a menu. "Man, this place is expensive. Is it always nine dollar beer night?"

"Yes, that's why I said I was paying."

"I'm not paying you rent, Amanda. The least I can do is buy you a drink."

"As I've said a million times, I'm happy to give you an opportunity to see how Washington actually works while you pay down the loans. And I'm happy to have someone to share the apartment with. It gets lonely sometimes. So, as I see it, *I'm* bribing *you* to keep me company. Besides, you can buy drinks another time. Today we're toasting to your first day at the Pentagon! How was it?"

"Let's see here," I said, making myself comfortable on the stool. "I forgot my deodorant, I found out that I'm no longer working on Afghanistan, my boss is a complete nightmare, I almost quit, I managed to get arrested, and my new nickname is 'Whiz Kid.'" I turned to the approaching bartender. "I'll have a scotch, please. Neat. Rocks on the side."

"Make it a double," Amanda said to the bartender. She turned back to me. "Arrested?!"

"They thought I was a terrorist," I said, shrugging off my jacket and hanging it on the hook below the bar. I caught a glimpse of my hair and another whiff of myself as I bent over. I closed my arms. "By the way, what do you do to combat this humidity? My hair—I look like a poodle."

"I use Sephora's anti-frizz spray," Amanda said, producing it from her purse. "Essential item this time of year. But nice try changing the subject. What's this about your boss being a nightmare?" Amanda asked. "Jim Townfield is an awesome guy—everyone thinks he's a great person to work for. Are they wrong?"

"I wouldn't know," I said, and sighed.

Amanda looked at me quizzically.

"Have you ever heard of a woman named Ariane Fletcher?"

Amanda involuntarily cringed as she set her glass of wine down on the bar, as if speaking Fletcher's name was like uttering "Voldemort."

"Fletcher?" Amanda said. "The Wicked Witch of the Pentagon?"

"That's the one. Guess who's lucky enough to be on her staff?"

"Please tell me you're joking."

"If only. And it gets better. She told me I was unqualified to work in the Pentagon."

"Unqualified? That's insane! Especially since Fletcher is an infamous psychopath who has made more than her fair share of *faux pas* over the years. Unbelievable. The only good news is that her direct boss is Assistant Secretary Chao—a great guy. He can restrain her. Sort of. I hope." Amanda grimaced.

"This morning, I thought I was going to be working on peacebuilding in Afghanistan. And now? I'm working on Moldova."

"Moldova?" Amanda asked, surprised. "Why Moldova, of all places?"

"From what I gather, she thinks we can use Moldova to stick it to the Russians."

"The Russians *have* been a problem recently," Amanda nodded and had another sip of her wine. "And General Braidenkamp in Europe testified on the Hill that the Russians could make trouble in the eastern part of Moldova. But I don't get it."

"Get what?"

"You're going to stay in the Pentagon?"

"I need the money."

I sipped my scotch and looked around the room. Young couples were flirting and work colleagues were arguing, all of them drunk on a heady combination of Washington politics, pheromones, and their libations of choice.

"I get that you need to pay off your student loans," Amanda said. "But you're talented. You could probably find some other way to do that. Why are you choosing to work on Moldova? Working for Fletcher? To stick it to the Russians? It seems a bit of a stretch for a card-carrying peacenik like yourself."

I sighed. "Strangely enough, I think I want to help."

"Huh? You want to help the U.S. government in its war-planning? Who are you, and what have you done with Heather?" Her eyes were playfully wide.

"I know, I know. It's weird. And I almost quit. I really did. I started thinking of going back to waiting tables like I did in college, and maybe doing some tutoring on the side, and how much money I'd likely make if I did that while I waited for the next school year to begin. But then I thought about Jon. What if, somewhere along the line, someone in the Pentagon didn't fight to get him what he needed? What if a Pentagon bureaucrat was more concerned with buying multibillion-dollar aircraft than finding ways to make Jon's body armor grenade-proof?" I wiped away a tear that slipped out.

"If Jon had someone like me back in the Pentagon, maybe he wouldn't have had to use his body to protect the soldiers around him. If someone like me was fighting for Jon back here, maybe he would still be with us."

We both remained quiet for a moment.

"That's a good reason to stay," Amanda eventually said. I noticed her lip wobble a little as she fidgeted with her old wedding ring that she now wore on her right finger. She took a steadying breath. "So, have you and Ryan set a date yet?"

I raised an eyebrow and stared at her. "Did Mom put you up to asking that?"

Amanda sighed. "She just wants you to be settled. That's all."

"Well, next time you talk to her, tell her I've got a lot on my plate right now. We'll pick a date when things settle down."

"You do realize you've been saying that for a while now."

"I've been busy! Teaching, moving to San Diego, and now D.C.... I can't plan a wedding on top of all these major life changes."

"Do you think Ryan's getting a little impatient?"

"Sure, but he also understands that the timing isn't right."

"Okay," Amanda said, doubtfully. "But you'd be doing all of us a favor if you'd just put something on the calendar. At this rate, you're looking at a three-year engagement."

"We're not in any rush," I said, sipping the last of my scotch.

"Clearly," Amanda said. She looked at her watch, and then signaled to the bartender for our tab. "Anyway. You may not be in a hurry, but now I am. I've got a dinner at seven."

"Hot date?" I asked, winking.

"No, not tonight. I'm headed to the British Defense Attaché's house. Do you want me to see if you can join?"

I sighed. Just about every time I asked Amanda about her dating life, she managed to find a way to change the subject. I remembered all those years ago, on their wedding day, when Jon and Amanda had stood at the front of the church and, through joyful tears, called each other their soul mates. It would have seemed cliché if it had been anybody else. But it was obvious to everybody in the chapel that for them, it was a simple affirmation of something as real and true as the blue sky or the green grass. After he died in Afghanistan, the wound of his absence was too fresh, too deep, and Amanda was busy putting one foot in front of the other. Dating was, understandably, out of the question. But after a couple years, after she'd put her life back together, she usually insisted she was too busy working. And on those rare occasions when she'd go out with someone, there was always something that held her back. He was too short, too tall, too dull, too crazy, too stingy, too chivalrous. In my heart of hearts, I knew Jon wouldn't have wanted her to put her life on hold, so every now and again I would ask her whether she'd really moved on. And every time I asked, Amanda insisted she was fine, that she was getting out there, but that D.C. was a dating wasteland for single straight women. Especially because she had standards she wouldn't compromise. I wasn't exactly convinced, but then again, pushing her too hard wasn't the right thing to do, either.

So I did what I always did: I followed her conversational lead. "The British Defense Attaché? That sounds super impressive and important. I feel intimidated just knowing you," I teased. "The right-hand woman to Senator McClutchy!"

"Stop it. You're just as impressive," Amanda said, although she clearly appreciated the compliment.

"And according to the press, your boss is definitely becoming a bigger deal. *Politico*'s number-one politician to watch in the country."

"If the number of dinners and social engagements I have to attend is any indication, you're spot-on right about that. Everybody wants a piece of the senator these days."

"Which means everybody wants a piece of you."

"Seemingly so. Anyway, did you want to come along?" Amanda asked.

"Thanks, but I'd better get home. I'm exhausted, and I need to do some research before I hit the hay," I said, gathering my purse and my suit jacket.

We headed out into the sticky, warm embrace of the Washington evening. The roads had a faint sheen, as if the pavement itself were perspiring, seeking some kind of relief from the intense heat that didn't go away with the sun. 18th Street was both alive and empty; the traffic was bustling with cabs, and the windows of the office buildings were occasionally lit up. Politicos, analysts, lobbyists, lawyers, all getting ready to burn the midnight oil. Or avoiding their homes. Or both. But the actual sidewalks themselves were empty, as if an unspoken curfew had been imposed: time either to go home or back to the office.

"I'll see you back at the apartment," I said, hugging Amanda before jumping into a cab with a Somali driver blasting music with a heavy African drum beat. I checked my phone. A text from Ryan was waiting for me:

So what's it like in the death machine? Ready 2 come home yet? Miss u I love u.

I sighed. How would I answer him? Amanda understood where I was coming from, and why I decided to stay in the Pentagon. But Ryan? He'd be a more difficult sell.

"Are you sure this isn't just your ego getting in the way?" he'd asked when I first broached the subject all those months ago.

Which, on the face of it, wasn't wholly off the mark. At the International Studies Association conference in D.C. about a year and a half ago, a member of the audience had asked me, in front of dozens of people, "How can you make recommendations about a peace process when you have never served in government?" If I hadn't been called out for my lack of experience in Washington, I might not have felt inclined to apply for the "year in government" fellowship in the first place.

"After Jon? *You're* seriously thinking of working in the war factory?" he'd asked when the fellowship committee assigned me to the Pentagon instead of the State Department.

I wasn't thrilled at first, either. But the additional income got me rethinking my position. Which was when I argued to him that, much as I loved academia, my long-term aspirations *didn't* include living just above the poverty line, and money had gotten really tight for us.

"Why don't you try the United Nations?" he'd asked. "You wanted to work for them at one point, right?"

I'd bitten my lip at that suggestion. While it was true, I'd briefly thought about joining the U.N.—a position in Angola had come up when I was finishing my Master's degree—I pursued my PhD instead. Ryan wanted us to live together, and so taking gigs in far-flung corners of the world wasn't in the cards back then. Fast forward, and he was already struggling with the idea of my being gone for a year in D.C. I doubted he'd be able to cope with my taking a U.N. position and being gone even further away, for an even longer period of time. But rather than raise those points, I told him that the application window for U.N. fellowships had already closed.

"Oh," Ryan had said.

Ryan's strength was what I fell in love with, all those years ago when we met in college. I was getting myself back on the right track after months of grief from losing Jon: going to classes again, running in the mornings, laying off the booze. But I was still a hot mess, trying to cope with that aching, Jon-shaped chasm in my chest. On those afternoons where I still couldn't get myself out of bed, Ryan was strong for me. He helped me put on my jeans and sneakers and took me for hikes in the countryside. He would help me find the spots of sunlight in my otherwise grey world. And slowly—day by day, inch by inch—the clouds over my life started to dissipate.

Also, I soon learned, he was strong in his opinions too—more a black-and-white rather than a shades-of-grey kind of guy. He'd never cared for violence, but soon after we'd met, and I told him about Jon, he decided he was a pacifist. It wasn't too long after that before he decided he hated *all* violence, because it violated the sanctity of life. It was a hop, skip, and a jump to veganism from there. We spent the rest of our relationship eating "dreamy tofu" ice cream, and doing our best to make vegan cheese taste like something other than rubber.

The idea, therefore, of the woman he loved—his future bride—working in the Pentagon was not something he was thrilled about, irrespective of the money. It was only after several conversations explaining that I'd be working on the Afghan peace process that he finally said, "I can get behind that." But I knew he'd only partly meant it. As he saw it, cozying up to the military—even if it was to work on peace-building—was a betrayal of our principles.

I remember breathing a sigh of relief that he was finally okay with my doing the fellowship. But now my stomach was in knots. How would I explain to him that I was going to be working on

Moldova instead of Afghanistan? In an office that prepared for war rather than planned for peace?

I was trying to find the right words to text back when I looked up and saw the Washington Monument appear on my right. I felt a sense of awe as I watched the ivory obelisk standing proudly in the center of the city. It reached up, touching the faintly peachy-purple sky that was dotted with the occasional star. It occurred to me that despite everything the day had thrown my way, I was about to be part of something bigger than myself—something enduring, something important.

I looked back at my phone and the text from Ryan.

Things are good. Long day, super tired. Headed to bed, I typed.

OK, love you.

I'd figure out another time, another way to explain my decision to Ryan.

"Love you too."

CHAPTER SIX

"MORNING," VOIGHT SAID, GREETING ME AT THE METRO ENTRANCE AT THE START OF THE NEXT DAY. "Let's get you badged up!"

"Hello, sunshine. You're awfully perky this morning," I said, bleary-eyed and clutching my empty travel mug. I hadn't gotten much sleep the night before. After getting home, I microwaved an overpriced vegan quesadilla and scoured the internet for everything I could find on Moldova. It was one in the morning before I knew it, which was way past my bedtime on any normal day.

"It's an act," Voight said as we entered the badging line. "If I don't pretend I like being here, I might lose the will to live."

"Gotcha. Pretend away." We moved to the front of the line. "By the way, thank you for escorting me."

"No problem. Are you going to get your in-processing squared away today?"

"Come hell or high water," I said, collecting my visitor badge. "It took me forty-five minutes to clear security through the visitor's entrance today."

"It's true. Security's getting to be an even bigger pain in the ass than usual, which is saying something. Last week a buddy of mine got stuck in the visitor's line so long they ended up conducting their meeting downstairs in the Metro."

"Short meeting, I take it?"

"Yep. It's amazing what you can get done if you don't use PowerPoint. One of the most productive meetings my friend has ever been in. And, bonus: afterwards they went to Sine's to get a beer instead of trying to get into this infernal place. Ready to head upstairs?"

"Ready as I'll ever be," I said.

"Do we need to take any potty breaks?"

"I decided to wear a diaper, so I'm good," I deadpanned.

"Nice. Thwarting the Pentagon Force Protection Agency, one pair of Depends at a time," Voight said, laughing. We swiped through the security barriers. "Coffee?"

"Definitely. So, Moldova."

"Yes? What about it?"

"I did some research on it last night."

"Overachiever."

"If only. The problem is I didn't come up with much. The most interesting thing I found was an article about taking down a cow-smuggling ring."

"Cow-smuggling?"

"Yeah," I said. "Some poor schmuck got caught stealing cows. One at a time."

"That seems…inefficient."

"No kidding. He'd steal one, stick it in the back of a car—it looked like a Fiat—and then move it to his farm about thirty miles away."

"There were pictures?"

"Yeah. The cow's butt was hanging out of the back. Poor thing—it couldn't have been very comfortable."

"Moldova: international capital for illicit bovine-trafficking. An epic national security threat, clearly." Voight checked his phone.

"See, that's kind of my point," I said as we climbed on the escalator. "Why does Fletcher care so much about Moldova? It doesn't have a whole lot going on. Aren't there better ways to push back on the Russians?"

"Beats me. But we'd better figure it out soon."

"Why's that?"

He held up his phone. "Because I got an email from Derek Odem."

"Who's that?"

"The Senior Advisor for Russian and Eurasian Affairs to the National Security Advisor," Voight said, scrolling down the screen.

"Senior Advisor? To the National Security Advisor? The one who has President Callahan's ear?"

"Yep—the advisor to the advisor." Voight sighed. "He wants to talk about why Fletcher is going to the mattresses over Moldova, apparently."

"When does he want to meet?"

Voight checked his watch. "Forty-five minutes." He rolled his eyes. "Guess we *don't* have time for coffee."

"Why? It'll only be a five-minute pit stop. We'll be upstairs in our office well before the meeting starts."

"If *only* it worked that way," Voight said. "We're pretty low on the totem pole. We go to them—not the other way around."

I felt a sense of apprehension as we walked from the Farragut Square metro stop toward the White House. I'd been to the White House one other time, for Jon's Medal of Honor ceremony. In a large white-and-gold room with parquet floors, President Bush stood on a platform and presented Amanda with the ribbon representing the nation's highest military award. I held her hand and an extra set of tissues, although Mom and I were the ones who needed them that day. Amanda's eyes glistened with tears, but she didn't let herself cry.

We all went to section 60 of Arlington National Cemetery afterwards. It was a grey November day. A damp chill was in the air, and I remember wishing I'd worn a thicker sweater under my wool jacket. I'd last been there when Jon was buried, and since then there were hundreds of new graves. It would have taken us a little while to find his marble headstone had it not been for Amanda. She knew exactly where to go. I hadn't been back to Arlington since that day. It was too much, seeing his name etched in stone instead of my vibrant, joyful brother who always knew how to make me smile.

I looked over to Voight, who was scowling. Or maybe it was a grimace? Either way, he didn't look too happy. "You seem annoyed," I said.

"Your powers of observation are keen, young grasshopper." He sighed. "Getting summoned by the national security staff. Derek should be working with our bosses directly. And our bosses' bosses. It's making me think that there's something up—something that we'd probably rather not be involved with."

"So you're saying that this is going to be a fun meeting."

"If verbal bludgeoning is your idea of a good time, then yes."

"Great."

We approached the iron railings surrounding the White House lawn. The park was dotted with tourists wearing wide-brimmed hats and fanny packs taking pictures of the White House. Four or five protestors lazily held brightly colored signs registering their vehement opposition to nuclear weapons, climate change, and genetically modified foods. They looked odd to me as we passed them; me wearing a black pantsuit, about to go to a meeting in the White House, them wearing flip-flops and shorts, their convictions to save the earth warring with their desire to escape the heat of the midmorning sun. It wasn't all that long ago that I'd participated in protests like theirs. What would they think of me if they knew I was one of them? Would they think of me as a turncoat? That I'd sold my soul?

"Must be frustrating," Voight said, noticing me watching them.

"Frustrating? Why?" I asked, as guilt washed over me for not joining the protestors. "They're trying to make a difference."

"Sure. But it's hard to change the world when you're sitting on the outside. Decisions are made on the inside."

I nodded, but remained quiet. Voight's point was so obvious; I wasn't sure why I'd never thought of it before.

"That's where we're going."

He pointed toward a massive grey stone building looming to the right side of the White House. At least ten floors tall and adorned with hundreds of columns, it more resembled a Victorian haunted house plucked from Transylvania and accidentally inserted squarely in the center of Washington, D.C., than a U.S. government building.

"There? Into Dracula's lair?" I asked.

"Ha! Nice one. Especially since it's filled with bureaucratic bloodsuckers. I hope you packed your garlic!"

"He's late," Voight said, tapping his pen against the dark wood table as we sat in a sunny, buttercream conference room of the Old Executive Office Building and distracting me from my study of an oil painting depicting a nineteenth-century naval battle.

"His assistant said he'd be a few minutes late," I said.

"That was twenty minutes ago. Doesn't this mean class gets cancelled?"

A brass doorknob turned and a younger man, perhaps in his early thirties, entered the room. He was immaculately dressed. His navy pinstripe suit had the faint sheen of fine fabric, his light blue shirt was perfectly coordinated with his light purple silk tie, and his brown hair was perfectly tousled. *Was this guy late because of a fashion shoot?*

"No such luck, I guess," Voight whispered under his breath.

"Sorry to keep you waiting. I was caught up in a meeting with the National Security Advisor." As he sat down at the head of the table, I noticed a pimple growing on his forehead. "I'm Derek. I appreciate your meeting with me at such short notice." He handed business cards to Voight and me.

This guy is the senior advisor? I thought, doing my best to keep my features smooth. *He's barely older than I am.*

"I'm really hoping we can resolve this Moldova question today," Derek continued. "Your boss is really pushing this hard, and we need to find ways to get her to throttle back."

"So, why don't you speak to Ms. Fletcher about this?" Voight asked.

"I'm hoping that you can help persuade her that Moldova is a bad option before any concrete proposals hit *my* level," Derek said.

"You want us to manage her for you," Voight said, with a soft, cynical smile. "Get her to back down."

Derek let a light smile cross his face but said nothing.

"You clearly don't know who you're dealing with," Voight continued.

"Trust me; I know her better than anybody. And what Ms. Fletcher is proposing to do will set back our efforts to support the Georgians."

"The Georgians? What do the Georgians have to do with any of this?" I asked.

Derek sighed. "Ever since Russia invaded Georgia in 2008—and annexed South Ossetia—the Georgians have been in a pissing contest with Moscow."

"And we've been supporting the Georgians," Voight said.

"Sort of. Previous administrations didn't want to give them too much help. They were worried about Moscow retaliating, especially after the Russians started the war in Ukraine."

"I'm still not tracking on what any of this has to do with Moldova," Voight said.

"Last week—after months of personally working on the issue—we decided to start ramping up our efforts to help the Georgians beef up their military. The idea is to help them get stronger before

Russia decides to annex more territory, start a proxy war or generally foment instability and chaos. Basically, we don't want them to have the opportunity to repeat their Ukraine playbook in Georgia."

"Sure, but we kind of shot ourselves in the foot with Ukraine, right?" I asked.

"How so?" Derek asked, his head jerking to the side as if I'd actually slapped him.

"I read that one of our top diplomats was so involved in getting Kiev to say 'screw you' to the Russians that they even handed out cookies to anti-Moscow protesters in the streets."

"Oh, yeah," Voight said, turning to me. "I remember reading about that. Wasn't that the woman who was caught on tape dropping F-bombs and talking about how useless the European Union is?"

I nodded.

"Classic. Good on her," Voight continued.

"I believe you're referring to our former Deputy Assistant Secretary of State for European Affairs," Derek said.

Voight raised his eyebrows. "I didn't realize she was *that* senior."

"Look," I said, leaning forward, "from everything I've read, our support emboldened the protestors and helped lead to the riots, which then led to the Russian crackdown."

Derek folded his arms and pursed his lips.

"Sure," he said, "we could have handled things a little better. But you overstate how much influence we had on the situation. And you understate how aggressive Moscow is these days. Not everything is our fault, contrary to what the foreign policy borg-people masquerading as 'experts' around this town would have you believe. But returning to the reason I asked you here. The enhanced

Georgia security assistance program will get going in the next month or two. And when Moscow finds out—"

"They'll have kittens," I said.

"The Pentagon is figuring out how to manage this so that we don't inflame tensions too much. So this isn't exactly the best time to launch a new effort for Moldova. Georgia is dicey enough— adding Moldova to the mix? Moscow won't like it. We need to pick our battles. Especially since neither Moldova nor Georgia are this administration's top priorities."

"Look, I'm just a staff flunkie," Voight said. "I don't really have a dog in this fight. But my boss, were she here—and she should be, by the way—would probably tell you that this isn't about Moldova *per se*. It's about checking the aggression of an increasingly volatile and dangerous Russia. A Russia with nukes that's recently told the world that the United States is enemy *numero uno*. Or however you say that in Russian."

"Supporting both the Georgians and the Moldovans at the same time is too provocative," Derek said. "Not to mention the fact that Fletcher is overstepping her boundaries. She's in charge of Coalitions now—not Russia and Eurasia policy."

"But what about the Moldovans?" I asked.

"What *about* the Moldovans?" Derek said.

"Shouldn't they have the right to live the way they want to? If they want help against Russian interference, shouldn't we give it to them?"

"Sure, they should."

"Really?"

"Absolutely. If you want to commit a hundred thousand troops to Eastern Europe and start World War III, that is."

"Oh," I said, and sat back in my chair.

"So, basically, you brought us here because you want us to tell Fletcher to cease and desist, lest she initiate Armageddon," Voight said.

Derek smiled. "Exactly. I'm glad we understand each other."

"I don't fucking understand," Fletcher said, taking off her reading glasses and setting them on her desk. "The NSC said *what?*"

"They're concerned that because we're enhancing our security cooperation program with Georgia," Voight said, "we'll *really* irritate the Russians if we start doing anything in Moldova."

"*Really* irritate? What does that mean?" Fletcher asked with a healthy side of sarcasm.

"Nuclear apocalypse," Voight said.

"*Who* at the NSC said that?"

"The Senior Advisor," I said, "to the National Security Advisor. Derek Odem."

"Derek Odem?" Fletcher was nonplussed.

Voight and I both nodded.

"You guys are telling me that *Derek Odem* is the toad in the road on this?"

"Umm, yes," I squeaked out.

"Derek Odem doesn't know his ass from a hole in the ground. Derek Odem is a bullshit artist with a poetry degree who somehow managed to land in the White House through his mommy's connections."

Fletcher's nostrils flared. For a split second, it seemed like she had turned into a dragon, smoke trailing from her snout, preparing to breathe fire. She stood.

"Lauren's hired a bunch of kids over at the NSC, too inexperienced to tell her anything but what she wants to hear," she said, looking out her window.

Voight and I glanced at each other, eyes wide, before turning back to watching Fletcher with equal parts terror and morbid curiosity.

"And you guys met with him?" Fletcher asked, turning to face us. "Without telling me first?"

The flip in Fletcher's rant was so abrupt that I felt whiplashed as my body tensed into "fight or flight" mode.

"Ma'am," Voight said, "I emailed you about the appointment as soon as I found out about it. Derek didn't give us a whole lot of time."

"*You* skipped several levels up the chain and met with someone who is at my level, if not Assistant Secretary Chao's level. You, Colonel Voight, know better."

"We did get valuable information," I said, trying to distract Fletcher from unleashing her wrath on Voight. "About why it's hard to get traction on Moldova."

Fletcher narrowed her eyes. "Go on."

"Well, Derek seemed personally invested in a Georgia program."

"Georgia? He's been pushing the Georgia package for almost a year now. It's not going anywhere—the Georgians already have a lot of support from us," Fletcher said.

"Not according to Derek. He says that an announcement is being made next month."

"An announcement?"

"He wasn't crystal clear with the details, ma'am," Voight said. "But he made it seem like a done deal. And with Georgia moving forward, Moldova would be a bridge too far."

Fletcher tapped her fingers on her desk as her face blossomed with the rosy hue of barely contained rage.

"And that little shit waited until I wasn't heading up Russia policy to move forward on his little Georgia program. Derek's getting too big for his britches, which is why, Colonel Voight, you should have come to see me first, before going across the river."

"I—" Voight started, clearly a little confused about how he ended up back in Fletcher's crosshairs.

"Let me tell you what *I* know," Fletcher interrupted. "I know that you decided to go above my head and meet with the NSC. And now the NSC thinks they've put our office in a box on Moldova. In other words, I know that your little adventure this morning set us back—a lot. We're going to have to go to war."

"With who? Russia?" I asked.

"Hell no. With the NSC. Now get out of my office. And don't come back until you've figured out a way to fix this mess."

CHAPTER SEVEN

A COUPLE WEEKS LATER, WE WEREN'T ANY CLOSER TO SOLVING FLETCHER'S MOLDOVA PROBLEMS, SO VOIGHT AND I AGREED MY TIME WOULD PROBABLY BE BETTER SPENT ATTENDING A THREE-DAY PENTAGON ORIENTATION TRAINING. Two and a half days in, I was as bewildered as I was my first day in the building, and beginning to realize that "death by PowerPoint" was more than a figure of speech. The orientation leader was a squat, barrel-shaped man named Ken whose physique and "high-and-tight" haircut proved you can take the man out of the Marines, but you can't take the Marine out of the man. He approached his briefing responsibilities with a military precision and gravitas, which would have been appropriate if he were talking about storming the beaches of Iwo Jima. Less so for the actual content of his briefing: the proper formatting of Pentagon memorandums (a page and a half, thirteen-point font, lots of "white space").

"A day's worth of information crammed into three days," Voight had joked.

No kidding.

On the upside, there had been plenty of opportunities to catch up on what was happening in the world, having swiped a printout of the *OSD Morning News* from the lobby each morning. The articles got progressively grimmer. One discussed a Russian plane that was downed in Syria. Another pontificated that Russia's decision to intervene in the Syrian conflict may have prolonged the war. Moscow supported the tyrant whose oppressive leadership led to the war in the first place, meaning it would be even more difficult to get the bastard to leave. Yet another article fretted about Moscow's simultaneous war in Ukraine—the latest Russian swipe at Ukraine was using cyber warfare to switch off the lights in the Kiev airport. ("What cyber-vulnerabilities do we have?" the author asked.) Maybe Fletcher was onto something when it came to Russia.

But the most horrible stories of all were the ones chronicling the latest atrocities committed by the Islamic State. In Syria, innocent people were starving—or worse. A lot worse. And the Islamic State seemed to be making more inroads into Afghanistan. True, the local warlords would probably be able to stave off the Islamic State for some time. The Afghans' experience hosting al Qaeda in the 1990s convinced a fair number of the locals that hosting radicals with agendas against the United States tended to lead to dire consequences. They were anxious to prevent a repeat performance. Still, it was becoming increasingly fashionable—if that's what you could call it—to close down girls' schools and enforce the strictest interpretations of Sharia law across southern Afghanistan. And by all accounts, Afghanistan was a chaotic place, often the victim of meddling by its neighbors, making it susceptible to outbreaks of violence and repression. All it would take was one thing going wrong—an assassination, a coup—and the whole place would go up in flames again.

"So, with that, are there any questions?" Ken asked, interrupting my train of thought.

I looked around the room; everyone else wore a slightly stunned look from being nearly bored to death. Nobody raised their hands.

"Okay then! You guys have officially completed—"

While I knew that everyone in the room wanted nothing more than to escape at that very moment, I couldn't help but raise my hand to ask the question I personally needed answered the most. "When are we trained on our portfolios?" I asked.

"What do you mean?" Ken asked, confused.

"Well, we're all new to OSD Policy. So, when are we going to be briefed on the administration's defense policies?" I noticed my colleagues perking up at the question.

"I'm not sure I'm tracking," Ken said.

"When are we going to be trained on how this administration sees the world?" I said. "What its priorities are and how we're supposed to carry them forward in our portfolios."

"You should know that already. You're the Subject Matter Experts."

I looked at him askance. *Is he being deliberately obtuse?* "Even after the reorg?"

Once again, Ken looked confused. It dawned on me that he wasn't being obstructive; rather, nobody had informed him about the reorg either.

"I guess I might be in a unique situation," I said, "but I was hired to do one thing, but I was told when I reported in earlier this week that I'm now working a completely different portfolio." I looked around the room at my colleagues; all of them were nodding their heads in agreement, as if they'd recently received similar news.

"So I wouldn't really consider myself a 'Subject Matter Expert,' and just want to get up to speed," I continued.

"Oh. Well, I'm sorry to hear that. But we don't really get into that in this course."

"We don't talk about defense policy in a training course for joining defense policy?" I asked, stunned.

It was one thing to be working on an issue I was utterly unfamiliar with; it was quite another to do so without any professional training whatsoever.

"Nope, sorry. But if you fill your evaluation form and put that as a suggestion, we can try to include it in future courses!" Ken said, helpfully.

"Unbelievable," Voight muttered at his computer, just loudly enough for me to hear as I walked toward my desk. It had been almost a week since I'd last seen him in Fletcher's office. Between getting my permanent badge and attending the obligatory four-day orientation seminar for new employees in OSD Policy, I hadn't been in the office much.

"Everything okay?" I asked, stopping in and leaning against the edge of his cube. Voight had been decorating. Sitting on his desk next to his computer screen was a large picture of him and his wife with their kids—two teenaged sons and a toddler-aged daughter—standing in front of the castle at Disney World. A small wooden rack held coins of different colors, shapes, and sizes. Affixed to the grey fabric wall of his cubicle was a small printout of a World

War II soldier holding a coffee cup and smiling. The caption read, "How about a nice cup of shut the hell up?" It seemed appropriate.

"Of course not," Voight said. "We're trapped here, for god's sake."

"True," I said, nodding. "But anything specific?"

Voight swung his chair away from his computer and faced me while taking a deep, cleansing breath. "I'm trying to book a trip."

"Vacation?" I asked.

"Already got our next trip to Disney World squared away last week—thank you very much. Now I'm trying to get my travel booked for EUCOM."

"That's in Germany, right? Stuttgart?"

"Bingo, although looking at DTS, you'd think it was on Mars. The routing they've given me is via Istanbul and Reykjavik."

"Yikes," I said. "What's DTS?"

"They didn't tell you about that in orientation?"

I cocked my eyebrow at him.

"DTS is the Defense Travel System. Imagine if Orbitz or Travelocity was designed by hundreds of sadistic, incompetent monkeys. In theory, it's great. In practice, it's only helpful if you like having four layovers and a middle seat on every trip—if, in fact, it even allows you to go where you want to." Voight sighed. "I can't tell you how many hours I've spent fighting with this damned thing. I miss the days when we could just call up a travel agent."

"Why don't they just make a system that's more efficient?"

"This *is* the system that's more efficient."

"Oh," I said.

Voight nodded.

"What are those coins, by the way?" I pointed to the rack.

"Those? Challenge coins. Just about every military unit has 'em made. Commanders give them out when they feel like it. A central feature of many a drinking game, back during the days of my capricious youth."

"Speaking of drinking, Germany has great beer. There are worse places you could be sent."

"True, but Lagunitas is my favorite, and I'd much rather drink one of those at home with my wife and kids. And a conference room there is exactly like a conference room here. Still, duty calls, and to be fair, a German *wiessbeir* will be the perfect way to round off a day of intense staff talks with European Command, wherein I try to convince them taking action in Moldova is a good idea, and they develop new and inventive ways to tell me to pound sand."

"Still haven't made any progress on Moldova?" I asked.

"Nope. Sending me over there—with my colonel's 'secret handshake' as she called it—is Fletcher's idea of a 'Hail Mary' pass."

"What does Derek think about all of this?" I asked, noticing Royle walking into Fletcher's office out of the corner of my eye.

"This is a covert mission—the NSC knows nothing. Besides, as Fletcher says, 'what Derek doesn't know won't kill him.' Unless, of course, we kick off the next apocalypse. Then all bets are off, I guess. But I'm pretty sure it'll be worth it."

"How so?" I asked, confused.

Voight smiled; a wisp of conspiracy crossed his features. "I made a deal with Fletcher."

"What kind of deal? Please tell me there wasn't any sacrificing of live chickens. Or soul-selling."

"Promise you'll hear me out? Don't get mad...." Voight's words were apologetic, but he still had a slight grin on his face.

"Mad?" I said, trying to fend off a sudden sense of dread.

"I kinda told her I'd happily go to Germany and work whatever magic I could...if she would officially make us teammates. I know, I know," Voight said, arms raised defensively with his palms out. "I shouldn't have forced your hand, or presumed to speak for you—"

"Are you kidding me?" I said, bursting into a grin. "This is fantastic news!"

Voight let out a breath of relief. "Oh, thank god. I was worried you wouldn't like being paired with a big, dumb knuckle-dragger."

"What's not to like? This is the best news I've gotten since starting here. But, honestly, I don't get it."

"Get what?"

"Why she let us be teammates. You're a colonel. You outrank me."

Voight looked at me curiously, and then burst into a raucous belly laugh. His face turned red and his eyes watered as he tried to gain his composure.

"Damn, Heather," Voight managed to choke out. "We're definitely going to get along great. You're hilarious and you don't even know it."

"What's so funny?" I asked, confused, but starting to chuckle along with him. I was pretty sure he was laughing *with* me?

"Well, for starters, you have a PhD," Voight said, once he'd calmed down a bit. "That's nothing to sneeze at. Second, I guess you haven't been here long enough to notice, but the only other place you'll see so many stars in one building? A planetarium. There's a ton of generals and admirals with stars on their shoulders working here. Colonels may be a big deal anywhere else, but around here we're a dime a dozen."

I quickly swallowed my laughter. Jon was an Army captain before he died. And according to him, colonels were a part of a lower pantheon of deities.

"But colonels run bases," I said. "And air wings. They captain ships. Lead brigades. And do other really important stuff."

"And here, in this god-forsaken place, colonels pour coffee and write memos. And book our own travel."

"That must be frustrating."

"No kidding. DTS is a freaking nightmare," Voight winked. "But I try not to think about it too much. Things could be a lot worse. Hell, my life just got a million times better, now that I'm officially teammates with a fifty-pound brain—one that's now freshly minted from Pentagon 101 training, no less. Speaking of, how was it?"

"How was what?" a man's voice behind me said. I turned to see Royle walking toward us, his chest a rainbow of ribbons and medals, his sleeves with six or seven lines on them coming up from the cuffs. I immediately thought of that time when Jon was back home in Carlisle with us for the holidays, a couple months before he was scheduled to deploy to Afghanistan. While doing the dishes as Mom and Amanda cooked, I could see through the window that a light snow kissed the Pennsylvania hillsides. Pans clean, I'd left the two of them working in tandem to get Christmas dinner ready and wandered through the house in search of Jon. I found him in his old bedroom, carefully affixing his newly won awards to his uniform.

"I got this one for passing Ranger school," Jon said, holding up a narrow arc-shaped patch that said "RANGER" in bright yellow letters. "Getting through that—man, it was a beast. I've never been that skinny before, and my feet will never be the same again."

Jon put down the RANGER tab and held up another patch. "And this one is for the unit that I'm about to go to," he said.

"The one in Italy?" I'd asked.

"Yep. The 173rd Airborne Brigade. It's going to go here," he pointed to his uniform's left shoulder.

Royle's patch, I noticed, was on the opposite shoulder as I shook myself out of the memory.

"I was just asking Heather about her Pentagon training," Voight said to Royle.

"Underwhelming," I said.

"Great," Voight responded. "Good to know that some things don't change." He turned to face Royle. "What can we do for you?"

"I just got word that OSD is doing a set of briefings for the incoming EUCOM commander. Fletcher wants to make sure our office is represented. Voight, can you take this?"

"No can do. I have DTS to wrangle," Voight said.

"I have a Joint Staff meeting," Royle said. "Maybe I could reschedule it..."

I looked back and forth between them, feeling like the last kid on the playground to be picked for the dodge ball team.

"I can take it," I said.

"Really? You think you're up for this?" Royle looked at me with surprise.

"Why wouldn't I be?" I felt slightly offended.

"It's true. Heather knows everything I know," Voight said. "More, in fact. Although that's not really saying much."

"Okay," Royle said, his voice laced with skepticism. "I've got the slides and talkers at my desk." Without waiting for me to respond, Royle turned and walked toward his cubicle, situated next to Fletcher's office.

I looked at Voight, my expression wordlessly asking him something along the lines of WTF? Voight shrugged, eyebrows raised in surprise. He was clearly caught off guard by Royle too.

Clearly, we're off on the wrong foot, I thought as I followed Royle to his desk. I decided I'd try another approach. Royle was already working on his computer by the time I arrived at his desk.

"I'm printing off a copy for you," he said without looking at me.

"Thanks. Your patch—I couldn't help but notice—my brother was in the 173rd."

Royle looked up and took a sharp breath. "Right," he said, before focusing even more intently on his computer screen.

"He was in Afghanistan—"

"Look, I don't have time for this right now," Royle interrupted. He stood up, walked to the printer, and collected the slides. "Here," he said, holding them out to me.

I stood, shocked. I'd never encountered anyone in uniform so utterly dismissive of my brother's service before. *What is his problem?* I bit my lip, trying to contain my anger. It was one thing to be rude to me; it was another thing entirely to treat my brother's sacrifice with such flippancy.

"Heather?" Royle asked, snapping my attention back to him. He was still holding out the papers.

I took the slides from him while taking a deep breath to keep myself composed. "I'll review these and do a little research before the brief."

"That's not going to work," Royle said.

"Why not?"

"Briefing's in ten minutes. Room 3C1034. Good luck."

"No problem," I said with a confident smile that masked a maelstrom of fury. "No problem at all."

Although Ken told us at the orientation briefing that navigating the Pentagon was pretty straightforward, somehow the passage that should have taken me between corridors eight and nine dead-ended into a blank, white wall. But only on the top three floors of the building. Ken also inconveniently neglected to mention the existence of *half*-corridors, which further complicated matters. Finally, after fifteen minutes of wandering the Pentagon's hallways, I finally managed to knock on the door of 3C1034.

I waited for thirty seconds and was about to leave when a Navy commander opened the door to let me in the conference room. Correction: an extremely *hot* Navy commander. He had steel blue eyes with blond, trimmed hair and the kind of chiseled features one could easily mistake for an ancient Greek statue of Adonis himself wearing a military uniform. He put his finger over his lips to indicate we needed to be quiet; the meeting was already in full swing.

Stop smiling. You shouldn't. You're engaged to Ryan. And then: *Quit worrying. You're engaged, not dead.*

We sat down next to each other on red leather seats next to the back wall—the only two that remained open—which also happened to be situated a couple rows behind the four-star general who was at the center of a U-shaped table. Several other one- and two-star officers flanked him. *Voight was right about all the stars around here.*

"Next slide," the general said, sipping coffee from a mug that looked like it was almost the size of my head.

I looked up toward the briefing, and my eyes widened; a perfectly coiffed and perfectly tailored Derek Odem was delivering the talk.

I guess the NSC will leave the White House to brief a four-star, I thought.

"Sir, as you know, we believe that the situation in Georgia is getting increasingly unstable," Derek said.

"That tracks with everything that I've been reading," the general said.

"Indeed, sir. We're increasingly concerned that Russia is going to attempt to create more instability in Georgia, the way it did in Ukraine in 2014."

"For what purpose?"

"It's difficult, of course, to interpret Moscow's behavior. But we think they want to warn the Georgian government not to align any further with the West."

"But the cat's already out of the bag on that one, isn't it?" the general said. "Haven't the Georgians signed a partnership agreement with NATO?"

"Yes, and Russia's been none too thrilled about that. We think Moscow wants to convince the Georgians to rethink their position, by using force if necessary."

"But aren't the Russians bogged down in Syria? And Ukraine? I mean, they can't do everything. Something's gotta give. Why ramp up our assistance to Georgia? Why now?"

"The 2008 Russian military campaign to take South Ossetia was, by many accounts, a debacle," Derek said. "It proved to Moscow—once and for all—that it *badly* needed to reinvest in its own military. A couple years later, Russia decides to get involved in Syria. And, although they've had some missteps, overall they've become a much more lethal fighting force."

"Great," the general said. "And there we were, at the end of the Cold War, thinking that Russia would no longer be a threat."

"Unfortunately, that doesn't appear to be the case," Derek said.

"Not anymore, no," the general agreed, quietly. "So we're going to help the Georgians shore themselves up against a possible Russian onslaught."

"That's the idea, yes."

"Won't that be provocative? Picking a fight? Won't the Russians want to swing back at us, somehow?"

Derek advanced to the next slide. It had a map of the Caucuses and the Black Sea.

"That's exactly the concern that I've been working to mitigate: shoring up Georgia's defenses without unnecessarily provoking Russia." Derek pointed to a country toward the right side of the map. "My—excuse me, *our*—solution is to build up a presence in Armenia, on the southern border with Georgia. We can invite the Georgians to train with us there, and we'll be able to rapidly respond in the event that Russia starts any shenanigans."

Something about the plan didn't smell quite right to me, but I was having a hard time putting my finger on just what was wrong.

"The added benefit to the Armenia plan is that we'll have a greater presence in the region, which will allow us to keep a greater eye on Iran and reinforce our troops operating in Syria and Iraq if needed."

"Logistics?"

"We'll ship our equipment through Turkey."

The general sat back in his chair, quietly staring at the screen. "Won't the Russians go nuts if they see Americans in Armenia? It's still their neighborhood."

"We'll do it through NATO, so our fingerprints aren't all over this."

"Great." The general nodded. "If you wouldn't mind, keep me posted on how this develops. It'll be good to have a heads-up as early as possible so I can give you the support you need."

"Actually, sir, that may be coming down the line pretty soon," Derek said.

"I see." The general was visibly annoyed. "Does Jim—the current EUCOM commander—know about this?"

"No. We've been working this as a close-hold initiative in the White House for a while now. Assuming we can get everything lined up with the Armenians, I expect the President's going to be making an announcement within the next couple weeks."

The general took off his glasses. "I would have appreciated a little more time to get up to speed in the command before taking on such a significant mission like this. And frankly, I'm not thrilled with your telling Jim—or me—how I'm supposed to use my forces, and where, without at least consulting me first."

"With all due respect, this is an initiative coming from the White House," Derek said.

"Is it really? If that's the case, I look forward to working with you further on this. In the meantime, I believe it's time to move onto the next briefing—from Coalition Affairs?"

I stood up.

"Ah, Dr. Reilly! Great to see you again," Derek said as I walked to the front of the room. "Over to you."

He handed me the PowerPoint remote and ceded the floor to me. He sat down at an empty seat at the table, a couple chairs down from the general.

I took a deep breath and squared my shoulders as I set my briefing notes down on the podium stand. My hands shook. Teaching had given me plenty of experience with public speaking, but teaching undergraduates—who didn't know much of anything about anything—was one thing. Briefing a four-star general, who had a hell of a lot of experience in global and military affairs, was an entirely different matter. Especially on a topic I was only loosely acquainted with. *What have I gotten myself into?*

I adjusted my papers in order to give myself a couple more seconds to calm down. It didn't work.

The only way out is through, Jon used to say.

I tried to advance to the next slide, but accidentally ended up on the map from the previous briefing. "Whoops, I'm sorry," I said, fiddling with the remote. The slide didn't move.

"Are the batteries working in this thing?" I asked, speaking to nobody in particular as I banged the remote against my palm in order to try and get it to work. I felt my cheeks redden as I pointed the remote toward the screen, the map still looming large instead of my own presentation.

And that's when it hit me.

I knew what was wrong with Derek's Georgia-Armenia plan.

Should I say something? I wondered. *They'll catch the problem eventually, won't they? That's what this huge bureaucracy exists for, right?*

"Turkey *hates* Armenia," I heard a voice say.

"What's that?" asked the general.

"Huh?" I asked, realizing that the voice I'd heard was, in fact, mine.

"What did you say?" the general asked, sitting forward in his chair.

Derek is going to hate me *for this.*

"Sir, I'm sorry. But—I…to go back to the last briefing. The Armenia plan—I don't think—It's just that it'll never work."

Derek sat up in his chair. Although his features remained passive, his knuckles started whitening as he strengthened his grip on the edge of the table.

"And why do you say that?" the general asked, eyebrow raised.

"You need Turkey to make this Armenia plan work, right?"

"Right," Derek said from the back of the room, steel in his voice.

"Well, when I attended a conference at Chatham House in London a couple years ago, we had a couple sessions on European security," I heard myself babbling.

"I'm not following," the general said.

"Right. Sorry—it's just that the problem with the plan is that Turkey hates Armenia. And vice versa. They're still squabbling over the Armenian genocide a century ago. They'd never support this mission. And Turkey's a member of the North Atlantic Treaty Organization. They'd *never* let NATO get involved in this."

The room hushed in stunned silence. Derek, now completely pale, somehow reminded me of a soda can that had been squashed from the middle.

"And that's not even the biggest problem," I continued. "Even if, against all odds, Turkey *did* go along with the plan, Russia hates NATO just about as much as it hates us. Getting NATO to run this mission is deeply provocative. It would be like waving a red flag in front of a bull. Or, in this case, a bear. A big, Russian bear."

Nobody said anything. The general looked down at the table, rubbing the bridge of his nose with his thumb and forefinger.

"I'm sorry. I shouldn't have—" I started.

"May I ask your name?"

"Dr. Heather Reilly," I said.

I felt awkward about using my title, but even more awkward that everyone in the room probably thought I was an idiot. I might be wrong, but at least the crowd would know I was an educated idiot.

"Dr. Reilly is right," the general said. "The plan is flawed."

There's a peculiar sound just as a flash of the blindingly obvious hits a crowd of people. It's a strange combination of low whistles under breath, pencils being put down on notepads, and the odd whispered expletive. Which is exactly what the room sounded like as the realization of what I was saying washed over the crowd.

"There may be some obstacles we have to overcome, but the plan is still solid," Derek argued, unconvincingly. He was a man drowning, searching for a life preserver...and I had thrown him overboard.

The Navy pilot in the back of the room grinned at me. My heart fluttered, just a little bit.

"You may want to wait a little while before you get POTUS behind this," the general said. "It'll be a cold day in hell before Turkey allows NATO to take this on, and it's liable to send Moscow into conniption fits. Back to the drawing board, ladies and gents." The general sipped his coffee and then turned back to me.

"Now, Dr. Reilly, shall we get on with your presentation?"

I got back to the office about an hour later, just as Voight was hanging up his phone.

"Hot damn! I heard you just kicked Derek's ass!"

"Wow. Word travels fast," I said.

"Einstein said that light speed is the fastest anything can travel. But Einstein didn't know about the Pentagon's rumor mill. Especially when the rumors involve telling the NSC to stuff it."

"Great," I said. "Derek's going to hate me."

"Maybe? You pulled a power move, definitely. But he probably thinks you were under instructions from Fletcher to scupper his plan."

"Well, that's a relief, I guess? But there may be a silver lining to all of this…" I said.

Voight raised an eyebrow.

"I think I just figured out how to move the Moldova plan forward," I said.

Voight grinned. "Man, it pays to be partnered with the Whiz Kid!"

CHAPTER EIGHT

AMANDA ASKED ME TO MEET HER AT A RECEPTION NEAR K STREET THAT NIGHT, AND SINCE THE ONLY THING ON MY CALENDAR WAS TO SECRETLY BINGE-WATCH OLD EPISODES OF *GAME OF THRONES*, I AGREED TO JOIN. The dark, oak-paneled bar of Sidecar Charlie's was filled with a potpourri of political Washingtonians—industrialists, lobbyists, Hill staffers, ambassadors, and executive-branch politicos—each contributing to the subtle, yet unmistakable scent of power floating in the air. A waiter wearing a neatly pressed waistcoat and a white apron down to his ankles passed me, carrying a tray of stuffed mushrooms.

"What's in the mushrooms?" I asked, feeling my stomach rumble.

"Perrano cheese and parma ham," the waiter answered.

I hesitated. I'd been vegan with Ryan for almost a decade by that point. But I was starving, and what Ryan didn't know wouldn't kill him. I took a bite. The ham, the cheese—real cheese, not the synthetic rubbery stuff I'd been eating for years—tasted divine. A waiter came by with another load of appetizers. This time, some kind of cheese on crackers.

I'd never really cared much about food. It was for eating. And you ate it so that you could get along and do whatever the next thing was that you had to do. Like running. Or studying. Or working. Which is why it hadn't been a big deal to me when Ryan asked me to go vegan. But that was *before* I had cheese and fig jam on a cracker. Or mushrooms stuffed with fancy ham and cheese. I could feel my eyes widen with surprise at the taste. I took several more, and then started circulating around the room to find Amanda.

I eventually found her in a corner, speaking to a man in a nondescript grey suit that I'd come to recognize as a defense contractor's uniform. Amanda was laughing—a little insincerely—at a joke he'd made as I walked up to join them.

"There you are!" Amanda said. "Tim, let me introduce you to my sister-in-law, Dr. Heather Reilly."

"Pleasure to meet you, ma'am," Tim said as he extended his hand to me. "Well, I'll let you two ladies catch up. But you'll pass on my thoughts to the senator?"

His smile widened larger than it seemed possible for his face, and for a split second his dark eyes and grey suit reminded me of a shark about to strike.

"I will, Tim. I'm sorry that he's not able to be here tonight."

"Well, I am too. But truth be told," he leaned in for a conspiratorial whisper, "I'm better off talking to you, anyway. You know how to get things done. And you're an awful lot prettier than the senator," Tim finished with a wink.

"I'm flattered," Amanda said with a strained laugh. "Enjoy your evening."

I ate another mushroom as I watched Tim melt back into the crowd, circling the room for his next target. It took me a moment before I noticed Amanda eyeing me curiously.

"What?" I asked.

Amanda eyed the mushroom in my hand.

"Those have ham."

I nodded guiltily. "It's true. They do. This will be our little secret," I said. "Is this what I've been missing for the last decade?" I popped the mushroom in my mouth.

Amanda laughed. "Vegan food doesn't taste quite as good?"

"Vegan food tastes like cardboard compared to this. I wonder if I could convince Ryan to ditch the diet?"

Amanda looked at me skeptically.

"Yeah, I didn't think so, either," I said glumly. "That would probably be a bridge too far. Especially with everything else going on."

"I take it you haven't told him yet?" Amanda asked. Another waiter came by, this time with glasses of red and white wine on a silver tray. Amanda took a glass, so I did too.

I sighed. "No, I haven't told him."

"Why not?" Amanda asked, trying to mask her incredulity. "It's been a couple weeks now. And he's your *fiancé*. You should be talking to him about this stuff."

"I know, I know. I need to. But I just don't know how to tell him I'm the brain child behind the Pentagon's new plan to stick it to the Russians."

"Sure, Ryan may have problems with what you're working on. But he knows you're trying to do something important while actually making a real salary, right?"

I sipped my wine. "Money—it doesn't really resonate with Ryan. I don't get it. He just thinks that things will eventually sort themselves out."

"Right," Amanda said, skeptically. "Look, I know you guys love each other. But you're making sacrifices to get yourself out of debt.

He's not. At least, not yet. And, from what you've told me, he's got some loans from law school that he's going to need to pay off too."

"His loans are worse than mine, if you can believe it."

"I believe it. And, by the way, you *are* working for a cause. Just not the one you thought you'd be working on when you moved to Washington. Speaking of moving here, have you been to Arlington yet?"

"No," I said, feeling guilty. Part of me wanted to visit Jon's grave. But another part of me—the part that was still hurt that he'd put himself in harm's way in the first place—held me back.

"Sometimes it's a good place to think. Clear my head. Maybe it would help you."

"Maybe," I said.

"Well, regardless, you have to give Ryan the opportunity to try and understand. You have to let him decide for himself whether he can deal with it or not."

"But what if he can't deal? What if he runs screaming?"

"That'll tell you something important, won't it?" Amanda said, cocking an eyebrow. "And besides. He'll definitely run screaming if you don't tell him what's going on—soon."

"Do you always have to be so wise?" I said, pretending to pout.

"It's in my contract. Section two, subparagraph a: roles and responsibilities of being a big sister-in-law."

"Ah. Of course." I took another sip of my wine. "Am I really worried about losing my fiancé because of my job at the *Pentagon*? Seriously? It's not as if I've decided to cultivate a heroin habit or something. How do I get myself into these messes?"

Amanda shrugged. "Ryan won't be the only one who's miffed that you're not working on Afghanistan."

"Huh?"

She grinned. "Only *slightly* miffed. But still. I'm trying to get Senator McClutchy to ask for hearings on Afghanistan and Pakistan. Which is becoming much harder now that I don't have an insider to give me the scoop."

"You mean, the news about the Islamic State in southern Afghanistan isn't enough?"

"Apparently not. Which is frustrating. And the reports that my contacts in the State Department have been bootlegging me? They aren't sticking."

"Bootlegging?" I asked. "Did you start selling pirated DVDs or something without telling me?"

Amanda considered that. "You know, selling pirated DVDs would probably pay more than my current gig. But what I was actually referring to is sending stuff without permission from the higher-ups. It's what makes this town work. Otherwise we'd never get anything done around here."

"Of course," I nodded. A couple months ago, it would have seemed bizarre to me that the only way to get anything done in Washington was to circumvent the system. But it made sense after working for a couple weeks in the Pentagon.

"So, what's this reception for?" I asked, changing the subject.

"It's being put on by 'Citizens for Fiscal Responsibility.'"

"Who are they?"

"It's a new lobbying group. Ultra-right-wing budget hawks. Think Grover Norquist meets the Tea Party. On steroids."

"These guys sound pretty conservative. Even for you," I teased.

"We can't all be lefty tree-huggers," Amanda said with a wink.

"More importantly, anyone here you think is cute?" I asked, scanning the room. As with most of the situations I'd found myself in recently, the women in the room were few and far between.

"Here? In a group with political leanings that are somewhere to the right of Attila the Hun?" Amanda was incredulous. "You said it yourself: I'm a conservative, but these are pretty right wing people, even for me."

"Sure, but *you're* here, and your politics are pretty reasonable. There may be someone who doesn't buy into it, either," I said. "What about that guy?" I casually pointed to a man with brown hair that was deliberately sculpted to look messy and carefree. He wore a pinstripe suit and clearly took his physical fitness seriously.

"Oh, him? That's Mike," she said. Just then, Mike looked up; they waved at each other.

"You *know* him? He's gorgeous! Why not ask him on a date?"

"I would, but I think his husband would probably have a problem with that."

"Figures," I said, annoyed.

"Washington is a career woman's dream and nightmare. It's a dream because there are incredible professional opportunities. But it's a nightmare because single, straight men are hard to come by."

"Really? Every meeting I've been in has had a five-to-one male to female ratio," I said.

"And just about all the men are either already married or gay. Or they have commitment issues, because they think they can just move on to the next highly successful, educated woman. Which they do."

"Ugh. That sounds dismal." I was beginning to see why Amanda made a point of changing the subject every time I raised the topic.

"It's not pretty. But at least it's easier to focus on my work."

"Speaking of, if we're not here to expand your dating horizons, why are we here?"

"The group throwing this shindig? They've started courting Senator McClutchy. They think he has a bright future. And as much as I've warned him against it—our party needs to reclaim the middle ground—McClutchy doesn't want to alienate them. Which is why I'm here instead of him," Amanda shrugged. "I don't agree with their politics, but I do agree with their open bar until nine-thirty. Speaking of which, did you want another drink?"

I thought about that for a second. True, it was a school night. But the drinks were free, and I wasn't ready to go home just yet.

"Sure," I said.

"Excellent. I'll flag someone down—what's *he* doing here?" Amanda asked, her eyes suddenly focused like a laser on someone that just entered the room.

"Who?"

"The senator."

"McClutchy?"

"Yes. Who's that with him?" Amanda asked, to herself before straightening her posture and forcing a smile. "Come on, let's go say hello to the senator and ask him what on *Earth* he's doing here."

Amanda charged off, dodging between waiters with canapés and politicos with martinis, determined to reach him before the rest of the crowd awakened to the fact that a United States senator had just entered the room. As I followed closely behind, I saw Tim shoot a confused look toward Amanda.

"Good evening, sir," Amanda said to the senator. "I didn't expect to see you here?"

"Why, hello, Amanda," he said. He was shorter than he looked on TV, with a little more grey at the temples and a few more wrinkles around his eyes as well. Still, he was striking: salt-and-pepper hair, dark eyes, and a brilliant white smile, as if he were the modern-day incarnation of John F. Kennedy himself. McClutchy exuded a confidence and charisma that was palpable, making it feel like ten men had entered the room rather than one. A short, squat man with flared nostrils, a thinning hairline, and an altogether striking resemblance to a toad accompanied the senator.

"Amanda, let me introduce you to Fred Wicker." He pointed to his toad-like companion. "Fred's joining our office as a consultant for a little while."

"Oh?" A slight glimmer of shock registered on Amanda's face, but was gone before anyone but myself noticed it. "Welcome to the team, Fred."

"Thanks," Fred grunted.

"Fred here thought I should get out of the office," McClutchy said, pointing at the toad-man. "He thought I might meet some new friends."

"Sure, but you need to be careful about which people you're seen with."

"Fred doesn't seem to think that's much of a problem. But speaking of meeting new friends…" Senator McClutchy looked at me and extended his hand.

"Of course!" Amanda said. "This is my sister-in-law, Dr. Heather Reilly."

"Sister-in-law?" McClutchy asked, while shaking my hand. "I've heard all about your brother. I want to thank you for your brother's service. And sacrifice."

"Umm, thanks." It still felt awkward and terrible and frustrating to be thanked for my brother's decisions—decisions that I thoroughly disagreed with.

The senator didn't notice my discomfort. "You know, I met Amanda at one of the Gold Star widows' meetings I visit with every now and again and I thought to myself, here's someone that's talented, and suffered such tremendous loss. Maybe I can help her direct her energy towards serving our country. I offered her the job then and there."

"That's kind of you," I said. For Amanda's sake, I swallowed my discomfort. "And hiring her was smart of you too. Amanda's the best there is."

"Indeed," the senator said.

Fred narrowed his eyes.

"Heather has just started at the Pentagon," Amanda said. "She has her PhD from Harvard and has written a lot on Afghanistan. We were just talking about the growing instability there."

"Well, I won't keep you ladies from your conversation. Fred, did you have anybody in mind that I should meet?"

Fred straightened up and pointed to another corner. "Yes, sir. The chairman is just over there—"

"Ladies, if you'll excuse us," the senator said. He walked off with Fred.

Amanda took a sip of her wine as she watched them leave. I could tell her mind was racing at a million miles a minute, assessing and analyzing the conversation we'd just had.

"Everything okay?" I finally asked.

"Everything's fine," Amanda smiled. "Just fine."

Amanda went into work mode after the conversation with the senator, mixing and mingling with the different power brokers in the room while keeping one eye fixed on her boss. I wasn't in the mood to keep up with her conversations, so I said my goodbyes and headed out at about eight o'clock. I was surprised that it was still muggy and light out; the bar, with its near-frigid air conditioning and cozy oak-paneled walls didn't have any windows, giving its patrons no real indication of the time—or the season, for that matter.

I decided to take the metro rather than take a cab. I was halfway to McPherson Square station when I felt a buzzing near my hip. I looked at my phone; it was Ryan. I took a deep breath to steady my nervousness and answered.

"Heather! I've been trying to get ahold of you," Ryan said.

"I was at a reception."

I fidgeted with a ragged nail on my index finger as we spoke. I felt guilty. For not having told Ryan about my decisions, for loving stuffed mushrooms as much as I did, and for the nagging feeling of anxiety that I felt when talking to him.

"You've been out a lot recently," he said.

"What's that supposed to mean?" I asked, stopping in my tracks.

"Sorry, that didn't come out right. I'm just saying that going out costs money, Heather. Isn't the point of you being in D.C. right now so that you can be in money-saving mode?"

"The food and drinks were free," I said.

"Oh. Well, you said that you'd be around this evening. That we could talk?"

My cheeks reddened. "Oh, right. Sorry about that."

"You've been hard to reach since you've gotten to Washington."

"I'm sorry. It's just been pretty busy."

"Too busy to talk to your fiancé?"

"No. Yes? I don't know," I said. "There's just been a lot going on—"

"What's up with you, Heather?" Ryan interrupted. "You're acting really weird. Is something going on?"

I paused. My moment of truth had arrived. But, somehow, I couldn't figure out what the words should be. Or how to say them. I looked across the street. Beyond the cars and cabs zooming to their destinations, students in jeans and Georgetown sweaters stumbled out of a dive bar.

Watching them reminded me of college, when Ryan and I stumbled into our own favorite dive bar after attending a lecture on the problems of an overmilitarized U.S. foreign policy. Sitting on dilapidated couches, surrounded by other students drinking cheap gin and tonics, the scent of stale beer in the air, Ryan told me he loved me. I took him home, and we made love all night.

It was the first time I'd felt much of anything after Jon died.

It should have been so easy. It should have been straightforward. *I decided to stay at the Pentagon to try and change things from the inside. I decided I wanted to help.* But somehow, I couldn't choke out the words.

"Heather? What's going on?" Ryan asked, snapping me back into the moment.

"I—I just miss you," I finally said. The words rang hollow because they weren't as true as I wanted them to be.

"Oh," Ryan said, sounding surprised. "I miss you too. We've never been apart this long. I could come out there. Visit you?"

"We've talked about that. We can't afford it, Ryan. You had to take a pay cut last year...."

"Well, Legal Aid's fundraising has gotten better this year, so I might be able to get them to bite on a 'research' trip to Washington," Ryan said. "I could see what our national headquarters is up to.... Besides, I saw some last-minute deals on Southwest."

"Really?" I said, trying not to wince, although I wasn't quite sure why. "Sure."

"Let me see what I can do," Ryan said, sounding excited. "And maybe we could set the date while I'm there."

"Date?"

"For getting married."

"Oh. Right," I said, suddenly anxious to change the subject. "Look, I'm about to get on the Metro. I need to let you go. Let me know about the trip, okay?"

"Will do. I love you."

"Yeah," I said. I hung up the phone and then walked the rest of the way down K Street to catch the train.

CHAPTER NINE

WHAT NOW? I thought, seeing my memo—the one on how to push forward the Moldova plan that I thought was already on Fletcher's desk—resting on my keyboard as I walked up to my cubicle the next day. It had tiny red writing scribbled all over it, along with a Post-it note that said "fix before briefing Fletcher this morning," and signed by none other than Colonel Royle.

Maybe it was because I was feeling a bit of indigestion after my dalliance with carnivorousness the night before, but as I surveyed his changes, I found myself feeling increasingly offended. While there were one or two good substantive points he thought ought to be addressed—and which I would happily incorporate—most of the changes he made were stylistic "happy-to-glads." In other words, they were insulting. Especially to someone who'd spent her entire career writing for a living. I decided I wouldn't give Royle the satisfaction of seeing his nitnoid changes incorporated into my memo verbatim. Immature? Perhaps. But I didn't care. These were the little victories of policy dorks like me.

"Pilgrimage to Mecca, Whiz Kid?" Voight said when he arrived in the office about half an hour later, looking freshly showered and setting down his gym bag on his chair.

"Sure," I said, hitting "send" on the memo. "We don't have to brief Fletcher for another hour."

"Awesome," Voight said. "Plenty of time."

We left the office and walked toward the Starbucks. Bright morning sunlight shone through the windows of the A-ring, illuminating the occasional dust mote as we walked. The lemony scent of disinfectant competed with the aroma of fresh coffee as we approached the food court.

"Ready to brief the plan?" Voight asked.

"The Moldova plan? As ready as I'll ever be. I mean, as far as ideas go, it's pretty out there. But I *was* feeling as confident as possible about it until Royle decided to shred the memo this morning. Now I'm just hoping I'll get through the meeting without Fletcher biting my head off. Or firing me."

"Don't let him get to you," Voight said. "Remember, I already sanity-checked this with our folks at EUCOM. They didn't like it, but they realized our idea isn't as bad as the Georgia-Armenia plan the NSC was cooking up. I'm just hoping that Fletcher signs off on this so I don't have to go to Germany. My little girl is starting school next week and I want to be around for that."

I thought about what it might be like if Ryan and I had kids, then immediately pushed the thought to the side. Mom, of course, had started hinting at wanting grandchildren years ago. But even if we decided to have them—and for me, it was still a big "if"—it would be a long time before our bills were paid off enough that we could afford to even contemplate procreating. My thoughts returned to Moldova.

"Do you think we're doing the right thing?" I asked.

"Sure," Voight said. "The alternative—not getting coffee—would be much, much worse."

I smiled as I rolled my eyes. "About Moldova."

"Oh. That. Beats me."

"Wait—what?" I asked, surprised. "Then why are you helping me push this plan along? What if the guy on the NSC is right? What if we end up starting World War III?"

"Are you kidding? After shooting down that goofy Armenia plan at the briefing the other day? I think you just might have prevented us from *really* provoking the Russians."

"Sure. I'm just worried. Is our plan really any better?"

"Look, I'm just a big plane driver. My job—until fairly recently—has been to make fun of the laws of physics by making sure that a multi-ton piece of metal flies through the air."

We stepped on the escalators. "Then explain my call sign," I said. "It took me a little while to get the reference."

"Reference? Moi?" Voight said, pointing toward his chest with the most innocent face he could possibly muster.

"Yes. *Vous.* 'Whiz Kid' *also* refers to the young brainiacs that Secretary McNamara hired in the 1960s to help him figure out how to win the Vietnam War and generally unscrew the Pentagon."

"Your point?" he asked as we turned a corner.

"My point, Voight, is that a relatively obscure reference like that would only come either from somebody as nerdy as myself, or someone who has really studied defense and military history. Or both. Which means you know a lot more about this defense policy stuff than you're letting on."

"Crap. I've outed myself, haven't I?" Voight laughed.

"Don't worry, your secret is safe with me. Latte?" I said, grinning, as we approached the counter.

"Yes, ma'am. Sleuthing me out is gonna cost you, big time. You're buying, Nancy Drew."

"With pleasure," I said, and then ordered our coffees—large lattes, but mine with an extra shot of espresso—as Voight went to find us a table. I noticed Royle joining the back of the line, which was at least fifteen people long. Royle caught my eye and waved a small, brief hello. I tried to smile in return, but barely managed a grimace.

Whatever. I grabbed our coffees and sat down with Voight.

"Anyway. Moldova? World War III? What do you think?"

Voight sighed. "I meant what I said back there. I have no idea. Because there's no easy answers to any of this stuff. All we can do is pick the least worst out of a universe of terrible options."

"Depressing."

"Sure is. And then, once we start down a particular path, we have to expect that something—if not everything—is going to go horribly wrong. And at that point, all we can do is course-correct."

"Then how do we know that what we're doing is right?"

"By knowing that doing just about anything else would be much, much worse."

"That's not reassuring."

"Nope. Not at all. So, back to Moldova. Which, ultimately, is about Russia, right?"

"As near as I can tell, yes," I said.

"Russia has been acting like a complete bastard since at least 2008. Invading Georgia. Annexing Crimea—right after it held the Olympics, for god's sake. Assassinating dissidents. Creating an army of internet trolls. Cutting off Ukraine's gas supplies—a place that gets really damned cold—in the middle of winter. Cyber-attacking Estonia so badly it shut down their entire government. Not to mention hacking our elections, starting a proxy war in Ukraine, and coming to the aid of the dictator in Syria. So, Fletcher's position is kind of understandable. If we don't draw—and stick to—some sort of line, somewhere, when will it stop?

"But here's the rub. The Russians will say that we started this mess in the first place. That the Kosovo War, the invasion of Iraq, and the bombing of Libya to get rid of Qaddafi were all examples of the United States' utter irresponsibility. That although these countries were run by scumbags, we didn't actually have the right to invade them. Not to mention pushing for the expansion of NATO to include countries that Russia previously thought of as 'theirs,'" Voight said, using air quotes. "Moscow is arguing that over the past twenty-five years, we've behaved like a bull in a China shop. And that, therefore, *we're* the ones that need to be taught a lesson."

"What if the Russians are right?"

"Well, if you look at what the Russians have been saying and doing, it's all pretty cynical. It looks to me like they want to restore their former glory before the whole country dies of HIV and alcohol poisoning. And invading a neighboring country isn't exactly kosher. That said, they very well may be right. But right and wrong are kind of immaterial, don't you think?"

I was shocked. "How can you say that 'right' and 'wrong' are immaterial?"

"Because the truth of the matter is that, if you go back far enough, everybody's fucked up. So we're probably both right, and we're probably both wrong. What matters is what we do from here.

Do we just pack up and go home? Let the Russians have their way? Or do we stand up for something?"

"Like what?"

"Maybe what we've always tried to stand for, at least in theory. Freedom."

"Seriously?" I felt myself getting agitated. "With the problems we have? *We* don't even have freedom. The one percent controls most of the wealth of this country. Mass shootings seem to happen nearly every day. And we have politicians who think that building a wall on the border with Mexico is going to magically solve our immigration problems. Things aren't that great here."

"I don't disagree that we have some serious issues," Voight said, setting down his coffee cup. "For one thing, I don't understand why our wall-building politicians haven't heard of tunneling. But every country has its issues. At least we have the freedom to screw things up in our own, unique way. And to change things, if we want to. We can vote. If you try to pull any stunts like that in Moscow, you're likely to find yourself in a very cold jail cell. Or dead. So, I'm not saying we've got things right—far from it. But I *am* saying that the world is a seriously fucked up place, and we've got things a whole lot better than just about anybody else out there."

"How does this apply to Moldova?" I asked.

"Well, maybe by giving the Moldovans an assist, we'll be giving them an honest shot at determining their own path for themselves. And, maybe in the process, we'll give other people the courage to stand up and choose their own paths too."

"So what distinguishes us is our idealism?" I asked.

"Something like that."

"You know, they say that the road to hell is paved with good intentions," I said.

Voight looked at his watch. "Actually, the road to hell is paved with polished concrete and leads back to Fletcher's office. Time to get back upstairs."

We arrived on time to meet with Fletcher. She, in turn, made us wait fifteen minutes. At last, her door opened, and a man I recognized as the Undersecretary for Personnel exited, looking a little flushed.

Voight and I looked at each other, eyes wide. He shrugged. He didn't want to know, and I didn't either.

"If you could get me that memo later today, Ariane, that would be great," he said, turning back to Fletcher.

"Yes, sir. Will do," she said. "Guys, you can come on in," she called out to us from behind her desk. Her voice was noticeably sweeter than any other time I'd heard her speak, which made the whole situation feel more, rather than less, tense.

We walked in and sat at her conference table while Fletcher finished up an email. "I'll be right with you," she told us, tapping away at her keyboard. When she finally finished, she turned to us. "Now, what's this I hear about a new plan for Moldova?" she asked, turning around to face us.

Fletcher's bright red lipstick was smudged. Just a little, but just enough to be totally obvious to me.

Really? Do you really have to play the cliché?

I took a deep breath to regain my composure and push the reason that her lipstick was smudged to the furthest corner of my mind.

"Your copy of the memo is right here, ma'am," Voight said, handing it to her. "Heather was the primary drafter on this, so she'll be leading the briefing this morning."

"I heard you put Derek in his place the other day," Fletcher said.

"The flaws in his plan were pretty obvious," I said.

"Good work," Fletcher said.

"Thanks. As you know, the U.S. has decided to assist Georgia as it shores itself up against the Russians. But the NSC wants to do that in a way that doesn't provoke the Russians."

"They don't want to start World War III," Voight interrupted.

"They *always* say that," Fletcher said, rolling her eyes. "They're drama queens. Scared of their own shadows because they might accidentally trigger an apocalypse. So, your plan is better?"

"Well, at least marginally better. If the goal is to support Georgia, without *completely* irritating Moscow, my idea is to put the training mission in Moldova."

"You're kidding me," Fletcher said, skeptically.

"Ma'am, hear Heather out," Voight interjected. "Putting the training mission in Moldova rather than Armenia scratches a number of itches. First, it supports the Moldovans, which makes us happy. Second, it supports the Georgians, which makes the NSC happy. Third, if we do it right, we'll minimize the chances of blowback from the Russians."

"Moldova is a lot farther away from Georgia than Armenia," Fletcher said, looking at the map on her wall. "It's clear across the other side of the Black Sea, in fact."

"True," I said. "From that perspective, this isn't ideal. But Voight's run the traps at EUCOM. It's not the prettiest logistical situation, but if the Russians make trouble in Georgia, we *could* rapidly deploy from Moldova."

"But, Heather, this gets us back to our first problem," Fletcher said. "NSC's objection is that if the U.S. has a training mission in Moldova, Moscow will go apoplectic because we're in the Russians' backyard."

"Right. That's why we should create a coalition—with some-one else in the lead—to run the training mission. That way we participate, and if there are issues with Russia we can quickly get to Georgia—or anywhere else, for that matter. But politically it doesn't look like we're there to challenge Russia."

"And, bonus!" Voight said, "As the DASD for Coalition Affairs, you'll be in the lead."

Fletcher cocked an eyebrow, "That'll make it hard for Derek to have his typical shitfit. So, what country do you have in mind to spearhead this coalition?"

"Nobody in particular. Just about anybody but us. Or NATO," I added.

"That's a pretty serious shortcoming in your plan."

"True. But I don't feel qualified to pick the right country. I figured you—with your insights and stature—would be the best person to answer that question."

"I see. What are the risks?" Fletcher was clearly suspicious about the compliment I just paid her.

"We might get pushback from people saying that we should just run the Georgia support mission through Turkey," I said.

"Because it has a border with Georgia?" asked Fletcher.

"Exactly. And, frankly, it's fairly likely right now that we'll go in that direction."

"Why do you say that?"

"Because it'll mean that the Joint Staff won't have to go completely back to the drawing board," Voight said. "They love the path of least resistance. Unless we tell them—soon—to start looking at other options."

"So you're saying we have a narrow window of opportunity to push Moldova as an option."

"Correct," I said. "But it's worth pointing out that the Turkey option isn't great either. Turkey's politics are pretty volatile these days. And Turkey's a NATO member. Russia isn't going to look kindly on a Turkish military buildup that points towards, well, Russia."

"There's also the risk that the Russians will see through what we're doing and call bullshit on us," Voight said. "But, to be fair, that was always going to be a risk for getting involved with Moldova. Or anywhere else in that region. This is just *slightly* less risky than all the other options."

"I feel like I've just entered the national security policy version of a circus freak show," Fletcher said.

"It's the least worst plan we've seen so far," Voight said. "At the end of the day, everyone pretty much gets what they want. Well, except for the Russians."

"Fine. Let's start socializing the idea," she said, standing up and dismissing us.

"That was weird," I said, once we got back to our cubicles.

"Which part?"

"Fletcher being nice to us. Maybe she doesn't breathe fire all the time?"

"Maybe," Voight said, skeptically. "Her being pleasant—it makes me itchy."

I nodded. "At least we got a go-ahead on our Moldova plan?"

"Which is also kind of weird. I expected her to tear it to shreds."

"Me too."

"Since she's on board, here's a question for you, Whiz Kid."

"Shoot."

"How in the *hell* are we going to pull this off?"

CHAPTER TEN

"I'M JUST A LITTLE WORRIED," MOM SAID OVER THE PHONE, JUST AS A CROWD OF TEENAGERS CARRYING BACKPACKS AND DRAGGING SUITCASES DECIDED TO WALK IN FRONT OF ME. I dodged and weaved my way through them as fast as I could in order to get to the passenger exit for Terminal C.

"What?" I asked, speaking loudly into my phone while plugging my ear with my right hand. The hard floors and open spaces of Reagan National Airport made for awful acoustics. "I'm sorry; I can't hear you."

"I said I'm worried. You, alone in that big city. It's not good for you and Ryan to be apart."

"Absence makes the heart grow fonder," I said, approaching the exit. I looked around. I couldn't see him anywhere.

"Absence makes the heart forgetful," she said.

"That's why he's visiting," I held my phone in front of me to check my texts. There was another one from Ryan: *"Finding coffee."*

"That's not what I meant. You two ought to be together right now."

"We've only been apart for a month, Mom."

"It's just not right for you guys to be separated. What about planning your wedding?"

I felt my annoyance build as we fell into that well-worn groove of a conversation we'd already had any number of times.

"We can't afford a wedding while we're under mountains of debt."

"You don't need a fancy wedding to get married."

"Do we have to go through this again?"

"Heather Reilly, I'm your mother. It's my job to worry until Ryan can take over the job for me. And besides, you need some stability in your life."

I finally spotted a familiar man with a familiar frame—tall, lanky, with thick glasses and wild, wavy brown hair—at the front of the line at a Starbucks.

"Right. I've got to go, Mom. I found Ryan." I was grateful for the reprieve as I hung up the phone.

"Hi there," he said, grinning at me as he finished counting his nickels, dimes, and pennies for the Starbucks barista. "Here you go, exact change." He scooped it all into his fist and handed it to the cashier.

Coffee paid for, Ryan sidled up to me, pulled me close, and closed in to kiss me. I turned my cheek to him at the last minute, although I couldn't quite understand why.

"What was *that*?" Ryan teased. "Did the Washington bureaucrats send you back to kindergarten? Make you forget how to kiss your future husband?"

"No—it's just, we're in a public place," I said, hoping to mask the fact that I was just as confused about my reaction as Ryan was.

"Man, this town is buttoned-up," said Ryan.

"Yeah. Let's get home."

"Sure. Lead the way."

"So, a woman working in the heart of the national security machine. Does this mean that you're like Carrie from *Homeland* now?" Ryan teased, burying his fork into his butternut squash curry. "This is great, by the way," he said, pointing his fork toward his food. "Just delicious."

I snorted. "Carrie is a vapid, mentally unstable lunatic who tries to sleep with her boss, and ends up sleeping with a terrorist who's trying to kill the President. Not exactly someone I want to be compared to."

"Okay. Sorry." Ryan put his arms up in a defensive position. "So if it isn't *Homeland*, what's it like?"

I struggled to put my impressions into words. *How do I explain a place that is at times profound, and at others mundane, and at all times utterly alien to most of the world?*

"Weird, I guess?"

"Weird?"

"It's pretty much like anywhere else. I work in a cubicle. My coworkers seem to be pretty obsessed with PowerPoint. And there's lots of memos. Except in the Pentagon they tend to be about things that could, you know, lead to war."

"But that's the reason you're there, right? To knock some sense into them about Afghanistan?"

I set down my fork. "About that. I need to tell you something."

"Okay, what's up?" He was clearly nervous.

"I'm not working on Afghanistan anymore."

"What?" Ryan asked. "Why not?"

"There was a reorg."

"Okay. Then what are you working on?"

"I'm working in the military coalitions office."

"But you don't know anything about military coalitions," Ryan said.

"I'm aware of that. Thanks."

"Don't get defensive. I just mean that you're an expert on conflict resolution. Not military coalitions."

"Believe me: I know. But real expertise doesn't seem to be required for a lot of the stuff I do."

"Well, that's comforting. No wonder this country is so messed up."

I kept quiet. He took another bite of his food, looking pensive as he chewed.

"Why?" he eventually asked.

"What do you mean?"

"Why are you doing it? This flies in the face of everything you believe, Heather."

Did it? I wasn't quite sure anymore. I looked up to my right. Jon's Congressional Medal of Honor—the blue ribbon with a gold star given to Amanda about two years after the funeral—was on the wall between the kitchen and the living room. I glanced back at Ryan.

"I think I can help, Ryan," I eventually said. "And besides, we need the money."

"Help the *military*? You're selling out?"

Something in me snapped.

"You're joking, right?" I asked.

"Why would I be joking?"

"Ryan, my debt—your debt—it's killing us. At least *I'm* doing something to climb out of it."

Ryan snapped his head back, as if I'd physically slapped him. "What is that supposed to mean?"

"It means that you can't get out of six figures' worth of debt with a job that pays thirty-five grand per year, Ryan."

"Heather, we've talked about this. They're student loans. It's good debt."

"There's no such thing as 'good' debt, Ryan. I'm teaching four classes every semester, all year-round, plus writing articles and books, and fighting for tenure. And even with all that work that I'm doing, we're barely making ends meet. Am I selling out? Maybe. But at least I'm trying to pull my weight. Which is more than you're doing."

"Excuse me? Not pulling my weight? I have a good job—"

"You're not making anywhere near what you could at a real law firm," I interrupted. "And I get that you're passionate about your work. That's important. But you're in even more debt than I am, and *pro bono* legal work at the clinic doesn't pay you enough. Something's gotta give."

Ryan sat back, stunned. "How long have you felt this way?"

"Since my first day at the Pentagon. I almost quit when they told me that I wouldn't be working on Afghanistan—"

"That's not what I meant. I meant, how long have you felt like I wasn't pulling my weight?"

I deflected. "Why do you think I applied for this fellowship?"

"Because you wanted to find a new way to have an impact," Ryan said. "You wanted practical experience so you could be a better teacher."

"Weren't you listening to me? How many times have I brought up the fact that we needed to come up with a get-out-of-debt plan?"

"Sure, but I thought we had things under control."

"We do, as long as our financial goal is to pay things off shortly before the second coming of Christ." There. It was out in the open. At last. I felt as if a tourniquet had been squeezing my chest for months—years—and was suddenly relaxed. I took a deep breath.

"If I'd known how much your debt was bothering you, I could have helped."

"How? You can barely cover your own loan payments."

"I don't know. We could ask our parents for help—"

"I am *not* asking anyone for money to bail us out of a situation we created for ourselves. Especially not our parents."

"So you'd rather sacrifice your principles instead? By helping the United States government build military coalitions?"

"That's not what it's like, Ryan."

"Isn't it?" I watched him as he sat in silence and fiddled with his fork, stabbing the occasional pea and carrot on his plate as he thought. After a minute or so, he furrowed his brow. "You said you almost quit your first day at the Pentagon?"

"Yes. It was horrible. But then I—"

"So your job changed on your first day, and you didn't think to tell me about that, either?"

I could see his jaw tense as he clenched his teeth.

"I wanted to tell you in person," I said.

"You've been lying to me, Heather."

"No—you don't understand, I just wanted—"

"Whatever, Heather," he said, standing up. "You clearly don't trust me." He turned and left the kitchen.

"Shit," I whispered, collecting the dishes and putting them in the dishwasher. I looked at the clock—it was just after eight forty-five, and Amanda wasn't home yet. Then again, her mandatory rotations around the D.C. cocktail party circuit made her evening schedules pretty erratic. I'd just finished wiping down the counter when I heard Ryan's footsteps climbing down the stairs. I looked up to see him standing in the doorway to the kitchen carrying his suitcase.

"Where are you going?"

"I think it's best if I stay somewhere else tonight."

"But where will you stay? We can't afford a hotel—"

"My *pro bono* law clinic gave me a travel allowance."

He tried to mask his anger, but I knew him too well. He was furious.

"Okay," I said, feeling shocked. I knew our fight was intense, but I hadn't thought it was so bad he couldn't stand to be around me. "When will I see you again?"

"I don't know, Heather. I'm going to need some time."

With that, he left.

I sat down in the hallway, facing the door. I kept waiting for him to knock, to come bounding in and hug me and let me know that he'd forgiven me. That we'd be okay.

But he didn't. Eventually, feeling shell-shocked, I changed out of my clothes, took a shower, and lay on my bed in the darkness. Tears occasionally streamed down my face as I tried to nurse my empty-feeling heart, in my empty-feeling bed.

CHAPTER ELEVEN

WHAT'S THAT BUZZING SOUND? I wondered as I stumbled toward consciousness before realizing it was my iPhone. It was five fifty in the morning, and I was pretty sure it wasn't the first time the alarm had gone off. I hit the snooze button again and flopped back into my pillow. After what happened with Ryan the night before, I just wasn't ready to face the day—at least, not for another nine minutes.

Forty-five minutes later, I woke up again to the realization that I'd accidentally turned the alarm off. *Crap*, I thought, and then sighed. I was tired. It was the kind of exhaustion you feel from crying too many tears, the kind that makes you feel like a balloon pricked by a pin that slowly lost all its air. Getting out of bed seemed almost impossible.

But if I didn't get up, Voight would have to deal with all of the Pentagon's craziness alone. And besides, it would be harder to dwell on all the things that were bothering me if I was busy at work.

I climbed out of bed and braced myself to face the day.

"You want me to do *what?*" I asked Royle in a more irritated tone than I'd intended. He was leaning with his shoulder resting against the top of my cubicle, giving me the impression that he was deliberately forcing himself to act casual.

"Write some talking points for Assistant Secretary Chao's meeting at the end of this week on Mongolia," Royle said.

"Yes, I got that much."

"Okay, then. What's the problem?" Royle did a double-take. "And why do you have a can of breadcrumbs on your desk?"

I looked to the side of my computer at the can of Japanese Panko breadcrumbs I'd found on my desk a couple weeks ago. A Post-it note with Voight's handwriting was attached to the top that read, "Thought I'd give you this to help you navigate the Pentagon."

"Long story. My problem is, have *you* ever been to Mongolia?" I asked.

"Nope."

"Neither have I," I said. "So I don't think I'm qualified to write these. Besides, I'm supposed to be working on the Moldova plan."

"You have a PhD, Heather."

"On conflict resolution. In Afghanistan."

"So?"

"Mongolia isn't Afghanistan."

"You can figure this one out. And besides, it's a softball. You'll be able to get back to the Moldova stuff later this morning. I'd do it, but I've got a meeting with the Joint Staff that's just come up. We're short staffed right now, so you'd be doing the team a huge favor."

"Fine, I'll do it."

"Great. The package will need to be at the front office by three. Don't forget to flash it in front of Ms. Fletcher. But I doubt she'll have much to say about this. You'll be fine." He looked at his watch and hurried out the door.

Right. I'll be fine. I took a deep breath and turned to my computer. It was 7:15. *Awfully early for a meeting,* I thought, feeling a small sense of pity for Royle. Checking Fletcher's calendar, it looked like she wouldn't be in the office for another hour and a half. Plenty of time. *Softball,* I thought. *Here goes nothing.*

Armed with my large coffee—with delicious real cream instead of soy milk—my rapid typing abilities, and my advanced research skills, I tackled my assignment by doing what any other doctoral-level analyst from one of the world's leading universities would do in my current position.

I typed "Mongolia" into Google.

After spending approximately an hour acquainting myself with all things Mongolian, I started writing. As my fingers flew across the keyboard, I started feeling good about the assignment—and, for the first time, about my decision to stay in the Pentagon. Royle was right; it was a comparatively small task. But maybe, in some small way, what I was writing at that moment would help pave the way for Mongolian and U.S. military forces to work together better. And maybe, somewhere down the line, I might be making it easier for our soldiers to get their jobs done.

Jon would have gotten a kick out of working with the Mongolians, I thought, and smiled as I hit print.

I cautiously peered my head into Fletcher's office and knocked lightly on the door. Fletcher, with her back turned toward me, held up a finger telling me to wait as she continued an angry conversation with a general, whose disembodied head appeared on a small television screen next to her computer.

"What the hell do you mean, *you can't clear on this?*" Fletcher asked, holding up a piece of paper to her webcam.

"Ariane—"

"You can call me ma'am."

"Yes, ma'am," the general said. Even though he was a tiny head on a small screen, I could tell his face was getting redder. "Ma'am, we're not yet in a position to—"

I'm glad I'm not him right now, I thought.

"Get into position. Figure it out," Fletcher said.

"We don't have the authority—"

"I said, figure it out," Fletcher said.

"I'll see what I can do," the general said, sheepishly.

"Good." She turned off the screen and then turned to face me. "What do you want?"

"Ma'am, I have talking points for you to review," I half said, half asked with an unintentional warble in my voice. "For the Mongolian Minister of Defense?"

"Let me see them." Fletcher held out her hand.

I straightened my shoulders and walked toward her desk. *She was actually fairly reasonable yesterday. Maybe the dragon-lady routine is an act?* I thought as I handed her the pages.

She pulled out her red pen, put on her glasses, and began reading. She took them off after five seconds. "What is this?"

"Talking points. For Assistant Secretary Chao?"

"Chao? I was told this morning that SecDef wanted to take the meeting."

"*The* Secretary of Defense? Secretary Sidwell?"

Fletcher looked at me with the kind of sneer that teachers reserve for their most annoying students.

"Is there another Secretary of Defense that I'm not aware of?" Her eyes glanced back down at the pages. "This document is five pages long."

"I wanted to be—"

"The meeting is only going to last fifteen minutes. This would take three hours to cover."

"Well, I—"

"This is why I didn't want to take you on, Heather. This isn't academia. We don't write dissertations here."

I felt my stomach tie itself in knots as it dropped through the floor and settled somewhere near the bottom of Marianas Trench.

Fletcher continued scanning my paper. "Yurts? You're kidding, right?"

"Well, it turns out those tents are Mongolian, and they're easily portable. I thought it would be a useful contribution—" I stopped myself as I looked at Fletcher. I didn't know it was possible for her face to reflect even *more* disdain.

"Why don't these talking points have anything about Moldova in it?"

I looked at Fletcher, confused. "Why would it?"

"According to *your* plan, we're looking for a non-NATO country to lead the mission in Moldova."

I was still confused. "Sure, but Mongolia?"

"Why *not* Mongolia?"

"But we haven't gotten anyone to bite off on the Moldova plan," I said. "Much less that *Mongolia* should lead the effort. Nobody knows about the idea yet, much less supports it."

"Except the Mongolians," Fletcher said.

Wait, what?

"Has there been some sort of development that I'm not aware of?"

Fletcher reached into a dark-stained wooden inbox—one that probably dated back to the 1960s, give or take—and produced a sheet of paper for me to read. It was a letter from the Mongolian Ministry of Defense in slightly broken English, offering to lead a military training mission in none other than Moldova.

"How——?" I asked, confused.

"Doesn't matter. Start over. Throw what you've got in the burn bag, and then talk to Voight. I want to see the version that's ready to go up the chain at 1300 at the latest."

"Right, ma'am," I said, feeling a combination of emotional whiplash and dread as I waited for her to dismiss me. It occurred to me that my earlier optimism about Fletcher was completely and totally misplaced.

"Well?"

"Yes?" I asked.

"Shouldn't you get tippy-tapping at the keyboard?"

"Right. Yes, ma'am," I said, turning on my heels and almost running out of Fletcher's office. But rather than returning directly to my desk, I made a beeline to the nearest ladies' room (which, by the way, was considerably closer than the one in which I'd been mistaken for a terrorist). Shaking with stress and sweaty with nerves, I ran through the room to the farthest stall from the door and promptly vomited in the handicap toilet. A million disjointed thoughts crossed my mind as I hung my head over the porcelain bowl.

This is the job from hell.

I'm not sure I can take this right now.

Thank god I didn't get any barf on my shirt.

"Shit," I said aloud as I flushed the toilet. I grabbed a paper towel on my way to the sink and dabbed my face to get rid of the cold sweat without smudging my makeup too badly. As I stood hunched over the sink, facing myself in the mirror and waiting to look presentable again, I wondered whether I was really up to working in the Pentagon. Whether I had the emotional stamina and intestinal fortitude necessary to deal with the lion's den that I'd somehow, despite all odds, found myself working in. And after that horrible fight with Ryan…

Is this really worth it?

The answer came to me from somewhere deep in my core: *Yes.* I stood up tall and decided then and there I'd be damned if I'd let Fletcher or Royle or anyone else get in my way. I had a job to do. I looked in the mirror one last time and put on my game face.

You've got to get it together.

You will *get it together.*

Memo in hand, I walked back to the office. "Voight, I need help. I've accidentally bitten off more than I can chew."

"I heard."

"You did? How?"

"Fletcher's voice carries."

"Oh," I said, feeling my face turn pink.

"So, what's all this kerfuffle about?"

"Talking points. SecDef is meeting with the Mongolian Minister of Defense. There's just three problems."

"Wait—Mongolia? As in, Genghis Khan, Huns on horseback, Mongol hordes, Mongolia?"

"That's the one."

"Neat! I binged that *Marco Polo* show on Netflix. It was awesome."

"Well, then you probably know more about Mongolia than I do. Which is the first problem. I'm not a Mongolia expert."

"Don't let that bother you. I have a buddy who was on the North Korea desk. His second day on the job? He was told to write North Korea talkers for a National Security Council meeting."

"Let me guess: He never worked on North Korean issues."

Voight nodded. "Not only had he never worked on North Korea, he'd never even been to Asia. He's an Africa specialist."

"Seriously?"

"You've been here a couple weeks now. Do you really think I could make something like that up?" Voight asked.

I shrugged in resignation.

"So, what's the next problem?"

"Guess who wants to use Mongolia to solve the Moldova problem?"

"Huh?" Voight said, confused.

"That's what I said. But—and I don't get this part—apparently, Fletcher has a letter from the Mongolians offering to do the job."

Voight looked at me with surprise and a dash of inspiration. "She *is* an evil genius."

"How so?"

"She must have done an end-run by asking the Mongolians to ask us for help. She's forcing the system to work—by going outside our system entirely. It's so dysfunctional it's poetic. When's the meeting?"

"Tomorrow."

"Ah. That's a *big* problem." Voight scratched his chin.

"Why?"

"It usually takes at least a couple weeks to get something up to the Secretary of Defense."

"A couple weeks?! For talking points?"

"Yep. Anything that comes out of the Secretary's mouth basically becomes policy for the Department. Now, the whole Moldova plan is completely new—not to mention, the Mongolia piece of it—so we've gotta get the right offices around here in OSD to sign off first. Without them, this'll go nowhere. That'll probably be the East Asia, Central Europe, and Special Operations desks. And then we've got to get the uniforms on the Joint Staff on board. And then we've got to get the State Department to clear. I'm not sure about the NSC. So, yeah. We're talking at least a couple weeks, if not a solid month to get this done."

"Excellent," I said. "We have eight hours."

"Well, isn't this a big bucket of awesome? We're going to be super popular." Voight held out his hand. "Let me see what you've got."

I handed him my memo and watched his eyes grow large and his mouth widen into a grin—an expression that I had come to learn was the telltale sign of pending belly laughter. I was right.

"What's so funny?" I asked after his laugher subsided.

"How do I put this? Let's just say that I've never seen the words 'neo-Foucaultian analysis' in a Pentagon memo before."

"But it needed an analytic framework. And the dynamics of the hegemonic relationship between the U.S. and Mong—" I started.

"They didn't give you the first clue in orientation as to what to write in these things, did they?" Voight ducked down and reached into his filing cabinet to retrieve a folder.

"All they said was to put lots of 'white space' between the bullet points," I said, weakly.

"I'm sorry, Heather. I promise, I'm laughing with you, not at you. Well, it's probably more accurate to say that I'm laughing with the version of you a week from now that will look at all of this and smile, in hindsight. But you get the point." Voight handed me a folder.

"What's this?"

"Talking points. We used these last week with the Germans."

"But that's Germany, not Mon—"

"I know. Use it as a template."

I looked at the package of documents, which consisted of three separate sheets of paper divided by hard paper tabs and an index card.

"These all say the same thing."

"Not quite, but close. One's a cover memo. The second tab has the actual talkers."

"These are written at a third-grade reading level."

"Yep."

"You know, Mongolia is a sovereign country. Some people have dedicated their entire careers to understanding Mongolia's culture, government, and people."

"And yet, all the complexities need to be condensed onto one sheet of paper. Using thirteen-point font. And lots of white space."

"Three sheets," I said, flipping through the package.

"Well, one really. The cover memo basically repeats the talkers. So does the index card."

"Voight, no offense, but these are written as if Secretary Sidwell is some kind of lobotomized talking monkey."

"None taken. It's so hard to get anything cleared around here, I consider it a victory if it's up to a third-grade reading level by the time it goes to the bosses. Second grade is safer. Fifth is unheard of."

"Why is that?"

"Too many cooks in the kitchen. Each office wants to put their stamp on stuff. And for whatever reason, everyone's afraid to send a memo up the chain unless everyone agrees with what's in there."

"Isn't that a recipe for getting to the lowest common denominator, policy-wise?"

"Bingo. I'm pretty sure that most of the stuff we send up the chain is utterly unreadable."

"No wonder we're so screwed up."

"Oh, that's just one reason. You'll find there are many, many more. Anyway, tell you what. I'll reach out to all the different offices we'll need to coordinate with to get this thing cleared and let them know this is headed their way. You can focus on rewriting the package. How long do you think you'll need?"

"To write a plagiarized memo fit for an elementary school kid? Twenty minutes."

"Great, let's get to work." Voight reached for his phone. "Oh, and Heather? I hope you brought your body armor."

"Body armor?"

"Competition is always fierce when the stakes are petty," Voight said. "This package is really going to get the carousel-o'-crazy spinning around here. But hell, at least you have a partner that'll be spinning around with you."

"Thank god for that," I said, sitting back at my computer. I took a deep breath and started typing. As the words flowed across the screen, and as I blatantly copied Voight's work, I could feel the academic in me dying a horrible, strangulated death.

"Don't worry," Voight said from over my shoulder. "Plagiarism is the sincerest form of flattery in government."

"That doesn't make me feel better."

My fingers moved furiously across the keyboard, switching out "Germany" for "Mongolia" in the appropriate places.

"Heather, are you just about done?!" I heard Fletcher bellow across the office.

I'm fucked.

CHAPTER TWELVE

AFTER MY CONVERSATION WITH VOIGHT, I WAS PREPARED FOR PUSH BACK ON OUR MEMO. I was prepared for weeping and gnashing of teeth. I was prepared to be told I needed to get out of the Central and Eastern Europe desk's lane, which was, I was rapidly learning, Pentagon-ese for "go to hell." After all, the Office of the Deputy Assistant Secretary of Defense for Central and Eastern European Affairs was in charge of the Pentagon's relationship with Moldova, and from their point of view, we were pulling a fast one on them. They were bound to be a little testy. I was prepared for that.

But nothing could have prepared me for the sight of the older woman, with copper skin, deep-set wrinkles, and short, slicked-back pixie-length hair standing behind the receptionist desk. Wearing a sleeveless red vinyl catsuit and a black choker around her neck. A feather boa was draped over her bare shoulders, as if it were a shawl protecting her from the frigid air conditioning. *Odd choice of attire for a receptionist at the Pentagon*, I thought. *Or, for that matter, an odd choice of attire for anywhere outside a kink club.*

She looked up at me. "Yes?"

THE HEART OF WAR

I blinked but quickly recovered myself. "I'm here to coordinate a memo?"

"Oh, are you from Fletcher's office?"

"Yes. I'm here to talk to the DASD? I was told she's expecting me."

"Indeed, she is," the woman said, putting a Post-it note on the computer screen behind her. It looked like a lunch order. She moved out from behind the receptionist desk and into another office on the other side of the room. A blue sign with "Deputy Assistant Secretary of Defense Jelena Krueger" written in white lettering hung on the door.

"Well?" I heard her call out to me from the office.

I followed the receptionist into Krueger's office, crossing the threshold in just enough time to see her sit down behind a large oak desk.

Which is when I realized my bondage-gear-clad escort was, in fact, the DASD I was looking for. I froze.

"So, Heather, is it?" Krueger said, squinting her eyes and jutting out her chin as she reviewed my package. "Explain to me why you're writing this, and not my office?"

"Because of the coalitions angle," I said.

"Yes, but this is for Moldova. That's *our* lane."

"Yes, but I was told to work—"

"I just spoke with Chairman Rodriguez, and—after congratulating me for my work on supporting the Ukrainians, of course—he asked me what more I could do with the Moldovans. So I really don't understand what you're doing here."

"The Mongolians are interested in leading a coalition to train the Moldovans," I said.

"Since when?"

"They sent a—"

"Never mind," Krueger said, waving a hand dismissively. I couldn't help but notice her talonlike hands were varnished with "vamp"-hued nail polish. *Of course.*

"Just a moment." Krueger stood up and walked to the small TV screen next to her computer. "Heather, you really aren't senior enough to know what's going on around here. I'm going to speak to Ariane about this."

She adjusted her feather boa, draping it across the back of her chair, making sure she didn't sit on the feathers as she video-conferenced my boss.

"Jelena, my dear! How are you?" Fletcher answered in a voice dripping with saccharine.

"I'm well, Ariane," Krueger said, her voice turning from sour to sweet. I wanted to turn away from the spectacle before me—two near-psychotic female senior Pentagon officials in an ass-kissing contest—but I just couldn't pry my eyes away from the sight before me.

"That's great! How can I help you, Jelena?"

"Well, Ariane, I'm sitting here with your staffer, and I'm wondering why she's been given this tasker?" Krueger tapped her nails against the desk as she spoke. "My office, after all, is in charge of Central and Eastern Europe."

"Well, Jelena, having held your job not too long ago, I know that all too well! Of course you're responsible for Moldova. But we're responsible for building coalitions. And Mongolia wants our help setting up a coalition to train the Moldovans."

I could almost hear Fletcher pulling out the knife.

"Sure, Ariane. But we don't want to get ahead of the Secretary on this," Krueger said, swiping her metaphorical claws at Fletcher. "If we move forward on this, we'll be jamming the Secretary."

"Of course we don't want to do that. But, if we do this right, we can use this support to the Mongolians in Moldova to help the Georgians too. And you know that supporting the Georgians is a priority for the President and the Secretary," Fletcher said, getting a jab in.

Krueger recovered quickly. "These things take time. Why don't our offices work together to build a coordinated strategy?"

And with that opening, Fletcher interrupted and went for Krueger's jugular. "Well, that's exactly it. We just want to support you, Jelena. I know you are extremely busy right now working on what we should be doing with Russia. After all, the strategic options you presented last month ended up being completely invalid, and the entire building is working to recover from your recommendations. You have a lot of catching up to do."

Holy crap! My eyes widened as I marveled at Fletcher's deft bureaucratic excoriation of Krueger.

Krueger knew full well she'd been defeated, so she sat back in her chair and quickly composed herself.

"Well, thank you, Ariane. I appreciate your support. I'll just make sure that my people work closely with yours to make sure that all our equities are represented."

"I wouldn't have it any other way," Fletcher said.

Even though the screen was ten feet away, I could see that Fletcher looked like the cat that caught the canary.

"Holy. Hell," I said, approaching Voight's cubicle.

"See anything interesting?" Voight said, grinning.

"You set me up! You knew I'd meet Krueger, didn't you?"

"Possibly. How was it?"

"You know those movies from the 1970s, set in Brooklyn? The ones where the gangsters tied their wrists to each other and then had a knife fight?"

"Yeah. Why?"

"I just witnessed the bureaucratic equivalent of that between Fletcher and Krueger."

Voight whistled. "Pink on pink…"

"What?" I asked, wondering if I should be offended or not. "I'm not following."

"It's an operational thing. You've heard of blue-force tracker?"

I shook my head.

"It's like a military version of Garmin. But it maps who's who on the battlefield. Friendlies are blue, enemies are red."

"Still not following."

"Right. It was a bit of an adjustment, working around so many women here in the Pentagon."

"Really? We're a fraction of the workforce here."

"Really. Which, by the way, is something that we've gotta fix, in my opinion. But I digress. At first I thought you ladies would be nurturing towards each other. All that talk of women's empowerment in the workplace, stuff like that. But wow, was I wrong. More often than not, you're vicious with each other, and I have no idea why. I call it 'pink-on-pink' violence."

"You know, sadly, that makes a strange kind of sense," I said, nodding and cringing at the same time. I furrowed my brow as I looked down at his desk. "Out of curiosity, why do you have an iron?"

"To iron my clothes. Obviously."

"You do your ironing at work?"

"Things get wrinkly, sitting here in the cube," he said, as if it were the most obvious thing in the world. "What? Looking this sharp takes work! Anyway. Back to your meeting."

"Right. Good news or bad news?"

"Good?"

"The good news is that I got Kreuger's office to sign off on the Moldova initiative. They cleared on the memo."

"And the bad news?"

"Their clearance depends on us incorporating their edits," I said, handing the memo to him.

Voight's eyes widened as he studied the paper. "Wow. I didn't know it was possible for a memo to be...eviscerated."

"Well, now you know."

"I mean, edits, sure. Comments, yeah. But look at this thing! They didn't leave a single sentence standing."

"Yep, I'm pretty aware of that."

"Oh, except for this one," he pointed to a sentence in the middle of the page. "Oh yeah, I was wondering. What's a yurt, by the way?"

"It's a Mongolian tent thing that's collapsible—you know what? Nevermind," I said, taking back the memo. "How was your meeting with the Joint Staff?"

"Entirely predictable. First they bitched that we're asking them for coordination at light speed. And then they bitched about springing a new military requirement on them to support the Mongolians."

"Did you point out that they'll be able to take the stuff they were going to put into Armenia and put it into Moldova instead?"

"Yep. So, once that throat-clearing was over, they had more 'conceptual' comments," Voight said, using air quotes.

"Which was?"

"Tell the Mongolians nothing." Voight grimaced. "But on the upside, they did like the yurts!"

"Great."

"Not to worry. I told my buddy on the Joint Staff—who you need to meet, by the way—that their proposed stonewalling approach wasn't exactly going to fly with our superiors. So they're working on language that would scratch the itch. In the meantime, we've got to head to State."

"The State Department? Why?"

"Because the Mongolians are foreigners. And State's in charge of dealing with foreigners. Let's go."

"What time is it?" Voight asked as we left the Pentagon and entered the blazing heat. It felt more intense coming out of the Pentagon, which, I then noticed, must have been kept at a temperature hovering just above tundralike conditions. The contrast to the outdoor heat was staggering.

"Five minutes after eleven."

"Crap. We've missed the shuttle. We'll have to cab it. Don't worry, the cabs are close by—in the next parking lot."

I was skeptical. My brief experience in the Pentagon had taught me that nothing was ever "close by"—at least, not in the conventional sense of the term. I was panting by the time we made it to the cab stand, but, on the plus side, I'd remembered to wear my deodorant that day. As we approached, Voight squinted at the one, lonely, bright orange cab patiently waiting to transport passengers to the far—and near—corners of the Washington metropolitan area. A look of recognition crossed his face. "Oh boy."

"What's up?" I asked.

"You'll see," he said as he opened the back door for me. "Hop in."

The interior of the cab was shabby from years—decades—of constant use and minimal repairs. The light brown seats were marked with the occasional streak of duct tape to keep the foam from exploding out of its dilapidated pleather skin. In the front, Styrofoam cups, fast-food wrappers, and the occasional newspaper littered the seat, surrounding the driver as if he'd constructed some kind of post-apocalyptic nest. Which seemed appropriate; the driver himself looked like he'd come to the Pentagon parking lot via the terrible dystopian future. He had long stringy grey-white hair, thick-rimmed glasses, and a thick coating of grey stubble masking yellowing teeth. The odor of cigarettes clung to everything in the car, refusing to submit to the odor of the pine-tree-shaped air freshener dangling from the rearview mirror.

"Where to?" the driver asked.

"The State Department," Voight said.

As the driver shifted the car into drive, Voight looked to me with wide, amused eyes. I, in turn, looked at Voight with confusion.

"So, do you two work at the Pentagon?" the driver asked, trying to start up conversation.

"Yes, sir, we do," Voight said.

"So then you guys must know about the secret submarine base."

"The what?" I asked, staring at the back of the driver's head in amazement.

"The secret submarine base. It's underneath the river entrance to the Pentagon," the driver cackled. "You guys, you guys work there, but you have no idea what's going on, do you?" His question came amid emphysema-laced wheezes.

"I guess not," Voight said, clearly entertained by the conversation. "Enlighten us."

"When Rumsfeld was there, he used the submarines to get out of the building on 9/11. Everyone knows that."

"But—" I started, before Voight stopped me, shaking his head and silently pleading with me to let the cab driver continue.

"Secretary Sidwell would've used it yesterday to allow him to get out of the building, but he was already at the secret Illuminati arctic base."

"But he was in Omaha yesterday," I said.

"Same difference." Voight shrugged.

"You guys, you don't know anything, do you?" The driver cackled again. "Bet you don't even know that the government is trying to cover up the last time we had contact with the aliens."

"The last time?" I asked.

"Yeah. There's been three contacts so far. But this time, with the internet, it's a lot harder to cover up. We've caught onto them," he said with a conspiratorial edge to his raspy voice. "We even know that they've been infiltrated."

"Infiltrated?"

"Half of the senior leaders in the Pentagon, they're aliens. Bet you didn't know that, either, did ya?"

After my meeting with DASD Kreuger that morning, I was almost willing to believe the driver was on to something. Almost.

"No, we didn't know that," Voight responded.

"Ha! Of course you didn't! Bet you don't even think anything's going on in Moldova right now!"

Voight and I looked at each other in amazement—and a little concern—and then to the driver.

"You're so dead wrong." Cynical laughter filled the cab. "So, so wrong."

"Okay, then," Voight said, taking the bait. "What do you think is going on in Moldova?"

"Russian Illuminati. Taking over the UFO landing spot. Prime real estate."

"I thought that was Area 51?" I asked.

"Ha! You would think that. But it's the Russian Illuminati that you've got to worry about."

"I'm not following," I said, with a slightly too sharp edge to my voice.

The driver scowled at me in response.

"I think what my colleague means," Voight said, trying to appease the cab driver, "is why would the Russian Illuminati make mischief *now*?"

"Well, their overall strategy is to get oil prices up in the Middle East. That way they can sell Russian gas at a higher price. And then fund their campaign for global control. And once they own the launch point, they can get stuff on and off the planet. Don't you guys know *anything* working in the Pentagon?"

I shrugged, deciding to remain silent.

"They tried to do the same thing after 9/11. That was an inside job too."

"That's an interesting theory," Voight said, *his* patience now a little tested.

"Ha! You don't believe me!" The cab driver was almost beside himself with glee, seemingly delighted with the fact that neither of us believed a word he was saying.

"I guess we don't, no."

"You'll see. One of these days, you'll see."

"I guess we'll find out later, then," Voight finished the conversation as we pulled up near the State Department. I climbed out, feeling like I'd stepped out of a parallel dimension and back into this one as I straightened my suit and tried to recover from the onslaught of paranoia I'd just escaped.

"He never remembers me, but man I love that guy," Voight said, watching the cab drive away.

"He's nuts!" I said.

"Which is why I love him so, so much."

"I'm surprised he wasn't wearing a tin-foil hat."

"I once tried to debunk his conspiracy theories by telling him the government is too dorked up to pull off a conspiracy. It was a spectacular exercise in frustration."

"Too dorked up?"

"Of course. You see, Dr. Reilly, you may have your fancy PhD, but I have my own theory about government."

"Which is?"

"Have you ever heard of Occam's razor?"

"Of course. All things being equal, the simplest explanation must be true."

"Right. Applied to government, all things being equal, the stupidest explanation must be true."

I laughed.

"You know it's true. Take today, for example. We can barely get our act together for talking points for the Mongolians. So how in god's name could we possibly pull off anything more complicated?"

"Point taken."

"There's all kinds of crazy in the Building. I sometimes wonder if the tin-foil taxi driver is onto something. But then I remember that he thinks we're lizard people."

"You mean, we're not?" I asked.

CHAPTER THIRTEEN

"RAFFAELLO! We're here!"

Voight knocked on a half-opened wooden pocket door of an office that looked as if Ikea had a field day doing the interior design. Light birch wood covered every square inch of the rectangular, narrow expanse with the exception of cream-colored carpets. The lightly floral fragrance of Earl Grey tea perfumed the space, giving the office a feel of delicate civility—a stark contrast to the Pentagon's more brutal aesthetic.

The pocket door slid fully open, revealing a short, brown-haired man in his late thirties with no-frame glasses perched on the end of his nose. His suit was impeccably tailored to his oversized frame.

"Hello, Colonel Voight. Dr. Reilly, I take it?" he asked, looking at me. "Please, have a seat."

He shuffled himself back to the chair behind his desk and we both squeezed ourselves into the seats crammed between his desk and the wall. As I looked around the tiny space, cluttered with service awards and family pictures and memorabilia from travels around the globe, it hit me that all of the key foreign policy decisions this country made were probably concocted in an office that happened to be a lot like this one: a glorified broom closet somewhere in the depths of the labyrinthine State Department. It made a kind of cosmic sense to me.

"I'm short on time, so let's get down to it," Raffaello said.

"Us, too. So yes, let's," Voight agreed.

"Dr. Reilly," Raffaello said, sitting back in his chair, his features smoothing into the kind of practiced, congenial smile that is the hallmark of a tough negotiator.

"Please, call me Heather."

"Heather. I know you're new around here, and that this is the first time we're meeting. But it would be helpful if you could walk me through your reasoning for asking the Mongolians for help training the Moldovans, rather than, say, just about anything else."

"Well, technically, it's the other way around," I said. "Fletcher has a letter from the Mong—"

"I know Fletcher has a letter. I also have a pretty good idea of who prodded the Mongolians into writing the offer letter in the first place."

"You do?"

Raffaello nodded, slowly. "So, why does the Pentagon suddenly care so much about Moldova?"

"Strategic sheep purposes?" Voight said. "Also, there's an illicit cow-trafficking network that needs to be shut down there."

Raffaello cocked an eyebrow.

"Fletcher wants to use Moldova to start pushing back against the Russians," I explained.

"The Russians have been a bit feisty these days," Raffaello said.

"That's an understatement," Voight agreed.

"The thinking is, Moldova is kind of near Russia. And it's kind of near Georgia. If the Mongolians set up a training mission, and we support it, we can be there in case Russia starts anything more serious."

"Yes, but why now? I haven't seen anything suggesting Russia's up to much in Moldova. Or, more precisely, not any more mischief than they're normally up to."

"Sure, but in that part of the world, *normal* is a whole hell of a lot," Voight said. "Perish the thought, but maybe Fletcher's onto something?"

"Oh-kay," Raffaello said, giving us the distinct impression that things were definitely not okay. "Regardless, I'm afraid this isn't going to work for us."

"Why am I not surprised?" I asked. "What, specifically, do you have an issue with?"

"Well, for starters, it's the Mongolians."

"Yes. We've established that much," Voight said.

"Mongol hordes? Genghis Khan? Scourge of the earth?" Raffaello said, taking his glasses off and wiping them on his handkerchief. "The Mongolians come with some serious baggage, particularly in that part of the world."

"We're going to shun Mongolian help because of Genghis Khan?" I asked, incredulous. "That was a long time ago."

Raffaello cocked an eyebrow. "Rumor has it, when the Mongolians deployed to Iraq the last time, their soldiers wore T-shirts that said, 'We're Back.'"

"Wow. Really?" Voight was amused.

"The shirts even had a pyramid of skulls on them."

"That definitely qualifies as baggage," I said.

"And then there's the whole matter that we haven't even agreed on our own strategy, or why Moldova suddenly needs to be a priority. We should wait to talk to others until we know what we're doing."

"But if we do something—whatever it is—we're going to want coalition partners there with us," I said.

"Right," Raffaello agreed.

"But don't we want to tell them what we're thinking? Give them a heads-up that we're going to want their help?"

"Not until after we've agreed we want their help. And how we want them to help us." Raffaello sat back in his chair. "Look, I appreciate where you're coming from. But if the Secretary of Defense delivers these points to his counterpart, he might as well grab a microphone and announce to the world that the United States is getting ready to kick off World War III in the not-too-distant future."

"Seriously? Why is everybody obsessed with World War III?" I asked.

Raffaello opened his mouth to speak.

"Actually, don't answer that. You know, this is better than the alternative."

"Which is?"

"Putting a NATO mission in Armenia to support the Georgians."

"You're kidding me," Raffaello said, wide-eyed. "*That's* the close-hold clever plan the NSC concocted?"

Voight and I nodded.

"Unbelievable. When are they going to put grown-ups back in charge there?"

Voight and I shrugged.

"Well, if that's the case, then you're right. This Mongolia-Moldova plan *is* better than the alternative. But that distinction isn't going to matter to the Russians. They're pretty paranoid."

"How are the Russians going to know anything?"

"If SecDef delivers these points, the first thing that the Mongolians are going to do is talk to their counterparts at other embassies here in Washington. And gossip spreads like wildfire here around the diplomatic cocktail party circuit. The ambassadors and defense attachés at the embassies can be worse than old ladies at a knitting circle." Raffaello looked at the memo. "What about this for a compromise? SecDef notes that we may or may not be interested in supporting the Moldovans and that we may or may not support the Mongolians if and when they set up a training mission in Moldova?"

"That's brilliant!" Voight said. "It would be like a choose-your-own-adventure talking-points memo!"

"So, basically we'd be telling the Secretary of all Defense to wish the Mongolians good juju," I said.

"And ask them for yurts," offered Raffaello.

"You actually know what a yurt is?" Voight asked.

"Of course. A collapsible Mongolian tent. Handy for disaster relief. Or refugees," Raffaello said.

"Of *course* you'd know what a yurt is. You're State," Voight said, impressed.

"That's why they pay us the big money," Raffaello said with a twinge of sarcasm.

"Hey, at least you get to go to the fancy cocktail parties!" Voight teased.

"Sure. When they aren't making us cover three people's jobs because of budget cuts. Did you know that the military has almost as many people serving in military bands as the State Department has diplomats? This computer here," he said, pointing under his desk, "I'm pretty sure it's powered by a hamster and vacuum tubes. And that, by the way, is an improvement—the result of a brief moment of budgetary inspiration shortly after the September 11th attacks. Don't spill anything on the carpets. We'll never be able to afford to get them replaced."

"Right. So morale is high over here, I take it?" Voight asked.

"As high as I've ever seen it," Raffaello said.

"Spoken like a true diplomat."

"On that happy note, I need to head to my next meeting," Raffaello said. "Are you okay with what we discussed?"

"Umm, no?" I ventured.

"It'll be fine. Just take out everything about Moldova. And a training mission."

"So, take out everything," I said.

"Basically. Except the yurts." Raffaello nodded. "Good luck!"

"What *is* this?" Fletcher asked, looking up at me from her desk as if I had the mental capacity of a half-eaten grapefruit. "This memo. There's nothing in here."

"Our counterparts thought it premature to talk about working with the Mongolians to train the Moldovans. They said we need to develop a strategy first. Evaluate different options."

"Wait for a strategy? That's what the State Department says anytime they want to slow-roll action. The Moldovan situation is developing *now*."

"Ma'am, they all said they'd withhold their concurrence on this memo unless we adopt these changes," Voight said.

"Nobody thinks we should be taking such a huge risk over Moldova," I added. "It's just not worth it."

The room suddenly plummeted to a temperature hovering just above absolute zero as Fletcher turned her gaze to me.

"You think this is a mistake?" Fletcher asked.

"I mean, *they* think it's not—" I stammered.

"Oh, really?" Fletcher said. I could just about make out the fog of my breath in the arctic chill that had now descended upon the office.

"What Heather is saying is that we can't—" Voight started.

"Like hell, we can't. We don't ask the Secretary of Defense to recite chicken-shit talking points. And that's what these are." She violently waved the papers in the air.

"But everyone agrees that this could make things worse. Lead to—" I said.

"World War III? And you believed them? This isn't going to lead to the goddamned apocalypse. That's just Derek in the background trying to sabotage us because we scuppered his idiotic plan. Things are *already* worse with the Russians. The Russians have been doing a damn good job of kicking off a war all by themselves. We just haven't been paying attention."

"But don't we need everyone to agree to the memo? To concur before we send it to the Secretary?" I asked.

"Bullshit. Getting everybody to agree on everything is why this Department has made such bullshit, lowest-common-denominator decisions. I am disappointed in you both," Fletcher said, looking at Voight, and then to me. "I expected better. And now it looks like I have to do your job for you. Now get out of my office. But don't go far. I'm going to want to see you again in fifteen minutes."

Mortified, we slumped out of Fletcher's office with my heart in my throat and my stomach at the bottom of the ocean.

"What do you think she's doing?" I asked.

"Singlehandedly solving the world's problems. Or, at least, that's how she sees it," Voight said.

"This is horrible."

"You're not wrong."

We sat in silence on the couch outside Fletcher's office for a minute or two before Voight muttered something that sounded a lot like "fuck this," and headed back to his desk. I decided to remain put, waiting for the inevitable with that excruciating anticipation I normally reserved for the dentist's office.

"Softball," my ass, I thought.

Fletcher's door opened. "Write this up—exactly as I've written it—and then send it to the Joint Staff and State. Tell them they have twenty minutes before it goes up our chain, and if they want it changed, they've got to contact me—not you, me—immediately."

"Yes, ma'am." I said, then scurried back to my desk, reading Fletcher's version of the memo as I walked.

"What does it say?" Voight asked.

I showed him. It was an entirely new document.

"Wow. Well, then. Our friends at State and the Joint Staff are going to have kittens over this one," he said, turning over the page.

"Yeah. It's exactly what they *didn't* want."

"Hey! She kept the yurts!" Voight said. "Good. I'm beginning to like those yurts. I think I'm going to try and get one for my kids."

"Are we sure we're doing the right thing?" I asked. "What if everybody in the interagency is right and this Moldova plan is wrong?"

"I'm not sure there's anything truly right or wrong in this business. Just action and inaction and then cleaning up the messes we've inevitably made."

"This could make a *big* mess if the Russians decide to make a stink over it."

"True. Another problem for another day. But hopefully they'll make less of a stink over this than they would have if we'd gone with the Armenia option."

"Right," I said doubtfully.

"Hey, this was *your* plan, remember?"

"It was *my* plan to make what we're doing in the Black Sea region a little less like a red flag to a bull. It was Fletcher's idea to use Mongolia to do this. And, for the record, I agree with just about everyone else. I'm not sure that Mongolia is exactly the right country to spearhead this for us. They're a little country to the east of Russia. What if they get intimidated by Moscow?"

"Yeah, well, too late now," Voight shrugged. "This train has left the station."

"Great. So once we make these changes, then what?"

"Then we get to walk it through each of the seven layers of bureaucracy between us and Secretary Sidwell."

"There's *more* coordination required?"

"Yep. Last round was horizontal. Now we've got to go vertical."
Voight looked at his watch and grimaced. "Looks like I'm going to be missing Sarah's soccer game tonight."

"I'm sorry. That sucks."

"Yeah, well. I swore an oath and wear a uniform for the privilege of exposing myself to this idiocy. Speaking of, we have another problem."

"Of course we do."

"We've run out of 'Tab A' folders."

"What's that got to do with anything?"

"They're folder-dividers. And god forbid we send a package up without the proper dividers."

"Or else?"

"Anarchy. Obviously," Voight said.

"Why the hell don't we have—wait, let me guess. Budget cuts?"

"Bingo."

"Okay," I said, shaking my head with frustration. "What do we do?"

"You're not gonna like this."

"How did I know you were going to say that?"

"Trash-digging. Maybe someone threw one away."

"Could this day get any worse?" I asked.

"Never say never," Voight said, starting to comb through the trash in the next cubicle over. I found a burn bag near the end of the row of cubicles and started sifting through it. *All this time and energy spent on a memo for the Secretary, and we're going to be thwarted in the end because we don't have a folder divider?*

"Found one!" Voight shouted across the office as if he'd discovered the Holy Grail rather than a bit of reinforced paper. It was bent, wrinkled, creased six ways to Sunday.

"Great. Now what are we going to do?" I asked, holding up the mangled tab.

"You've got me," Voight said. "Maybe flatten it with something heavy?"

"Flatten it," I said, suddenly struck by inspiration. "Flatten it! Voight, your iron!"

Voight's confused look was eclipsed by a grin as he put the pieces together. "Heather, you're a genius!"

"I'm just glad that all this higher education I've got is being put to good use," I said, setting the paper on the floor and testing the bottom right corner to make sure the iron didn't leave scorch marks. "It works."

"Heather! Voight! Is the package moving yet?!" We heard Fletcher's voice scream from her office.

Voight smiled at me with a bright, fake grin. "It's just a typical day here in the Pentagon!"

"So now what happens?" I asked as we assembled the package.

"SecDef either uses these points, or doesn't."

"So we may or may not be going to Moldova after this?"

"Pretty much. We'll know more tomorrow. Maybe."

"You're telling me all this work may be for nothing?"

"Entirely possible. But hey, I learned what a yurt is, so that's got to count for something. Now let's get this package up to SecDef so we can get the hell out of here."

CHAPTER FOURTEEN

"WHY IS IT SO NOISY IN THE BACKGROUND?" I asked, cradling the phone between my shoulder and my ear as I sat down on my bed that evening.

"I'm at the airport." Ryan paused. "I'm—I'm going home."

"What? Without saying goodbye?"

"I tried calling you, but I couldn't get through. And then today got pretty crazy. I just barely got here in time to catch my flight."

"Why, Ryan?"

"The office needs me back home."

"Okay. What's the real reason?"

"Do we need to rehash this?"

"Yes."

"Look, you don't trust me, and I'm—I'm not sure that I can trust you either, Heather."

"Oh," I said, fiddling with a loose thread on my bedspread.

"That's all you have to say?"

I sighed. Part of me wanted to bring up how frustrated I was that he'd left the night before. That he still didn't seem to want to take my concerns about our finances seriously. Or how maddening it was that he didn't even attempt to understand why I'd been so nervous about talking about my job change. Rather than work through any of those issues with me, he'd turned the tables and found a reason to make me feel like the guilty party. But as I felt the day's exhaustion spreading through my body and weighing down my shoulders, all I could manage to say was, "Right now? Yes."

"Huh," Ryan said, clearly disappointed with my response. "Look, I think we need to take a break."

"Take a break? What does *that* mean?" I asked, suddenly exasperated.

"I just think that we need some time and space apart to re-evaluate things."

"We live in different cities. We *are* apart."

"That's not what I mean. We need to think about our *priorities*."

There was something about the way he said "priorities" that rubbed me completely the wrong way. Suddenly my nerves were on fire with something close to righteous indignation.

"You're kidding, right? Let's just call a spade a spade, Ryan."

"What do you—"

"*Don't* interrupt me. I don't want to be with a partner who can't face up to the facts. Who won't support my decisions. And I sure as hell don't want to be with someone who would rather walk away right now than hammer things out." The weight lifted from my shoulders while a lead ball simultaneously formed in my stomach.

"Don't you think this is a little sudden, Heather? Let's just take a breather—"

"No, Ryan."

"Right. I guess this is goodbye, then. I wish things were different."

"Me too."

I noticed my hand shaking as I hung up the phone. I was numb; I was furious. I felt disconnected; I felt weighed down. Everything was a jumble as my heart screamed in both relief and pain at what had just happened. *Ten years down the tubes in a short twenty-four hours.* I was furious at myself for letting things get to this point, and even more furious at Ryan for betraying everything we'd built. For being so quick to run away.

My best friend is gone.

Looking for a distraction from the hurricane whirling around inside me, I changed into my pajamas, picked up my laptop, and begun digging into the pile of books on my floor. The last time I checked the clock was eleven; sometime after that I passed out, surrounded by my notes and scribbles and research.

CHAPTER FIFTEEN

I NOTICED THAT I HADN'T MISSED ANY CALLS WHEN I WOKE UP THE NEXT MORNING. I stretched, accidentally knocking some books that were perched on the edge of my bed onto the floor. After the prior evening's turmoil, I felt surprisingly calm. Numb. Which was probably a good thing. I took off my engagement ring and put it in the drawer of my night stand.

I grabbed my favorite towel—the one Jon gave me along with a copy of *The Hitchhiker's Guide to the Galaxy*—and made my way to the bathroom in the hallway. I leaned my head against the tile of the shower as both the water and recent memories washed over me. It suddenly hit me: *Mom is going to be devastated....*

I shook my head. *Moldova. Mongolia. Russia.* Those were easier things to think about as I lathered up.

Shower over, I wrapped myself in my towel and made my way back to my bedroom. I was just about to close my door when I heard Amanda's open. I turned to say good morning to her.

But it wasn't Amanda who was leaving her bedroom. It was a man.

Good for her! At least one of us has a love life! I thought as my heart swelled with happiness for her. I was about to close my door again but then decided to leave it ever-so-slightly ajar. While I was feeling off-kilter, that didn't mean that I wasn't up for a bit of good-natured spying. I pressed my eye to the crack in the door. His back was toward me, but I could tell that he was slender but not skinny; tall, but not too tall. He wore a dark grey suit that looked slightly rumpled, undoubtedly a product of being carelessly thrown on the floor the night before. He gently shut her door and then turned around to find his way out of the apartment.

I saw his face. My eyes widened. I felt an inexplicable nervous twinge—something like anxiety mixed with something like jealousy—spike through me.

It was Royle.

I shut the door before he could see me, and then leaned against it as I tried to recover myself. *Of all the men in Washington, she had to pick him?*

Seriously? Is all this some kind of cosmic test? I swept my hair into a bun and put on my lipstick. Especially with what Amanda had said about the shallowness of the dating pool, she would need me to be supportive. And I would be, somehow. *But Royle? Honestly?* I thought about Royle's complete disinterest when I tried to mention Jon's military service. Would Amanda really want to be dating someone who didn't care about Jon's sacrifice? A guy who repeatedly threw me under the bus?

I faced myself in the mirror. I looked like hell.

Moldova. Mongolia. Russia.

"I guess I owe Raffaello five bucks," Voight said, startling me as he entered his cubicle. I heard him set what I presumed was a mammoth-sized Starbucks coffee on his desk.

"Why do you say that?" I asked.

The loud *thunk* of the A-section of *The Washington Post* landing on my desk forced my attention away from the computer.

"News *does* travel fast," Voight said. "Check it out."

I looked at the newspaper. Voight had used a red pen to draw circles and exclamation points around an article about how the Mongolians had decided to lead a coalition to train the Moldovan Armed Forces. It further reported that the U.S. was about to massively increase its presence in Moldova as part of that effort.

"The meeting was...this morning, right?" I suddenly felt removed from normal conceptions of space and time.

"Yep. Ended five minutes ago."

"Did they make the decision about Moldova before the meeting or something?"

"Nope. Not to my knowledge."

I blinked. "Okay, then. So now what?"

"Buckle our seat belts and wait for the crazy?" Voight said.

"Sounds about right." I said, shrugging.

"Dr. Reilly? Colonel Voight?" Royle suddenly appeared, as if stepping out from an invisible curtain. It was confusing to see him there in his dress blues, when it had been only hours before that I'd seen him leaving Amanda's room. As he smiled at the both of us,

I did my best to keep a lid on the odd sense of panic that suddenly welled in my stomach.

Voight looked at his watch, and then to me. "Right on schedule. What can we do ya for?"

"Fletcher's been asked to brief the Vice Chairman later this afternoon, and she needs you guys to help her with her slide deck on Moldova."

"Okay, what does she specifically need us to do?" Voight asked.

"She asked me to ask you guys to 'beef it up,'" Royle answered. "It needs to be sent to the Vice Chairman's office in a couple hours so they can preload it into the PowerPoint deck."

"But, *Washington Post* story notwithstanding, we don't actually know what we're doing in Moldova. The meeting between SecDef and the Mongolians just ended," I said.

Royle looked to me; his eyes flashed to my hands and widened in surprise as he noticed I wasn't wearing my ring. I flushed a little as I quickly hid my hand behind my back.

"Right. Well, I wouldn't worry too much. She's already got all the basics down," Royle said, deciding not to mention anything. I let out a small sigh of relief as he walked away.

Voight and I watched him go, and then looked at each other.

"You know, he told me that the Mongolia thing was going to be a softball," I said.

"Yeah, well, you never know what kind of curveball this place is going to throw at you. Let's open up the deck and see what we've got," he said, moving behind me so we could both look at my computer screen. I checked my email and found the slide deck sitting at the top of my inbox. I opened it and scrolled through.

"Uh, Voight?"

"Yes?"

"I have a PhD."

"That is factually accurate, Dr. Reilly. Why?"

"Because I have no idea what half of these—words? Acronyms?—whatever they are, I have no idea what they mean. 'Building Partner Capacity?' 'MOOTW?' What is this stuff?"

"You know, I have no idea either. I mean, I've heard people say this jargon before. Hell, I've even used it. But now that I think about it, nobody's been able to actually explain it to me. Or, at least, not in a way that makes any sense."

"All these words, they're so vague that they're meaningless."

"That's probably intentional," Voight observed.

"Great. How are we going to figure that out in time to turn these slides?" I asked, annotating my questions on the slides using colorfully snarky language. "And how are we going to figure out what happened at the SecDef meeting this morning?"

Voight looked to me. "How would you like to engage in a little bit of bureaucratic espionage?"

Twenty minutes later, Voight and I stood in a nondescript hallway, in front of a nondescript steel door, ringing a nondescript doorbell. Carrying a box of donut holes.

"Why do we need these?" I asked, pointing to the donut holes.

"We're about to try and pry information out of the Joint Staff, which is even harder than squeezing blood from a stone. We need all the help we can get."

"So tell me: Why do we need to talk to the Joint Staff? Can't we take care of this without them?"

"Well, my dear Dr. Reilly, the thing about the Joint Staff is that, unlike OSD, their different sections actually talk to each other, rather than hoard information like it's leprechaun gold."

"Leprechaun gold?"

"I'm tired. Work with me. The trick is getting our Joint Staff counterparts to clue us in on what's actually going on in this building. Lord knows we won't figure it out by talking to other offices in OSD."

The door opened. A large, pale, grizzled Navy captain with a nametag that said "Fitzgerald" and a five o'clock shadow at eight in the morning loomed over us through the entryway.

"Hi, Pumpkin!" Voight chirped.

Pumpkin? I pressed my lips together to contain my confused laughter as I looked at Voight in shock. Voight smiled.

Pumpkin took a deep sigh. "Real name's Bob, of course, but if you called me that, no one would know who you're talking about." He turned to Voight. "I didn't know Dunkin' Donuts delivered."

"Only the best for our Joint Staff brethren," Voight said.

"Uh-huh. You guys owe me after the Mongolia thing yesterday."

"Mea culpa?" Voight said, holding out the donut holes.

Pumpkin eyed the box. "Yeah, fine. Free donuts. Wins every time. Come on in."

Voight winked at me.

I'd imagined of all places in the Pentagon, the Joint Staff—the backbone of the entire U.S. military—would resemble something out of the movies. That it would be some sort of cross between *The Hunt for Red October* and a J. J. Abrams flick: television screens everywhere, inexplicably bluish lighting, and lens flares. Instead, as Voight and I followed Pumpkin through the office, I found myself walking through yet another cubicle farm. I was underwhelmed. Again.

The folks in Hollywoodland really need to do better research before designing their shows, I thought as we walked.

Pumpkin opened a door at the far end of the cubicle bay, and we entered his office.

"So, how's your family?" Voight asked Pumpkin.

I looked around as the two of them caught up. It was a small office, barely bigger than a cubicle, but at least it was enclosed. CNN played a story about Afghanistan on a small flatscreen TV on the corner of Pumpkin's desk. The Afghan president was speaking to a gaggle of reporters outside of a palace in Kandahar, asking for assistance from the international community to help deal with internal terrorist groups. The Afghans were still in dire straits, but Washington had moved on to the next issue du jour—Russia. Or Moldova. Or whatever.

"So I hear your boss is briefing our boss later today," Pumpkin said, interrupting my focus on the news. "I take it you guys are the lucky stuckees preparing her brief?"

Voight looked at me with a see-I-told-you-they-know-everything look. I nodded, feeling like we'd unwittingly entered some sort of freakish poker game, and Pumpkin was holding all the good cards.

"Royle said something about this when he dropped off his paperwork this morning," Pumpkin continued.

"Paperwork?" I asked.

"They didn't tell you?" Pumpkin asked, incredulous. "Royle's moving to the Joint Staff. He's transitioning to the Chairman's advisory group. Starts Monday."

Voight and I looked at each other, stunned.

"But I'm guessing Royle's new assignment isn't what brought you guys down here."

"No," I said, quickly recovering myself. "We actually have a few questions."

"Questions?"

"We have no idea what any of her brief means," Voight said.

"It's all meaningless jargon," I added.

"*Most* things in this building are meaningless jargon," Pumpkin said. "We have no idea what any of that stuff means either. We just know that the bosses like to say it a lot. Mostly because your bosses on the civilian side of the house like to hear *them* say it. We're good to let you guys spin up, changing 'happy' to 'glad' and having fights about the definition of 'is.' It keeps you Policy guys busy. And the busier you are, the less likely it is that you'll do something that affects our equities."

"So, you guys pretty much run interference down here?" I asked.

"For the stuff that doesn't really matter, yes," Pumpkin said.

"And Moldova?" I asked.

"Doesn't matter." Pumpkin popped a donut hole in his mouth. "We've got other, more pressing things on our plate right now."

"If it doesn't matter, then you won't mind letting us know what happened at the SecDef meeting this morning," Voight said.

"They really don't tell you anything up there, do they?"

"You know how it works up there," Voight said. "Information flows up, not down. If we rely on our bosses to tell us anything, it'll be at least a week and a half before we have a clue what happened."

"So you're screwed," Pumpkin said.

"Pretty much. Help us out?" Voight asked holding out the box of donut holes.

Pumpkin ate another donut hole, but was obviously skeptical.

"Think about it this way," Voight explained. "If you don't tell us what happened—and we have to go with what we've got—then Fletcher will be pissed."

"So?"

"She'll start winging it."

Pumpkin sucked in a breath.

"We're talking full-throttle bull-in-a-china-shop winging it, too. Nightmare," Voight continued.

"Which means we'll have lost *our* opportunity to protect *your* equities on Moldova," I said.

"So, whaddaya say?"

"*Pumpkin?!*" I asked as we finished tweaking the slides.

Voight laughed. "Rumor has it, the poor bastard had a spray tanning debacle. Right before Halloween too. And you thought Whiz Kid was bad."

I nodded, eyes wide. "Okay. That's one mystery solved."

"There's another one?" Voight asked.

"Around here? There's millions. But the one I'm thinking about is how did the *The Washington Post* know about the outcome of the SecDef meeting before it even happened?"

"Easy. They didn't," Voight said.

"Then—?"

"I'm becoming convinced that we work for the female incarnation of Niccolo Machiavelli," Voight said.

"How do you mean?"

"Well, either the Secretary himself decided to do a private late-night presser, or someone leaked the story. And nobody cares about this issue the way Fletcher does."

"Interesting theory." I cleaned up the next slide, replacing my earlier notes on the banality of phrases like "Building Partner Capacity," with more polished language. "Then why did she ask us to fix these slides, if she knew what SecDef said and we didn't?"

"Good question. I have no idea. Ready to hit 'send?'"

Even though I reviewed the presentation countless times, I took one last peek to make sure everything was in order. I was immediately glad I did; "Coalition" was misspelled on the title slide.

"Good to go," I said after correcting the mistake. I sat back in my chair. Afghanistan was falling apart, but I'd spent the morning chasing after information my boss probably should have told me, on an issue that seemed to pale in comparison to the Islamic State trying to take over another country. *Maybe Ryan is right*, I thought, before pushing the thought to the back of my mind. *Moldova. Mongolia. Russia.*

The Vice Chairman's conference room was completely full when we walked in, save for the two chairs behind Fletcher's seat at the far end of a U-shaped table. Voight and I scooted through the row to make our way to the seats, attempting to be graceful but instead awkwardly stepping on toes as we went. When we finally sat down, I observed how stark the room was. No pictures on the bright white walls, no patterns in the grey industrial carpet, the fluorescent lights giving everything a pinkish-bluish cast. The only feature distinguishing the room was the number of clocks on the wall. Each one reflected a different time zone. I noticed Afghanistan wasn't one of the clocks. I turned to look behind us and saw Royle sitting next to Pumpkin against the back wall. *What is Royle doing here? I thought he wasn't working on Moldova?*

The meeting started. Soon, it was DASD Fletcher's turn to brief. My first clue that something was horribly wrong hit me at precisely 15:46, according to the first clock on the wall. "Coalitions" was still spelled incorrectly on the first slide. *Did I send the wrong file?* My face blushed as I froze in fear, praying to any higher power that would listen that the spelling mistake was the only manifestation of the version control problem that I clearly had.

As Fletcher advanced to the next slide, I was brutally confronted with the fact that the lord on high hadn't paid any attention to my silent pleas. Because now, prominently displayed on the screen in front of the Vice Chairman and several constellations' worth of generals and admirals, were our snarky annotations on the briefing. Phrases like "Can't we figure out a better acronym?" "This is jargon," and "God help anyone who has to actually implement this," peppered the bullet points that outlined Fletcher's Moldova strategy. Almost everyone in the room involuntarily gasped.

"Fuck," Voight whispered.

"We're fucked," I said at the same time.

"What the fuck is this?" Fletcher asked, turning to us.

CHAPTER SIXTEEN

"I'M SO EMBARRASSED," I SAID, SIPPING MY FAT TIRE.

"Why's that?" Voight asked.

"Pick a reason. The fact that we sent the wrong version of the slide deck. The subsequent wire-brushing by Fletcher. And don't forget the cherry on top: me crying after Fletcher reamed us out." Before forty-eight hours ago, the last time I cried was after Jon died. Now it seemed like I couldn't turn off the waterworks.

"Yep, today pretty much sucked," Voight said. "You know, for a minute there, I thought we might be able to avoid the ass-chewing."

"Why's that?"

"Didn't you notice the flowers on her desk? Thought they might put her in a better mood. Boy, was I wrong."

"Ah. You don't think they're from—"

"Her workplace paramour? Indeed I do."

"Ugh," I grimaced. "What does he see in her?"

"Probably not anything even remotely like what we see. She's a kiss-ass up, kick-ass down kind of woman."

"Truer words," I said, then took another sip. "Did I mention the fact that I cried?"

"I was there."

"Right." I polished off my beer. I looked around. The heavy oak bar and stenciled Gaelic phrases made the place feel like it should be in the middle of a small Irish village and choked with cigarette smoke. But, of course, because nothing in life seemed to make sense anymore, nothing could be further from the truth. Sine's, the Irish pub, which I'd recently learned was the *de facto* Pentagon officer's club, was situated in the corner of a shopping center in Arlington, a couple hundred yards from the Pentagon.

"So, how are you doing, kiddo?" Voight asked.

I looked at him quizzically, trying to hide the fact that I knew exactly what he was asking about.

"You don't need superhuman powers of observation to notice that you're missing a piece of jewelry. Everything okay?"

I sighed. "I called it off with my fiancé yesterday."

"Holy mother of Christ. I'd be busting out the waterworks, too, if I were you! You *have* had a turbulent couple of days, haven't you?"

"Yeah, that seems like an understatement right now."

"What happened?"

"He and I—we're moving in different directions, I guess. There's a bunch of reasons I called it off. But this particular moment? The one that's really bothering me is that he doesn't get why I'm in the Pentagon."

"Ah. You aren't the first and you won't be the last to face that problem. Being in and around the military takes its toll, and sometimes the spouse back home doesn't get it."

"How do you do it?" I asked.

"Do what?"

"Survive the Pentagon."

Voight snorted. "Great question. I've pondered that one countless days and nights," Voight waved his hands as if he were some kind of grandiose, albeit theatrical, philosopher. "And although I've dreamt up all kinds of theories and mantras, when it comes down to it, it's pretty simple. You have to embrace the suck."

"Embrace the suck?"

"Yep. Embrace the suck. Once you make peace with the fact that the Building will find new and inventive ways to make your life miserable, it gets a lot easier."

"So, if I accept the fact that things will suck, life will suck less?"

"I don't know whether it will suck less *per se*. More that it'll be easier to deal with the utter absurdity of this place. The entire damned system was designed to be dysfunctional."

"Explain."

"Our founding fathers—wise though they were—were fearful of government, right? So they designed the U.S. government to be dysfunctional: separating out congressional, the executive, and the judiciary branches. They wanted to make it difficult for any one part of government to act quickly to do anything."

"But that's a good thing, right? Prevention of tyranny? Government should fear those who are being governed."

"Sure. Until you're in the position where you have to do really complex stuff that requires regular coordination across the U.S. government. Like win the 'hearts and minds' of the Afghans. We got so caught up in our own legalese and bureaucracy, we almost forgot that we were fighting an enemy. We fought—we fight—ourselves instead. You think the Pashtun tribal networks are confusing? They've got *nothing* on Washington."

My eyes widened. "You know, I'm terrified by how much sense you're making right now."

"No shit," Voight agreed. "Don't get me wrong. Most people working here are pretty stellar. But there's a limit to what even the best of people can accomplish when surrounded by bureaucratic ineptitude."

"Why do you work here, if you hate it so much?"

Voight set down his pint, turning the glass on the table a couple times while he thought about what to say.

"Honestly?"

I'd never seen his features so serious. I nodded.

"Okay, well, you hear a lot about deployments, and how they strain Army and Marine Corps families. But truth be told, it doesn't really matter what service you're in. We all deploy or get sent away. And as I said before: it all takes its toll."

I thought about that. Jon and Amanda had been apart more than they were together after they got married. Which must have been awful for both of them.

"The fact of the matter is that I pushed for this assignment. As god-awful as the Pentagon is, I've been gone from home a lot over my career. I wasn't around much for my boys when they were growing up. But then Jamie got pregnant again. Total accident. And I kind of felt like it was an opportunity to do it right this time. So when Sarah was born, I tried to find a job that would let me spend more time at home."

I was both surprised, and not surprised at all, by Voight's candor. He reminded me of Jon more and more by the day.

"And I guess the other thing is that most military bases are in some pretty backwoods places. I wanted my boys to go to a really good school for a while. Be exposed to culture and the monuments. They haven't really had that before. And I've dragged Jamie to the boonies any number of times. When the position in space policy opened up, I thought, hey! It's a nine-to-five, in a good location—relatively speaking—and so I pushed for it."

"So, you're here in the Pentagon for your family," I said.

"That about sums it up."

"But if you hate it, why don't you quit? Do something else?"

Voight looked at me strangely. "Wearing the uniform is a calling, Heather. I can't walk away."

I thought about Jon—about how he decided to continue serving rather than get out after four years. At the time, I couldn't quite understand why he'd choose to spend so much time away from Amanda. After he died, I thought his decision was selfish. So much pain could have been spared if he'd just left the Army to do something—anything—else. A couple months prior, I would have told Voight he was nuts to stay in uniform. Instead, I said, "I think I'm starting to get what that means."

"Good. You'd be one of the few civilians in Washington that does. Anyway, why do you ask?"

I struggled to get the words out. After everything that Voight just shared, how could I express that I was having second thoughts about my decision to stay in the Pentagon? "I guess I'm just struggling—"

"I'm sorry, Heather—my phone's buzzing. I'm waiting to hear from Jamie. Do you mind?" he asked, taking his phone from its holster along his belt and fiddling with the device.

"Not at all." I was grateful for the reprieve. I used the opportunity to check my phone. There was a voice mail from my mother, but nothing from Ryan.

"That was Jamie. She and the kids are going to be out longer than expected tonight. So I've got a little bit more time. Where were we?"

"Let's see here. Bureaucratic dysfunction and ineptitude?"

"Ah, yes. Given how depressing things are, there are essentially three reactions you can have in the face of all of this: anger, depression, or laughter. How you react is up to you. I choose laughter. And of course the occasional adult beverage," he said, holding up his empty glass. "Speaking of, want another? I've got time for one more pint."

I checked my watch; I had another hour before I was supposed to meet Amanda.

"Sure, why not?"

As Voight scooted out from the booth and made his way to the bar, I began seeing him in a new light. Sure, he reminded me of Jon—a class-clown type that could always make me smile. But now...it was almost as if he were the military's version of a Buddhist Bodhisattva, cursing himself to the cycle of bureaucratic rebirth in order to steer people like me toward the Pentagon's version of enlightenment. I half expected him to start projecting some kind of ethereal glow. Assuming that Buddhas glowed, of course.

Instead, he projected hairy knuckles as he set down our pints. "I'm going to see a man about a horse. I'll be back."

I checked my phone again for messages from Ryan. Still none. I was tempted to call him, but instead I distracted myself by watching the screen with the D.C. United game projected on it. Although sports weren't my thing, after the Women's World Cup a couple years ago, I'd developed a soft spot for soccer. I quickly got absorbed in the game. It was a close one against the Colorado Rapids, with D.C. in the lead.

"Heather?" said a man who appeared out of nowhere.

I gasped in surprise; it was Royle. He wore dark, fitted jeans and a button-up shirt that brought out the steel grey in his otherwise bright blue eyes. I grudgingly admitted to myself that he looked great. *I suppose Amanda could do worse?* I thought.

An awkward silence passed between us. Finally, he managed to choke out a few words. "I—I saw you over here, and just wanted to say hello."

"Congratulations—I heard about your new assignment."

"Thanks," he said. "Even though I'm the Joint Staff, I'm sure we'll end up working together again. I have a feeling things are going to get pretty intense."

"Great," I said, trying to hide the fact that the prospect of working with Royle again was not something I'd consider "great" by any stretch of the imagination. I couldn't take any more of the professional turbulence that he'd undoubtedly inflict on me.

"Voight is on his way back in a moment, if you'd like to say hello to him," I said.

"Oh, thanks, but Kristen and I were just about to head home," Royle said, pointing to another table across the room. Sitting alone, sipping a glass of white wine, was a stunningly attractive woman. She was tall and slender, with straight golden blonde hair that fell just beneath the shoulders of the Kelly green dress that hugged and flattered her curves as if she'd just stepped off a catwalk.

My eyes widened in shock. I'd been annoyed, irritated, peeved, exasperated with Royle before. But looking between him and his supermodel of a girlfriend, I was livid. Royle had just spent the night with Amanda. How could he be so callous? I remembered what Amanda said about men in D.C.: "Gay, married, or on to the next." *Indeed. Asshole.* And then it occurred to me that he probably didn't know Amanda and I were roommates. Otherwise, why would he flaunt this other woman in front of me?

Unless he *did* know? That would make things even worse.

"Heather?" Royle asked, disturbing me from my thoughts.

I bit my lip. As much as I wanted to give Royle a piece of my mind, starting a scene with one of my colleagues in a public place was probably not a good idea.

"Have a good night," I responded with as much venom in my voice as was humanly possible.

"You too," Royle said, looking confused. "And please tell Colonel Voight I said hello." He walked back to his table and Kristen, watching him approach, put on her short denim jacket that worked spectacularly well with her dress. *Of course.* The pair walked out into the early Washington evening.

I was still stewing when Voight returned to the table a couple minutes later.

"So, did I miss anything?"

CHAPTER SEVENTEEN

"ARE YOU OKAY?" Amanda said before I could get a word in edgewise about Royle. We hugged each other, not really caring that other visitors to the Willard Hotel would have to maneuver around us to get up the steps and inside the building. Nearby, doormen both greeted guests and bid them goodnight, gracefully hustling them along toward their destinations while somehow steering them clear of Amanda and me. It was the perfect public place-for a private conversation.

"Not really?" I wiped the beginnings of a tear from my eye. "It's over. He wanted to take a break, and I told him we should call it quits. He said he doesn't know if he can trust me."

"Seriously?" asked Amanda. "That's rich."

"How do you mean?"

Amanda suddenly reminded me of a kettle that had just boiled a full head of steam. "He's financially irresponsible, he makes you feel bad for doing your job, he's been completely unsupportive, and now he says that *he* can't trust *you*? That's one hell of a mind fuck."

My eyes widened; Amanda never dropped the F-bomb.

"I'm sorry. You're going through a lot, and I don't want to make it worse," she said, calming herself down. "But from my own experience, I can tell you that life throws you a ton of curveballs. A real partner will stand with you when life gets tough. Ryan's clearly lacking in that department."

"Thank you," I said, hugging her; no one in the crowd seemed to notice our affectionate moment. They were all too busy hobnobbing with each other.

"For what it's worth, I always thought you guys were a weird pair anyway."

"What? Why didn't you say anything?"

Amanda shrugged. "You said you loved him, and I wanted to be supportive."

"Right. Well, for the record, next time, feel free to give me that kind of heads-up before I spend ten years with the wrong guy," I said with a small laugh.

"Will do. Have you told Mom?"

I grimaced and shook my head. "She's going to freak."

Amanda nodded, slowly. "Yeah, I can see that. You know what will get your mind off things?"

"A pint of ice cream, pajamas, and booking a one-way ticket to Ulaanbaatar?" I asked. "I hear they have yurts there."

"A nice dinner with your best friend, followed by retail therapy. Washington style," Amanda said. "And fortunately, we're in the right place for the dinner part. Let's go."

We walked from the bar into the lobby of the Willard; the memory of the last time I was there flooded over me. It was a year and a half ago when I'd encountered one of my more cantankerous mentors—an older, spindly American academic—at the International Studies Association annual conference. Although the conference was at the Marriot next door, we'd escaped to the Willard to catch up, away from the menagerie of policy wonks and academics studying various and sundry aspects of international relations.

"He's right, you know," my mentor said, agreeing with the portly gentleman who had publicly excoriated my ideas earlier that day because I didn't have any real-world experience.

I felt like I'd been slapped.

"How can you say that? I have a PhD—more than that guy can say."

"You've never worked in government," he said, taking a sip of his Glenfiddich.

"So?"

"So, you're smart, Heather. But you're part of the problem. Most of these people," he said while waving his hand dismissively toward the crowds around us, "have no idea what it's like to work in the bureaucracy. All these good ideas about how the world should work, and all of them completely miss the point."

"And what, do you think, is the point?" I asked.

"Probably only point-oh-one percent of the bright ideas coming out of this place are actually achievable. And that's being generous."

"Why not?"

"Maybe some day you'll figure that out. If you have the guts to get in the game," he murmured, before changing the conversation to our different research projects.

At the time, I'd simply thought he was trying to provoke me. But over the next couple of weeks, what he said really started to eat away at me. I'd never thought of myself as timid, or someone who would back down from a challenge. And I began to wonder what I was missing. What was it really like, working in the belly of the national security beast? A couple weeks later, I'd sent off my fellowship application.

I subsequently convinced myself—and Ryan, too, I supposed—that I'd applied for financial reasons. But now, I had a creeping sense that the money was only a small part of my reasoning for moving to D.C.

As I looked back at the chairs where we'd sat, I realized exactly how right he'd been. Everything in the Pentagon seemed to be much harder than it needed to be.

The Willard looked much the same: a taste of Old World décor in the beating heart of new world politics. Fresh flowers scented the air, and the occasional palm tree was nestled against the marble columns holding up the embossed, gold-leafed ceiling. Following the signs to the National Defense Industrial Association annual gala dinner, we made our way down the red-carpeted corridor and into the ballroom. It was full with people in suits and dress uniforms, all trying to find their namecards in the sea of tables.

Crystal chandeliers lit the room and gold-painted boiseries covered the creamy yellow walls, lending the room a warm, yet sophisticated, eighteenth-century French aesthetic. It took a fair amount of time for us to actually make it to our seats; as Senator McClutchy's point person on national security and defense, legions of lobbyists and businessmen wanted to make sure they were seen by—and said hello to—Amanda. "You're already the best date ever." Amanda turned her back to the crowd as if to physically shield us from the hordes of defense industry wonks. "If I'd been alone, I'd have had to actually talk to these people."

"Groveling's not your cup of tea, I take it?" We sat down.

"You have no idea. All they want me to do is relay messages to McClutchy. Steer him in their direction. And it's only going to get worse."

"What do you mean?"

Amanda shook her head, indicating that then and there was the exact wrong time and place to say what she really meant. Instead, she lifted an event program resting on her plate and opened it to the first page: Senator McClutchy was the keynote speaker. It was at that moment that the convener of the evening walked up to a podium in the front of the room and asked everyone to take their seats at their tables.

Over the crisp white linens, crystal wine glasses, and silver dining ware, I noticed we were two tables away from McClutchy's in the center. Fred sat next to him.

"I checked—they only have a vegetarian, not a vegan, option tonight. I'm sorry about that," Amanda said, eyeing Fred at the other table.

I looked at the menu. Every course had some kind of meat on it; steak was the main course. Suddenly, the idea of stabbing into a steak seemed exactly what the night called for. *Screw it.*

"That's okay. I'll take the risk. I'll stick with the regular menu."

Amanda raised her eyebrows in surprise. "Turning over a brand-new leaf! I like it!"

I felt better—important, somehow—sitting there amongst the fine linens and floral arrangements. We made small talk with the people next to us as we ate our prosciutto-wrapped asparagus. Everyone registered their shock at Russia's buildup in Eastern Europe, followed by polite yet firm assessments that the world was becoming a much more dangerous place as we daintily nibbled on our asparagus stalks. Our steaks were served just in time for some chatter about how the United States was no longer the world leader it once was. I nodded and smiled at the conversation, pretending I was listening, as I almost died with joy as the steak melted in my mouth. I'd just finished when Senator McClutchy came to the stage to deliver the keynote address.

For being a slender man, McClutchy seemed to fill the entire stage.

"It is absolutely unacceptable that President Callahan is presiding over the most serious decay in American leadership in our lifetimes." I looked to Amanda. She tried to hide her agitation, but I could read it spreading across her face.

"We are facing an astonishing period of American retrenchment, even as crises around the globe are mounting, and the need for U.S. leadership is greater than ever."

As the crowd murmured its agreement with McClutchy, I turned to Amanda. "What does he want us to do? Be globo-cops? Put more soldiers in harm's way?" I whispered.

Amanda gave a brief nod—one that anyone but me would have missed—and sipped her wine.

"President Callahan has shown astonishingly poor judgment!" McClutchy continued. "Failing to submit a budget to Congress that represents compromise. A budget that would fully fund our defense department. And now the chickens have come home to roost. We're not able to protect our homeland, and we're losing our credibility abroad."

The audience clapped. Fred beamed. Amanda grimaced.

"Let's get out of here," she whispered after our chocolate mousse with raspberries. We politely made our excuses and escaped into the Washington evening.

"Explain to me why we're here?" I asked as we headed up the escalator to the Designer Shoe Warehouse in Pentagon City.

"This is my happy place. So many pumps! And I think we could both do with some retail therapy," she said as we reached the top and entered the warehouse-sized room full of shoes. Heels, boots, flats, and sneakers of all different shapes, sizes, and colors were organized into long, neat rows. "And yes, I realize this makes me a cliché. I, personally, don't care."

I'd never really bothered investing in nice shoes, largely because I'd never needed to. Sneakers were good enough for academia, and the flats I wore around the Pentagon were just fine too.

"So, what's bothering you?" I asked, as we entered a row dedicated to different styles of high heels. I wanted to bring up Royle and ask her what was going on between the two of them, but it seemed like there were more pressing matters to discuss.

Amanda pursed her lips, as if she was physically trying to prevent herself from saying something she might regret later.

"Amanda, it's me," I said, reassuring her. "Whatever you say stays between us."

"I know. I'm just having some…challenges…at work." Amanda paused, distracting herself with some royal-blue, peep-toe heels, before responding. "I'm beginning to think that the senator and I don't exactly see eye to eye on the issues anymore."

"What's up?"

Amanda sighed. "I wrote the speech."

"Really?" I was shocked. McClutchy's bloviating didn't sound like something Amanda would write.

"Well the first draft, at any rate. Fred must have gotten his hands on it. It was supposed to be about responsible American leadership. Instead, he behaved like a monkey flinging its poop at anything and everything."

"That's got to be incredibly frustrating." I followed Amanda as she turned down another aisle. "Is he going to move forward with an Afghanistan hearing?" I asked.

"Of course not. Afghanistan is yesterday's news," Amanda said with a clear note of frustration in her voice. "Anyway, enough about me." I knew better than to push her once she was done sharing. "Now that you've put a couple hours between you and the day from hell, how are you?"

"Wondering whether Ryan is right. I came to the Pentagon to work on Afghanistan. And instead, I'm working on Moldova and ironing pieces of paper."

"Ironing?"

"Don't ask. The point is: Maybe I am better suited to academia."

"You may be better suited to academia, but that doesn't mean that you're not capable of working in the Pentagon. You've got to make it work, Heather."

"But what if I can't?" I asked.

"Nonsense. You can. You will. You're tougher than you give yourself credit for."

"I don't feel very tough right now."

"Are you kidding?" Amanda said. "You're one of the toughest women I know. Look, sometimes you're the windshield, but right now, you're the bug. It happens to all of us. You can get through this. And you will."

"What makes you so sure?"

"Because you *need* to. You really want to make the world a better place, and you're genuinely dedicated to our military service members. Not everyone around here thinks the way you do. That's important."

"But I'm just a peon."

"Maybe. But you're a peon in a really important place, with a portfolio that you can use to make a real difference. And if you choose to give that up, or choose not to help, then you'll have to live with that forever. Besides, just because your day job is focused on Moldova, doesn't mean that you can't keep up on Afghanistan. You're used to working jobs on the side, right?" Amanda winked. And, think about it. You have a PhD; you're a smart cookie. If you're having problems getting the hang of it, don't you think everyone else is too?"

Amanda's phone buzzed. "Excuse me, I need to take this. I'll be right back." She dashed to a corner that was full of purses, wallets, and handbags.

I wandered aimlessly through the aisles and found myself surrounded by fancy heels: pale with sequins, silver with rhinestones, all designed to make a ball gown pop. They were the kind of shoes that I never considered buying. Fancy heels were for formals, and Ryan and I never went to anything that even remotely resembled a gala affair. "They're for the one percent," Ryan said when I suggested we splurge and go to a ball one New Year's Eve. We made vegan nachos and watched the ball drop on TV instead.

I watched Amanda pace back and forth as she talked on the phone, looking a little tired but nevertheless stunning. I had always considered Amanda's style to be something unattainable for me. Meticulously put together with a kind of attention to detail that I couldn't fathom. And her high-heeled shoes—which always complimented the suits she wore—looked painful to me. And besides, I'd always rationalized, my colleagues would judge me for my ideas rather than my looks if I dressed a little on the conservative—okay, a bit frumpy—side.

It was at that precise moment that I saw them: a pair of red, patent leather pumps. They were three inches tall and totally outrageous, at least by my standards.

I started to walk away, and then stopped myself.

Trying on a pair won't kill me, I thought. I found a pair in my size; they fit perfectly. I walked around to gauge how they felt on my feet and realized that the shoes were surprisingly comfortable—even more so than my black, squat heels. And as I caught myself in the mirror, standing taller with my shoulders squared and a gorgeous pop of red on my feet, I felt strangely empowered. More ready to embrace the changes that had just overturned my life. I just might be able to become the windshield rather than the bug. Cliché? Probably. Did I care? Not so much. I'd take what I could get.

Amanda found me at the cash register. "Nice pair!" she said, eyeing my new shoes. "Ready to head home?"

"Actually, if it's okay with you, I'm going to give that a miss," I replied, feeling a new burst of energy. "I think I'm going to go back to work for a couple hours."

Amanda smiled. "That's the right attitude."

Three hours and a mocha latte later, I finished writing a memo about the implications of our Mongolia-Moldova move, and some thoughts on what the U.S. strategy to deal with Russia in Central and Eastern Europe might be. Wanting to ensure I wasn't wildly off base, I hit "send" to a couple colleagues that I knew through academic circles that worked in Washington think tanks. I was about to leave when I had a sudden burst of over-caffeinated inspiration and decided to write out my thoughts on the worsening situation in Afghanistan in an email to Amanda. Maybe she could use the points to make the case for a hearing on Central Asia.

Finally, at one thirty in the morning, I was intellectually and physically spent. Despite my exhaustion, I walked out of the Pentagon feeling better than I had in days or weeks, perhaps even years.

CHAPTER EIGHTEEN

I'D SPENT MOST OF THE WEEKEND IN THE OFFICE, SO I WAS MORE TIRED THAN NORMAL BY THE TIME I GOT TO WORK THE NEXT MONDAY. It therefore took me a moment to figure out what was wrong with my desk. It appeared that some kind of canvas cloth covered my cubicle, with a pole sticking out from the top in the approximate location of where my chair ought to be. Even more incomprehensible: how to actually enter the tent-like construction covering my desk. I set down my coffee and began working with the leather straps that were apparently fastening the door to the makeshift tent.

"Like it?" Voight said cheerfully when I finally made it inside. He was sitting on the floor, reading the newspaper and sipping his coffee.

"Why are there sheepskins on the floor of my cubicle?" I asked. I took another sip of my coffee. "And where is my chair?"

"Rolling office chairs ruin the yurt's aesthetics," Voight said. "Duh." He rolled his eyes.

"Obviously."

"I thought it a fitting way to pay tribute to the fact that our crazy little Moldova plan is actually moving forward. Us and the

Mongol hordes. And anybody else that wants to join our merry band of Moldova-supporting misfits. I think Pumpkin is working on a 'free yurts incentive plan' for any country that contributes to the coalition."

I nodded. "Makes sense. I'd join." I yawned.

"Need more coffee?"

"Definitely. I was here pretty late. Burnt some serious midnight oil."

"Over the weekend? Doing what?"

"Writing memos."

"On what?"

"Just some thoughts on the Moldova plan and how Russia might react—and what we could do about that. I mean, that's ultimately what all this is about, right? Standing up to Russia?"

"Yep. Well, standing up to the Russians, behind the Mongolians. Kind of like the world's lamest ventriloquist."

"Right. So, if all of this is about standing up to the Russians, I'm guessing the Russians aren't going to like Plan Moldova."

"Probably. But remember: Plan Moldova is less terrible than Plan Armenia. So, we've got that going for us. But, hang on a second. You spent the whole weekend here writing memos?"

"Yep."

"You must be exhausted."

"You're not wrong."

"Excellent. You're therefore in perfect mental condition to go to the Joint Staff. Pumpkin called; they want one of us to join him for a meeting on Moldova."

"I'm happy to take it, but wouldn't it be better if you went? You're the one wearing the uniform."

"I've got to go with Fletcher to a meeting with the Georgians. The Russians won't be the only ones unhappy with Plan Moldova. The Georgians are pretty upset that they're not going to have a contingent of Americans in Armenia, just over the border from them."

"How did they find out about it?"

Voight cocked an eyebrow.

"Oh. Right. *The Washington Post.*"

"Anyway, you'd better get down to Pumpkin's office. Meeting starts in twenty."

"Pumpkin, where are we going?" I asked, struggling to keep up with his pace in my bright red heels.

"To the NMCC."

"Oh! Right. Of course," I said, doing my best to hide my sudden excitement. The National Military Command Center was one of the most important places in the entire Department of Defense. If the Joint Staff was the backbone of the U.S. military, the NMCC was its brain.

"That's why I had you meet me at my office," Pumpkin said as we stepped onto an escalator. "The NMCC's kind of hard to find. You pretty much need a trail of breadcrumbs to make your way in and out of there the first couple of times."

"Shoot. I left my breadcrumbs on my desk," I said. "So, why do you want me at this meeting?"

"Running interference. At this stage of the game, the more you know about what's about to go down, the easier it will be for us to do our jobs," Pumpkin said.

"You guys have precooked how you're going to do Moldova, haven't you?"

Pumpkin smiled but didn't say anything.

We arrived at a large set of steel doors. A seal, easily half as tall as me, with four swords crossed behind a shield with the stars and stripes, was situated on the wall to our right: the seal of the Joint Chiefs of Staff of the United States of America. As Pumpkin worked with the guard to secure a visitor's-access pass for me, I couldn't help but feel awestruck. Years ago, standing at an anti-war protest on a rainy Boston day, I never in my wildest dreams would have imagined I would be standing there, about to enter such a vitally important place for the nation's—and the world's—security.

"Heather?" Pumpkin asked, interrupting my train of thought while handing me a badge. "Shall we?"

Pumpkin nodded to the guard, who buzzed us through the steel doors. I involuntarily held my breath; I couldn't help but speculate that whatever lay beyond those doors would have a profound impact on me. The discussions we would have, the decisions we would make would affect thousands of men and women around the globe. I felt humbled; I was about to be part of one of the most important conversations going on in the world at that very moment. Humbled, but also alive with a sense of purpose. *This is why I decided to stay in the Pentagon.* I was ready for anything and everything.

Everything except feeling underwhelmed. Again. *Dammit.* I'd entered yet another fluorescent-lit cubicle farm, with yet more people hunched over their desks, as if their computer screens were a kind of physical crutch their lives depended upon. The only difference between this office and every other in the Pentagon that I'd seen so far was that the men and women in the NMCC had darker circles under their eyes, paler skin, and deeper grimaces etched on their faces. It was as if the NMCC was turning everyone into their own personal versions of Gollum. The bitter scent of coffee that had been on a burner since roughly around the time the Pentagon itself was constructed wafted through the air.

Pumpkin noticed my surprise. "Yeah, that's why we don't let these NMCC guys out too much. You think it's bad now? You should have seen this place *before* the renovation. It was like a dingy, dank, janitor's closet. With PowerPoint."

"I'm pretty sure that sounds like my own personal version of hell."

"Mine, too. But apparently, the Army staff is even worse. Or, at least, that's what they tell me," Pumpkin said, opening a door. "Thank god I joined the Navy. After you."

We entered another nondescript conference room. Large, faux-wood conference tables formed a "U" shape in the center of the room. Cheap chairs with green cushions lined the walls behind the tables and were organized into several rows in the back of the room. To the front of the room was a massive screen with a Power-Point presentation already projected upon it. Pumpkin's attention was suddenly distracted by an Air Force officer entering the conference room.

"Hey, do you mind if I leave you alone for a couple minutes?" Pumpkin asked. "I've got an issue I need to sort out with Lester over there."

"No problem. I'll be fine."

"I'll be right back."

"Okay." I fished my notebook out of my purse and sat back to take in my surroundings. Clusters of men in uniform gathered together, presumably to hammer out the issue du jour, while quickly darting glances in my direction.

"Excuse me, ma'am?"

I looked up and smiled when I saw the gorgeous Navy Commander I'd seen a couple weeks ago at the Georgia—Armenia strategy meeting. And once again, I was awestruck. His eyes looked more green than blue under the Joint Staff's fluorescent lighting, but otherwise he looked the same. Stunning.

Stop it, Heather! You're engaged.

Wait. No, I'm not.

"Ma'am?"

I could feel my cheeks burning. I'd definitely been caught staring.

"Uh, yes?" I said, trying to calm down.

"May I?" He gestured to the other seat next to me.

"Of course."

"Thanks. I'm Matt, by the way," he said, extending his hand toward me with a smile.

"Heather," I responded, setting down my notepad. As I shook his hand, it was as if all my hormones had been on ice for, well, forever. And they'd just been thawed.

"What are you doing here?" a familiar, if unwelcome, voice to my right asked. I turned around. Royle was towering above me, with an expression on his face that bordered between annoyed and angry. "Who told you about this? You're not supposed to be here."

"This—" Matt started.

"Pumpkin *asked* me to be here," I interrupted. I could fight my own battles without my new friend Matt's support.

"Pumpkin?" Royle responded, almost confused.

"Captain Fitzgerald."

"Right," Royle said, then pursed his lips. He turned on his heels, obviously annoyed, and walked to the other side of the room.

"What's his problem?" I muttered under my breath.

Matt overheard me. "That guy? Royle? Everyone knows he's difficult. He's been that way for a while."

"That's an understatement," I said, watching Royle angrily speak to a lieutenant colonel on the other side of the room.

"I wouldn't worry about him, though. The captain outranks him."

With that, the room suddenly stood to attention as a general— bald and broad, with his uniform stretched almost a little too taut against his chest—walked into the room.

"All right, gentlemen," the general said. "Let's get down to business." He indicated that everyone should take a seat.

I sat back down. On my notebook. Realizing there was no way to delicately or gracefully retrieve it, I stood to fish it out from underneath me. Which is how everyone else noticed that there was a woman in the room. A woman that wasn't in uniform. I immediately felt as out of place as a penguin in the Sahara.

"Colonel Royle, I understand that you are delivering this brief?" the general said.

"Yes, sir," Royle said.

"Over to you. Let's get this show on the road. Give me the SITREP."

"Right, sir," Royle said, getting down to business. "As you know, last night SecDef authorized a mission to support the Mongolians as they train the Moldovan Security Forces. The overall plan is to redirect the force package we were spinning up for Armenia and placing it in Moldova instead. But we've also received guidance that the mission is contingent upon the establishment of a coalition presence there joining us."

That was news to me. I'd thought we were going into Moldova with the Mongolians, regardless. It was a good caveat for the mission—one that I was planning on recommending to Fletcher later that day.

"The purpose of our mission is twofold," continued Royle. "First, to prevent Russian interference in Moldovan affairs, and second, to build another logistical hub in case the Georgians need help repelling a Russian incursion on their territory. An added benefit, of course, is that we'll have better visibility on the rumored uranium-trafficking, if there is any."

Uranium-*trafficking? I thought their major problem was cow-smuggling.*

The briefing continued, and I felt a quick punch to the gut as I watched my argument—Fletcher's argument—for building a presence in Moldova become real. As real as blue sky and green grass and the hard granite of the Pentagon's walls. The implications were suddenly, starkly clear. American soldiers were going to be positioned in Moldova as a bulwark to Russian aggression. The region was already volatile. What if Russia crossed a line? For that matter, what *was* the line?

"Unfortunately, we diverted assets away from the EUCOM AOR in order to focus on PACOM issues as part of the pivot, particularly ROK/DPRK, respectively. Our understanding of developments in the region is therefore unsat. But we're working on it. The Chairman has requested—and CENTCOM and EUCOM have agreed—to temporarily divert all intel assets from Afghanistan and Pakistan in order to cover down on the Black Sea region and give us better SA."

Diverting assets from Afghanistan and Pakistan? My heart froze. *I thought the plan would be to divert stuff from Georgia?* I wouldn't have recommended Moldova at all if I thought that doing so would mean taking our eyes off Afghanistan, even if briefly. True, Russia was a problem. But the civil war in Afghanistan was getting worse and worse, and the Islamic State was getting stronger and stronger.

"What *do* we know?" the general asked.

"We're hearing through diplomatic channels that Russia has gotten wind of our involvement in the Moldova-Mongolia mission, and they've already started reacting."

"How so?

"From what we can tell, they're starting to send some of their proxies into Eastern Moldova—the Transnistria region. We're getting reports of men that look an awful lot like out-of-uniform Russian Special Forces."

I frowned. The situation that Royle was outlining was getting close to the nightmare scenario I'd written about in my memo. The punch to my gut that I'd felt earlier was now twinged with nausea.

"But we haven't even arrived in Moldova yet," the general said.

"That doesn't seem to matter to the Russians. They're also stepping up airstrikes against the U.S.-trained forces in Syria."

"Didn't they agree to a ceasefire there?"

"Yes, sir, they did. But according to them, the conditions of the ceasefire let them designate anybody they want as either the Islamic State or the al-Nusra Front."

"So they're retaliating by bombing our guys and calling them ISIS?"

"Seems so, sir.

"All this seems like a massive overreaction, don't you think?"

"The Russians are known for that, sir."

"Dammit, all this is making my head hurt. What's the status of the interagency?"

"Sir, it's a kabuki dance on the other side of the river. State is in the middle of a class-one FLAILEX over the Russian's response. They're a soup sandwich over there. But for our purposes, they're working overflights around the region. They're also reaching out to anyone and everyone to build out this Moldova coalition. The NSC is still smarting from the fact that this package isn't what they initially had in mind."

"Yeah, Derek's a good guy, but he can be a pain in the ass when he doesn't get his way. Where are we on options?" the general asked.

"Well, the bottom line is that the force package we were planning on sending to Armenia is being redirected to Moldova. Now we're looking at mitigating implications and risks," Royle said.

"Specifics?"

"At 0800 this morning we sent out the order to CENTCOM and EUCOM in order to develop a series of COAs for response to the Russian-Moldovan-Syrian situation."

Wait—what?

"We're looking at establishing a JTF for conducting ops in theater, if necessary. JAG is reviewing legalities. BLUF: depending on the COA that SecDef chooses, with TRANSCOM and SOCOM support, we are prepared to conduct anything from CT to SASO in the EUCOM AOR."

Was any of that English?

"We're spinning up to deploy teams with twelve hours' notice; SOF would be part of any initial strike force package. CENTCOM is also spinning up to do an RFF once we have greater fidelity on what's available. In any case, we can have BOG within forty-eight hours of SecDef signing a DEPORD."

I have my own acronym for you guys: WTF.

The general nodded, comprehending everything. I, on the other hand, was mystified. I looked around the room. All the other officers were nodding in rapt attention. The feeling of nausea in my stomach was now sidekicked with a generous helping of near-existential dread as I realized I had no clue what my colleagues in uniform were talking about. And this was precisely the kind of meeting that Fletcher would want to be back-briefed on. I decided to furiously take notes verbatim and pray Voight could help me translate them later. And because I was furiously scribbling in my notebook, transcribing the discussion without actually understanding what any of it meant, it took me a minute to hear, and then recognize, the general's remark.

"Colonel Royle, I need to interrupt you for a moment," the general started.

"Yes, sir."

"During my workout, I read a memo that popped into my inbox this morning. It's a piece about the consequences of our Moldova decision. It argues that the only way to squelch Russian retaliation to our involvement in Moldova is to get as many coalition partners as possible involved, as quickly as possible."

"I'm sorry, sir. I haven't read it," Royle said.

"It basically says that the more countries that have boots on the ground alongside the Mongolians and ourselves, the harder it will be for Russia to get away with shenanigans in Moldova. And with an increased presence in Moldova, near Russian bases around the Black Sea, it'll be harder for Russia to get away with murder in Syria."

"Because we'll be positioned to ring-fence them in," Royle said, tracking the logic of the idea.

Thank god, I thought, as I made a note at the bottom of the page to track down this strategic-implications paper they were talking about. It would be great to have someone—anyone—to compare notes with. Someone who'd spent more time than me thinking about this Moldova situation.

"Exactly," the general said. "State may take the lead for a lot of this stuff, but this memo I was reading raises a number of important points we need to factor in now as we plan and execute this mission. Quite frankly, it's one of the most insightful pieces I've seen on this subject."

I breathed a sigh of relief. From the general's description, my thinking on Moldova tracked quite closely with this mystery expert's, so my own memo wasn't completely off base.

"I'll forward it along to you, Royle, so that you can circulate it to this group," the general said, pulling out his folded hard copy from a pocket on the side of his uniform. The paper looked wrinkled and worn, presumably from his workout. He took his reading glasses from the same pocket and inspected the paper. "It's by a... Dr. Heather Reilly. Have you heard of her?"

Wait, what? I dropped my pen in shock.

"Sure," Royle replied. "She's sitting behind you."

CHAPTER NINETEEN

ALTHOUGH I'D LEFT THE JOINT STAFF MEETING OVERCOME WITH BEWILDERMENT—THE GENERAL WALKED UP TO SHAKE MY HAND AFTER THE MEETING WAS OVER—BY THE TIME I GOT BACK TO MY OFFICE, I DEFINITELY HAD A NOTICEABLE SPRING IN MY STEP. After the morning's victory, I was looking forward to getting back to my desk and getting to work.

Unfortunately, getting to my desk proved a little more challenging than I'd expected. I opened the office door to find most of my colleagues loitering in the waiting area in front of Fletcher's office. I pushed through the crowd, overhearing my colleagues awkwardly making small talk about the weather, their kids, their family vacations—any topic that would prevent them from actually communicating with one another. Voight, in the meantime, hovered back near the cubicles, somehow staying out of the fray and giving himself plenty of personal space. I bumped and nudged my way through the crowd in order to join him.

"What's happening?" I asked.

"Fletcher's called a snap meeting," Voight said. "Supposed to start now."

"On time as usual, then."

Voight nodded.

I suspected that we still had at least ten minutes to wait before the meeting started. I walked back to my desk and checked my email. It was empty when I left the office the night before. Now it contained three hundred and eighty-two messages.

My mouth dropped open.

Starting at the bottom of my inbox, I saw that one of the colleagues I'd sent my paper to—James at the Atlantic Council—was at a conference in Warsaw and had therefore responded to my message last night almost immediately. He, in turn, had forwarded my message and memo to some of his colleagues. And then they'd sent it on to some of their colleagues. And so on. From there, it was apparently circulated to an email distribution list called the "Warlord Loop." I lost track of where it went after that. At least a hundred emails were from complete strangers, asking me to clarify points or giving me additional feedback. Another hundred or so simply said "great stuff," or something similar. All of them, in total, suggested that my piece had gone "viral"—or, at least as "viral" as something could possibly go in the uber-dorky national security community.

I was stunned. Five or ten specialist scholars in my field—at most—had read my academic writings; I'd never authored a piece that had been read by so many people before in my entire life. I didn't know what to make of it.

"Everybody, come in," Fletcher said loudly as she opened her office door. I turned off my screen and joined my twenty-odd colleagues as we all stuffed ourselves into the space that was designed to fit ten people, max.

"Thank you all for being here on such short notice," started Fletcher. "I need to share with you some news that's going to have a big impact on all of us. Last night, Assistant Secretary Chao suffered a heart attack. He's now in critical condition, and it's not clear that he'll recover anytime soon."

I'd never met the man, so all I knew about him was what Amanda had told me. But given my colleagues' reactions, Amanda's favorable opinion of the man was widely shared; most of the people in the room appeared genuinely distraught by Chao's situation.

"This morning, the Secretary of Defense asked me to take on the role of Acting Assistant Secretary in ASD Chao's stead, at least until they can determine whether he'll be able to return to work. So, effective immediately, I am both the DASD for Coalitions Policy and your ASD."

"Acting," Voight said, with barely disguised snark in his voice.

"Yes, of course. Acting," Fletcher admitted, without any hint of recognition that she'd just been admonished. "Let me be clear: I expect nothing but excellence from all of you. They've asked me to take this on because of my reputation for getting things done."

I didn't doubt that she had a reputation, and that she was known for getting things done. Whether those things were the right things to get done? I had my doubts.

"I will be working you even harder than before; we have long hours ahead of us," Fletcher continued.

I looked over to Voight. His expression was pained, and I noticed he was twisting his wedding ring.

"But that is what our nation needs at this historic, if difficult, moment. Are there any questions?"

Historic?

The silence from my colleagues was deafening, with the notable exception of Voight, who whispered, "fuck," under his breath.

"You're dismissed," Fletcher said. I was almost out the door when Fletcher stopped me. "Heather, could you please come here for a minute?"

Voight and I looked at each other; Voight slightly shrugged before leaving the room.

"I've seen your little memo that you've circulated to our senior leaders," Fletcher said.

"Ma'am, I didn't mean—"

"I don't want to hear it, Heather. Just know that it shows remarkably poor judgment on your part."

I was confused. "But the Joint Staff liked—"

"Your memo could be mistaken for this administration's policy," Fletcher interrupted.

"Ma'am, I just wanted to get some colleagues to take a look at my arguments before sending it to you."

"Exactly. You sent a pre-decisional document outside the building. Uncoordinated. Uncleared." Fletcher took off her glasses. "I've been doing damage control all morning on this."

"Damage control?" I asked.

"Yes, Heather. Damage control. So, I think this goes without saying, but don't *ever* do that again. This is not academia. This is not a think tank. This is the U.S. government, something that I'm still not sure you fully grasp. People watch our every move, trying to discern what we will do. And you just broadcasted we're worried that our Moldova move may destabilize our relationship with Russia."

Fletcher's words struck me as either ironic or hypocritical—I wasn't sure which. After all, the Moldova issue hit the media because of Fletcher, and we'd moved forward despite the overwhelming objections of just about every other office in the United States government.

"But we *are* worried about the Russian reaction, aren't we?" I said. "Don't we need to figure that part out?"

"Broadcasting we're worried exposes us, Heather," Fletcher said, crossing her arms. Despite her trim and relatively small physique, she managed to loom over me. "What you did was give the Russians an avenue to exploit. They're watching."

I wanted to give Fletcher a piece of my mind. I wanted to tell her that an honest dialogue among national security professionals about how Moldova might affect our relationship with Russia would only help make our policy proposals stronger. And that they'd get more traction in the long term if the broader community—including Capitol Hill—got behind what we were doing. And the best way to do so was by circulating memos like mine and starting the conversation.

Instead, I said, "Oh."

"Due to your poor judgment, both yesterday and today, your position here in this office is even more...precarious than it was when you started."

A spike of fear shot through my heart. After everything that I'd been through recently, leaving the Pentagon before my fellowship ended was a non-starter as far as I was concerned. "Ma'am, I apologize. It won't happen again."

"To be clear, this is the only document you've sent outside the building, correct?"

Shit. I sent that email on Afghanistan to Amanda.

For a split second, I remembered Jon telling me that honesty was the best policy after I'd been caught shoplifting a Snickers bar when I was seven years old. The ensuing punishment for my petty crime—grounding by my parents—paled in comparison to Jon's disappointment in me. But as Fletcher stared me down, with my job hanging by a thread, I realized that Jon never had to contend with—nor was nearly fired by—DASD Ariane Fletcher.

"That's correct," I lied. "I only sent out the Moldova memo." The lie tasted bitter in my mouth, especially after being accused by Ryan of untrustworthiness. But I was fairly certain that Amanda probably hadn't even looked at my email yet. I might still be able to pull it back. And if not, Amanda knew how to keep things close hold.

"Good. You're dismissed."

"Are you sure you want to sit down for lunch?" Voight asked while we waited to place our orders at what he called the 'secret' Subway sandwich stand. It was nestled between the third and fourth corridors on the third floor, and would have been completely hidden were it not for the line of people waiting to enter.

"Yeah, why?"

"Because I'm pretty sure you don't have an ass left after that chewing you got from Fletcher," Voight winked.

"Right."

Voight munched on his sandwich. "I wouldn't worry about it too much. She's been on a tear this morning."

"Why? What happened?"

"Let me put it this way. I'm a full-bird colonel. I've commanded an air wing. I don't want to brag, but it's generally considered a rank of authority. At least, outside of this god-forsaken place, it is."

"And?"

"And this morning she made me carry her purse on the way to the meeting with the Georgians."

"What?" I said, shocked. "I wouldn't ask *anyone* to do that."

"I wish I was kidding. And then halfway through the meeting, she kicks me out," Voight said while opening his pack of Sun Chips. "Which is never good. That's when things normally go off the rails, and today was no exception."

"What did she do now?"

"She went off script. All the time and effort I spent prepping talking points, and from what I understand from our Georgian friends, she totally ignored them. She apparently offered them a Humvee factory. I'm going to have to spend a week and a half cleaning up this mess."

"A Humvee factory?"

"Yep. A Humvee factory."

"Does she have any authority to do that?"

"Nope."

"Great," I said. "So, it's not just me?"

"No. It's not just you. And, if I'm honest, I'm not sure it's her either."

"*Not* her?"

"She's always had the reputation for being a tough boss, right? But there's a difference between being tough and being a terror, and she's definitely trending towards terror. Sometimes I wonder whether she's a nightmare because the building's craziness is forcing her to become that way."

"If that's the case," I said, "then adding in the pressure of this new gig of hers? She's going to go from 'tough' to 'batshit insane.'" I rubbed the bridge of my nose and then pushed my sandwich away.

"Which, by the way, is why it's going to be even more important that we stick together," Voight said. "Safety in numbers. Besides, if I go it alone, I'll never get home on time. Jamie's going to kill me as it is."

"Why's that?"

"Just…it's important for me to try and spend some time at home, is all."

"Anyway, this morning," I said, changing the subject. "From what I could decipher, the Joint Staff is charging full steam ahead on the Moldova plan."

"Good. They know how to follow orders."

"There's just one problem."

"When *isn't* there a problem?"

"Besides the Mongolians and their yurts, we don't *actually* have a coalition yet."

"Ah," Voight said. "Yep. That's a problem. We should probably figure out which countries are going to join us." Voight polished off his sandwich in one swift bite. "And we should probably figure out what our big bosses are thinking about the whole thing."

"Can't we call Derek or something?"

"Ha! If only. He'd rather let us hang out to dry at this point."

"All right, then. How do we figure all this stuff out?"

"Tell me, Dr. Reilly," Voight said, raising an eyebrow and cocking a smile. "How do you feel about religion?"

CHAPTER TWENTY

"THIS DOESN'T LOOK LIKE A CHURCH," I SAID TO VOIGHT AS
WE STOOD OUTSIDE THE OMINOUS, MONOLITHIC BUILDING
ON SCOTT CIRCLE A FEW DAYS LATER. With its grey-white
concrete and dark-tinted windows, it looked like it could be the
headquarters of sinister government's intelligence agency. Or
the Illuminati. Or both. The only thing that made me reconsider
whether I was, in fact, entering the headquarters of the New World
Order was the seal above the doorway that had an emu and a
kangaroo on it.

"We're here for prayers."

"But Voight, it's a Friday night. And I'm not religious."

"Doesn't matter."

"I don't understand. Did the Australian Embassy somehow
become a religious site and I didn't notice?"

"Ha! The Aussies? Never."

"Then what are we—"

"'Prayers' is what the Aussies call their embassy's happy hour.
And yours truly has an invite. An invite that allows me to bring a
plus-one."

"Why isn't Jamie coming?"

"She's having a girls' night. Besides, she's been to any number of these things before."

"I really want to meet her sometime," I said.

"Well, it won't be at one of these things. The excitement wore off a while ago. Now she finds them kind of boring. Not that I blame her. They *are* pretty boring. Unless you're a total nerd. Which is, of course, why I thought of you."

"Thanks. I think. But, what exactly are we doing here?"

"Because the only people who have a reasonably good guess as to what's *actually* happening in the U.S. government are the embassies. They're watching us so hawkishly, they know what we're doing, even before we do."

"Right. So we're spying on the people who are spying on us in order to figure out whether they might join us in Moldova," I said as we entered a large, wood-paneled meeting room at the far end of the first floor of the embassy. Floor-to-ceiling windows along the far wall let in the sunset. "Makes perfect sense."

"Pretty much. I gotta hit the little boys room. See you in a minute," Voight said before disappearing.

I walked through the crowd, almost running into a large, blue plastic bucket on the floor filled with more beer than ice. The occasional waiter passed out hors d'oeuvres on silver trays: pigs in a blanket, mini quiches, pizza bagels, and taquitos. It occurred to me that I was squarely in the middle of the diplomatic equivalent of a college kegger. I took a taquito and then turned my attention back to the bucket.

"Whatever you do, don't drink the Foster's. Dreadful stuff," said a man behind me with a British accent.

It was the kind of accent you hear in the movies; one that comes from having a double-barreled last name and a "cottage" in the countryside that turns out to be bigger than several European microstates. Fittingly, he was impeccably dressed, wearing a khaki seersucker suit and pink tie with matching handkerchief. He was truly a peacock among pigeons.

"I don't know why you Yanks love it," he continued.

I smiled. "Good thing I was reaching for the Fat Tire, then."

"Indeed!" He stuck out his hand. "I'm Colin Harding-Spencer. British Embassy. Defense section."

"Dr. Heather Reilly. How long have you been here in Washington?"

"This is my second week on the job, and third in this country." He paused to loosen the double-Windsor knot in his tie. "I must admit, I'm not at all used to this weather."

"If it's any consolation, none of us are. My hair will never be the same again."

"You know, I haven't spoken to anybody in this town who hasn't complained about this oppressive heat. It's quite uncivilized," he said as we shuffled toward the visitor entrance. "Did you know that the British Embassy in Washington was considered a 'tropical hardship' posting until the 1970s?"

"Really?"

"Yes, well, you Yanks, in your infinite wisdom, decided to build your national capital in the thick of a swamp."

I hadn't thought of it quite that way before. Maybe it said something that our Founding Fathers decided to situate the heart of their new nation's political life squarely in the middle of a barely drained bog.

I noticed Colin eyeing me intensely.

"Sorry, you said your name was Dr. Heather Reilly?" he asked.

"Yes," I said, surprised.

"I *thought* I recognized you. I believe I attended a conference with you? At Chatham House, yes?"

"You mean, the one a few years ago? With the panel on Afghanistan?"

"Precisely."

I felt a small burst of pride that I'd made an impression. "Aren't you supposed to keep our participation secret?" I teased. "'Chatham House Rule?'"

"What Chatham House doesn't know won't kill them, will it?" Colin said with a grin.

"It's kind of like the first rule of *Fight Club*, isn't it?"

"Indeed!" Colin laughed. "Complete with academics and policy wonks beating each other up. Metaphorically speaking, of course."

"Of course."

"Anyway, I heard you speak just before I was headed back out to southern Afghanistan for six months. Your remarks were quite good. Refreshingly candid."

"Didn't I say that if we didn't do more, the situation would become hopeless?"

Colin grinned. "Yes. As I said. Candid. Anyway, where are you working now?"

"I'm in the Pentagon's coalitions office."

"Well, how *fortuitous* we should meet now. My job involves managing our embassy's relations with the Pentagon, which, as I gather, normally means figuring out whether and how to tag along with you lot on your military adventures," he said, fishing out his business card from a lightly tarnished holder in his inner jacket pocket. "Excellent memo on Moldova, by the way."

"You read that?" I asked, cringing.

"Who hasn't? It's brilliant. If you Yanks would just implement what you put down on paper, this whole coalition business would be much, much easier. Although why you decided to reach out to the Mongolians—of all people—is quite beyond me. And everyone else."

I almost choked on my beer. "Yeah, let's just call that a 'target of opportunity.'"

"Still, it's an odd choice. My minister almost went ballistic when he heard about that."

"We think their yurts could come in handy," Voight said, joining the conversation.

"Voight, this is Colin from the British Embassy," I said.

Colin looked up and down Voight's uniform as he stretched out his hand. "Colonel *Tom* Voight?" he asked.

"That's what the name tag says," Voight said.

"Well, isn't this a small world? It's a pleasure to finally meet you."

Voight looked confused. "Finally? Are you sure you don't have me mixed up with someone—"

"Colonel Farrell is a very good friend of mine," Colin interrupted.

"Oh," Voight said, quietly. He pursed his lips as a cloud crossed over his face. "I see."

Colin turned to me. "You see, Heather, your colleague here is a true hero."

I raised my eyebrows, somewhat—but not totally—surprised. "Really?"

"Really. He rescued a number of people during the September 11th attacks. Including our own Colonel Farrell. How many people did you end up getting to safety?"

Voight sighed, then reached down to an ice bucket for a beer. "Not enough."

"Farrell said it was eight."

"As I said. Not enough." His discomfort emanated off him in waves.

"Anyway," I said, changing the subject to give Voight a reprieve, "as you were saying. Aren't you here to investigate these delightful Costco Taquitos?" I took another from a waiter that walked by. "If so, you're missing your opportunity to sample the delicacies surrounding us."

"You caught me," Colin said smiling. "As it happens, my job this evening is to figure out what in the world you lot are doing on this Moldova issue."

"Well, it's actually pretty clear," I said. "The Mongolians are organizing a coalition and we're supporting them."

"Right," Colin said, skeptically. "That's one view of the matter. Others take an entirely different perspective."

"You mean, your government doesn't support the coalition?" I asked.

"*My* government?" Colin said, laughing. "My government doesn't yet know what to think. I'm talking about *your* government."

I noticed Voight perk up.

"Your counterpart at the NSC is out there telling everybody that this coalition of yours is a damn fool idea."

I winced, as if someone had physically punched me in the gut. "Derek Odem?" Voight asked.

"That's the chap. Nice bloke. I need to find out his tailor," Colin said. "In any case, I have to figure out which horse Her Majesty's Government ought to back: the Pentagon or the NSC."

"And *have* you decided?" I asked.

"Not yet. The Powers That Be back in Whitehall aren't exactly thrilled with the Moldova idea."

"But it's just a training mission," I said.

"They're worried it will provoke the Russians. Which will naturally lead to Armageddon."

"Seems like all roads these days lead to Armageddon."

"Indeed! In any event, after the Iraq debacle, my masters aren't quite as keen to follow you lot wherever you decide to go. It's going to be a hard sell, I think. But anyway, on to more important matters. Would you like another drink? I think you two are the only Americans *not* drinking that Foster's swill."

"You are observant, aren't you?" I said, nodding.

"Indeed. You'll have to tell that to my ambassador. Otherwise how will they know I'm 'earning my keep' around here, as you people say?" Colin said, turning to hunt for another beer.

I saw a familiar face on the other side of the room, deep in conversation. "Actually, gents, if you'll excuse me, I just saw a friend that I need to say hello to," I said, and then bobbed and weaved my way through the crowd. Soldiers and civilians from a variety of nationalities—Hungarian, Spanish, Indian—all mingled with each other, most of whom looked like they wished they were at a barbecue and wearing khakis and flip flops rather than suits and uniforms. I narrowly missed a collision with another ice bucket on the floor before joining Amanda.

"I didn't expect to see you here!" Amanda welcomed me to the conversation. "This is Ambassador Jawad."

"From Afghanistan, yes," I said, shaking his hand. "It's an honor to finally meet you, sir."

"The pleasure is mine, madam," he said, then took a sip of his orange juice.

"The ambassador and I were just talking about how we're getting concerned about the security situation in Afghanistan," Amanda said.

"The Taliban is making a comeback," he said. "I'm worried that we're going to lose territory to them this year. Helmand Province is already teetering on the edge."

"Yes, I've been reading about that," I said. "What about the Islamic State?"

"We're worried about that, too. We just don't have enough forces to keep them at bay. We need more U.S. troops to help us."

"Forgive me for asking, Mr. Ambassador, but what good do you think putting more troops in Afghanistan will do? If you guys can't secure your country, how can we?"

The ambassador smiled. "I get that question a lot. And it's understandable. Here is how I think of it: When you are teaching someone to ride a bike, you give them training wheels. For us, the training wheels were removed before we were truly ready to ride on our own."

"But would the Afghans ever be ready?" I asked. "Is there really anything we could do to help?"

"I believe so, yes. But I also believe that there were many mistakes made in the past that make securing Afghanistan a formidable challenge. Still, it must be done. Too many terrible things have happened to your country and to mine when the region has been neglected. But I'm not sure we have the capability to bring peace to Afghanistan alone. I fear for what will happen."

"I do too," I said.

"If you ladies will excuse me," the ambassador said, his eyes sparking with recognition at someone in the crowd. "It was very lovely speaking with both of you."

I turned to see who he recognized: Amanda's colleague Fred had just entered the room, looking rounder and puffier than the last time I saw him.

I looked at Amanda, curious.

"Fred is taking a greater interest in the senator's foreign policy positions these days," she said, eyeing him over her glass of wine.

"I see," I said, skeptically.

Amanda nodded. "It's temporary, though."

"Temporary?"

"He'll be in our office long enough to dispense wisdom to the senator about positioning for the next election. And then he'll move on to the next candidate."

"I didn't realize Senator McClutchy anticipated having a tough re-election."

"Oh, this isn't for the Senate. McClutchy is setting his eyes on the presidency."

"Wow," I said, overcome with the light, albeit powerful, thrill of knowing insider political gossip before the rest of the world caught on. "That's exciting!"

"Yes. Intense, but exciting."

"That will put you in an incredible position if he wins," I said.

Amanda slowly nodded. "That's the plan."

"And the way things are headed, you'll be just in time to do something about Afghanistan. Things really are getting worse over there."

"Just before you got here, the ambassador was telling me that the Islamic State makes dealing with the Taliban look like a walk in the park. It's a mess over there. But you already know that. Thanks for your email, by the way. Really helpful."

"Oh yes! About that," I said. "You didn't get it from me. It's extremely close hold."

"Sure. No problem."

"I mean, if-it-ever-sees-the-light-of-day-I'm-probably-fired, close hold," I said.

"Got it," Amanda said. "Don't worry."

I sighed as I felt the knot that had been tightly wound in my stomach—the one that had been there since my morning encounter with Fletcher—start to unravel, if just a little bit. I took another sip of my beer.

"There's something else I've been meaning to mention," I said, taking a deep breath. Delivering bad news was always a bit painful; especially so when delivering tough news to someone as amazing as Amanda. "And I don't know how to say this. But I noticed Royle in our apartment the other morning."

"Oh! Sorry about that," Amanda said. "Next time I'll leave a note under your door to let you know what's going on."

"No, it's not that. It's just that I saw him again. With another woman."

"Okay," Amanda said, confused. She sipped her drink. "Have you heard anything more from Ryan?"

Changing the subject, right on cue. I pursed my lips and folded my arms.

"No."

"It's probably better that way. Well, my dear, I need to run."

"Another dinner?"

Amanda nodded. "Lockheed Martin is hosting a dinner at the Army-Navy Club. I'll see you at home later. And if you *do* hear from Ryan, stay strong, okay?"

I nodded as Amanda gracefully made her way out of the reception, as if the crowd instinctively knew to part as she approached. I looked around the room. Voight was with an Australian general; the two were chatting away with the wild enthusiasm of teenage boys talking about video games—a conversation I didn't feel like interrupting. Colin, in the meantime, was lurking to the side of the room, talking with an Army officer whose back was toward me. I walked over to rejoin him, grabbing another beer as I walked.

"Why, hello again, Dr. Reilly," Colin said.

The officer turned to face me: It was Royle.

"Hi, Heather," he said with a smile that seemed to be tinged with a wisp of concern.

"The two of you know each other?" I asked, unable to contain my surprise.

Royle nodded. "We were in Iraq together. And then Afghanistan."

"That's understating things somewhat, don't you think?" Colin said.

"Perhaps," Royle said, with a barely perceptible smile.

Colin laughed. "It's a good thing I know you rather well, Royle. Otherwise I'd think you're a total arse."

"Good thing, then," Royle said.

"Well, I'm ready for another ale. Can I get you two anything?" Colin asked.

"I can go with you," I said, putting my very-full beer down by my side. "Keep you company?" I gave Colin a look, silently pleading for telepathy to work so he could read my mind and know that I didn't want to be left alone with Royle.

It didn't work. *Of course.*

"If you'll just excuse me," Colin continued before turning to swim his way through the crowd to find an ice bucket. Royle and I watched him go, standing in silence for a moment, allowing the moment to become ever-increasingly awkward.

"I read your memo that the general liked," Royle finally said. "I think something's missing."

"Oh really?" I asked, a clear note of frustration in my voice. *Who kicks off a conversation that way?* "What, exactly, do you think is missing?"

"It seems to me that you actually probably downplayed what the Russians are likely to do in response to this."

"My memo argues that they'll be pushing back pretty hard on us," I said, feeling my irritation mount. His condescending tone was always tough to take. But he clearly had no respect for me, or for Amanda, or for anyone for that matter, and I was getting fed up.

"True," Royle said. "But they've been saber-rattling with their nukes. So I'm thinking they'll push back a lot harder on this than even your memo suggests."

And that's when I lost my grip on my patience. Admittedly, it was pretty feeble in the first place.

"Listen, Royle. You're not telling me anything I'm not keenly aware of. That memo? It was just a way for me to organize my thoughts. But now I'm catching hell from Fletcher for writing it. I don't need you piling on too. I'm just trying to do my job. I'm new, and I'm just finding my feet, but every time I turn around, Fletcher wants me fired. You're not helping. And to top it off, my personal life has fallen apart. So I'd appreciate it if you'd back off, and cut me some slack for once."

"So you're not engaged?" Royle asked, a little too quickly.

"No." I said, caught off guard by his question.

Royle stood dumbfounded while I took a sip of my beer.

"I didn't mean to offend you," he eventually said.

"Really? You've got a funny way of showing it."

"What are you talking about?" Royle asked, his body stiffening except for his hand; it was trembling ever so slightly.

"You seem to be doing everything you possibly can to make my life miserable," I said, my anger radiating off me in waves. "You set me up for failure, and then tell me that my work isn't up to your standards."

Royle pursed his lips, his eyes wide with shock.

"I'm sorry—that wasn't my intention."

"Sure. Fine."

I'm not sure whether it was my fatigue, the fact that I hadn't eaten much that afternoon, or the fact that Amanda was the sweetest, most genuine friend on the planet. Either way, I couldn't help but say, "You missed Amanda, by the way. I don't know what you're playing at, Royle, but if you hurt her, you're going to have to answer to me."

Royle's face paled and his voice fell to just above a whisper. "You think I'm playing games with Amanda Reilly? Your sister-in-law?"

His question was so out of left field, I physically shook my head in confusion.

"Wait—how do you know she's my sister-in-law?" I asked.

Royle took a step back, as if he'd just taken a body blow from a linebacker.

"How does who know what?" Voight asked as he walked up to join our conversation. "Good to see you, Royle." He slapped him on the back.

Using the interruption as an escape route, I chugged my beer and set it on a tray. "I'm just a little tired now. So, if you'll excuse me, I'm going to head out."

"Already?" Voight asked, perplexed. "Are you okay?"

Instead of answering, I fled out the door.

Even though it was twilight, the air was a blanket of stiflingly muggy heat as I stepped out of the embassy. Even so, it felt refreshing to be outside, away from Royle and all difficult feelings of inadequacy and anger that he'd stirred up in me. Part of me felt guilty for unleashing on him. But I just couldn't help it. He'd simply pressed too many of my buttons.

I looked up to the scarlet-purple sky and saw the remnants of a striking sunset. I'd read somewhere that sunsets were going to be beautiful for the next couple days; a volcano exploded somewhere in the Philippines and the ash, now having dispersed through the atmosphere, heightened the colors and hues of dusk. As I stood on the sidewalk taking in the view, I marveled at how something so destructive could, in the end, create something so beautiful.

"Fancy seeing you here," said a familiar voice from behind me.

I turned around to see Matt—of all people—putting on his white hat as he walked out of the Australian Embassy. He looked even better in his all-white uniform, adorned with ribbons and bright brass buttons.

"The party inside looks like it's winding down," he said, looking through the embassy's windows to the reception area. "Want to get a drink?"

I thought about my conversation with Royle. And my situation with Ryan. And the problems I was having with Fletcher. And although part of me wanted to climb into bed and forget the week had ever happened, instead I found myself saying, "Sure? Why the hell not?"

CHAPTER TWENTY-ONE

AN HOUR AND A HALF LATER, WE FOUND OURSELVES
CLIMBING THE ESCALATORS OF THE SOUTHWEST D.C.
Metro station. After stopping at a bar downtown—D.C. Coast—
for a glass of wine, Matt insisted on playing the gentleman and
escorting me home. I, of course, didn't mind the company. For
starters, it was nice to hang out with someone besides Amanda.
And being escorted by a gorgeous man definitely helped cut the
edge off my emotionally tumultuous day.

Matt looked around, temporarily losing himself in thought.
"How do you feel about a five-minute detour? Just a stroll."

We walked past the Arena Stage, and jaywalked across Maine
Avenue to reach the Southwest Waterfront. We navigated a jungle
of construction—rebar and cranes and concrete—before finally
making it to the waterfront. Laughter emanated from somewhere
near the Potomac River.

"Where's the party?" Matt asked, smiling.

"Sounds like it's coming from Cantina Marina," I said, pointing to
a bright blue sign with whimsical yellow lettering. "Have you been?"

"Don't think so," Matt said, looking down toward the Cantina.

"Me neither. I've only heard about it from Amanda."

"Should we stop in?"

"Definitely."

The Cantina was a mostly open-air restaurant situated over the river, painted with light blue pastels and decorated with string lights and paper lanterns. It was the perfect dockside bar; a place that felt like it should be somewhere in the Caribbean rather than spitting distance from the middle of downtown Washington, D.C.

We sat down at a table at the edge of the dock, overlooking the water. The air was still steamy, and despite the humidity's best attempts to crowd out the stars, they fought through the haze to pinprick the evening sky. Occasional heat lightning flickered above. The Potomac was calm except for the occasional boats lazily making their way up the river, back to their slips for the evening.

"I don't know what it is about nights like this," I said. "Everything is just...peaceful. It's easier to forget everything."

"And what do you want to forget?"

I thought about Ryan. And Royle. And the memo I'd written. And Fletcher. "Let's see here. Just about everything?"

"Well then. It sounds like we need some margaritas. Waiter?" Matt said, flagging him down. "We'd like two margaritas, please."

"Coming right up."

I turned my gaze back toward the river. We were almost directly across from Reagan National Airport; I watched the planes as they took off and landed. Ryan had been on one of those planes, just a few days ago.

Ryan was gone.

I felt relieved. I felt lighter. I felt free. I laughed out loud.

"Just so you know, there's no better way to forget a shitty week than tequila shots," Matt said.

"Sounds like a plan," I said, shrugging. "Besides, I have all weekend to nurse my inevitable hangover."

"That's the spirit," he said. He scampered off to the bar and returned with at least four rounds of shots.

I raised my eyebrows in surprise.

"Don't worry. We don't have to drink them all. I just thought it would save the hassle of going back and forth."

"Thank you, Matt. That's quite...thoughtful of you. And prescient," I said, taking a shot and downing it. "Hot damn, that stuff is awful!"

"It's not too bad," Matt said.

"Says the Navy guy, who probably drinks tequila like it's water."

"Well, we sailors have many talents."

"Do you now?" I winked, then giggled. I shrugged off my suit jacket, and unbuttoned the top two buttons of my blouse.

This isn't terribly professional of me.

I really don't care.

"I thought you were supposed to be in a bad mood," Matt said.

"I was," I said, snapping back into the moment. "I mean, I am. Sorta. It's just...you said you know that guy Royle, right?"

Matt looked at me with an expression of curiosity mixed with a twinge of irritation.

"Yes, why?"

"Oh, I just wanted to know what his deal is. He and I kind of had it out at the Australian embassy."

Matt downed another shot and then sucked in air through the sides of his mouth.

"Huh. Well, I'm probably the wrong person to ask about him."

"Why's that?"

"It's just…. He and I don't tend to see eye to eye on things, is all."

"Okay. That was cryptic."

"Fine," he said, his voice getting quieter. "We're drinking, so this stays between you and me. I used to fly close air support missions over Afghanistan. And there was this one mission, I remember the Special Forces guy on the other end of the line was asking me to drop on a location that was pretty near an Afghan village. It didn't meet the rules of engagement. So I held off."

"What happened? What does this have to do with Royle?"

Matt sighed. "There was an investigation into what happened. We lost some people that day—soldiers that shouldn't have been out there near an Afghan village in the first place, if you ask me. Anyway, that guy on the ground? It turns out that it was Royle."

"You're *kidding* me." I was stunned; I hadn't realized it was possible to feel angrier toward Royle. But to know that he'd been so cavalier with the men under his watch, placing them in a situation that wasn't covered by the rules of engagement? It was infuriating. *And Royle got away with this?*

"Wish I was. Anyway, it's not just you. In my experience, Royle is a hard-ass toward just about everybody." Matt's voice drifted off a bit as he sat still for a moment, gazing at the lights of the city reflecting in the waters of the Potomac.

"Unbelievable. I think I need another drink. Another shot?"

"Yes, ma'am."

"Excellent." We both downed our tequila, and while Matt was stoic about it, I squinted and squirmed as if I'd just accidentally ingested turpentine. Which, I supposed, was probably not far off given the quality of the tequila. I put my hand flat on the table as I absorbed the shock of the alcohol; I could feel every inch of its movement as it made its way down my throat and nestled somewhat violently in my stomach.

Matt put his hand on mine, distracting me from the tequila pains. He looked me in the eye, and moved a stray hair from my face. And then he kissed me.

I'd never been kissed like that before. My body automatically responded to it, deepening the kiss. Part of me wanted to pull away. The collapse of my relationship with Ryan was so recent, and the wounds were still so fresh. But that was only a very small part of me. Because I felt alive, for the first time in what seemed like forever.

"You have no idea the power you have, do you?" Matt asked, gently pulling away and playing with my hair.

"What?" I asked, both flattered and confused.

"I remember when I first saw you a couple weeks ago during that Armenia brief. You stood up there and shredded the plan, right before their very eyes. And you were right, Heather. So, I guess I'm saying that you're beautiful, brilliant, and funny. A rare combination around the Pentagon. You're powerful."

My heart melted. Nobody had ever said something like that to me before.

"Walk me home?" I asked.

"With pleasure."

It took me a minute or two to figure out where I was. My head felt like it was filled with slam-dancing elephants, and I was more than a little nauseous. My eyes felt crusty, as if the Sandman himself had decided to sprinkle a beach on my lids, and my mouth was parched.

In other words, I was well and truly hung the hell over.

When I finally mustered the courage to pry open an eye, my field of vision was covered with bright red spots. Rather than panicking (my head hurt so much that a strong reaction to anything was physically impossible), I contemplated my loss of vision for a moment. Was this what going blind was like? Was the headache causing my impaired vision? Did this mean that I would have to get glasses? If so, I could start rocking a sexy librarian look….

I noticed an itch on my nose; after carefully extracting my hand from somewhere underneath the covers I delicately scratched my nostril.

The spots moved.

Curious.

I scratched my nose again and slowly realized that my finger was touching something that was resting precariously on my face. I slowly pried my other eye open while removing the alien object. It took another second for me to realize two things: first, I had 20/20 vision again, and second, I was now clutching my red lace panties.

How the hell did they get there?

I struggled to recall the events of the previous evening, but in my current state was coming up short. So I decided to do an inventory of my current situation. I lifted my covers and noticed that I wasn't wearing pajamas; indeed, I wasn't wearing anything at all. On the plus side, the panties-on-head mystery was beginning to unravel. On the down side, I was having a hell of a time remembering why I was naked.

Curious.

But there were much more pressing matters to contend with at that precise moment. In particular, how to make the insane pounding in my head stop. This presented quite the dilemma; any possible solution necessarily involved getting out of bed and making my way first to the bathroom (for the painkillers) and then to the kitchen (for a blessed can of hangover-curing Coca-Cola). I would have to dig deep in order to muster the courage to face these seemingly insurmountable obstacles.

I was about to make the bold move of putting my feet on the floor when I noticed a large glass of water and five ibuprofen on my nightstand.

And a can of Coke.

My sheer joy at that very moment was comparable to that of the Israelites upon discovering they'd been saved from starvation by manna from the heavens. I grabbed three of the ibuprofen and delicately cradled the glass of water, drinking half of it before moving onto the soda. Three sips and my nausea started to dissipate; another three and the throbbing in my head started to lessen.

Divine intervention is the only explanation for this miracle, I thought. I subsequently flopped back to the middle of my bed and shut my eyes. Today would just have to be a two- (if not three-) starter.

I'd almost gotten back to sleep when I heard my phone buzz. I was tempted to ignore it, but then heard it buzz again. Someone was texting me repeatedly. I decided to investigate, if for no other reason than to turn off the infernal device.

After groping around the covers and coming up empty, I looked to the floor. I could just see the phone peeking out of my rumpled suit. After a minute or two of contortions and stretches, I finally reached the phone with the tips of my fingers, then another bit of nudging and I had the phone in my hands.

I looked at the messages. One from Voight asking if I'd made it home safely, and one from Matt.

Which is when the evening's events all came back to me in a solid wall of memories. The Aussie embassy, Royle, Cantina Marina, tequila shots, Matt, stumbling into my bedroom, the crazy sex....

Wait. Crazy sex?

I sat up; I was suddenly, and completely alert. Memories of Matt taking off my shirt, almost ripping off my bra, throwing my panties—apparently toward my pillows—washed over me. As I wondered how it was physically possible to perform the previous evening's athletics, I found myself wrapped in a feeling of delicious, guilty shame.

My walk down memory lane was interrupted by a knock at the door.

"Are you awake?" Amanda asked.

Hearing Amanda's voice brought me back to reality: I hadn't been single for even a week before sleeping with a coworker. *Yeah, I'm handling this breakup really well.*

"Come on in," I answered, voice warbling.

Amanda opened the door, wearing an ear-to-ear grin and carrying two steaming mugs of coffee.

"I thought you could use this," she said, stepping over the rumpled suit to hand over one of the mugs.

"Thanks," I said, taking the mug gratefully. "I feel awful."

"I'm not surprised. I heard you come in pretty late last night."

"Did you—?"

"Coca-Cola and ibuprofen?" asked Amanda. "That was me. This morning. After he left."

"You really ought to be canonized for that. I'm calling the Pope," I said, sitting up. I promptly decided that was a bad idea, and returned to my reclining position. "I'll call him later."

Amanda laughed. "You're welcome. So, what happened?"

The buzzing feeling that had been humming since I woke turned into a cacophony of emotions that was simply overwhelming. Instruments of all different shapes and sizes screeched out their own off-key notes in an orchestra of raw, shattering embarrassment. "I ran into a colleague after the embassy shindig. One thing led to another.... Sleeping with a colleague? So soon after Ryan? You must think I'm a total mess."

Amanda put her coffee mug on the nightstand and leaned back on my bed. We sat in silence as a small tear worked its way from my eye and onto the white linen sheets.

"Am I losing it?"

"Maybe a little. But maybe that's a good thing."

"A good thing? How can losing control like this be a good thing?"

"Sometimes you've got to let your hair down. Blow off some steam. You've had a lot going on, and for the first time in your entire adult life, you're not in a relationship."

With everything going on in my life, it hadn't actually occurred to me that I was single for basically the first time ever. Or, at least, I hadn't thought about it in such stark terms.

"What if I end up sabotaging myself? Screwing myself over somehow?"

Amanda looked at me curiously. "What's to say that you weren't screwing yourself over while you were with Ryan? Didn't you want to work for the United Nations at one point?"

I nodded. "Ryan didn't want to be apart."

"That's exactly my point. You can't know if you're sabotaging yourself if you don't know what you really want in the first place. So I guess the question is, what do you want, Heather?"

"Want?" The question felt alien to me, somehow.

"Exactly. You've never really thought about that before, have you?"

"I guess not."

"So, maybe you should start doing what you want to do, rather than what people like Ryan or Mom expect you to do."

I nodded, then sat back in the bed, more confused than ever. I'd always been good at researching and figuring out problems. But this? Discovering what I wanted? As opposed to what I was *supposed* to do?

I didn't have a clue where to start.

CHAPTER TWENTY-TWO

"FLETCHER SHOULD BE HERE IN FIVE," I SAID, APPROACHING VOIGHT FIRST THING MONDAY MORNING. He was standing to one side of the ivory marble steps of the Russell Senate Office Building. It was only after he turned and held up a finger while cradling his phone against his ear that I realized he was speaking to someone.

"I already told you I feel terrible for missing her game yesterday," he said, hunching over his phone again. "Sure. Listen, can we talk about this later? My colleague just got here."

I felt embarrassed for accidentally listening in on Voight's conversation, so I walked a few feet away and distracted myself by taking in the view of the Capitol Building. It was a bright, crisp morning, the kind that signals autumn is just around the corner. The breeze would have made me feel chilly were it not for the warm sunshine beaming on the spot I was standing. It was a moment of serenity in my otherwise complicated life.

After mostly recovering from my hangover Saturday afternoon, I'd spent the rest of the weekend in the office with Voight trying to avoid thinking about exactly how complicated my life had become. Fortunately, there was plenty to do. After I'd left the reception on

Friday, Voight had learned that it wasn't just the Brits that were waffling. Military officials from other countries quietly conveyed to Voight that the prospects of building a coalition for Moldova were getting dimmer by the minute, due to the fact that Russia was already having apoplectic conniptions over the training mission. Not to mention Derek Odem's work behind the scenes to sabotage the whole thing. It turned out that Royle was right; Moscow had already started with its nuclear saber-rattling in response to the Moldova mission. So, at Fletcher's urging, on Saturday night, Secretary of Defense Sidwell decided to go to London in order to start shoring up British support for the coalition, in the hopes that doing so would attract other participants.

Still, in between projects and memorandums, the thoughts that I'd been trying to squelch crossed my mind. *How am I going to tell Mom? What if Matt told everybody we worked with about Friday's adventure?* Which is when I would return my attention to the memo I was working on, grateful for the distraction.

Voight, however, seemed increasingly agitated that he'd been called into the office instead of watching Sarah's soccer game. "As much as I love being around you, Heather, this is complete bullshit," he said, just about every half an hour on the dot.

Saturday night, just before going to bed, I heard a buzz and quickly checked my phone. It was a text from Matt.

That's when I learned why there's so much hype about sexting.

I'm going to hell, I thought, just before I fell asleep at two in the morning.

By Sunday afternoon, Voight and I were halfway through the prep work for the trip when the next fly in the ointment popped up: how DOD was actually going to *pay* for the Moldova mission.

There was some kind of accounting or legalistic blip that we weren't expecting, the full details of which I didn't quite understand. But what had become clear was that we were going to have to ask Congress to include a separate line item in the Defense budget for operations in Moldova.

Which is why we were standing in front of the Russell Senate Office Building at that very moment, bright and early on a Monday morning, waiting for our boss. I stifled a cringe as I braced for encountering Fletcher.

The wind caught Voight's voice, and I couldn't help but overhear him say, "Yes, of course you're my priority." He whispered a couple more things that were mercifully inaudible, and then hung up the phone.

"Fletcher's on the way?" Voight asked.

"So says the email I just got. She's in a car now," I said.

"Brace yourself," Voight said. "I think she's getting close to popping."

"Like a pressure cooker without a release valve," I said as Voight acknowledged someone walking up behind me.

And suddenly, the morning went from bad to worse.

"I take it the Joint Staff flicked this booger to you?" Voight said to Royle as he joined us. I did my level best to hide my annoyance.

Royle nodded. He looked like hell, and was studiously avoiding looking at me.

"We can cover down on this and report back," I said to Royle's back. "There's no need for you to waste your time here."

Voight laughed. "Heather, the Joint Staff can't run interference unless they keep close tabs on what's going on. And given

Fletcher's reputation for stirring things up, they want to keep *very* close tabs on her."

A black sedan pulled up, and Fletcher stepped out. She was on the phone, alternating between English and Spanish during a very intense conversation. She raised her chin to acknowledge she'd seen us as she walked past and set her purse on a nearby concrete planter. She fished out a folder, presumably her talking points, and then handed her purse to Voight.

Voight's face turned grey as he pressed his lips into a thin line. Royle looked angry. I felt embarrassed for Voight and furious at Fletcher for treating a U.S. military colonel like a college intern. Fletcher, of course, didn't notice any of this; she charged into the building as she talked on the phone. We followed.

"How did the pre-brief go?" Royle asked.

Voight laughed without a hint of mirth. "There *was* no pre-brief."

"What?" Royle said.

"Our legislative affairs team was swamped," Voight said. "They've lost five people in the past month, and can't hire any replacements. Total nightmare. They're treading water on the best of days. If you want to witness human misery firsthand, hang out in their shop for a day or two."

"Given that the world's pretty much on fire these days, that's a hell of a thought," I said.

"I might be stating things a touch dramatically. But still. The sheer volume of inane requests for information, reports, and other assorted crap that the different members of Congress make.... It's staggering. All the man-hours we spend answering their questions.... We could staff a Wal-Mart for the next century with all the requests for information they send our way."

"But surely they need to ask these questions. You need information to do oversight, and oversight is what Congress does," I said.

"No argument here," Voight said. "With all the insanity back in the building? DOD *definitely* needs to be watched like a hawk by Congress. I'm just saying the way they go about exercising their responsibilities usually results in flailing. We spend more time reporting on our jobs, rather than doing our jobs. So it *sucks* to be the folks dealing with Congress. Then again, Leg Affairs probably isn't the worst place in the building to work. I'm pretty sure that designation goes to the Army staff. Now *there's* a soul-crushing place. I'm pretty sure their offices are located in the half corridor between the third and fourth rings of hell."

"Sounds about right," Royle agreed.

"Which part?" Voight asked.

"All of it," Royle said.

"Does it matter that there was no pre-brief?" I asked.

"Let's hope not," Voight said. "Remember my meeting with the Georgians the other day? Fletcher has a habit of...winging it. Sometimes it works, sometimes it doesn't. I mean, you really don't want to just come up to the Hill without knowing *exactly* what to say—and what *not* to say. That's like turning up to a shark tank wearing a raw red meat bathing suit. These folks will eat us alive if we don't have our shit together."

"Great," I said.

Voight started humming the tune from *Jaws*.

Fletcher stopped, turned around, and covered her phone. "Where are we going?"

The three of us were taken aback; we thought *she* knew. Voight and Royle immediately turned to their phones to look up the location.

"We're late," Fletcher said. "Why didn't you guys figure out the location of the meeting before we left?" She seemed to miss the subtle point that she was the cause of our group's tardiness.

"It's in Senator McClutchy's office," Voight said, reading the email.

Finally, a small break. Feeling myself stand a little taller, I chimed in. "Ma'am, I know the way. Follow me."

I led them through the creamy marble corridors, up two flights of steps, and around several gaggles of school children before finally reaching Senator McClutchy's office. Progress was slow; Fletcher was wearing her Louboutins. Thank god Amanda had showed me the way to her office when I first got to D.C. She wanted to make sure I could always find my way to her in case she was stuck and couldn't come escort me.

Amanda was waiting for us when we arrived.

"Hi, Heather," Amanda said, a warm smile spreading over her face.

"Colonel Royle. And DASD Fletcher, I presume?" Amanda continued, turning to the rest of the group. I was surprised that her reaction to Royle wasn't a little more extreme. Then again, Amanda had a good poker face.

"*Assistant* Secretary of Defense," Fletcher said, curtly.

"I wasn't aware that you'd been confirmed by the Senate," Amanda responded.

Nice one. I couldn't help but crack a smile. Voight, situated behind Fletcher and out of her line of sight, was openly grinning.

"Yes, I'm Acting Assistant Secretary." For a moment, I thought Fletcher looked somewhat admonished. But if so, it was fleeting.

"The senator will be with you in a minute."

"Just one senator?" Fletcher asked.

"Is there a problem?" Amanda asked.

"I'm a senior Pentagon official," Fletcher said. "I thought there would be more members here for this briefing."

"Am I to take it that you think meeting with a prominent member of the Senate Armed Services Committee isn't worth your time?" Amanda said, her voice now ringing with a note of irritation.

"No, no," Fletcher hastened to add. "It's just that I was hoping to establish a rapport with as many members as possible today. But of course, I'm honored that Senator McClutchy can take the time today to meet."

I watched in awe as Amanda dominated the conversation while Fletcher anxiously backpedaled. Voight was biting his cheek to contain his laughter, and even Royle's normally stoic expression slipped for a moment as he watched the two alpha females clash. My heart swelled with pride.

"Why don't we all get situated while we wait for the senator to arrive?" Amanda said, showing our group toward the conference room. I moved to follow behind the group, but Amanda pulled me aside before I entered.

"I spoke with Mom last night."

I winced. "You did?"

"Don't worry. I figured out pretty quickly that she didn't know about you and Ryan splitting up, and didn't mention anything. But when are you going to break the news to her?"

"I don't know. Soon. When things settle down a little bit."

"You're in the Pentagon, Heather. What if things never settle down?"

"I'll figure it out," I said, trying to squirm my way out of the conversation. "Let's get this meeting over with."

Offices were assigned to members of the Senate based on seniority and power, and while McClutchy hadn't been on Capitol Hill very long by Senate standards, he was clearly a powerful man. His cream-colored walls were adorned with degrees, military decorations, and photographs of himself with dozens of high-powered officials and celebrities. But perhaps the clearest indicator of his status within the Senate: his nearly unobstructed view of the Capitol Building from his office's large windows. On top of the royal red carpet, a large, wooden rectangular table sat to the side of the room, with eight heavy leather chairs stationed around it. Smaller chairs, presumably for overflow, were situated against the wall.

The room, while big, suddenly felt smaller as Senator McClutchy—with his larger-than-life presence—entered it.

"Senator McClutchy, it's an honor to meet you," Fletcher said, moving across the room to shake his hand as he walked in.

I looked at the configuration of the table; Fletcher would want to sit opposite of the senator. I placed my notebook and pen at the seat next to Fletcher's and stood behind my chair, waiting for the meeting to begin.

"Ariane Fletcher, is it?" McClutchy asked.

"Yes, sir, that's right."

"Glad you could join me, Ms. Fletcher. We've got a lot to talk about today, I think," McClutchy said, taking a seat at the center of the conference table. Amanda sat to his left; Fred, the toad-man, having just entered the room, sat to McClutchy's right.

"Yes, sir, we do," Fletcher said, taking the seat opposite him.

McClutchy caught my eye as I sat down next to Fletcher. "Well, hello, Dr. Reilly. Good to see you again."

He remembers who I am? I thought. I could feel Fletcher's displeasure rolling off her in waves; she was clearly not amused that I knew the senator before she did.

"Yes, sir. Likewise." I heard a coughing sound behind me. It was Voight, his eyes were widened; he was trying to communicate something to me—but I had no idea what it was.

"Let's get down to business, shall we?" the senator said.

Why is Voight sitting in the back row against the wall? I wondered. Royle apparently wondered the same thing; as Voight continued to use his eyes to communicate something indecipherable to me, Royle sat down on Fletcher's right-hand side.

"Let's get down to business, shall we?" the senator asked. "There's a lot of rumors flying around about what you guys intend to do in Moldova. Or is it Georgia? Armenia? Frankly, this administration is all over the place, and I'm not sure what the hell is going on. All I know is that the Russians are going nuts—which, by the way, leads me to believe that you must be doing *something* right. But still, I don't quite get it. Why don't you enlighten me?"

"Sure," Fletcher started, pouring herself a glass of water and then taking a sip. "The bottom line, Senator, is that we're taking an indirect approach to managing what appear to be growing security concerns in that region."

"Which are?" McClutchy said.

"Russia is getting increasingly aggressive, and they're expanding south and east. And let's not forget how they tried to sabotage our elections in 2016. Russia is back, in a bad way. And it's only a matter of time before they start trying to push the envelope again. They've been conducting 'snap' exercises on their borders with other countries, which is making the Georgians—and others in the region—worried that Russia is getting hungry for more territory. This is in addition to all the 'snap' exercises they've been doing in the Baltics. They're deliberately provoking us."

"My understanding was that the initial idea you guys had was to do a mission in Armenia?"

Fletcher grimaced. "That bright idea originated at the NSC, not DOD. It's off the table now. The Russians and the Armenians are strengthening their relationship. The Russians have even started stationing some of their fighter aircraft near Yerevan, the capital of Armenia. It was a dumb idea to begin with, and one that we've thankfully put to bed."

"Well, let me play devil's advocate with you," McClutchy said. "According to the Russians, none of this is a wise course of action. We've been provoking them. They're still upset about NATO's expansion to their doorstep."

"Of course they are. Because it means they have less control over the countries on their borders. Moscow wants to dominate its near-abroad the way it did during the Cold War. But these countries chose to join NATO because they wanted to start charting their own path as sovereign nations. They wanted to be free. Now

Russia's trying to reverse all that. Are we going to stand by and watch them bully and intimidate them? Or are we going to take a stand?"

So much for needing a pre-brief. She's knocking it out of the park, I thought. I looked back to Voight. His eyes were wide, and his pencil was down. Evidently, he shared my assessment.

"But you could make the case that by arming the Moldovans, we're going to be provoking the Russians further," McClutchy said. "In fact, I think I read a memo recently that made that very argument."

I flinched. *That's my memo.*

"I've read it." Fletcher's nostrils flared as she glanced in my direction. "I don't buy the argument. I believe it mistakes how much influence our decisions on Moldova have had on the Russians. Moscow was going to do this stuff anyway. They're just now using the Moldova situation as a political pretext."

"Fine then. So how do the Mongolians play into all this?"

"In a lot of ways, that was taking advantage of an opportunity. They happened to be visiting, and they happened to want to find a way to work closer with the United States. But it also strategically makes sense. Russia can't complain about the Moldova effort too much if it's an international coalition—with cats and dogs from all over the globe—doing the mission. They also can't say it's a threatening, NATO-led coalition that's designed to challenge Russia."

"Even though it kind of is."

"Not politically, it's not," Fletcher said. "And that matters. Our Ambassador in Moldova has already secured the basing rights for the coalition, which might not have been possible if we'd waited much longer. And it's important to make these moves in relative peacetime. If we wait until there's an actual crisis, doing these things is going to be much more provocative."

"So what do you need from me, Ms. Fletcher?"

"Well, we have enough left over from last year's budget to get the mission started. But we need to create a line in next year's appropriations bill so we can continue the Moldova mission."

"How much do you think you're going to need?"

"Our budget guys are telling me five hundred million dollars. But the important thing is that we'll need some flexibility in the way we spend it, in case something happens in the region."

"I see. So how is that coalition coming along?" McClutchy asked.

Fletcher grimaced. "We have some work to do on that front. Our allies are getting wobbly but the Secretary is going to Europe this week to shore up support. We believe that if Secretary Sidwell can convince the Brits to come on board, others will join as well."

"I do hope so, for your sake. Your entire plan, Ms. Fletcher, is predicated on the delicate notion that an international coalition will be doing this work. If you don't get them, you'll have a serious political—and military—mess on your hands. And may I remind you that this country has little appetite to become involved in spurious ground wars in regions we don't care much about. You can tell your boss Secretary Sidwell that I said that."

"I will, Senator."

"I'll see what I can do about the money. But I can guarantee you that you won't see a dime of it unless you pull off this coalition. Now, if you wouldn't mind," McClutchy said, looking around the room. "I need to move on to my next appointment."

We all stood up to leave.

"Amanda, could you let our next guests in? I'm not going to need you for this next one. Fred, you can stay."

Amanda looked to the senator; McClutchy nodded, dismissing her. A mixture of anger and frustration registered on Amanda's features, but although she was livid, she remained quiet. By the time I'd made it out of the conference room and into the waiting area, Amanda had already left, presumably to get back to her office.

"How do you think that went, ma'am?" Voight asked as we walked out of the Russell Building.

"It went fine, despite the fact that I had to do even more damage control." Fletcher turned and looked directly at me. "And Heather, only principals sit at the table."

"I'm sorry?"

"You heard me. Don't sit at the table."

"Ma'am, I sat at the table too," Royle said.

"Royle, you were there representing the Joint Staff. Heather, on the other hand, is my subordinate." Fletcher turned to me. "Don't do it again." Then she turned to make a call on her phone.

"Understood, ma'am," I said, falling a little behind the others as we walked back through the corridors of Capitol Hill.

Royle hung back. "Don't—"

"Don't *what*, Royle?" I snapped without meaning to.

"Don't let her get to you," he said with a kind of quiet tenderness I'd never heard from him, before walking ahead of our group.

I shut my eyes and frowned. Although I didn't like Royle much, there really was no excuse for being rude. Again. Especially since he was, for once, just trying to be nice to me. I wondered—not for the first time—whether the job was officially getting to *me*. Maybe it wasn't just Fletcher who was a pressure cooker.

Fletcher stopped and turned toward the group. "Voight, what are you doing this week?"

"I'm on vacation. Disney World."

"Cancel it."

"Can't."

"Why not?"

"Non-refundable plane tickets."

"DOD can reimburse you."

"Ma'am, with all due respect, I would strongly prefer not to miss this vacation."

I immediately felt worried. Something about the way Voight's voice slightly wavered sounded disconcerting. It was clear that taking this week off was really important to him. Which meant it was important for me to make sure he got it.

"Fine."

Fletcher looked up; her gaze fixed on me for a moment. Fletcher seemed to be contemplating the upsides, the downsides, the benefits, and drawbacks of something important. I, in the meantime, felt as if I were being studied under a microscope, which would have been thoroughly uncomfortable under any circumstances, but particularly so after being chewed out less than five minutes earlier.

Eventually, Fletcher's expression suggested she'd come to a decision.

"Okay, Heather. You're coming to London with me."

"Oh." It took a moment for me to register what Fletcher was saying. I blinked a couple times as my heart entered my throat with excitement; eventually I regained the capacity to speak. "I'd be honored."

"Go home, Voight," I said, looking at the clock. It was eight. If Voight didn't leave soon, he wouldn't be able to tuck Sarah into bed, or help his boys with their homework.

"Are you sure? I don't want to leave you hanging."

"Thanks, but we're almost done here. I'll be fine. Go."

Voight didn't need to be told again. He was out of there in a hurry. After he left, I finished up the talking points I was working on and then did some further reading on the dynamics of the Moldova-Georgia-Russia-Turkey-Syria-Armenia-and-god-knows-who-else situation.

Our travel people had warned us to keep quiet about the itinerary before we left—security protocol—so I couldn't tell anyone, including Amanda, what I was up to. But I couldn't wait to fill her in on the details when I got back.

Before I knew it, it had just gone past ten o'clock at night, and I had been completely alone in the office for at least an hour and a half. I was about to close out of Outlook, shut down my computer, and quit for the evening when a message popped up from a new sender.

TO: Heather Reilly <heather.reilly@osd.mil>
FROM: Matthew Brown <matthew.brown@navy.mil>
SUBJECT: Hello.

Hi Sunshine,

I hope you don't mind, I looked you up in the global. How was the rest of your weekend? I hope you're not stuck here in the office like I am!

Matt

I couldn't help but grin ear to ear as I read, and re-read, his message. Before I knew it, I was crafting a response.

> TO: Matthew Brown <matthew.brown@navy.mil>
> FROM: Heather Reilly <heather.reilly@osd.mil>
> SUBJECT: RE: Hello.
>
> Dear Lt Cdr Brown,
>
> I've spent most of my weekend here in the office! Although Saturday morning was a bit... difficult. And yes, I am definitely still at my desk. Unfortunately.
>
> > Heather

Approximately thirty seconds after hitting "send," another response was in my inbox.

> TO: Heather Reilly <heather.reilly@osd.mil>
> FROM: Matthew Brown <matthew.brown@navy.mil>
> SUBJECT: RE: RE: Hello.
>
> I'm about to head out of here. If you're going to be a little while longer, mind if I stop by your office on the way out to say hello?

As the cursor blinked on my screen, I thought about how to respond. About whether I *should* respond. On the one hand, I was tired, and my brain felt like a sponge that was saturated with water. On the other hand, the memory of the other night was just too delicious, and I'd never experienced anything near that amazing with Ryan.

> TO: Matthew Brown <matthew.brown@navy.mil>
> FROM: Heather Reilly <heather.reilly@osd.mil>
> SUBJECT: RE: Hello.
>
> Don't mind at all. 5E682.

What am I doing? I thought, after hitting send.

Ten or fifteen minutes later, the doorbell to the office rang. As I opened the door, I saw Matt was wearing his khaki brown uniform. Despite the fact that his hair was closely trimmed by normal standards, he was pushing the boundaries of what was an acceptable Navy haircut.

"Hello, Matt," I said, smiling. It suddenly became an awkward moment. Should we shake hands? Hug? Kiss on the cheek?

"Hello, Heather," he answered as he entered the office and then kissed me.

That solves that problem, I thought.

"How was your day?" Matt finally asked after breaking the kiss.

"Long. But getting better. Let me grab my things, and then we can go somewhere?"

Matt took my hand and gently pulled me toward his chest. "You know," he said, putting his hands on my waist. "DASD offices are secure."

"Secure?"

"No cameras. Soundproofed. Secure."

"So?" I asked as I felt his lips on my neck. "Oh. OH!" I said, finally getting what he was talking about.

I let him lead me into Fletcher's office and shut the door. I felt an unexpected sense of rebelliousness. I'd never in my life done anything remotely as scandalous as what I was engaging in at that moment. The consequences of being caught were unthinkable—which made it all the more exciting.

"Now, what did you say that you liked in your texts the other night? Oh yes, I remember," Matt said, murmuring into my hair. And with that, my inhibitions were cast aside along with my blouse, bra, and his shirt. Eventually, Matt led me to the conference table and undid the button of my pants, letting them spill to the floor.

This never would have happened with Ryan, I thought. Hell, the last time we'd done anything remotely risqué was when we'd snuck a quickie during his parent's Christmas party last year.

I was about to completely lose myself to the feeling of him when we were interrupted by the sound of a phone ringing.

Matt suddenly pulled away from me. "Hide!"

"What?"

"I said, hide!" he exclaimed, pulling me underneath the conference table. He held his finger to his lips; his eyes were wide.

"Ariane, are you there?" DASD Kreuger's voice rang over the Tandberg VTC screen on Fletcher's desk.

"Hello?" Krueger asked. "I guess she's not there yet," she said to someone off screen. "We'll call back in five," and then hung up.

"Hurry! Grab your clothes!" I whispered to Matt.

I scrounged on the floor on all fours, picking up my pantsuit, blouse, shoes, and bra, while Matt grabbed his things. Doing one last check to make sure everything was in place, we dashed to a cubicle that happened to be on the very far side of the office. We'd just gotten into a hiding position when I heard the front door of the office open.

"Is anyone here?" Fletcher called out.

Shit. Shitshitshitshitshitshitshitshitshitshit. "Ma'am, I'm here," I called out while putting on my pants as quietly as possible.

"Heather, is that you?"

"Yes, ma'am," I frantically put on my bra and shrugged on my blouse with lightning speed.

"You're not at your desk. Where are you?"

"Just trying to find something I left over here," I grimaced at the lameness of my response. "I'll come see you before I head out?"

"Please do," Fletcher said before going into her office and calling DASD Krueger on the VTC.

Oh, thank god, I thought with relief as Matt laced up his shoes before leaning in to kiss me.

Scandalous is fun, but doing this? This isn't me.

"I can't—," I said, pushing him away.

"Can't what? Can't wait to get out of here?" Matt asked, confused.

"No. I can't do *this.* I only recently broke it off with my fiancé."

"But, you're single, right?" Matt asked, moving back toward me.

"Yes. And while I'm up for some adventure, this is a little much for me."

Matt sighed with a clear note of disappointment, then slowly nodded.

"Okay."

"Great," I responded before turning my attention to the next problem at hand. "Now, how am I going to get you out of here?"

Matt looked at me with wide eyes, and then smiled. "Let me handle it. Follow my lead."

"'Follow my lead?' What, do you think we're in some kind of cheesy Hollywood flick or something?" I whispered. Matt didn't hear me.

Matt, now fully clothed and fully oblivious to my disbelief, walked to the main waiting area.

"Thanks a lot, Dr. Reilly, for helping me out with that memo," he said, loudly enough for Fletcher to hear. "It's going to make coordination a lot easier."

My eyes widened. What the hell was he doing, announcing that he was there in the office with me?

"Uh, yes. No problem. Thanks for coming by," I said, cringing at my own awkwardness.

I watched as he opened the door and left, and stood for a minute waiting for the flames in my cheeks to calm down. Eventually, I walked into Fletcher's office; Fletcher was sitting at her desk, already back at work. Her hair was down and she was wearing her reading glasses, reviewing a document with her Mont Blanc pen.

I took a minute to scan the room. Thankfully, nothing seemed out of place.

"Ma'am, you wanted to see me?" I said, moving to the conference table chairs and pretending to straighten them.

"I want to review the SecDef briefing book tomorrow afternoon at the latest," Fletcher said without looking up.

"It's ready for your review now if you would like," I said.

Fletcher raised her eyebrows in surprise. "Okay, then. Bring it in. Oh, and Heather?"

"Yes, ma'am?"

"Your lipstick is smudged," Fletcher said with a wisp of a smile crossing her lips and a hint of admonishment—or was it amusement?—in her voice.

I immediately covered my mouth. *Oh dear god.*

Fletcher's smirk hardened. "Just in case you're thinking of letting yourself get distracted right now, let me make something abundantly clear, Heather. If this trip doesn't go well, it's *your* job on the line."

CHAPTER TWENTY-THREE

ALTHOUGH IT HAD ONLY BEEN A COUPLE DAYS SINCE I'D
FOUND OUT THAT I WAS GOING TO LONDON, WHEN THE DAY
OF THE TRIP ARRIVED, IT FELT LIKE A COUPLE YEARS HAD
PASSED. My eyes were tired; the newly formed bluish circles under
my eyes felt like they were being pulled down by lead weights. But
despite the exhaustion, my brain buzzed with the electrical energy
of adrenaline-washed nervousness. I ran through every detail of
the trip—and the proposed Moldova coalition—in my head as I
wheeled my suitcase into the Pentagon and made my way up to the
office. Despite the mental double- and triple-checking, it still felt like
I was missing something. I chalked it up to nerves.

Voight was running late, so I made the bleary-eyed pilgrimage
to Starbucks on my own. Coffee couldn't wait. And after all the
recent chaos in my life, a quiet moment by myself with a morning
latte seemed like a good way to organize my thoughts and mentally
prepare for the trip.

I checked my phone as I walked. Matt hadn't texted me after the
previous night's escapade. Which was both a relief and annoying
at the same time. *On to the next?* Amanda's description of the D.C.

dating scene seemed to be getting more accurate by the minute. *Whatever.* I had better, more important things to focus on.

Like surviving this trip, I thought as I stepped into the coffee line.

Which was a lot better than thinking about the other thing nagging at the back of my brain. Even though I'd started to move on, it still stung that Ryan hadn't even bothered to check in on me. *All those years. Did I mean nothing to him?*

And then: *London. Moldova.*

There were at least a dozen—maybe fifteen?—people in front of me. Which was fine. I could use the delay to straighten out my thoughts before joining the whirlwind that was undoubtedly waiting for me upstairs.

"Where's your partner in crime?" said a familiar voice behind me. *Royle.* I closed my eyes and pursed my lips as I composed myself. As much as I wanted to tell him to stuff something—preferably spiky—in an orifice where the sun didn't shine. But the angel of my better nature restrained me. *Popping off isn't going to solve anything. Try and be nice. He's a colleague.*

I turned to see him smiling at me. I grudgingly admitted to myself that his smile lit up his face, making him even more attractive. *I can see why Amanda went there*, I thought. *Maybe she needed to let her hair down too?*

"Voight's running late—he'll be in later."

"Ready for the big trip?"

I sighed. "As I'll ever be, I guess."

Royle nodded. "You'll be great."

Wait—why is he being nice to me?

"I briefed the Chairman on your trip earlier today, and what you guys are hoping to get out of London. Things are definitely getting messy with Russia. We're counting on you."

"Great. No pressure or anything."

Royle looked at me, quizzical. "Pressure? Heather, if there's anyone who can help pull this off, it's you."

I blinked. *Have I stepped into an alternate universe?*

"Thanks for the vote of confidence. But it kind of feels like I've screwed up at almost every turn." *Often thanks to you, by the way.*

Royle narrowed his eyes. "No more than everybody else around here. Seems to me that you've fared pretty well. Let's be honest: Fletcher is not an easy lady to work for."

"There's the understatement of the year. You, at least, got to bail. Voight and I are stuck with her."

Royle snickered. "Well, the Chairman of the Joint Chiefs of Staff outranks Fletcher, by a lot. And I have to admit, I was pretty okay with him pulling rank and putting me on his team."

We approached the front of the line. "Here, let me buy," Royle continued. "Large latte with an extra shot, right?"

I looked at him, confused. "How did you know that?"

"I'm observant."

The whole situation was getting too weird for me. "What's going on, Royle? We haven't had this long of a conversation, well, ever. Is there something that you need? Something that I can help you with?"

Royle let out a small laugh before his features went more serious. "No, no. It's just—I thought a lot about our conversation at the embassy. And I guess I think we got off on the wrong foot.

For the record, I like you, Heather. And I want to see you do well. So if there's anything you need help with, just let me know, okay?"

"Uh, thanks," I said, picking up my latte and trying to disguise the fact that I was utterly floored.

"I've gotta run back to the basement. Have a safe trip, okay?" With another smile, he left.

A small piece of my heart—the part that was still a nerdy fifth grader with an insane crush on the most popular boy in school—fluttered with the sight of his smile again.

One nice conversation doesn't mean he's not a jackass. I promptly stuffed that part of me back in a box, and then walked back to the office.

"So? You ready?" Voight asked as he placed my binder into the wheeled leather briefcase.

"I went through the trip briefing book five times this morning and studied up on all the meetings. I can't believe that I'm about to go on a trip with the Secretary of Defense! What if I screw something up?"

"You'll be fine. I've been on SecDef trips before. Just remember—"

"Embrace the suck?" I finished for him.

"Well, that too. But I was actually going to say that there are three rules to travelling with the Secretary of Defense."

"Which are?"

"One, never miss the convoy. Two, never miss the convoy, and three, never miss the convoy."

I laughed.

"You think I'm kidding! My buddy Mark got left in Budapest because he got confused about when the Secretary was leaving a meeting. Total pain in the ass. His luggage and passport were on the Secretary's plane, and he was stranded downtown. Couldn't speak a word of Hungarian either. Poor bastard had to sing "The Star-Spangled Banner" to convince a local to drive him to the embassy. So as long as you remember those three rules, you'll be fine, Heather."

"I wish you were going, Voight."

"Yeah, well, you're in luck."

I looked at him quizzically.

"Much to the irritation of my wife, Fletcher had me cancel our vacation plans," Voight continued, pointing to his own little briefcase on wheels.

"Fantastic!" I exclaimed, as the prospect of what lay ahead of me suddenly seemed less overwhelming. Voight, on the other hand, looked pained. "I'm sorry. I know this vacation was important to you," I said.

"Thanks," Voight said, sighing. "I'm going to owe Jamie big time."

"We'll find a way to make it up to her, okay?"

Voight checked his watch. "Good. Because we'd better get going. Wheels up at two. Let's go kick some ass. And figure out what the fuck is going on around here in the process, shall we? I'm dying to know whether, and how, we're going to pull off all this Moldova stuff without instigating the apocalypse."

"You and me both," I responded. "You and me both."

Voight and I decided to carpool to the base together. Fletcher announced she would meet us there, saying she needed to pick up a couple things along the way, which was a relief to both of us; the prospect of spending even more time with Fletcher than was absolutely necessary wasn't a happy one. Unfortunately, since Voight was driving, he had control of the music. Which meant that we had to listen to what he called his "awesome tunes:" AC/DC's "Highway to Hell," as we drove down Suitland Parkway. I just hoped that Voight's musical selection wasn't the universe trying to tell us something.

At exactly twelve thirty, we pulled up to the gate of Andrews Air Force Base. Brown brick buildings formed neat rows along perfectly perpendicular, perfectly parallel two-lane roads, dotted by the occasional Subway and Burger King.

"So," I said. "You've been on these trips before. What's about to happen?"

"We'll go to London, have some meetings, then come back," Voight said.

"No, I mean, what *do* we do on the trip. Do we brief the Secretary of Defense?"

"No."

"Oh," I said, a bit disappointed. "Do we at least get to meet the Secretary?"

"Probably not."

"Do we get to *see* the man?"

"Yes. We'll definitely *see* him at some point or other on this trip."

"Then why, exactly, are we here? Are we just supposed to sit here and look pretty?"

"Exactly. Think, Victorian schoolchildren. Fletcher will do the talking. We're just supposed to be encyclopedias on legs. Don't worry; it gets better."

"It does?" I asked, unable to contain the note of desperate optimism in my voice.

Voight glanced at me with a smirk. "Of course not. I was being sarcastic. When we're not looking pretty, we're going to be working our asses off."

"Doing what?"

"Taking notes. Drafting thank-you notes. Writing reporting cables—basically, glorified meeting summaries, broadcast to other parts of the U.S. government with an interest in what took place."

"Oh." I thought about that. I'd basically been doing nothing but taking notes and writing reports all my professional life. "That doesn't sound too bad."

"You'd be surprised. My advice: Sleep when you can."

"Now what?" I asked, setting my bags down in the VIP lounge of the Andrews passenger terminal.

"Now, we wait," Voight said as he looked around the room.

I wandered over to a table that held cookies, coffee, and the day's newspapers, picking up a copy of the *Post* and settling into a chair overlooking the flight line. Heaps of bags and equipment were prepositioned near the exit in front of me; plainclothes Pentagon police members and other assorted staffers worked quickly and efficiently to prepare the Secretary's departure.

I turned to my newspaper. The top story was about Russia's foreign minister declaring that the United States was overstepping and encroaching on Russia's "natural" borders. He further threatened to protect all ethnic-minority Russians, regardless of where they lived, from their oppressors.

Does that extend to the Russians in Brooklyn? I wondered. *That* would make some headlines.

The Islamic State's spread to Libya and Afghanistan was the second story. Too depressing. I turned the page.

"Are you traveling with us today?" A red-headed man with a clipboard asked, interrupting my reading. He reminded me of a cruise director, except that he herded defense dorks from one side of the planet to another instead of old people and tourists.

"Yes, I am." *I'm traveling with the Secretary of Defense of the United States of America,* I thought. "Dr. Heather Reilly."

"Glad to have you with us today," he said, ticking off my name and handing me a set of luggage tags with my name and the Secretary of Defense's seal on them.

As he walked away, it hit me: I was *supposed* to be there. They were expecting me. It wasn't some freak clerical accident that sent me to Andrews that day. They had baggage tags for me and I was listed as part of the Secretary's delegation on a clipboard. I let out a deep breath that I didn't know I'd been holding; my participation on the trip was official.

And then I saw the plane. It took my breath away.

Because it wasn't just a plane. It was *the* plane. The one I'd seen in any number of news broadcasts: a massive, light blue and white E4-B with "United States of America" written along its fuselage. The late afternoon sun bathed the aircraft, giving it a golden-kissed brilliance. I watched it move down the runway and into position several hundred yards away from where I was sitting.

All the petty politics, interpersonal squabbles, and emotional battle scars that had become my day-to-day life...simply dissipated. I was transported to a moment of clarity, a feeling I hadn't experienced since seeing Jon's patch on Royle's shoulder, my first day in the Pentagon. The angst, the stress of my own insecurities, melted away as I realized that I was there to help the Secretary of Defense figure out the best possible way forward for the President and the American people. I was part of a team that would determine the direction of U.S. foreign policy for years to come. In small and big ways, I would help shape, and be shaped by, the historic events about to unfold in front of me.

"Cookie?" Voight asked, waving a chocolate-macadamia-nut Otis Spunkmeyer in front of my face. "They've got 'em free over there." He pointed toward the opposite side of the lounge, mouth full of crumbs.

"I'm good; thanks."

"Suit yourself." Voight sat down next to me to watch the airmen and the security detail load the plane. "It is pretty impressive, isn't it?"

"Yeah. It's pretty impressive."

Voight smiled. "It never gets old. I didn't even want to be here, but now that I am...well, it's not so bad."

"Puts things into perspective, doesn't it?"

"Yeah. It does," I answered.

Voight noticed a group of people beginning to make their way to the door out to the runway. "Well, then. I guess it's about time to get this show on the road. Shall we?"

We grabbed our bags and followed the group across the runway to an entrance at the belly of the plane. I never thought that a several-hundred-yard walk could be so thrilling. But that brief moment conjured an excitement in me that was nearly impossible to contain: feet hitting the tarmac, engine noises humming in my ears, walking past the enormous jets, walking under the fuselage. For all the ups and downs I'd experienced since starting at the Pentagon, this made everything worth it. I suspected everyone else walking up to the plane felt the same way.

After climbing several sets of narrow stairs, I found myself inside a plane that was beyond anything I could have ever imagined. Because never, in all my wildest musings, could I ever have envisioned the Secretary of Defense of the United States of America traveling in a plane that looked like it came straight out of the late 1970s. Minus the faux wood paneling.

This is it? I thought, quickly followed by: *I need to stop being surprised by this.*

After I set my briefcase down next to my designated desk, I stopped to look around. Before me was a glass wall, overlooking what I presumed to be a briefing room that, strangely enough, resembled a movie theater. Rows of blue-cushioned seats were gradually filling up with faces. Some I recognized from TV news; others, I didn't. Most were carrying bags with logos announcing their respective affiliations: CNN, NBC, Voice of America. Behind me were what appeared to be IT guys, beavering away at computers. And all throughout, there was harsh fluorescent lighting that gave the whole place its own uniquely sterile-feeling atmosphere.

"These desks look like they're older than I am," I said, pointing to my console.

Voight considered that. "They very well might be."

"What are these buttons?"

"I have no idea. You probably shouldn't touch them, though."

"This console looks like it's from *Star Trek.*"

"No, it doesn't. It's not that sophisticated looking."

"The original one. With William Shatner."

"Oh. Yeah. Right." I could feel Voight watching me as I studied my terminal.

"What are you doing?" he said.

"Looking for the floppy disk drive."

"Cute. Buckle up. We're about to take off."

"Wait—where's Fletcher?" I asked after I felt the plane ascend.

"I'm guessing up front with the boss. She must have driven in with him," Voight said as they approached cruising altitude. "Don't worry; we'll see her soon enough."

"Colonel Voight?" An air force major approached us. "You've got a phone call in the back."

As Voight left to take the call, I unbuckled my seat belt and stretched my legs. The journalists in the movie-theater-turned-fish-bowl-turned-briefing-room were, for the most part, frantically checking their laptops and handhelds, trying to figure out the stories that would dominate the headlines during this trip.

A silver-blonde man wearing clear glass spectacles and a grey three-piece suit walked through the fish bowl and toward me. I'd never seen a man in the Pentagon so impeccably dressed. He gave both Colin and Derek Odem a run for their money—or at least their tailors.

"Excuse me. Have you seen Ms. Fletcher?" he asked.

"Not since I left the building. I think she's up front with the Secretary?"

"Oh really? Great," said the man, looking both nervous and relieved. "I'm Jeremy, by the way. Secretary Sidwell's special assistant."

"Heather."

"Nice to meet you. Hey, just so you know, we'll be needing Ms. Fletcher to do the Secretary's pre-brief in ten minutes."

"Thanks. I'll let her know," I said. I steeled my nerves as I pulled out my briefing book. It was at least four inches thick, and there was no way that I could recall—or need—everything in there. Still, it was a great, brick-shaped safety blanket. And given that I was about to be in the same room as one of the most powerful men in the world for the first time, having a safety blanket was probably no bad thing. So I spread out the book over the desk in front of me, and began sorting through the items containing minor and major details that Fletcher might need while briefing the Secretary.

"So, do you want the good news or the bad news?" Voight said, interrupting my last-minute study session.

"What's up?"

"Well, the good news is that we're not going to have to deal with Fletcher for the next six hours."

My stomach dropped. "No…"

"Yes. Guess who forgot the three rules of traveling with the Secretary?"

"She didn't…" My eyes widened.

"She did. That was her on the phone."

"What happened?!"

"Caught in traffic. She was twenty minutes away when the plane was taking off. She's driving to Dulles now to catch the first flight to London."

"Oh, my god. She's supposed to do the Secretary's pre-brief in five minutes!"

"Ah, crap," Voight rolled his eyes and grimaced. "They didn't already square that away back in the building?"

"Apparently not," I said.

"Let me go talk to Jeremy," Voight said.

I sat back down at my desk and flipped through the briefing book, eyes skating over the pages but my mind completely unable to take in any information. I was nervous—nervous that I was entering a meeting with the Secretary without Fletcher, nervous that Fletcher would be a nightmare when we caught up in London, nervous that I'd say something stupid in front of the Secretary, nervous that I would draw a blank if and when it came time to say something. My nerves snowballed, getting bigger and bigger with every second, rolling into an avalanche of all-consuming anxiety.

"So, I spoke to Jeremy," Voight said, interrupting my nearly full-blown panic attack. "He's going to do the brief instead of Fletcher. So, once again, we just get to sit and look pretty."

Relief mixed with the tiniest hint of regret washed over me. On the one hand, I wouldn't have to speak and risk embarrassing myself in front of the Secretary of all Defense. But if I was being honest with myself, there was a teeny—barely discernable—part of me that had looked forward to the challenge.

"Ready?" Voight asked.

"Not at all."

"Me neither. Embrace the suck."

CHAPTER TWENTY-FOUR

VOIGHT AND I PICKED UP OUR BINDERS AND NOTEPADS AND WADED OUR WAY THROUGH THE MASS OF JOURNALISTS AND EQUIPMENT TO MAKE OUR WAY TO THE SECRETARY'S PRIVATE CONFERENCE ROOM. The seal of the Department of Defense loomed large on the far wall. Other staffers, some with faces I recognized from Policy, others complete strangers, started trickling into the room—all told, there were about six of them. Voight, as usual, was talking to someone he knew. I was beginning to suspect I could go anywhere in the world and play "six degrees of Colonel Tom Voight."

A door near the head of the table opened and in walked a shorter, slightly heavyset man with salt-and-pepper hair and black plastic-rimmed glasses that amplified his sparkling brown eyes. He was wearing khakis and a button-up dress shirt and, I noted with amazement, black Converse shoes. As I stood along with everyone else while he walked to his seat, I was surprised; Secretary of Defense Edwin Sidwell didn't *look* very intimidating. In fact, the man seemed like a pretty amiable, relaxed guy. All of my assumptions were thrown upside down; given the endless lengths I'd gone through to ensure that every single sentence of every single memo was perfectly crafted and formatted, I'd thought he would exude a more hardass-Type-A vibe. That he'd have a pocket protector and a ruler to identify all the mistakes his staff made. Instead, he looked like the kind of guy who wouldn't really care whether he received a briefing package with a wrinkled Tab A.

Secretary Sidwell sat at the head of the table; his three-star senior military assistant, General Park, sat to his right, and Jeremy sat to his left. Everyone else took their seats; Voight and I were the only people situated against the wall. I pulled out my notepad and rested it on my briefing book, ready to take the kind of extremely detailed notes that Fletcher would expect when she arrived in London.

"How is this going to work?" Secretary Sidwell asked Jeremy.

"Sir, as you know, Acting ASD Fletcher missed wheels-up. So I'll be doing the briefing, assisted by Dr. Reilly and Colonel Voight over there."

Secretary Sidwell looked over at the two of us. "Why are you guys sitting against the wall?" he said, motioning with his arms for us to join the table. "Come sit with us."

"Yes, sir," Voight said.

As we switched seats, I involuntarily looked around the room, suspicious that Fletcher would somehow find out that I'd sat at the big-kids table.

"That's better," Secretary Sidwell said. "Jeremy, please continue."

"Right. As you know, on this trip we are going to London, then on to Germany, and finally to Egypt. Then back to Washington."

"When we initially considered the London leg of this trip, our thinking was that we would be announcing our enhanced cooperation with the Brits on building a new nuclear weapons capability together. But recent events have put the question of a Moldova coalition on the front burner."

"Where are we at on that?" asked the Secretary.

"Sir, I'd have to turn to Ms. Fletcher's team to elaborate on that."

I was so focused on scribbling notes in my notebook that I'd almost missed Jeremy steer the conversation in our direction. I looked up to see every eye in the room staring at Voight and me.

Voight leaned in to respond. "Sir, my colleague Dr. Reilly has been tracking the Joint Staff's planning quite closely, and has done considerable work to map out our strategic options. Of all of us, she is best prepared to walk you through that."

At that very moment, I fully understood what it was like to be a deer facing an approaching car, frozen in headlights and about to be flattened. As I stared unblinking at my colleagues, I felt myself unable to speak, unable to say anything. If I contradicted Fletcher in any way, I'd have hell to pay later. Not to mention the fact that Fletcher had made it abundantly clear that I was not, in any way, supposed to interact with the higher-ups. Hell, I felt uncomfortable sitting at the same *table* as the principals after the ass-chewing I'd gotten from Fletcher the other day.

But just as I felt myself about to completely choke, I remembered what I said to Amanda when I'd started at the Pentagon: *I want to help.*

"Dr. Reilly?" Jeremy asked.

I looked up. Fletcher be damned, the Secretary of Defense was asking me to speak. And it's hard to say no to the Secretary of Defense.

"Yes, sir," I said. "Sorry, I was just organizing my thoughts."

"No problem," Secretary Sidwell said. "Dr. Reilly—why do I know that name? Oh yes! You wrote that memo a little while ago. About our options on Moldova and regional implications, right?"

"You *read* that, sir?" I asked, eyes wide.

"I did. Excellent work. Anyway, please continue."

The Secretary of Defense read my work and liked it? If I could have gotten away with it, I would have leapt up and danced on the table with joy. Instead, I sat up a bit straighter and said, "Thank you, sir."

"You're quite welcome," the Secretary said. I looked at Voight; he was beaming.

"Anyway, sir, as you know, the United Kingdom is one of our closest—if not *the* closest—ally we've got," I started.

"Right. Ariane seemed to think that this trip was necessary to help our counterparts get over their own politics. And that, when it comes down to it, this should be a walk in the park."

I grimaced as I recalled my conversation with Colin at the Embassy. He was flippant—as usual—but as I thought back to that evening, it felt like he was telling me that things were much more difficult than he was allowed to let on, even without Derek trying to sink the whole thing.

"I take it you don't agree, Dr. Reilly?"

I have got *to work on my poker face.*

"Sir, while I agree with you and Ms. Fletcher that it should be easy, everything I've heard and read tells me that it's going to be a much harder sell than we initially thought. If tensions escalate, the Brits worry they will be forced into a war with Russia over a country that they don't care that much about. And they've already got their hands full with Brexit."

"But that's the point of all this, isn't it? Preventing Russia from letting its eyes get too big? If we all threaten to retaliate to Moscow's provocations, the Kremlin might think twice about its next steps."

"Yes, sir. But Britain currently gets a lot of its natural gas supplies from Russia. Not to mention that according to some sources, Russian oligarchs own half the property in London. The two countries are intertwined in some frankly uncomfortable ways, at least from our perspective, if not theirs. There's also the fact that the Russians have already escalated this issue, at least rhetorically."

"Meaning?"

"Threatening nuclear war," I said. "Which is, of course, serious business. But it's also a threat they've been making pretty routinely recently. I think they threatened Denmark last year."

"With nukes?"

"Yes, sir."

"Christ, all this because of *Moldova?*" The Secretary turned back to Jeremy. "What do you think?"

"Sir, I tend to agree with Heather on this one. It's going to be a tough sell. Politically, the Brits want to support us of course. But the whole country's in turmoil as it figures out how to leave the EU. And after the debacle in Iraq, as well as in Afghanistan, the left wing of the Labour party wants to maintain a bit of distance. And they're running the government right now."

Secretary Sidwell sighed. "Those wars are going to continue to bite us in the ass, aren't they?"

"It seems like it, sir. But this is a winnable debate. And if we get them to join us in Moldova, it's likely that a number of other countries will also join."

"In other words, we need to do our best not to screw this up."
Secretary Sidwell sighed. "Remind me again why I approved this
Moldova plan?"

"Sir, you approved it if we can assemble a coal—" started
Jeremy.

"Don't worry, Jeremy. I'm not wobbling. Well, then. I think
that's about all I need to know for now. Let's rest up. I have the
feeling that this is going to be a fairly tough trip." Secretary Sidwell
stood up and the rest of the room rose as well.

"Oh, and Dr. Reilly?"

"Yes, sir?"

"Could you print off a copy of your memo? I'd like to read
it again."

"Absolutely, sir," I said. I couldn't help but radiate a shocked
sort of pride as the Secretary left the room.

"That was incredible!" Voight said.

"I didn't embarrass myself, did I?" I said, feeling a quick spike
of fear.

"Embarrass yourself? Hell no! You kicked ass! Fletcher's
going to go nuts when she hears about this!" He smiled with smug
satisfaction.

"Oh, goody. Can't wait."

"Don't worry about it now," Voight said as we made our way
back through the press pit to our desks. "Besides, it was her fault
she missed the flight. Now let's get some rest and brace for the
storm. I have the feeling this is going to be an interesting trip."

I awoke when the plane came to a halt. Suddenly, the aircraft was buzzing with activity as everyone quickly gathered their things and made their way down the stairs out of the aircraft and into the cool London Heathrow night. The yellow-orange lights of Heathrow's sprawling terminals pierced the fog hovering over the tarmac that bathed everything in a Prufrock-like glow. The roar of the cooling engines muted all other sounds around me, so I followed the crowd as we quickly made our way to a set of—eight? ten?—cars situated approximately one hundred yards from the aircraft.

I was about to climb into one of them when I felt a pull on my shoulder. Voight was waving toward the back of the line of cars and beckoning me to follow him. We walked past all the other cars in the line until we finally reached a tall minibus with a sign on the window that read, "Staff Van 2."

We climbed aboard. The van was already full of journalists and staffers; no two seats were empty together, so I sat next to a woman in her mid-thirties who was fiddling with her seat belt. She looked familiar, although it wasn't until we were both strapped in and the bus started accelerating that I finally recognized who I was sitting with: Janna Pessin, CNN's defense correspondent.

I decided to introduce myself by striking up a conversation.

"So, is this your first trip with the Secretary?" I asked, before kicking myself for saying something so stupid. Of course it wasn't. I'd had watched her coverage of SecDef trips any number of times.

"Me? No. I've done this a dozen times, at least. I've been covering the building for CNN for three years or so."

"So, just another day at the office?"

Janna chuckled. "The hours are long, but at least it's better than riding a desk in Atlanta."

Through the glass window behind Janna, the lights and sights of Heathrow whizzed past. "Is it safe to go this fast?" I wondered aloud.

"The police cleared the highway for our motorcade," Janna said. "Standard procedure."

Sure enough, every minute or so, I saw another cop on a motorcycle, stopping traffic to let us go past.

"What are you doing on this trip?" she continued. Her question was blunt, but her tone of voice was kind.

"I work in Policy."

Smelling an opportunity, Janna involuntarily perked up, alert for details.

"So, then maybe you can answer me: Why are you guys so obsessed with Moldova—of all places—these days? Doesn't seem to make that much sense."

"I'm not allowed to talk about that," I said. It probably wasn't the best idea in the world to let a member of the press know how U.S. strategy for the region hung on the outcome of this trip.

"Damn. I thought maybe I'd got you before they gave you the 'don't talk to strangers' briefing, or whatever it is you guys do."

"Sorry, too late. But out of curiosity, what is the outside world saying about all of this?"

Janna settled back into her seat, clearly a little disappointed that I wasn't about to give her a scoop.

"The usual. You government folks are pretty predictable. You want to stand up to the Russians so they don't start treating their neighbors like a kid would a candy shop, gobbling everything they can get their paws on. And the rest of the world is scared that going down the path you're charting will lead to another Cold War. Or worse."

I nodded. Janna was happy to continue.

"In the meantime, while the U.S. is distracted by this Moldova situation, Afghanistan is going down the drain, and the rest of the Middle East is on fire. The Islamic State is creating franchises faster than McDonald's."

"What are you hearing about Afghanistan?" I was caught off guard. I wasn't used to anybody *else* raising the question of Afghanistan.

"You guys basically left Afghanistan to its own devices and let the region descend into chaos afterwards. Again. The craziest of the crazies took over running things. They're even worse than those lunatics in Syria. And after all the lives we lost trying to build that place into somewhere stable…. It's a tragedy."

"I couldn't agree with you more," I said, once again wishing I could work on Afghanistan before turning my gaze back to the window and watching the darkened buildings of London speed in and out of view.

It was just before one in the morning when we reached our hotel, yet somehow the white marble lobby of the Royal Horseguards Hotel was bustling with people, most of whom I recognized from the Secretary's plane. Jeremy was standing next to the worn, brown leather couches situated in the center of the lobby; Secret Service members hovered near the plush red chairs near the window. A couple new faces were talking intently with the Secretary's travel team in a nook between the fireplace and what appeared to be a corridor to the rest of the hotel. After figuring out when to meet Voight for breakfast the next day, I went to my room and unpacked my bags.

I put my head on my pillow, but sleep eluded me. Too much was at stake, and the next day wasn't going to be pretty. So when my phone buzzed and I noticed it was my mom calling, I decided to answer.

"There you are! I was worried!" Mom exclaimed.

"Hi, Mom."

"Why haven't you been taking my calls? It's impossible to reach you these days."

"I know, Mom. I'm sorry. I've been overwhelmed at work."

"That's no excuse. You know how worried I get about you. And now with Ryan here and you there, you don't have anyone to look out for you."

"I have Amanda, Mom," I said, dodging the points that I was neither in Washington nor engaged to Ryan.

"Yes, but Amanda is living her own life. As well she should. She's got plenty to do, working for that senator of hers. I saw him on CNN last night. He was looking very presidential."

"His politics are moving to the right of Attila the Hun, Mom. And last I checked, you were a lefty."

"Who votes on politics anymore? Our politics are so screwed up, I don't know who stands for what."

I remained quiet. Sometimes Mom managed to hit the nail right on the head.

"What's new with you, Heather?" Mom continued. "How's work? How's Ryan?"

I took a deep breath to try and contain the tsunami of painful emotions that were suddenly flooding my heart, body, and mind, the emotions that I hadn't yet allowed myself to feel. How many times had Mom told me that she loved Ryan? That we were a perfect couple, as far as she was concerned? That she was so thrilled that I was settled? That we were living the life she'd hoped for me?

How many times hadn't Mom said that it all mattered so much to her because after losing Jon, she was desperate to see her daughter live a long, happy life? That she couldn't wait to meet her grandchildren? At that moment, I realized that these fiercely held dreams she had for me formed such a core part of the fabric of our relationship that they didn't ever need to be voiced aloud. They were just there, real and part of the universe of our relationship.

And I was about to throw our little universe into chaos.

After the grief and turmoil of Jon's passing, I swore to myself I'd never make her feel pain. She'd already had enough. A tear slipped out of my eye as I realized I was about to hurt her. But it couldn't be helped.

"Heather, are you there?"

"Ryan and I separated, Mom."

"Of course, you're separated. He's in California, and you're in Washington. But that's only temporary."

"No, Mom. We broke up. I'm not engaged anymore."

Mom gasped. Then, silence. Tears welled in my eyes and streamed down my cheeks as I heard her heart practically stopping on the other end of the phone.

"But Ryan is a good man. Why would he do this?" my mother eventually asked with a warbling voice.

"I ended it, Mom."

"Oh. I see," Mom said, her voice now cracking with the onset of tears. "I'd better go, Heather."

"I love you, Mom."

"I love you too. Always," she said, a little too hastily, and then hung up.

I set the phone next to my pillow and allowed myself to fall into my grief, crying aloud as my body convulsed with heavy sobs. It was one thing to talk to Amanda, who had been privy to the ins and outs, ups and downs of my life for years. It was an entirely different matter to admit that everything had fallen apart to my mother. To disappoint her. Because voicing the breakup aloud to my mom gave form and permanence to the end of my relationship with Ryan, and signaled the end of a phase of my relationship with my mother that I hadn't realized that I was in.

I was no longer a fiancée.

I was no longer a child.

The question was, what had I become? And was I strong enough to handle whatever life threw at me next?

CHAPTER TWENTY-FIVE

I WOKE UP AT FIVE FEELING BOTH WORN OUT AND FILLED WITH NERVOUS PENT-UP ENERGY. As always, the light of morning after sleep brought a new, fresh perspective on things. And despite the pain of my conversation with my mother just a few hours before, I felt better. Relieved, somehow, that it was finally out there. As if I'd let out a breath that I didn't know that I'd been holding. Fletcher wouldn't arrive for a couple of hours, and I didn't want to hang around in my room, so I decided to put on my workout gear and get some exercise.

I was pretty out of shape—all my hours of being chained to my desk at the Pentagon were catching up with me—and I was jogging at a snail's pace compared to my former speeds. But it felt so good to feel my feet against the pavement, pushing myself just a little harder. As I ran along the river, it struck me as funny: a former peacenik, in London, with the Secretary of Defense, looking at Big Ben and the Houses of Parliament. I stopped and jogged in place for a moment as I took in the appropriately ornate palace of representative democracy—the thin lines of its tan stone crowned with gold adornments, all of it washed with the rosy sun of the dawn. I smiled and started jogging again.

I looked at my watch: I still had about half an hour before I needed to shower and get ready. I decided to keep going. I turned corner after corner, marveling at the hodgepodge of architecture—some buildings were centuries old, others looked like they'd been built less than ten years ago. There was something inspiring to the city's resilience; I'd read that huge swathes of the city had been bombed out during the Battle of Britain. But Londoners weren't going to let that stop them, apparently. They carried on. They filled the gaps and crannies left over from the blitz with new buildings and modern designs, and the city of London slowly, but surely, found its beating heart again.

I'd lost myself in thought so thoroughly, I hadn't realized that I'd become actually, physically lost. I pulled out my map, but couldn't seem to place myself on it, so I wandered around a couple more streets to see if I could locate one of them—any of them—on the map. I didn't. I was just about to give up when I saw a wrought iron sign that pointed in the directions of Buckingham Palace (to the left, approximately half a mile) and Parliament (to the right, also approximately half a mile). Deciding not to overdo it, I half jogged, half walked to Parliament and then made it back to the hotel.

When I got back to my room, I was actually pretty pleased with myself that I'd managed to find my way around in a complicated city like London. After showering and changing, I discovered that I'd forgotten some of my toiletries, including my industrial-strength anti-frizz spray. *This doesn't bode well*, I thought, as I tied my hair back to prevent it from turning into a cotton-ball-like halo around my head.

At seven I met Voight, and the two of us had a pleasant English breakfast: eggs, sausage, a roasted tomato, baked beans, and fried toast. Even though baked beans weren't exactly my top choice for breakfast foods, the sausage was a nice way to revel in my newfound carnivorousness. It was pleasant, or it had been, until we heard a shrill voice echoing through the hotel lobby and up through to the restaurant.

"What do you mean my name isn't on the roster? I'm a part of Secretary Sidwell's delegation!"

"Incoming," Voight said, drinking the last few sips of his latte.

"Bracing for impact," I said, signing for our breakfast. We stood up and walked into the lobby to see—and hear—a frustrated and frazzled Acting Assistant Secretary of Defense yelling at a poor, hapless concierge.

"Where is your manager? I demand to speak to your manager. This is unacceptable."

"Ma'am?" Voight ventured.

"Finally! Where have you been?" Fletcher said.

"We were—"

"Nevermind. When is the day brief?"

"Eight thirty," I said.

Fletcher looked at her watch. "That's fifteen minutes from now. Walk with me." She turned to Voight. "Please tell me you know what room I'm in."

"Of course, ma'am. I have your key right here," he said handing it to her as we entered the elevator. "Room 604."

"Now, Voight," Fletcher said, turning her body to face away from me, "Tell me what's been going on."

"Okay, then," Voight said, as we walked behind Fletcher toward her room. "Our meeting with the Secretary on the plane went well. Heather ended up doing most of the talking—"

"Heather?! Briefing the Secretary?" Fletcher looked at Voight in horror. "Why didn't you do the brief? You're the colonel." Fletcher turned to the door and swiped her key card unsuccessfully while I took a moment to take a deep, cleansing breath. After a couple more tries, the light turned green.

"Finally," Fletcher said, storming in and throwing her suitcase on the bed. "What did the Secretary ask about?"

"He asked how the coalition is coming along." Voight said. "He thinks that getting the U.K. to join is going to be a tough sell because of the Russia factor."

"A tough sell? That makes this sound like we've made the Secretary of Defense the Action Officer on this issue. He's doing *your* job. Did you create this mess?" Fletcher asked, looking at me.

I'd braced for impact, but this was definitely a larger explosion than I'd expected. My frustration was bubbling to the surface, and it was everything I could do to contain it.

"Ma'am, he asked for my opinion—"

"*Your* opinion? You've got to be kidding me." Fletcher turned to Voight.

"Ma'am, she didn't—" started Voight.

"What else do I need to know before the day brief?" Fletcher interrupted.

Voight must have realized that mentioning me was like waving a red flag in front of a bull. Because as he continued to recount the salient details for Fletcher, he conveniently left out the fact that the Secretary had personally requested my Moldova memo.

"I'm going to finish getting ready," Fletcher said after Voight finished, taking her suit into the bathroom with her. "Voight, wait outside. I want you to come with me to the day brief with the Secretary. And Heather, just so you know, we are going to have a *serious* chat when we get back to Washington. In the meantime, don't screw up again. This is your second formal warning, is it not?" she said, her voice so sharp I could almost feel it cutting my skin.

My odds of staying in this job have just gotten a lot worse. A couple months ago, that might not have bothered me so much. But now, the thought of being fired felt like a death sentence.

Having nothing better to do, and needing to get my mind off the fact that my boss hated me, I decided to walk back down to the lobby and wait for the day to begin. Voight remained upstairs in case Her Highness needed anything. I sat down at one of the large leather sofas and flipped through my briefing binder that contained just about everything the principals could possibly need for their meetings with the Brits that day: maps, the military requirements for the Moldova mission, what we thought the Brits could contribute to Moldova, Russian force dispositions in Ukraine and near the Georgian border, fact sheets, talking points—just about everything related to the topic that I could physically stuff into a three-ring binder.

Soon, members of the Secretary's delegation started to trickle into the foyer. Almost as if I'd acquired a radar for it, I could hear

Fletcher's shrill voice as it assaulted the lobby's acoustics. I looked toward the staircase just in time to see Fletcher rounding the corner and stomping down the stairs. Voight was three steps behind her, carrying her purse.

"There you are," Fletcher said, approaching me. "I need a map of Iranian Revolutionary Guard training camps across the Middle East. The possible Iranian response to our Moldova plan is a major sticking point with the Brits. As a countermove to our Moldova plan, Russia is flooding Iran with military equipment."

"Which is making Syria more unstable, and the Saudis uncomfortable," I said. "Got it."

In my memo, it was one of the possible outcomes I'd discussed. Voight and I had discussed including materials on the Middle East dimension to the Moldova situation, but in the end we decided not to include a map like that in our briefing binder. For one, there wasn't enough time for the mapmakers in the bowels of the Pentagon to build it before the trip without them screaming bloody murder at us. Second, bringing along a map like that would, according to Voight, mean that we'd have to "pack our hazmat suits" to handle a product with that high of a classification level. But I didn't want to leave that aspect uncovered, so in the absence of a map I wrote some talking points instead.

"I have some talkers on that issue right here," I said, feeling smug as I set my binder on the table and flipping through to find them.

"I don't want talking points. I want a map," Fletcher said, irritated.

Shit, I thought as I continued to flip through the binder, hoping—praying—it would magically appear. It didn't.

"Unfortunately, ma'am, I don't have those details with me." I said, resigned while internally scolding myself for my binder-preparation hubris. Of *course* Fletcher would ask for one of the few things I didn't actually have on me. *Did I do something terrible in a past life? Is this the universe wreaking some sort of karmic justice on me?*

Fletcher was visibly annoyed. "Fine. Get them to me ASAP," she said, walking off to take a phone call.

Voight, meanwhile, walked up to me and then sat down on the couch, looking more than slightly shell-shocked.

"What *happened* up there?" I asked while watching Fletcher huddle in the corner of the lobby near the door.

"To her? Or to me?"

"Her."

"She's absolutely, one hundred percent having a nervous break-down," Voight said. "And after what just happened upstairs, I think *I* might be on the verge of a collapse."

"Why?"

"Before we went to the day brief, she demanded that I come to the room and pick up a bunch of papers from her."

"So?"

"She answered the door in a blanket."

"What do you mean, in a blanket?"

"She was wearing a blanket."

"A blanket?"

"Yes, a blanket. That was it. All she was wearing. A blanket."

"Good god. The horror."

"I'll never be able to un-see that."

We shuddered as we watched Fletcher argue with some poor bastard on the phone on the other side of the room.

"Some people have quiet, internal nervous breakdowns," Voight said. "Graceful. With lots of meds to keep it manageable. But not Fletcher. She's detonating."

"And we're caught in the blast radius."

"Ground zero," Voight agreed.

"What brought this on?"

"You mean, *besides* the fact that she's trying to suck up so she can get the ASD job, and managed to horribly embarrass herself by missing the plane? The day brief made her pop. Jeremy and the Secretary led off the meeting by saying how hard they thought it would be to win over the Brits. And then the Secretary talked about your memo. Apparently, he *did* re-read it last night."

"Fantastic," I said in a tone of voice that reeked of sarcasm. "That memo is the gift that keeps on giving."

Voight set Fletcher's purse on the couch next to us. "Oh, and the rest of this trip is off."

"Wait—what?"

"SecDef is needed back in Washington. POTUS wants him back for an early morning meeting tomorrow. Frankly, I think it's a relief to most of the team. The weather guy thinks there could be a major tropical storm on Tuesday, when they were scheduled to fly home."

"So, we're headed back this afternoon?"

"Yep. Right after the press conference."

"Wow. I guess we're not going to have much time to check out London, are we?

"If by 'not much time' you mean 'absolutely zero,' then yes," Voight said. I could feel his grumpiness with the situation mount.

"We won't even be able to go through the duty free shop at Heathrow. So much for getting a gift for Jamie."

"So….we have a bit of a problem," I said.

"*Another* problem?" asked Voight. "Haven't we already reached our quota on problems?"

"Apparently not. Guess what Fletcher is asking for?"

Voight blinked.

"The map that we decided *not* to have made. On IRGC training camps."

"The one that would have taken our intel guys months to put together?"

"That's the one."

"Does she know that putting together a product like that—in a format we'd feel even remotely comfortable handling outside of a secure facility—would literally take an act of God?"

"Would it matter if she did?"

"Point taken," Voight said, rubbing his face. "All we can do is email the Joint Staff, I guess."

"And say what? It's only four in the morning back home. And we don't have a way to get that kind of classified material while we're in the Ministry of Defense."

"Let the folks back in Washington figure that out," Voight said. "We have bigger things to worry about."

Secretary Sidwell passed through the lobby with his security detail, starting his walk down the street toward the Ministry of Defense.

"Like what?"

"Like avoiding blankets. And the blast radius. Surviving today, basically."

CHAPTER TWENTY-SIX

AFTER STARING AT MY PHONE FOR A COUPLE MINUTES, I FINALLY SENT A NOTE OFF TO PUMPKIN ASKING HIM FOR HELP. I'd been tempted to reach out to Royle after his offer the other day, but when push came to shove, I didn't want to feel like I owed him anything. Besides, Royle wouldn't be able to do anything that Pumpkin couldn't do. SOS sent, I joined the rest of the delegation as we walked to the Ministry of Defense.

Thirty minutes later, we were loitering in a nondescript rectangular conference room, at the heart of the thoroughly ugly Ministry of Defense Main Building, drinking underwhelming coffee out of short white porcelain cups. "This stuff is terrible," I said, sipping my coffee.

"Brits aren't exactly known for their coffee, Heather," Voight said.

"True. Tea is for civilized people," said a somewhat familiar voice. Colin, whom we'd met at the Australian embassy, looked dapper as ever. "Coffee is for upstart colonial rebels. But at least it's caffeine."

"Caffeine is about all that this brown swill has going for it," I said, forcing down another swallow. "But putting that aside, what are you doing here, Colin? Why aren't you back in Washington?"

"You must be joking! I wouldn't dare miss the excitement! Mind you, if this was a normal meeting, we'd have had this already scripted, and I wouldn't have bothered."

"And now?"

"No idea what's going to happen. My political masters here haven't got the foggiest what to do. Brilliant, isn't it?"

"Surely you've picked which horse to back by now?" I asked, recalling our last conversation at the Australian embassy.

"*I* have. But your colleagues in the White House haven't been helping you. Our good friend Derek Odem happens to be good friends with the Prime Minister's confidential advisor. And Mr. Odem has not been terribly helpful to your cause, I'm afraid."

"Well, sure," I said, trying to downplay the tribal warfare-like dynamics between the different U.S. government departments. "He had a different idea about how to counter the Russians. But that's just a policy disagreement. Happens all the time."

"Policy disagreement? Sure. But as I understand things, it's personal too. Didn't you know that he's angling for Assistant Secretary Chao's position? The one that your current boss is currently—temporarily—filling?"

Although I did my best to keep my features smooth, my eyes involuntarily widened in shock.

A flicker in Colin's eye told me that he understood exactly how surprised I was.

"It all seems rather cloak-and-dagger to me," Colin continued. "Which seems to me to be a little distasteful, frankly. But the question that really matters to you—and to us, I suppose—is whether my bosses here in Whitehall have decided. I don't think they have."

"It would be a shame to have the Secretary of Defense come all this way only to have his closest allies turn into wet noodles," I said, regaining my poise.

Colin cocked an eyebrow, and smiled ever so slightly. "Indeed. There're a couple options on the table right now. What the Prime Minister ultimately decides, however, is entirely up to how hard your man pushes the Defense Minister. Ah, my director just walked in. Let me go say hello to him. I'll see you afterwards."

I looked around the room's white walls, grey carpets, and large wood conference table. Two miniature flags, one British, one American, crossed each other in the center of the large rectangular table. Two placecards, one for the Secretary, the other for the Minister, were situated opposite each other at the center seats of the table. Fletcher and her British counterparts loitered near the coffee stand near the entrance to the room, but Voight and I decided to steer clear of the gaggle, lest Fletcher be tempted to dress us down—again. Instead, we hovered near the seats against the wall, directly behind Secretary Sidwell.

On the surface, the task before us didn't seem like a whole big deal: listen to a meeting, take notes, write them up. But with everything that had already happened on the trip, I couldn't help but worry that something else, somehow, would go wrong. My head was starting to buzz with nervousness and I choked down the last of my coffee. We both watched as Fletcher schmoozed with General Park on the other side of the room—smiling, laughing, joking, flirting?

"It's like Jekyll and Hyde, isn't it?" I said, nodding my head in Fletcher's direction. "Do you think her lover would be upset to see her like that?"

Voight froze. "I have no idea. Let's never speak of that again."

"Right. Changing the subject. I guess we now know why the Moldova plan has been so hard to pull off."

"Odem. He wants the ASD job." Voight paused for a minute. "Which means—"

"Exactly. Killing the Moldova plan embarrasses Fletcher and takes her out of the running."

"Aw, hell." Voight rolled his eyes. "It's funny. In school they teach you that our government is like, united. And professional. You know, the grownups who know the right thing to do."

I nodded. "They left out the part about the senior leaders that act like they're on a kindergarten playground half the time. Either way, none of this bodes well for us."

All of a sudden, Secretary Sidwell and Minister Dutton swept into the room, laughing with each other.

"Let's get down to business, shall we?" said the Secretary, moving to his seat at the center of the table. "We've got a lot to get through."

"Agreed." Minister Dutton took his seat opposite; the Minister's staff—including Colin—filled up the ten or so chairs on the British side of the table as the Americans started to find their seats.

I watched Fletcher try to take a seat next to the Secretary, yet the size of the table, compounded by the width of the chairs, made it impossible for her to squeeze by the Secretary without asking him to move—a request that was somehow understood by all as verboten. So the Secretary's military assistant sat to the Secretary's right, and then Jeremy, and then Fletcher next to him. But all the chairs to the left of Secretary Sidwell were unfilled.

I was horrified. Not only was sitting behind the Secretary completely unworkable—his chair was a mere three inches from the one I had planned to sit in—but leaving the left of the Secretary of Defense's side of the table empty just looked awkward—like a wide open smile suspiciously devoid of teeth in one quarter of the mouth.

Voight noticed the weirdness too. "What do we do?"

"You sit next to the Secretary. I'll sit next to you. And we'll pray that Fletcher has other things on her mind."

"Gotcha," Voight said, taking his newly assigned seat.

I was equal parts terrified and nervous as I pulled out my notepad while the Minister and the Secretary exchanged further pleasantries. And so to alleviate my nerves, I retreated to my tried-and-true strategy: feigned invisibility. I hunched over my notepad, pretending I wasn't actually there.

Voight stifled a cough, distracting me from my critically important doodling. His expression was one of amusement and agreement as he glanced at my paper: it had "Help me. I'm in hell" scribbled all over the margins.

Why aren't we getting started? I wondered, briefly glancing up to look at my surroundings. I couldn't see Fletcher, which, I hoped, meant that Fletcher couldn't see me. Thank god. *Maybe we'll get away with this*, I thought, with a spark of hope beginning to form in my chest....

Hope that was just as quickly obliterated when the doors to the room opened, and the international press walked in to take photographs of everyone sitting at the table. Janna smiled at me.

So much for getting away with it, I thought, trying to turn my face away from the cameras as much as possible. A million expletives floated through my mind as I tried to pretend I wasn't there by scribbling even more furiously on my notepad. It was as if my chicken scratch was either the most important writing in the history of the English language, or my lifeline. Or both.

"That's enough," Jeremy eventually said, either three hours or thirty seconds later. I wasn't exactly sure. "We have work to do here."

The photographers left, shutting the door behind them.

"So, Des," Secretary Sidwell said to the Minister. "You know that our relationship with the U.K. is critically important to the United States. We've tackled any number of challenges together. So I'm not going to beat around the bush, not with you. Where are you and the Prime Minister on Moldova?"

"Ed, you know it's a tricky one for us."

"Des, when *aren't* things tricky?"

"Look, we don't want to send troops. The Prime Minister doesn't think we ought to be picking fights with the Russians."

"A little late for that, don't you think? The Russians have already picked a fight with us over Ukraine. They're picking fights with us over Syria. It looks like they're trying to pick a fight over Georgia—again. And they're intimidating the hell out of our allies in the Baltics. They're not going to stop this foolishness unless we stand up to them."

"Yeah, but you're talking about building up a presence in Russia's back yard."

"Look at the map, Des. It's actually next door to Romania. Which means it's in NATO's back yard, not Russia's."

"Still, it's a provocative move," Minister Dutton said.

"We've got to start standing up to Russian aggression somewhere."

"Sure, along NATO's borders."

"So we're just going to cede everything that's *not* part of NATO to Russia? That's crazy, Des. You know that's only going to embolden Moscow. We need to start making it much more difficult for them to do whatever the hell they want. Besides, building an international coalition will make it much harder for Russia to use this as a political football."

"What if the Russians want to join the coalition?"

"We'll let 'em join."

"Doesn't that defeat the purpose?"

"Not at all. Actually, the opposite. We'll be able to watch Russian maneuvers in that part of the world much more closely."

"Yes, we'll be able to watch as we give them the political pretext to arm the Iranians to the teeth, heighten their proxy war in Ukraine, and possibly start another world war," Minister Dutton said. "Frankly, I'm not convinced."

Secretary Sidwell sighed. "You know, we may have to just go to the French instead of you guys."

"The *French*?" Dutton said, beside himself. "You're joking, surely."

"They're actually willing to *do* stuff these days rather than sit on the sidelines."

"Let's not get too hasty, Ed. There are other options we could consider."

"Okay, then. You mentioned earlier that you won't send *troops*. Do you have something else in mind?"

Minister Dutton smiled. "As a matter of fact, I do."

"Do *you* think what they're proposing is enough?" I asked Voight as we walked outside of the Ministry of Defense building, en route to the press conference at a local think tank. It was drizzling, and I didn't have my umbrella—a rookie move in London—so I carefully wrapped my head with a scarf as we shuffled down the pavement toward Whitehall. "I mean, I know the Secretary is pretty unhappy with what just went down in that last meeting, but what do you think?"

"I'm with the boss on this one," Voight said.

"But why? Sharing the intel they've gotten through their networks in the region will be helpful, right?"

We turned a corner. Nelson's column in Trafalgar Square stared down at us from a couple blocks to our right; a couple blocks to our left, the Houses of Parliament and Big Ben loomed even larger.

"Sure. There's just two problems with their proposal."

"Which are?"

"One, they probably would have shared that intel anyway. And two, if they don't send troops, it doesn't help us politically. Which is one of the big reasons we want them involved. But they're not putting any skin in the game. These are our closest allies, and they're giving us the cold shoulder."

"It seems to me they're trying to find the middle ground between us and the White House," I said as we walked through the grey stone columns surrounding the heavy wooden doors of the Royal United Services Institute. "Doing something, but nothing too risky."

"Agreed. I think we can *also* agree that Derek has managed to really screw us," Voight said. "The U.S. government: one team, one fight? My ass."

"Heather! Voight!" Fletcher screeched from a nook near the coat racks as we entered the lobby.

"Yes, ma'am?" My nerves stood completely on end.

"Did you find what I asked for?" Fletcher asked.

"We're still waiting, ma'am," I responded.

"Why are you just standing here, then? Why aren't you on the phone tracking it down? You need to be more aggressive, Heather."

"Of course, ma'am," I said.

"Also, I'd like a summary of the Georgian armed forces and the Russian buildup along the border."

My eyes lit up. "Here," I said, reaching into my binder.

"I'd also like a summary of what we're requesting from the Brits."

"I've got that handy as well," I flipped to another section of my notebook and removed the pages.

Fletcher nodded and stomped off.

Is all this some sort of elaborate Pentagon hazing ritual?

Voight and I looked at each other; Voight shrugged his shoulders in defeat.

"I'll just go ahead and email Pumpkin again," I said. "See you upstairs."

I wandered to a quiet corner and pulled out my phone. After sending the urgent request for information to Pumpkin—along with several lines of "I'm sorry to do this to you" and "thank you so much"—I had a quick scroll through my sixty new emails to see if any of them were from Pumpkin or anybody else on the Joint Staff. None were. Great. I sighed, feeling deflated.

I watched as reporters and camera crews filtered into the building, dragging their equipment, reviewing their notes, and buzzing with the energy of a major, unfolding story. I followed the crowd up the wide white and black marble staircase and into the library. I was immediately awestruck: I'd just entered a defense nerd's version of Hogwarts. Two stories of books, neatly housed on wooden bookshelves, ran along the walls of the ovular room. Red carpeting made the room feel regal; it wasn't just a library—it was a palace for books.

"It's impressive, isn't it?" Voight said, appearing behind me.

"It truly is," I agreed. "Anything from Pumpkin?"

"Not yet."

"Where are we sitting?"

"Up there, on the side of the stage," Voight said, pointing to the raised dais that held two podiums. Three chairs were situated near the left edge of the platform.

"Are you sure we're allowed up there? On the platform with the Secretary and Minister Dutton?"

"That's where I was told we should be."

"And Fletcher?"

"I haven't seen her yet, so in the absence of any course correction from her, I'm just following orders. Anyway, we should probably get seated. They'll be getting started in a minute."

We stepped behind the red velvet cordon and walked up to our seats. "There're a lot of people here," I said, looking down into the crowd.

"Yeah. Looks like fifty or so."

"Is that Geraldo in the front row?" I asked.

"He's still alive?" Voight asked, squinting. "I'll be damned. Yeah, I think it is. Our press corps will have kittens—he's not part of our delegation. Anyway, it looks like we're about to get started."

The Secret Service agents walked in with Secretary Sidwell and Minister Dutton close behind. Both men looked agitated as they climbed the platform and took their positions behind their respective podiums.

"Ladies and gentlemen, it's been a great honor to welcome my friend, the Secretary of Defense here in London today...." I found my mind wandering as I watched Minister Dutton speak.

We've got to find a way to get Derek back in a box.

Will Fletcher fire me during, or after, this trip?

"We'll take your questions now," Secretary Sidwell said.

The journalists, quiet and demure during the speeches, were suddenly like a pack of jackals that had just been served raw red meat on a platter. Between their leaping and shouting for attention, I almost missed the new addition that had just entered the back of the room. I nudged Voight and nodded in the direction of the newcomer; in turn, Voight's eyes widened and his head snapped back as the shock registered across his body.

"What in the fresh hell?" he whispered.

"I have no idea," I whispered in return. I looked to the Minister and the Secretary just in time to witness their own "WTF?" moment.

Because there, calmly making its way down the side of the library toward the dais, was a chicken. Or, more precisely, a man dressed in a chicken costume.

"How do you think they got that in here?" Voight whispered.

"I didn't *see* a chicken walk in."

"I have absolutely no idea. It's got a pretty big head, doesn't it?"

I watched as the white-feathered bird stopped at the velvet cordon, closest to Minister Dutton. The Secret Service agents were beside themselves, unsure whether to start laughing or start worrying. The journalists, in the meantime, were torn; on the one hand, they wanted to maximize their time with the two officials speaking on the record publicly.

On the other hand, there was a chicken.

Secretary Sidwell's eyes were wide with shock as the chicken hovered near the dais. Minister Dutton evidently decided that the show must go on, and ignored the feathered intruder. He pointed to a balding, middle-aged man wearing a pinstriped suit who happened to be sitting near Geraldo.

"You, there."

"Thank you, Minister Dutton. Jake Wolfram from the *Daily Mail.*"

The *Daily Mail?* *Uh-oh,* I thought. I looked to Minister Dutton; he apparently had the same thought as I did.

"I'm actually here with our feathered friend over there," he continued. "Since you're being such a chicken about supporting our American friends on Moldova, he wants to know when you'll be coming home to the coop."

CHAPTER TWENTY-SEVEN

"IT'S TOO BAD THAT THE CHICKEN GOT KICKED OUT," VOIGHT SAID AS WE LEFT THE ROYAL UNITED SERVICES INSTITUTE AND WALKED THROUGH THE HAPHAZARDLY NARROW ALLEYS LEADING TO THE PUB WHERE THE DELEGATION WOULD CONTINUE TO MEET OVER LUNCH. "They should have let him hang around longer."

"Yeah, well, I'm not sure the Institute has much of a sense of humor," I said. "They seem like a pretty conservative bunch."

"Apparently. Still, lame," Voight said, checking his phone. "It's trending, by the way. Whatever that means."

"What is?"

"Chickengate. It's all over the news," he said, scrolling through the CNN website. "See? The article says it's 'trending' on social media.'" Voight handed me his phone.

Sure enough, #chickengate was the top trending hashtag on Twitter at that very moment. There was also a piece by Janna at CNN on exactly how much #chickengate was trending on Twitter. Thousands of people had retweeted the photo of the Minister, the Secretary, and the chicken. I looked at it more closely.

"Oh, god. We're in the picture."

"What?" Voight said.

"Right here," I said, zooming in on the photo that was bouncing all over the world as we spoke. "And my hair looks awesome," I said with a thick layer of sarcasm.

In fact, my hair looked like it had taken on a wild, weird life of its own. My curls, frizzy from the humidity, had escaped the hair tie and stuck out in every direction.

"It's not too ba—yeah, it's pretty bad," Voight said, inspecting the photo. "But, whatever. Anything from Pumpkin?"

"Nothing yet, I said. I just tried calling, no answer. Do you think the Brits are going to come around?"

"Well, reading the dynamics in the room during our meeting earlier, I'm not sure anyone besides the Prime Minister knows what Britain is going to do."

"Quite right," Colin said, appearing out of nowhere. "Unless your boss makes a more compelling case, I'd suggest that this trip might end badly for you lot. That said, bringing up the French? That just *might* have done it."

"This is going to be an awkward lunch, then," I said.

"Undoubtedly. Which, by the way, is the worst thing in the world for us Brits."

"Lunch?" Voight asked.

"Awkwardness," Colin said.

I felt my phone buzz.

"Oh, great," I said, scrolling through my phone. "My mom just emailed. She's seen the #chickengate photo too."

"Well, that's not the worst way for her to find out that you're on a SecDef trip, I guess?" Voight said.

I nodded. "She's not too thrilled that I'm out of the country. And she's underwhelmed by the fact that my hair looks like a poodle."

We turned a corner, and lo and behold, the chicken was standing on the opposite side of the road, head balanced on the wall he was leaning against, smoking a cigarette.

"I'll catch up with you," Voight said, and then dashed off toward the chicken.

I nervously checked my email again as we walked—still no word from Pumpkin. There was nothing I could do, of course. But that didn't stop me from fretting, wishing that there were some way I could put together the map by myself. But I couldn't. How was I going to recover with Fletcher? It seemed to me like Fletcher was getting worked up about fairly petty minutiae, getting unhinged about stuff that in the long run didn't matter, and placing my sanity and Voight's in serious jeopardy as she did so. But she was the boss. On some level, I figured, it didn't really matter whether Fletcher was right or wrong to demand the impossible. It was just a fact of life.

We entered a pub called The Ship. It was dingy, with wood paneling and an oak bar situated to the side. Maritime paintings and horse brass decorated the walls, making it feel as if they'd been magically transported out of London and into an *actual* country village pub. The smell of fish and chips in the air sparked hunger pangs in my stomach. I sat down at a table with Colin and prepared to eat my pain away.

"Heather! Come here," Fletcher commanded, beckoning me from a few feet away.

I excused myself, then stood up and walked over to Fletcher.

"What, exactly are you doing?" Fletcher asked.

"I was just—"

"What makes you think you have time to sit here? Why aren't you tippy-tapping at the keyboard right now? You have cables to write. And my map to track down. Your job isn't done, not by a long stretch."

Why does she keep referring to 'tippy-tapping' at the keyboard? "Ma'am, I thought—"

"You thought wrong," Fletcher said. "Once again, you're displaying remarkably poor judgment—"

"Excuse me?" interrupted a rather flustered young man—who couldn't be a day over twenty-two. Had he any idea who Ariane Fletcher was, he would have waited for her to finish dressing me down before interrupting. But, fortunately for me, he didn't recognize Fletcher in the slightest. "Is either of you Dr. Heather Reilly?" he asked.

"I am," I said, stepping forward.

"I'm from the Embassy," he said. "This is for you." He held out a manila envelope.

"Thanks," I said, taking the package from him. Relief poured through me as I opened it up. *Pumpkin came through,* I thought, as I pulled out a note on top of the dossier of documents. It was from Raffaello at the State Department.

Dear Heather,

Requested documents, including map, enclosed. We scrubbed them so they're unclassified, but they should provide what you need for now.

Just so you know, we've gone through hell to get this to you. You've got some powerfully tenacious friends on your side.

Regards,
Raffaello

I felt chagrined by Raffaello's note, but there really wasn't anything that could be done about it. I was just doing what my boss asked of me, and I'd just have to owe Raffaello—and Pumpkin—a beer. Or twelve. I squared my shoulders and turned to Fletcher.

"Here's what you asked for, ma'am."

Fletcher took the papers from me without batting an eye. "Thanks," Fletcher said, before returning to her normal state of frenzied terribleness. "You're not off the hook, though. You need to get to writing the cable. When does Minister Dutton get here?"

"Any minute now."

Fletcher walked away and sat herself next to Secretary Sidwell, who was enjoying a well-deserved pint with Jeremy while waiting for Dutton.

I grabbed my bag from the chair and turned to leave the pub. I'd just about made it out the door, when I ran into Voight.

"Where are you going?"

"Back to the hotel," I said. My voice warbled with frustration.

"Didn't you just deliver the package that Fletcher wanted?"

"Yes. But Fletcher wants me to work on the cable."

"Bullshit. You're going to sit here and get something to eat. And *then* we'll go back to the hotel and work on the cable. Together." He eyed the table where Fletcher was seated. "Besides, she's so happy to be sitting with the Secretary, she won't notice that we're here if we sit in the corner."

"Voight, I'm tired of catching hell from her."

"We have to draw a line somewhere."

"And that line is lunch?"

"As a matter of fact, yes."

"I'm already skating on very thin ice with her," I said. "She's got her sights set on me, and I think she's looking for any reason to get rid of me."

"Well, you know what? Let her."

"Excuse me?" I said, shocked.

"I said, let her. If you get fired, so what? After this trip—and after impressing Secretary Sidwell as much as you have—you'll land on your feet somewhere. You'll be okay."

I had my doubts about that. But then again, I was in London and I really didn't want to pass on no-kidding, authentic fish and chips. So I stayed, promising myself that I would leave the pub and get back to the hotel before the rest of the delegation.

"Where'd you go, by the way?" I asked, changing the subject.

"To talk to the chicken. And then make a phone call—checking in on Jamie. Couldn't get through to her, but she's probably on a ride or something with the kids." Something about the tone in his voice made me think that something was wrong.

"Everything okay?" I asked.

"Yep, everything's fine." I could tell he was lying, but this didn't seem like the time to push it.

Although we were in a corner, from our vantage point we had a direct view of Fletcher and the Secretary as we ate our fish and chips. It was perfectly fried, with the right amount of crispy batter to take on the salt and vinegar. My mood improved. Yes, I might work for a psycho. But at least I was in London—if briefly—having proper pub food, and watching the psycho-in-question use the materials I'd been able to deliver to brief the Secretary.

Eventually, Minister Dutton walked in and ordered a pint of ale before sitting near Secretary Sidwell. It was only one in the afternoon, but Dutton looked absolutely exhausted, as if he'd stayed up for three nights and then gotten into a brawl.

All eyes in the room were on their table.

"All right, Edwin," Dutton announced. "I've just gotten done with speaking to Number 10. Let's just work this out, the two of us, shall we?"

"Certainly, Des," the Secretary said, dismissing Fletcher, who moved to sit at the next table with Jeremy. I noticed Fletcher left the manila envelope on the table with Secretary Sidwell.

With that, all of us in the rest of the room turned to our colleagues at our tables in order to give the principals some space amid the crowd. The two leaders huddled over their pints, and eventually fish and chips, talking quietly about a way forward, and occasionally referring to the materials in the envelope. Frustration gave way to satisfaction, which gave way to laughter as they hashed out a workable solution for both countries.

"And that, Heather, is proof," Voight said as we walked through the drizzle back to our hotel ahead of the rest of the delegation.

"That beer was invented by God himself?"

"Exactly," Voight smiled. "We just watched its magical hoppy goodness prevent a full-blown diplomatic incident."

After what I'd just witnessed, I couldn't argue with that.

"Oh, and I heard from Derek at the NSC," Voight continued. "He's *pissed.*"

"Again? Why now?"

"Besides the fact that Moldova is now on? He blames Fletcher for Chickengate. If we'd just gone along with his initial Georgia plan, the Secretary wouldn't have been embarrassed like this. Or so he says."

"Huh. That seems like…like he's grasping."

"Of course he is. He's getting boxed into a corner. The only question is whether he's going to take down this ship as he sinks."

My phone buzzed. It was a message from Amanda.

"Senator McClutchy is calling for a hearing on Tuesday, and the Senate Armed Services Committee chairman agreed to hold it," I said. "Status of Moldova. He's asking SecDef to testify."

"There goes our weekend," Voight said, frustrated.

"Why's that? Can't we get the testimony squared away tomorrow?"

"Sure, if it wasn't for Fletcher. But she's aiming for the ASD position, right? She'll have to be confirmed by the Senate. Which means that the hearing is going to have to go perfectly—otherwise Derek is going to have good reason to scuttle her nomination. In other words, she's going to freak the hell out."

"When *isn't* she freaking out?" I rubbed the bridge of my nose in frustration. "Can we go home yet?"

"Soon." As we approached the hotel, we could see the motorcade and Staff Van Two getting into position, readying to whisk us back to the Secretary's plane.

"We're almost back to Kansas, Dorothy," Voight continued. "Just hang on a little longer."

CHAPTER TWENTY-EIGHT

THE SKY WAS ALREADY A DARK GREY BY THE TIME I ARRIVED AT THE CAPITOL HILL COMPLEX. It turned out that the Secretary's staff had made the right call on canceling the trip; the tropical storm they'd been tracking had been upgraded to a category-four hurricane the night before. People across the Washington metropolitan area were taking care of their last bits of business—whether it be buying milk and toilet paper or conducting hearings on Moldova—before the early September storm hit.

I walked over to Amanda; she was waiting for me at the entrance of the Dirksen Senate Office Building. She was a welcome sight—a relief from the stress and self-inflicted chaos on the other side of the river.

"So how are you?" Amanda said as we walked through the brass doors of the building. "It seems like it's been days since I've seen you!"

We walked past greyish marble edifices and brass-door elevators, ostensibly designed to convey an impressive aesthetic. Instead, the low ceilings and polished concrete floors conveyed the impression that the place was squat. Sturdy. If the Capitol Building itself was a graceful ballet dancer, the Dirksen Building was a rough-and-tumble wrestler that was spoiling for a fight.

"It's been a rough couple of days," I said. "Being at the office pretty much nonstop since we got back from London? It pretty much sucks. You wouldn't believe the hoops I had to jump through to get you the key points from the Secretary's testimony so you could prep McClutchy."

"I can only imagine," Amanda said, sympathetically.

"On the plus side, Secretary Sidwell gave us his own personal challenge coin on the flight back. So, there's that."

"Wow, that's a real token of honor."

"Yeah. I never realized what a commodity those things are in military circles. The more you have, the better. Voight has dozens of them."

"Well, that's nice that you got a coin, but does that make up for the long hours you've been putting in?"

"Not really. But I tell myself otherwise."

The weekend had truly been an ordeal, especially since Voight wasn't around. I'd told him to get on a plane to Disney World to meet his family as soon as we landed back at Andrews. He'd halfheartedly pushed back before heading for the hills, but I had insisted.

"Changing the subject, have you heard anything more from Mr. Right Now?" Amanda asked, teasingly.

"You mean Matt? The fling?"

"That's the one."

I thought about my near-disastrous escapade in Fletcher's office and felt a little nauseous. But now wasn't the time to bring up the gory details.

"Yeah, I saw him briefly in the Pentagon. But we haven't really spoken since I left for London."

"Well, that's the good news about flings—you can fling them away from you when you want. Any more news from Ryan?"

"No."

"Nothing? Not a word?"

"Zilch. Is it weird that I feel a little angry that he hasn't bothered to reach out?"

"It's not weird at all, Heather. You guys were together for ten years. Have you reached out to him?"

"No," I admitted.

"Well, for whatever it's worth, he's probably pretty hurt too. It's probably good that you guys aren't in contact. It'll help both of you move on."

We turned a corner and entered the Hart Building. It, too, was different. Quiet. Tall, white pillars framed massive interior courtyards that were surrounded by senatorial offices that climbed at least six stories. We rounded another corner to enter the Senate Armed Services Committee's main hearing room.

"It's amazing," Amanda said. "All this over Moldova?"

"Well, it would all probably be slightly saner if we didn't have to contend with Fletcher's freak-outs. They're now happening every two hours, like clockwork. Voight thinks it's because she's hoping for the nod for the ASD position."

"Ah. That makes sense."

"By the way, quick question: Did anything change overnight on your end?"

"I don't think so," Amanda answered. "McClutchy's book is prepped, and so is the Secretary's. I think we've both covered all the bases."

We arrived at the hearing room for the Senate Armed Services Committee and parted ways. While I took a seat two rows back from the Secretary, Amanda took her place on the dais, behind McClutchy's placard. We both watched from opposite sides of the room—and, effectively, opposite sides of the U.S. government—as journalists set up their cameras and interns helped guide people to their seats. Senators began meandering in from a door behind the dais—first McCain while talking to Cotton, then Kaine, and then McCaskill.

Secretary Sidwell walked in, with General Park and Jeremy. Fletcher was not far behind them. Secretary Sidwell sat at the witness table; the other three of them sat directly behind the Secretary, prepared to support him in case he wanted more information, or coffee, or a stiff martini, depending on how the hearing went.

"Good morning, ma'am," I said, as Fletcher sat in front of me.

"Good morning. You've got your briefing book?"

"Right here," I said, holding up the four-inch binder that now contained information on Iranian Revolutionary Guard positions across the Middle East.

Senator McClutchy walked in, and the hearing started. He made some introductory remarks, and then turned the floor over to Secretary Sidwell. The Secretary, in turn, made his points about Moldova. About how the international community needed to stand up to Russian aggression. That the Moldova strategy was the best way to ensure that Moscow knew it couldn't play great games, slicing up the territory of its neighbors when it felt like doing so. That involvement in Moldova was preventive.

The Secretary then turned to his points about his U.K. trip. How the Brits were joining us, as were a number of countries from across the Middle East. And how the U.S. would authorize additional weapons sales to its Gulf Arab allies should Russia continue sending arms and equipment to Iran. If Russia wanted to use the Moldova mission as a pretext for arming the Iranians, the U.S. could play at that game too. We had options, and the Secretary and the President were not afraid to use them.

As I watched the various senators nod their heads, I realized that on balance, the hearing was going really well.

After the Secretary's testimony, the questioning went in a number of different directions. Some senators asked about the latest, most-expensive-in-history fighter aircraft that was widely viewed as a debacle; others asked about plans to consolidate or close military bases. Senator McCain asked about Russia's dangerous nuclear rhetoric; Sidwell responded, saying that we shouldn't allow ourselves to be intimidated by a nuclear bully, especially when there were countries in the region like Moldova that wanted a chance to determine their own path, without Moscow's interference.

Eventually, it was Senator McClutchy's turn to ask questions.

"Secretary Sidwell, thank you for sharing with us these insights on how the Department of Defense is going about doing its duties. This has been a very informative exchange for all of us."

"Thank you, Senator McClutchy."

"And I am particularly gratified that you have been able to assemble a coalition to support us in Moldova. This is excellent news, as I understand it was a critical component of your overall strategy."

"Yes, that's the case," said the Secretary.

"I just have one final question about your priorities, and whether they are being directed in the right manner."

"Excuse me?" Sidwell asked.

"Well, you see, while you've been focusing on Moldova, the situation in Afghanistan has deteriorated considerably. Wouldn't you agree?"

"Yes, I would agree."

I put my pen down and instinctively leaned in, as if doing so would allow me to better hear the exchange.

"And Afghanistan is a deeply unstable country. It's a country—it's a region—that we have spent a lot of blood and treasure trying to rescue from itself over the years. And we appear to be abandoning it to its own devices. We don't even have much in the way of intelligence assets positioned there any longer. So while I understand you're prioritizing Moldova, I don't understand why you're dropping the ball on Afghanistan."

Senator McClutchy's arguments were beginning to sound eerily familiar to me. Like they were derived from my own email on Afghanistan that I'd bootlegged Amanda.

I looked at Amanda. Something was wrong. Her face had gone white, her lips were pursed, and she was biting the bottom of her cheek.

I began to panic. Something was definitely wrong.

"Senator, we developed a drawdown strategy that allows the Afghans to take responsibility for their own security," Secretary Sidwell said. "It's hard to see what impact we would have had if we maintained a more robust presence in the region."

"Let's speak candidly, Secretary Sidwell. You don't believe that. Your staff doesn't even believe that."

"Excuse me?"

"I have the email right here," Senator McClutchy waived it in the air. "Written by a woman by the name of—let me just check here—Dr. Heather Reilly."

I don't remember the rest of the hearing. I was in too much shock. Because the moment Senator McClutchy said my name, I knew how the rest of my hour, day, week, month, year would play out. There would be castigation, and then my resignation, and then finally my relocation out of D.C. I felt a brief stab of nausea and shock and betrayal.

Amanda said she wouldn't share my memo, I thought, just before the numbness set in.

It started with the Secretary's staff looking back, staring at me in surprise, at the mention of my name. Furious did not begin to describe Fletcher's expression.

The castigation started immediately following the hearing. Fletcher pulled me into the hallway outside to scold me as other members of the audience shuffled out of the hearing room. Passersby turned their heads and stared as Fletcher used phrases like "undermining the Secretary" and "violating protocol" and "think about your future in policy" while pointing out that I had lied to her about sending out the email.

I said nothing. I just stood there and took it, admitting I'd messed up. Part of me wanted to cry, but that would mean allowing myself to feel the body blows I was sustaining. So, instead, I let my body and mind shut down. I would reel from the hits later.

Fletcher left. Amanda approached me, tears welling in her eyes and muttering apologies. I watched her mouth make the words, but they didn't resonate. They didn't connect.

"Aren't you going to say something?" Amanda asked.

"I thought you were going to keep the email close hold?" I asked.

"I was—I did. But things at the office—I never imagined he would do that—"

"I don't think I have a job anymore."

Amanda looked at me; tears were in her eyes.

"I think I'd better get home and pack."

I could feel the rain sprinkling on my face and hands as I stepped out of the Southwest D.C. Metro. The clouds were dark with bellies full of rain and the wind was picking up. Gusts were blowing hard enough to show the silver undersides of the maple leaves, and, occasionally, nudge me forward as I briskly walked toward the apartment.

I don't have an umbrella, I thought. A rookie move, again. But that hardly seemed to matter.

It looked like a typical afternoon storm—so common at that time of year in Washington. Normally, they would blow out as quickly as they'd blown in, dropping buckets of rain and giving the ground a reprieve from the sweltering heat. But this was the beginning of a hurricane. And as the lightning crashed overhead and the sky turned an eerie pinky-purplish color, it looked to me like Hurricane Josephine really had picked up steam in the past twenty-four hours. It was going to be particularly fierce. This was the kind of weather that tore apart trees, flooded roads, and left thousands without power in their homes. I started sprinting toward the apartment—this was not a storm I wanted to get caught in.

With about a block further to go, the heavens opened in sheets of brutally heavy rain. As I wiped my sticky wet hair from my eyes, I could feel little pinpricks of hail as they pelted my head and face. Within a matter of seconds, the sidewalk became a river, forcing me to slosh the remaining hundred feet home.

I was drenched by the time I entered the apartment. I stripped off my clothes, hung them in the bathroom, and then grabbed some sleeping pills from the medicine cabinet. I took three with a glass of water, put my phone on airplane mode, and then let the blackness of induced sleep take me away.

I woke up in the middle of the night. I took another three pills and went back to sleep.

The slam of a branch at my window woke me up the next day. The storm was raging. I checked the time on my phone; it was just after ten in the morning. I couldn't bring myself to panic about being late for work, especially because the federal government was probably shut down due to the weather. And especially because it didn't really matter if it wasn't shut down; I wouldn't have a job in the government for much longer anyway.

I rolled over and went back to sleep.

The next time I woke, I found a sandwich next to my bed, along with a glass of water. I wasn't hungry, but drank the glass of water in a series of swift gulps. I checked the time: It was one thirty.

I was done wallowing. It was time to rip off the Band-Aid and finally face whatever was in store for me in my inbox. I turned off airplane mode.

There were ten voicemails and over a hundred emails waiting for me. I wasn't surprised at the volume. A fuck up of that magnitude was usually followed by a shitstorm that rivaled the hurricane currently battering the D.C. metropolitan area.

I took a closer look. The first emails were from Voight. He saw the hearing. He was worried.

Ryan also sent a message earlier in the day, saying that he was flying to D.C. and wanted to meet me. The earliest flight he could catch was Thursday afternoon—less than twenty-four hours away. *Why is he coming out here? Did he hear what happened? What does he want?* Part of me felt curiously relieved. *Maybe I could go back to my old life?*

Then there was a request from Fletcher to see the email that I'd bootlegged to Amanda a couple weeks ago, followed by more emails from people I'd never heard of asking for it. And then I saw a note from Pumpkin, requesting my presence at a meeting down in the NMCC that took place two hours prior.

I was confused. Was this some sort of inquisition?

I heard a knock at the door.

"Are you awake, Heather?" Amanda asked.

"Not really," I said, groggily.

She opened my door. Dark circles surrounded her bloodshot eyes.

"Look, I don't want to talk about it right now," I said. "I'll start packing tonight—"

Amanda interrupted. "I've been running interference for you for the past hour or so. I've told them you are sick. But they're getting insistent. And I think I now know why. The story just aired five minutes ago. Come downstairs. There's something you need to see."

Something in the tone of Amanda's voice made me sit up. I followed her downstairs to the living room, where the TV was switched on to CNN.

"The news just came in," Amanda said, studying the screen. "There have been attacks."

"Attacks?" I said, looking at the TV. Images of smoke and blood and bodies of school children assaulted the screen. Suddenly, a familiar reporter's face appeared; Janna was briefing from somewhere near the Pentagon press room.

"We are getting reports of multiple, coordinated attacks on American schools around the world. Britain, Switzerland, Saudi Arabia, all experienced massive explosions about half an hour ago. We don't know the full extent of the damage, but all are reporting significant casualties."

The camera returned to Wolf Blitzer. "In all my years, this is probably one of the most horrific attacks I've ever witnessed."

"Indeed, Wolf. What makes this attack particularly insidious is the fact that these are the children of diplomats from around the world, including the United States. They struck at the heart of the

U.S. diplomatic service—and at the hearts of many governments worldwide."

"Do we know if anyone is claiming any responsibility?" Wolf said.

"Yes, Wolf. The Islamic State in Khorasan—Afghanistan—is claiming responsibility."

Oh no, I thought, as I sank into the couch. A tear slipped from my eye as I watched a child, no more than eight years old, crying and holding his bloodied arm.

"I think this is why they've been asking for you," Amanda said.

I looked up at Amanda, quizzically.

"You were right about Afghanistan," Amanda said. "Your email was *right*. And because Senator McClutchy broadcast your conclusions during the hearing, the entire Pentagon knows it."

Amanda handed me a cup of coffee.

"Your entire career has built to *this* moment, Dr. Reilly. It's time for you to get back in the game."

CHAPTER TWENTY-NINE

THE STORM LOOKED LIKE IT WAS BREAKING AS I WALKED INTO THE PENTAGON.

My heels clicked and clacked as I walked through the corridors; it was the same distance I covered every other day of the week, but somehow time stretched itself.

Ryan texted me to make sure I was okay, and to tell me that flights were still running despite the attack—although security was extremely tight. I let him know I was fine, and then refreshed Twitter.

The news kept getting worse.

Another series of bombs had gone off, this time attacking the first responders who had come to rescue the children and teachers of the American schools.

It was chaos.

The Islamic State issued a message that the attacks were revenge for ruining the lives of their children through airstrikes and drone strikes and Western moral corruption.

Over one hundred fifty children were now dead.

I couldn't tell if it took me seconds or hours to get to my office. And while I had no idea what I was about to face, for once that was okay. I felt strangely calm. A calm that was born more from determination than from paralyzing fear. There are moments in life when you can feel something momentous is about to occur. For good or bad, better or worse, the universe is about to shuffle the deck, and the cards will lie where they fall. And, either way, life will never be the same again.

This felt like one of those moments.

But first things first. Fletcher wanted to meet with me. And if Fletcher wanted to take me out of the game, I'd find another way to help.

I squared my shoulders as I knocked on Fletcher's door.

"Yes?" Fletcher's voice echoed through the doorway.

"You wanted to see me, ma'am?"

"Ah. Heather. Yes. Come in and close the door."

I shut the door, sat on the couch, and watched as Fletcher finished an email. Her TV, on mute, blasted more scenes of the attacks. I could feel my pulse pounding with every second as the wait got more and more excruciating. I wished that she would just get it over with. Whatever the outcome, after this conversation I'd be able to figure out my next move.

Eventually, Fletcher calmly stood up from her desk and sat in the leather seat next to the couch.

"There's a lot going on right now, so I'll be brief. I understand the Joint Staff wants you to join them for their planning meeting right now."

"Yes, that's correct."

"This is exactly why we need to talk. You have consistently demonstrated poor judgment, Heather. Making the wrong decisions, preparing atrocious packages for the Secretary, and stepping out well beyond your place as an Action Officer."

"But, ma'am—"

"Your ill-thought-through comments during the Secretary's pre-brief on the plane, as well as your ham-fisted memos, caused a huge uproar here in the building. It's taken a lot of my time and energy to smooth all the feathers you've ruffled around here."

"I'm sorry, ma'am, but I was just—"

"In fact, you're just as bad as I was when I first joined the Pentagon, years ago."

Wait. What?

"Heather, make no mistake. It's a man's world, particularly here in the Pentagon. This building will eat you alive and spit you out if you're not tough."

I was genuinely confused.

"I'm sorry; I don't quite understand what you're getting at. I thought you were firing me."

"And if I chose to do that, I'd have good reason."

Has Fletcher been hazing me this entire time?

"But you're learning and growing from your mistakes, Heather," Fletcher continued. "And while I'm disappointed you lied to me about your email, I'm not stupid. I know why you did that. I can be extremely aggressive. But that's because I want excellence for our organization. It may seem like the men and women in uniform are far away, but they depend on us making the right strategic choices."

Pigs flying. Gravity taking a holiday. The four horsemen of the apocalypse marching through the corridors of the Pentagon alongside the Army and Navy bands. All of these things were higher on my "list of things that might probably occur in the universe" than what was taking place in Fletcher's office at that very moment.

"I hope you know I've been tough on you in order to make you stronger," Fletcher continued. "Women are held to different standards than men. I didn't get to where I am today without being tougher than all the men around me. But, of course, when a woman is tough, she's seen as bitchy. Demanding. It's not fair, but that's the way it is. I know I've pushed you guys to your limit. But I haven't done anything that I haven't had done to me, or seen my male colleagues do to their teams. And I've done so because at any moment, the United States might have to go to war, and we've needed to deliver the best possible work to the Secretary under extreme pressure. Which brings us to the here and now. Royle shared your background with me. About your brother, Jon. He tells me that you're in this business to serve men and women in uniform like him. I like that about you."

Why would Royle be talking about me? Besides, I thought Royle didn't want to know anything about Jon. Maybe Amanda told him? *But I thought they just had a one-night stand or something. Maybe it was more?* I wondered. I shook my head. There was too much going on at that moment to put the pieces together. I'd figure it all out later.

"And that, plus the fact that you didn't flinch, or make excuses, when I called you out the other day after the hearing tells me that you're the right person."

"For what?"

"To be my lead—to be policy's lead—on Afghanistan."

"You're not firing me?"

"No, Heather. I'm promoting you."

I blinked, taking in this stunning turn of events.

"What about Moldova?" I asked.

"Moldova is a lesser priority. For now."

"I see." I looked back at her TV screen. At the innocent children that were victims of the atrocity. My anger and outrage cooled themselves into a resolve of steel.

"I'd be honored, ma'am. When do I start?"

"Now. Your meeting with the Joint Staff is in ten minutes."

The NMCC's conference room was completely full by the time I arrived. On the periphery of a massive briefing screen were windows with CNN, NBC, Al Jazeera, and Fox News, all reporting the devastation. Janna was still on the air. Everyone was quiet, watching the horror unfold: screaming, bloodied children and their parents helpless to protect them.

At least ten American schools across Europe, the Middle East, and South Asia had been bombed. Some were mobbed as well. Casualties mounted, as did outpourings of grief around the globe. It would take days to sort through the rubble and identify all the bodies.

A man holding a rifle described the attacks, and why they were perpetrated, in a grainy video published by the Islamic State of Khorasan.

I took a seat in the back of the room, next to Pumpkin. Perhaps unsurprisingly, Colin was there. He gave me a quick wave "hello" from across the room. Generals from Australia, Canada, and Britain sat at the table, along with their counterparts from the U.S.

Navy, Air Force, Army, and Marine Corps. The shockwaves of the day's attacks were reverberating around the world, and America's closest allies were unquestionably, unwaveringly, there to support.

Matt was in the far corner of the room. I grimaced a tight "hello" to him, and he waved back. We both knew that this was neither the time, nor the place, to be distracted by our personal drama.

Before long, a question nagged at me.

"Pumpkin, can I ask you something? Why do you guys want me here? Aren't you supposed to be keeping policy away from meetings like this?"

"I told you. We run interference on things that *don't* matter."

"And?"

"This matters," Pumpkin said. "Time to up our A-game."

I pursed my lips. "Right. By the way, I've been meaning to thank you—"

"Dr. Reilly?" interrupted a familiar voice. It was Royle.

Unlike the last time I saw him, when by comparison he looked more haggard and worn, this time he had a nervous energy. Adrenaline was coursing through him. He no longer looked lost; he looked like a man with a purpose.

"Yes, Colonel Royle?"

"I believe your seat is at the table," he said, pointing to a chair two away from the center. A placard with my name rested at the edge of the table.

"Right. I just wanted to say hi to Pumpkin," I said, trying to cover my shock. I moved to the table, then pulled out my notebook and waited for the meeting to begin.

A minute or so passed before a three-star admiral—Admiral Stammer, I noticed from his nametag—entered the room.

Everyone stood, including me. Stammer waved everybody back into their seats.

"Let's do this, ladies and gents," he said.

"Right, sir," Royle said, getting down to business. "As you know, parts of Afghanistan—the south, under the control of ISOK—were used as a staging ground for the terror attacks today."

"ISOK?" the admiral asked.

"The Islamic State of Khorasan. The Islamic State's franchise in Afghanistan and parts of Pakistan."

"What the hell has been going on over there?" the admiral asked.

"Unfortunately, we diverted assets away from that area in the past two years, and most recently because of the Moldova issue. So we're still building our intel picture."

"What *do* we know?"

"Sir, I'm not qualified to give you the overall political picture," Royle said. "But we happen to have Dr. Reilly here, who knows quite a lot about Afghanistan."

"Dr. Reilly, would you care to share your assessment of the region?" the admiral asked.

Every eye in the room focused on me. I took a deep breath to steady my nerves—to sift through the hundreds of hours of research I'd done on the region in order to identify the things that no-kidding mattered. *Game time.*

"Sir, the region is endlessly complicated, with thousands of years of tribalism preceding decades of exceedingly brutal conflict. I don't want to bog you down with details, but I'm happy to go into them if you'd like. With that in mind, there are four things you need to know.

"Since we withdrew from Afghanistan, the government has been run by a somewhat competent, although fairly corrupt, politician named Zalmay Popal. His deputy, Atal Popal, was known for getting the job done. But Atal didn't have enough power. It wasn't long before Zalmay came under attack for being unfair, corrupt, and predatory toward the Afghan people. Crucially, it became difficult to resolve disputes as government judges were paid off by higher authorities. The local tribes became angry and wanted a government that would keep them safe and be fair arbiters of quarrels."

"You're saying they wanted fair courts and basic safety?" the admiral asked.

"Yes, sir," I said. "Which leads to my next point. Judicial fairness took priority over moderation. Which created a window for the Islamic State to take control. It started about a year ago—Islamic State clerics would turn up in local villages with a Koran and listen to local cases. And then make a swift judgment based on available facts. Punishments were sometimes brutal, but according to the locals, they were fair because the clerics wouldn't take bribes."

"I think I'm tracking," the admiral said.

"Right. Once the Islamic State ran the *de facto* court system, they were in place to challenge the Popal government. Which they did. And they had local Afghan support."

"So the entire country is radicalized?"

"No. Once the Islamic State thugs consolidated their control, they became unhinged. It was almost as if they wanted to prove how utterly brutal they could be. They make those folks in Iraq and Syria look like pansies by comparison. They crucified—literally—any of their opposition, and executed any Shia Muslims who happened to live there. Needless to say, the local Pashtun Afghans got more than they bargained for. The Islamic State has become like a cancer to the Pashtuns, eating them alive from the inside."

"Dr. Reilly, do you think the Islamic State could pull something like this off?" the admiral said, pointing to the television screens.

I frowned. "They certainly have the intention—these guys have a 'bring on the apocalypse' philosophy. And they certainly don't like the U.S. very much after we droned the hell out of them. The capability? Numerous camps have been reported, where the Islamic State has been training as many people as possible to wage global jihad. But the scale of these attacks? Probably not without some outside support. Unfortunately, there's plenty of that. Wealthy oligarchs from across the Middle East—Syria, Iraq, Yemen—tend to fund these guys."

"Sir," interrupted Royle, "what Dr. Reilly is saying tracks with what we've learned through our British colleagues."

A Chief Petty Officer abruptly entered the room, carrying a piece of paper. He handed it to the admiral and then scurried out. Stammer read the note.

"Ladies and gents, I regret to tell you that it appears that, as tragic as today's events have already been, they're about to get worse. There's no easy way to say this. Several of our diplomatic compounds across the Middle East have just been shelled with what appear to be chemical weapons. It hasn't yet hit the airwaves, but it's only a matter of time."

The room went silent. Admiral Stammer set down the paper, but remained quiet as well. At first, I thought he was pausing for reflection. But as I studied him, I saw he was shaking, ever so slightly. He wasn't pausing for reflection, I realized. He was trying to contain his rage.

Eventually, he spoke. "They have attacked our families. Our innocents. And we don't know a goddamned thing about that area—besides what's in Dr. Reilly's head—because we've been so busy spinning up on Moldova, of all fucking things." He pounded his fist on the table. After a moment, he said, "I'm sorry, Royle. Please continue."

"We are pretty sure we know where the attack was staged." Royle clicked a button in his hand and flipped through several briefing slides before settling on a map of Afghanistan and Pakistan. He pointed to an area toward the bottom right of the map. "Here, in Kandahar, is where they're headquartered."

"WMDs?"

"Probably chems. There may also be dumping grounds for radiological debris dotted across the country. You're shaking your head, Dr. Reilly."

I hadn't realized I was physically expressing my disbelief.

"Sorry. I agree with you on radiological dumping grounds. But chemical weapons? They may have some kind of stockpile rotting somewhere. But the kind of chems that they could mortar our consulates with? Those would have to have come from somewhere else. Like, Syria, for example."

"So all this points to external support for these radicals in Afghanistan."

"Yes, sir," Royle said. "Which brings us to the here and now. POTUS has asked for military options. What we've developed so far focuses on eliminating the terror camps in Afghanistan while sending a signal to the rest of the world that the United States will not tolerate state sponsorship of terrorism.

"There are basically three different strike packages. The first is to take care of the objectives through drone strikes. While there would be minimal risk to our troops—we wouldn't be putting boots on the ground, after all—what would be at risk is our ability to achieve the mission. Without some human presence on the ground, it will be difficult to determine whether there are any targets that we've missed."

"Not to mention the fact that part of the reason we're in this mess is because of drone strikes in the first place," the admiral added.

"Right," Royle agreed. "Though drones are precision weapons, the risk of collateral damage is high, particularly since the camps and storage depots for radiological materials appear to be in and around Kandahar, which has about half a million people.

"The second option is to send in Special Forces teams to comb through Southern Afghanistan after air strikes take out the major sites. While there would be a higher chance of mission success— we would have hands-on knowledge of whether we took down all the critical targets—the risk is that we would lose some guys to urban fighting in Kandahar. And, as you know, sir, urban fighting is always extremely challenging."

"What's the third option?"

"Roughly the same as the second, but utilizing either the Marines or Army rather than Special Forces. They would deploy at least a battalion-sized element, if not a brigade. That's anywhere from one to three thousand troops. So there would be strength in numbers, of course. Quantity has its own quality after all, and both the Marines and Army have been training to do urban operations."

"Will we have coalition support?" Admiral Stammer said, looking at the foreign officers in the room.

"Admiral, you guys could decide to invade the moon, and we'd be right there behind you," an Australian officer said.

"Dr. Reilly, what do you think?"

I was about to speak, but before the words were about to leave my mouth, I thought I saw Jon out of the corner of my eye. I turned to face where he was, but he was gone. It must have been my imagination. But imagination or not, it was still enough to remind me of the stakes at play. I thought about his grave in Arlington, surrounded by so many other white marble tombstones laid out in their final, precise formation. I thought about my anger and rage and confusion and pain that filled the Jon-shaped hole in my life after he left. I thought about those tear-filled nights with Amanda, hugging each other tightly, knowing that those hugs were the closest we'd ever get to being with Jon again.

Would it be better to let the Afghans fight it out for themselves? To walk away, but prevent the loss of U.S. service members' lives? Or would inaction bring its own set of further, terrible consequences?

I thought about the day I met Ryan, all those years ago. About the protests we'd attended together; about all our late-night chats over coffee and vegan biscotti about U.S. foreign policy and warmongering and how violence was never the answer.

What would Jon want? I wondered.

And then I decided to speak from my gut.

"Frankly, I think they're all bad options," I said.

"Why do you say that, Dr. Reilly?" asked the admiral, surprised.

"Well, first off, this is eerily similar to what we did after 9/11, which kicked off a series of events that led us into this mess. But second, I mean there's a total absence of strategic planning, as well as post-operation planning for this. Not to mention a plan for working with the Afghans—and after we left last time, it's not going to be easy to rebuild their trust. I mean, the Islamic State is awful, of course. But if we're not careful as to how we go about this, we may end up deposing the Afghan government, only to find that they're replaced with even *worse,* even more radical, thugs. We might get some short-term wins, but make the whole region much, much worse in the long run. And without a broader strategy, it's hard to describe these options as doing anything more than playing 'whack-a-mole.'"

"So you think we shouldn't go to war over this?" the admiral asked.

I hesitated, then made my decision. Saying the next few words would be physically painful, but they had to be said.

"Sir, that's not it. If we don't strike back—and strike hard—these radicals are going to learn the wrong lessons: that they can get away with murdering our people. And if we leave Afghanistan alone, they'll only get worse. The Islamic State is a disease that will bring the entire region down."

"I'm not tracking, Dr. Reilly. What are you saying?"

"Our military strategy needs to be integrated with a political one. My thought would be to find a way to support Atal Popal, assuming the Afghans want that, of course. To bring him into power after eliminating the hardcore Islamic State guys, and reconciling the more moderate ones."

"Talk to these terrorists? Are you kidding?"

"They're not all terrorists. And if we're going to make Afghanistan stable, we're going to have to bring as many people as possible into the tent."

The admiral nodded.

"Colonel Royle, please make sure you incorporate Dr. Reilly's thoughts into the courses of action you develop for the president. Coordinate it with State. Whatever the president decides to do, make no mistake: We are going to make those sons of bitches pay for what they did to us."

Stammer stood up; we all stood with him. The room felt heavy, as if its gravity had increased and weighed heavily on everyone.

"Now let's get to work," he said, and then walked out of the room. Everyone else gathered their things and made their way back to their desks as quickly as possible.

I was halfway back to my office when Pumpkin caught up to me.

"Dr. Reilly?"

"Pumpkin, call me Heather."

"Sorry. Heather. Hey, I just wanted to thank you."

"For what?"

"For making your argument back there. If we're going to lose people, we need to make sure their sacrifices matter. Not playing whack-a-mole, as you called it. I thought you should know that folks like us in uniform really appreciate what you did back there."

"Does this mean you won't be running interference on me anymore?"

"Not a chance," Pumpkin grinned. "Gotta watch out for you policy types."

"By the way, I've actually been meaning to thank *you* for your help during the SecDef trip," I said. "We wouldn't have survived without those documents, and I know you had to bend over backwards to get them to us."

"Oh, that. Yeah." Pumpkin said, a bit sheepishly. "I'd love to take credit for that, but that was actually Royle's doing."

What?

"How so?"

"Well, when your request came in at zero-dark thirty, I forwarded it on to Royle. He was in the building within a half an hour, working on turning it around. I've never seen anyone work so aggressively to get a package like that cleared. I thought it would be impossible, but he managed to pull it off."

I was thunderstruck with surprise. Between this, and the good word he'd apparently put in for me with Fletcher, I was beginning to feel like the world's biggest jerk.

"Then I'd better thank Royle," I said. "Do you know where I can find him now?"

"You can't. He's on his way out of the building now. He's off to CENTCOM Forward in Qatar—this was his last brief before being sent forward."

"What are you doing here, Voight?" I asked when I got back to my office. "Aren't you supposed to be in Florida?"

I looked at him more carefully; his face was a sullen pale and his eyes were bloodshot. Something was seriously wrong.

"You can talk to me, if you want," I added quietly. "We're in this together, after all."

Voight looked up; I could swear that I saw a drop or two well in his eyes.

"My wife. She's leaving me. Taking the kids too."

"What? Why?"

"She's tired of all this, Heather. She said that work was always my priority. That she needed to prioritize herself."

"Is this because you went to London instead of going on vacation?"

"Yeah. That was the straw that broke the camel's back, I guess." I could tell Voight's throat was starting to close up from the heartbreak he was enduring.

"But, the thing was," Voight continued, "it wasn't a vacation…"

"What do you mean? Where were you going?"

Voight sighed. "We were supposed to go to a marriage counseling retreat."

"Oh, no…."

"And I skipped it."

"But you didn't have a choice!"

"That's the whole point, Heather. I didn't have a choice before, when everything went crazy after September 11th. It was already getting hard to spend time with the family—this office kept sucking me back in. And now, with these attacks? She said she's been on this merry-go-round before. And she wants off."

"I'm so sorry, Voight. Where is she now?"

"Heading to her mother's in New York." Voight pounded his fist on his desk, making his monitor bounce and toppling over his mug of pens. "The irony is that this was supposed to be the tour where we could put our family back together. Being around Washington, having all the culture to explore…. We were going to have dinner dates and the kids were going to go to museums and great schools. But instead, this goddamned building has torn us apart."

"Do you love her?" I asked.

"With all my heart. She's the other, better half of me. We make each other better."

I was reminded of Jon and Amanda. They loved each other with the kind of intensity that Voight loved Jamie.

"Then you'll get her back. You'll have to work hard at it, but you'll get her back. Voight, you are one of the best, most sincere, most caring people I've ever met. You are a good man, a good father, and a good husband. We all have issues, and yes, this job takes its toll on us. At the end of the day, if you've still got the love, and you support each other, you can get through just about anything, can't you?"

"Even this?"

"Even this." I looked at my watch. "So. How long does it take to get to her mother's house?"

"It's about an eight-hour drive."

I looked Voight squarely in the eye.

"Get out of here. I'll cover down for the both of us until you get back."

Voight looked at me, stunned.

"Are you sure? Things are only going to be getting more crazy around here."

"I'm absolutely certain. And that's precisely why you need to go now to fix things with her. If we do end up going to war, we're both going to need to give this job everything we've got for a while."

"Do you think it's going to happen? Going back into Afghanistan?" Voight asked.

I thought for a moment, then nodded.

"Yes. I do. And soon. So hurry back, okay? And bring your wife with you. We need you—*all* of you—here. Which includes your other, better half."

"Thanks, Heather," Voight said, picking up his bag. "I owe you one."

He grabbed his hat and coat, and dashed out of the office. Watching him go, I knew deep down that he would figure it out. The burning need to put his family together would be the glue that would once again bond them again, somehow.

I realized at that moment that I'd never felt the same burning intensity for Ryan. And that ultimately, he'd never felt that way for me. *So, if that's the case, why was he coming here?*

Later that morning, an email informed me that my paperwork had been successfully pushed through and that I was now a civil servant rather than an academic fellow. It was, apparently, a step that needed to be taken in order to allow me to have the necessary access and clearances that would be required in my new position. So, despite the fact that governments around the world—including my own—were still coping with the terrorist attacks that day, I found myself sitting in another nondescript cubicle farm, somewhere off of the E-Ring of the Pentagon. It felt poetic.

A balding man, with facial hair resembling a bushy cat's tail across his upper lip and wearing one of those horrendous dark blue shirts with a white collar and cuffs, approached the waiting area.

"Dr. Reilly?" he said loudly to the room. I was the only person there.

"Yes, that's me."

"Come on back. Do you have everything?"

"I think so," I said, pulling out my stack of paperwork at least an inch thick.

He immediately began disaggregating my neatly paperclipped documents and flipping through them. A copy of my security clearance paperwork—130 pages detailing my life history, complete with fingerprints and phone numbers and everywhere I'd ever lived—ended up in its own separate pile. I sat in silence and stared at the "Hang In There" poster of a fluffy ginger kitten precariously dangling from a tree branch on the wall opposite me.

At last, the man finished. "Well, it looks like everything's in order here. You're very thorough, Dr. Reilly."

"Well, I wouldn't want you to miss any obscure details about my life history," I said. "My kindergarten years—it's riveting stuff."

"Let's hope not," said the man.

"I was joking."

The man blinked, and then shuffled my paperwork again.

"Are we almost done?" I asked. "I need to get back to work."

"Almost," he said, turning to a desk behind him and picking up a miniature American flag. "We need to swear you in."

"Swear me in?"

"Yes. You're joining the government. You need to take the oath."

"What?" *Swearing an oath? To the Pentagon?* "Nobody told me that I had to swear an oath."

The man was confused; clearly nobody had ever questioned the wisdom of pledging allegiance to the Pentagon.

"What if I have a crisis of conscience? What if I see somebody doing something wrong?"

"But you need to take the oath," he said. He handed me a piece of paper and held up the postcard-sized American flag.

I read what was on the sheet.

"Oh," I said.

It wasn't an oath to the Pentagon. It was an oath to defend the Constitution. To defend principles that I believed in, against anybody, anywhere, that might threaten them. A chill came over me and, for a split second, it felt like Jon was in the room. Which is when it hit me: Jon must have taken the same oath, all those years ago.

For so, so long, I'd been angry. Angry that Jon died. And angry that he died while fighting in a pointless war that we never had a chance at winning, because we didn't even know what winning looked like. Angry because we had decided to spend our soldiers' lives supporting an Afghan government against the Taliban, when the Afghan government was just about as predatory as the Taliban itself.

I'd talked to Dan—one of the soldiers in Jon's unit—a couple years after the funeral. Over a couple of beers at a TGI Friday's, he told me they'd pieced together why that Afghan man threw the grenade that day. It didn't take long for him to confess. The man had a daughter—eight years old—and the local security chief wanted her. The father refused; the chief abducted the daughter.

The Americans supported the security chief. The father, therefore, targeted the Americans.

"Fucked up," Dan had said, then finished his beer. "No wonder they hated us."

I'd been angry before that conversation; outrage gnawed at me for years afterward. "Why Jon?" I'd asked, over and over and over again. Why did Jon—who burned so bright, who made everyone laugh, whose warmth filled a room, who couldn't wait to have a family, who was loved by everybody—why did *he* have to be the one that came home in a casket?

I looked down at the words on the paper. *Because of this oath.*

People told me during the funeral that he'd died because he believed in something bigger than himself. For years, I thought they were patronizing me. Or deluding themselves. That they were just saying that to make sense of something that was so senseless. It all seemed so cliché. But that moment, sitting in a fluorescent-lit office with Equal Employment Opportunity posters on the wall, I realized that it was true. Jon died because he believed in the freedoms, rights, and values of the United States, as spelled out in our Constitution. A tear slipped out.

"Dr. Reilly, are you okay?"

I looked up at the balding man with the bushy moustache. The anger that had been seething in the background for years—so ever-present that I'd forgotten it even existed—crescendoed and broke, leaving me feeling both relieved and unsettled. And with a newfound sense of responsibility. If Jon had been willing to lay down his life to protect our Constitution from all its enemies, I needed to honor that vow. I needed to do what I could to make sure his—and others'—sacrifices, if they needed to be made, wouldn't be made in vain.

The words on the sheet gave me a new sense of purpose. Just as they'd given Jon a sense of purpose all those years ago.

"Sorry. I'm fine," I answered, managing to compose myself.

"Are you ready?" he asked.

"Yes," I said. As I opened my mouth to speak, I could feel Jon behind me.

"I do solemnly swear that I will support and defend the Constitution of the United States against all enemies, foreign and domestic."

Tears welled in my eyes and my throat constricted, making it hard to speak.

"That I will bear true faith and allegiance to the same."

I stopped. For the first time since his passing, I could feel the warmth of Jon's smile behind me. The smile he'd given me when I caught my first fish after he'd taught me how to cast. The smile he gave me after seeing me act in my first high school play.

Managing a shaky smile through tears, I continued on.

"That I take this obligation freely, without any mental reservation or purpose of evasion; and that I will well and faithfully discharge the duties of the office on which I am about to enter…"

I miss and love you so much, Jon, I thought.

"So help me, God," I finished.

Jon was gone.

The man sitting across from me—who clearly wasn't used to new employees spouting waterworks—had a slightly terrified look on his face.

"Uh. Tissue?" he asked, grabbing a roll of paper towels from a stand next to the white board.

"Thanks," I said, taking a sheet and wiping my eyes with the course paper.

"Congratulations on joining the U.S. government and the Department of Defense."

CHAPTER THIRTY-ONE

DESPITE THE FACT THAT DOWNTOWN WASHINGTON WAS BUSY WITH TOURISTS, IT SEEMED TO ME THAT THE STREETS OF D.C. WERE EERILY QUIET. Even the groups of schoolchildren coming from and going to the Metro were silent, or speaking in hushed tones as a strange sort of depressive fog settled over the town.

Ryan was already seated by the time I arrived at *Off the Record*, the pretentiously named bar in the basement of the Hay-Adams hotel, just across the way from the White House. I thought of all the preparations and deliberations and discussions that were happening at that moment in the situation room in the West Wing and in the Pentagon. Today had been a long day, and there still wasn't any end in sight. It had just gone past seven o'clock, and, although the sun was still setting over Washington, in the bar it felt like it could have been midnight in the middle of winter. The plush red velveteen couches rose three quarters up the wall, giving the room a cozy, conspiratorial feel. Which, I supposed, was the point. Photographs and caricatures of some of the journalistic and political luminaries that had frequented the establishment over its many years of existence covered the wood-paneled wall on the other side of the room. The message, to anyone really paying attention, was clear: *Off the Record* was a place to be seen, but not heard.

Men in suits and women in summer dresses compared notes and political gossip as they sipped their overpriced drinks. The whole place had a strange feeling of disconnectedness, as if the terrorist attacks had happened on another planet, to another country. Life had already moved on for these people, if it had ever stopped.

Their carefree attitudes inspired a deep frustration in me.

Ryan looked out of place among the Washington wonks sipping their martinis as he played with his phone while snacking on wasabi peas. He, too, didn't appear much affected by the day's events. His hair was a bit scruffy, and he wore his favorite jeans and his Ramones T-shirt.

I took a deep breath to steady my anger, and then walked to his table.

"Sorry I'm late," I said. "It's been a long day at work."

"I can only imagine." He gestured to the glass of wine sitting before the empty chair at his table. "I got you a glass of wine. The bartender said it's a nice Pinot Noir."

"Thank you," I said, accepting the glass.

"Thanks for meeting me here. This is where I'm staying, by the way."

"Here? The Hay-Adams? This is one of the most expensive hotels in Washington, Ryan. You can't afford this."

I took a sip of the wine; far from being nice, it tasted bitter in my mouth.

"Actually, I can."

I looked at him, puzzled. "I don't understand."

"I took what you said to heart, Heather. I've been offered—and accepted—an offer at Pritzker and Filch."

"The biggest law firm in San Diego?"

"Exactly. The work isn't anything I'm really passionate about. But I'll be able to pay off our debts in no time, and then I can get back to what I love."

"That's great, Ryan. Congratulations."

"Which means that you won't have to sell out anymore, either, Heather," Ryan said, excitedly. "You can come home. Where it's safe."

I felt as if I'd been walking along a sidewalk, only to tumble off a curb that I hadn't previously noticed.

"Come home? Ryan, what exactly are you doing here?"

"I've been thinking a lot about things, Heather. About us. About what went wrong. I know that I wasn't always the best partner for you. And that there's a reason that you didn't feel like you could tell me what was going on in your life. I'm sorry about that, Heather. And I miss you."

I sat back, stunned, as a tear formed in the corner of Ryan's eye.

"I handled things so badly," Ryan continued. "I was selfish. I guess I was having a hard time being apart from you."

"And so your solution was to push me away completely?" I asked.

"Yeah. I know. It makes no sense," Ryan said, putting his hand on mine. "Watching the news, the terror attack, I just realized what's really important to me, Heather. *You.* Your smile. The way you fight with your hair in the mornings. The way you dedicate yourself to your work. Your bottomless need for coffee and your guilty obsession with nerdy sci-fi shows." Ryan smiled. "All the big things and the little things that make you who you are. And the thought of spending my life without you…. It fills me with….." He choked up as his eyes welled up with tears.

My heart broke more and more with every word of his. Because the woman I was just a couple months ago would have leapt at the opportunity to return to San Diego with him. But she wasn't me anymore.

"We've been together for so long, Heather," Ryan continued. "And we've had some amazing times. We're great for each other. And I want to fix us. I've figured out how to deal with our finances. I mean, you'll have to go back to teaching, of course. But I can pay off your debts in the meantime. You don't have to stay in the Pentagon anymore."

"Oh." I took a deep breath, and pulled my hand from his as I tried to figure out what to say next. How could I explain how different things had become? That I'd found my purpose? That what mattered most to me wasn't, I suspected, what mattered most to him? In the end, I settled on: "Ryan, I *am* home. I want to stay here."

"I don't understand," Ryan said, looking at me as if I were some kind of alien object. "But after those attacks? D.C.—it isn't safe. Why would you want to stay?"

"Because I need to serve my country, Ryan. It's as simple as that."

"But we may go to war, Heather. You need to get out of here before you're a part of that. Before you compromise your principles."

"You're right. We are going to war. And I need to make sure that I do my part to protect the men and women that are about to fight it, as best as I can. The President is going to get on the television tonight—in about twenty minutes—and make a speech. He's going to announce that the United States is going to start conducting military operations in Afghanistan to eliminate the

Islamic State, and once we, and the Afghans, eliminate those hard-liners, we will help them reconcile with the more moderate Taliban that we should have been talking to for years."

"How do you know all this?" asked Ryan.

"Because I helped craft the strategy."

Ryan sat quietly as a shadow of confusion and deflation over-came his face. It was as if his sails, which had been full of the wind just a moment before, had suddenly begun luffing as he turned in to face a maelstrom.

"Who *are* you?" he finally asked.

"Excuse me?"

"After Jon? You crafted the strategy for the U.S. to go to war? More violence isn't going to solve anything, Heather. All you're doing is putting our soldiers'—and Afghans'—lives on the line. How many thousands of Afghans died the last time—'civilian casualties' we called them?" Ryan laughed, cynically. "You've drunk the Kool-Aid, Heather. You've become just as bad as one of the terrorists."

I involuntarily gasped; Ryan might as well have hit my solar plexus with a sledgehammer, but I'd be damned before I'd let him see that he'd delivered a body blow.

"I'm sorry you feel that way," I said, standing up. I took my engagement ring out of my purse and put it on the table, next to my half-finished glass of wine. "Thank you for all the happy times, Ryan. For being a wonderful partner. But it's clear we want different things out of life. I wish you all the best."

I left him sitting in the bar and went back to work.

CHAPTER THIRTY-TWO

THE DAYS BEGAN BLURRING TOGETHER, AND FOR THREE NIGHTS STRAIGHT I SLEPT AT THE PENTAGON ON A COT THAT SOMEONE SCROUNGED UP FOR ME. I showered in the Athletic Center, jogged a little bit and then got back to work. With Voight gone, Pumpkin, for whatever reason, decided that it was now his responsibility to make sure my basic needs were taken care of—food, laundry, and even the odd toiletry or two from CVS. It was nice. I was beginning to understand what Voight was talking about the day we met, when he first escorted me into the Pentagon: the building was designed with all the amenities in mind so that if you had to stay and work, you wouldn't need to leave.

And, just like Voight, I also began to wonder if it was a trap.

Despite the frenzy at the Pentagon as it prepared to go to war, the fact that Derek Odem had been sabotaging the Moldova plan somehow reached the ears of Secretary Sidwell. It was apparently the worst possible timing for the Secretary to hear that news. Fed up and frustrated, he called the National Security Advisor herself and demanded that Odem be fired.

In between planning sessions and briefings, Fletcher had a wisp of a grin on her face for the next couple days.

One thing I managed to do in between writing memos—with a great deal of satisfaction—was make my first, 1,500 dollar payment toward my student loans. Only twenty-five more payments like that, and I would be debt-free. So that was nice. Another unexpectedly nice development: Matt stopped reaching out. He'd sent an email or two, but I didn't answer. It was all too much to deal with. Of course, I felt slightly guilty. After all, ghosting was rude. But with everything else going on, I simply didn't have the emotional energy to do much else.

It was ten at night when I finally returned to the apartment a couple days later. The lights were out and the apartment was quiet; Amanda was probably asleep. I took off my red heels and was almost to the stairs when I heard the sound of a glass hitting the hardwood floors. Curious, I walked back to the living room where the sound came from, and turned on the lamp next to the sofa.

Amanda was sitting on the floor, in her pajamas, squinting at the light of the lamp in the now-brightened room. A bottle of whiskey sat next to her. Judging by how much whiskey was left, as well as the fact that her legs were akimbo, it seemed like Amanda had gone through enough of the bottle to give her quite the buzz.

Amanda slowly rolled her head to look up at me. "You're here."

"Yes, I'm here. Amanda?"

"Yes?"

"What are you doing on the living room floor?"

Amanda's face crumpled and her shoulders shook as her tears started falling uncontrollable sobs. Her carefully crafted mask—a mask forged pretending things were okay when they weren't, and hadn't been for a long time—suddenly cracked, falling off her face. Amanda was in terrible, terrible pain.

"I'm so sorry," she said as the tears fell down her face.

I did the only thing I knew to do: sit on the floor, hugging her tightly as Amanda cried and cried and cried.... Eventually, when Amanda had no more tears to cry, she sat back against the cabinets and took a sip of her whiskey. I decided to pour myself two fingers as well. It was only when I leaned my back against the wall that I realized that Amanda was directly facing Jon's Congressional Medal of Honor.

Amanda sighed. "I'm a mess, aren't I?"

"I've seen you in better shape. What's going on?"

"I've got to quit."

Everything clicked into place. "Fred's not temporary, is he?" I asked.

"No. I can't stay in Senator McClutchy's office any longer. He pulled us into the office this afternoon for a strategy session. Fred recommended—and McClutchy agreed—our talking points need to use the phrase 'carpet bombing.'"

I gasped. "Does he know that's a war crime?"

"Does it matter? Fred is McClutchy's right-hand man now. Fred doesn't trust me, and so neither does McClutchy. He's shutting me out of meetings, disregarding my opinions. Anyone who contradicts him—even if it's only to help strengthen his own arguments—gets ostracized. I thought.... I thought that he would take me with him if he went into the White House."

"And now?"

"Now...I'm ostracized from a team that I helped build." Amanda sighed.

"Is that why—"

"The email? Yes. I shouldn't have showed it to him. I'm so, so sorry."

"It's okay, Amanda."

The betrayal still stung a little, but after everything was said and done, I knew the sting would fade. I'd get over it.

"I'm so tired of it, Heather."

"Of what?"

"Everything I am, everything I've become. I look at myself in the mirror and I don't like what I see. I don't want to be the person that sells out her friends to score points at the office."

"You did what you did, Amanda. But you're a good person. Jon knew it, and so do I."

Amanda smiled, eyes shining with tears. "Thank you. I'll do better, for both of you. I promise." She twisted her wedding ring, losing herself in the thoughts and memories of the man who brought us together. By law, Jon had made us sisters. But after his passing, our shared memories—and shared grief—forged our bond into something, I now knew, that was stronger than steel.

"I remember our first date," Amanda eventually said. "We went bowling. I kicked his ass. Later he said he'd let me win, but we both knew he was lying through his teeth about that. We were leaving the bowling alley when he pulled out a quarter and stuck it into one of those candy machines. The kind with the red metal tops, but one that had toys rather than bubble gum. He twisted the handle, retrieved the plastic cup, and out popped a plastic ring with a pink flower on top. He put it on my left ring finger and told me I'd better get used to wearing a ring there. At first I was a little weirded out…but then he won me over." Amanda smiled, her eyes shining through tears.

"He was always pretty persuasive," I said.

"Yeah," Amanda said with a small laugh. "The problem now, I guess, is that I'm *too* used to wearing the ring. I can't take it off." I watched as Amanda lost herself to her tears. "I miss him so much. Every day. Losing him, it wasn't like losing a part of me. It was like I lost *myself*. As if he was in my DNA. And getting over him would mean rewiring my genetic code. Who I am."

"I know. But it's been almost ten years. I miss him, too, but it's time to move on, one step at a time," I said, putting a hand on her shoulder. "Just like you're moving on from McClutchy."

The two of us sat in silence. And then it occurred to me that I'd been so wrapped up in work, my extracurricular flings, ending things with Ryan, and feeling sorry for myself that I'd forgotten to check in on my very best friend, a woman with such grace and love and grit in her that it was sometimes a heartbreaking joy to know her, kind of like how it hurts to stare at the sun too long. My dearest friend had been in pain, and I hadn't known.

"You've been going through so much, and I haven't been there for you through all of this…. It must have been awful keeping it to yourself…."

"Well, one other person knew."

"Who?"

"Royle. He and I get together every now and again."

"I didn't realize you guys had gotten back together," I said, wondering how I could have missed them getting close.

"Together?" Amanda asked.

"You and Royle. You're dating, right?"

"Royle? No! If anything, I thought *you* had a bit of a crush on him," she said. "I thought that was why you kept bringing him up."

"Me? No way," I said, perhaps a little too quickly. For some inexplicable reason, I felt elated at hearing that he and Amanda weren't together.

"Well, regardless, we never dated."

My heart was somehow thrilled, but also totally confused. "But—"

"Heather, Jon died to save him."

I heard Amanda's words, but they didn't register, not at first.

"Royle and I met at the Medal of Honor ceremony," she said. "He was torn apart with guilt, and wanted to apologize. We've been in touch ever since."

"Jon threw himself on the grenade for Royle?" I asked, still unsure how to understand what Amanda was telling me. A tear slipped out, but I only noticed it when it landed on my hand. "How did I not know that?"

"The investigation, it was classified. I didn't know until Royle opened up to me about it. He probably shouldn't have, but he was kind of a mess. It was brutally unfair. It almost wrecked him."

"Unfair? How so? I'd heard that he kind of deserved to be investigated."

"The parents of one of the other soldiers that died that day—they demanded Royle's head on a platter. Said that Royle had ignored the rules of engagement, and that he unnecessarily put soldiers in harm's way. But the thing was, Royle's planning for the mission was sound. And his detachment had coordinated the operation extensively with Jon's unit. It was just that they didn't get the close air support they needed at the time. And because they didn't have any backup from the air, that's when things went haywire. And in the chaos, Jon gave his life to save his buddies. And Royle."

My stomach dropped. *No…. It couldn't be. Was Matt ultimately responsible for Jon's death?*

Amanda sighed. "Royle told me that the firefight was one of the worst he'd ever been in. And they needed to find another way back to their base because they didn't have the close air support. The grenade wouldn't have been a problem if they'd gotten the help from above they'd asked for."

I lost my breath. I didn't know how to comprehend what Amanda was telling me. I reached for my whiskey as I put the words together and my stomach spiraled itself into a dark, nauseating hole.

"I don't know how to say this, Amanda. But 'Mr. Right Now?' I think he was the pilot that day."

Amanda sucked in a breath. "You're kidding."

"I wish I was."

I thought about the meeting in the Joint Staff a month or so ago, when I sat next to Matt, and Royle looked furious. Royle's anger—it wasn't directed at me, after all. It never was.

"I always forget how small this world is," Amanda said. "The best and the brightest in the military always have to serve in the Pentagon before they can wear stars on their shoulders. So it tends to be a small place. But this?"

"This is insane," I said, feeling like I wanted to take a shower. *The next time I hear from Matt….*

"Well, what's done is done," Amanda said, ready to move beyond our realization that I'd let the man who'd played a part in taking Jon from us into our home. "And in any case, Royle is always looking for ways to help us out. He keeps saying that he wants to 'do right by us.' So, almost a year ago, over lunch, I mentioned that you might be looking to come to Washington. He helped you get the fellowship in policy."

"He *what?*" Black was becoming white, and white was becoming black.

"He didn't want you to know. He thought it would be weird, somehow. Like you might feel like you owed him something. But he made sure you got pulled in. And when the reorg happened, he made sure he got switched to Fletcher's office so that your job would be protected. He said it was the least he could do."

"So then why did he sleep over that night?" I asked.

"I bumped into him at a reception. Things have been getting pretty bad with the senator. I got tipsy that night, so when he asked me whether there was something wrong at work, I told him everything. Afterwards, he brought me home and took care of me. He promised he wouldn't tell anybody that I was on the outs with the senator. So, after I'd cried my eyes out to him, he put me to bed and made sure I drank some water. He must have slept on the couch that night."

I sat back, stunned. "I—I think I owe Royle an apology."

"What for?"

"Long story. I'll tell you some other time."

"Right, well, enough about me." She wiped her cheeks with the bottom of her T-shirt. "How was the Pentagon?"

"Intense. There's a pretty decent chance I'll be asked to go… away…for a little while."

Amanda let out a small laugh before her eyes watered again.

"Of course you will. You're so much like him, you know that?"

"I try to be."

"Take his medal," she said, pointing to the frame with the medal commemorating the moment that took Jon from us both. "Maybe his memory—it'll help keep you safe."

"I can't. That's yours, Amanda."

"Take it," she said, walking over to the medal in its frame, picking up a book from the coffee table as she moved. She stood in front of the medal for a moment, and then smashed the glass with one resounding clash; shards skittered across the floor. She reached into the casing and retrieved the medal, wrapping up its light blue ribbon in her hand and resting its gold star on her palm.

"Please, take it," she said again. "And please, *please* be careful."

"I will."

But after everything we'd already been through, we both knew all too well that it was a promise I couldn't necessarily keep.

CHAPTER THIRTY-THREE

A COUPLE DAYS LATER, I ROSE AT DAWN, PUT ON MY RUNNING SHOES, AND WALKED TO THE NATIONAL MALL. The air smelled sweet and fresh, with dew-kissed grass that reached up to embrace the cool mist of the mid-September morning. The footsteps on gravel of joggers of different shapes and sizes punctuated the quiet calm of pre-rush-hour D.C.

I looked to my right; the sun was rising behind the Capitol Building. I turned left and continued walking.

I remembered my first day at the Pentagon; it was the last time I'd really studied the Washington Monument. As I walked, the ivory obelisk, now rosy with the morning sun, stood in front of me, above the mist and the grass and the everyday fracas of the city. And much like before, the monument's size, its permanence, made the squabbles and strife of D.C.—of the Pentagon—seem less important. The only difference between then and now, I supposed, was that I had a better grasp of how all-consuming the day-to-day of government business was. But then again, the things worth building are also the things worth fighting for. Worth all the petty frustrations and anxieties and doubts, too. And I was finally a part of building something.

I kept walking.

I crossed through the World War II Memorial. I thought about what I'd learned about that war from my teachers and history books. America's greatest generation fought and died during an existential crisis that threatened to swallow Europe, then the world. But it had only seemed existential in retrospect; at the time, President Roosevelt was reluctant to stick Americans in the thick of battles so far from American shores. What use was it? Why should we fight their wars? I supposed that in the end, Roosevelt was confronted with the same hard truth that I was now facing: to protect our country, our people, we had to be sentries on a wall. Let our guard down, and we'd risk being badly hurt. Roosevelt passed away before he could be confronted with the horrors of the Holocaust and the many other Nazi terrors; instead, the rest of the world grappled with the price of inaction. The Trotsky quote hummed through my mind: "You may not be interested in war, but war is interested in you."

I kept walking.

I passed the Lincoln Memorial; the president's face was awash with sunlight that had now turned golden white. Families were torn apart by the conflict that pitted North versus South; the conflict that determined *e pluribus unum* was not a pledge to be taken lightly. I thought of my own family, when I went home to visit them in Carlisle the other day. The way that mom's lip shook when I told her that I was going to Afghanistan; the way the tear slipped out of her eye and down her cheek. I knew that I was doing exactly what she didn't want for me, and that it scared her tremendously that I was about to go.

"I don't like this, Heather," she'd said. "Not one bit. But, I'm proud of you." Which is when I realized I was no longer a child to her; I was a woman. And a woman that she respected.

"Just focus on staying safe out there," she continued. That's when her voice choked up and she excused herself.

I kept walking.

I crossed the Arlington Memorial Bridge, and entered the cemetery just after it opened at eight. I made a left, and followed the path through hundreds—thousands—of uniform, white marble graves, finally crossing into section 60. For a cemetery, it felt alive. The remnants of other visits—flags and flowers and trinkets and full beer bottles and pictures of loved ones—adorned the graves of the men and women that died in our nation's most recent wars, in deserts and mountains halfway around the world. I trudged through the still-wet grass through the tombstones and, after a couple of wrong turns, found him.

Fresh flowers and Amanda's wedding ring were on the grass in front of the tombstone.

"Hi, Jon," I said, kneeling down as a tear pushed its way out of my eye. "It's been a long time. I'm sorry about that. You must think I'm an awful kid sister. I guess—it just took me a while to get it. But now I do. You can't ignore the call to service, can you?"

I reached into my pocket and pulled out the coin that Secretary Sidwell gave me.

"I thought you'd get a kick out of this," I said, putting it on his grave. "Your little sis, the former vegan peacenik, with a SecDef coin."

I placed my fingertips on the etching of his name.

"I'm going there, where you were. Look out for me, okay? And don't worry. I'll keep looking out for Amanda for you. She's got to move on, but you'll always be part of her. Of us. Always."

I sat there on the grass, my jeans soaked through, for another hour or so watching the sun rise through the sky over the city and telling my brother Jon stories from the past ten years since his death. I told him about Ryan. I told him about graduate school. I told him about teaching. I told him about the Pentagon. Some stories were small tremors, others were tectonic shifts, but it felt good to tell him about all of it.

Finally, I stood up. The enormity of where I was about to go, what I was about to do, fell over me like a wave I'd been watching from afar, approaching the shore and breaking against my body. A wall of water was crushing me, pushing me toward the shore while a silent undertow pulled my legs deeper out into the surf, further into unknown depths.

"I just hope I make you proud, Jon."

CHAPTER THIRTY-FOUR

TWO AND A HALF DAYS AFTER VISITING ARLINGTON, I WAS SURROUNDED BY MOUNTAINS IN THE CENTER OF ASIA, AT THE EDGE OF THE WORLD, ACCIDENTALLY DISPLAYING MY LEOPARD-PRINT PANTIES TO ROYLE, OF ALL PEOPLE. *Of course.* I zipped up my fly and pulled my shirt flat against my body in a vain attempt to use my body armor to de-wrinkle myself. I took a deep breath; the air was laced with musty-scented dust and diesel fuel that tasted bitter in my mouth. The blades of the helicopter I'd just been dangling from were still spinning as it moved down the runway toward the military side of the airfield. I could faintly see the grey hulks of other military aircraft in the distance, obscured by the layer of smog that shrouded the base of the mountains.

I shrugged off my backpack and it landed near a rose bush. It felt strange, being closely surrounded by the reds and pinks and peaches of the blooms amid the sights and smells and sounds of war. I noticed a smaller Afghan man—white beard, wearing a long tunic and flowing cotton pants—hunched over a rose in the corner, carefully tending to it, almost as if it were a family member.

I looked over to Royle; he looked stronger, more confident, than I'd ever seen him. He was still talking to the Afghan guard through an interpreter, showing him some papers and pointing to me. I started to wonder if there was a problem. It would be just my luck to run into Afghanistan's version of a bureaucratic stickler for paperwork before I even got into the country.

A rundown bus full of passengers pulled up to the terminal building on my left. It looked like they were from the Air India plane a couple hundred yards away on the opposite side of the airstrip. Men with shaggy hair and dark complexions, who were wearing crisply tailored business suits, shuffled alongside women with their faces and heads and bodies covered in their full-length abayas and the occasional bright blue burqa.

A man who was holding his toddler-aged daughter's hand looked at me. Even at a distance, I could see his leathery mouth tighten. His brown eyes tired, sad. He pulled his daughter closer to him and walked alongside the rest of the crowd into the terminal.

A stab of fear ran through my gut as it registered exactly how alien, yet exactly how familiar, I looked to them. They'd seen this show before. The Afghan harbinger of war: an American woman wearing khaki pants, boots, and a helmet instead of a headscarf.

Royle finished his conversation with the Afghan guard and walked over to me.

"We'd better get going."

"Everything okay?" I asked, nodding at my papers.

"As okay as it can be, I guess." Royle pointed to the crowd. "The guard wanted you to go through the airport terminal along with everyone else, but it's not that safe right now, and you're mission-essential."

"Oh." I felt a strange sense of relief at hearing him say I was "mission-essential."

He led the way out of the rose garden nestled on the side of Kabul's commercial airport. The airport complex was busy, with Afghans congregating in twos and threes, sending off their loved ones to distant places, or perhaps greeting them. The bright neon signs looked worn down, clearly no match for the thick Afghan dust.

"Are we heading to the embassy first?" I asked as Royle opened the door to the up-armored SUV for me. A Marine Lance Corporal was waiting for us in the driver's seat. It was the only car in the lot that wasn't beaten up. The SUV was a status symbol. It occurred to me that status symbols in war zones were probably easy targets.

"Yeah. It's only a couple minutes from here," he said, putting my bag in the back of the car. He climbed into the rear passenger seat next to me, and the Lance Corporal started driving.

I turned to face Royle. "So what are you hearing?"

Royle shook his head, silently indicating to me that we'd talk later.

I pursed my lips, embarrassed. Rookie move.

The car stopped and started as we entered traffic. We passed dilapidated buildings, carcasses of concrete stuffed with Afghans selling fruits, vegetables, and bread. We dodged a man driving a donkey cart that was laden with cordwood in the center of the road; we swerved to miss a gaggle of burqa-clad women on our right. The occasional LED screen—the ones that worked, anyway—advertised an Afghan cellphone network.

After negotiating the crowded traffic around the Masood roundabout, we eventually pulled into a gated compound after showing our IDs to enter. We drove a little farther, then pulled into a mustard-yellow-walled compound. The bright sun shining on the white concrete pavement added to the compound's feeling of Spartan austerity. I stepped out of the car; a hushed silence blanketed the vast courtyard. It felt a little smothering compared to the hustle and bustle outside on the streets.

"This is it?" I said, taking off my helmet.

"Welcome to the fortress that is the U.S. embassy," Royle said. "Do you want to get showered and changed first?"

I briefly considered the offer. But earlier vanity—worrying about my mascara and hair—seemed inappropriate. Amateurish.

"No. Let's get started," I said, tying my hair back.

Royle nodded, then beckoned me to follow him. After clearing another round of security guards, he led me into a smooth grey atrium that served as the foyer of the United States Embassy in Kabul. I was surprised. Although the compound looked desolate outside, inside the embassy was humming with people scurrying back and forth, alive and abuzz with an adrenaline-induced sense of urgency. Royle nodded at several people as we walked up a number of stairs to the top floor.

"Is that the ambassador's office?" I asked, pointing to a set of glass doors that we were passing. "Yes. He's in a meeting with the Afghan president, or he would be joining us."

I raised my eyebrows. I might have gotten a promotion, but I still figured that I was pretty low on the totem pole. So it was surprising that an ambassador—the President's personal representative to Afghanistan—would want to be in a meeting with me.

The corridor narrowed, eventually ending with a steel door. Royle knocked at the door; after waiting a moment, a mousy looking man, brown-haired and balding, opened it.

"It's all ready for you," the man said.

"Great. I'll let you know when we're through," said Royle.

"No problem," the man said. "I'll need your phones." We handed them over as we walked into the secure room. The man shut the door behind us.

"Sorry for not talking about what's going on while we were driving. I wanted to make sure we have this conversation in a secure facility."

"I shouldn't have prodded out there," I said.

I sat down at the heavy, honey-lacquered conference table that dominated the windowless room. A video screen displaying the logo of the Department of State was against the far wall. Eight chairs were squeezed around the table, leaving barely enough room for anyone to sit and adding to my claustrophobia.

After maneuvering around several other seats, Royle sat down at the table across from me.

"So what's going on?"

"It's complicated."

"Situation normal…?"

"Exactly. But this…." Royle sighed. "This kind of takes the cake."

"Tell me everything."

"Well, the good news is that the initial strikes are over, and they were successful. Our Special Forces teams were able to rapidly take out some stockpiled chems, and we found some radiological stockpiles too. Small, but significant. The Islamic State is on the run after we bombed the hell out of their headquarters and training camps, and our teams are sweeping up the mess, finding the bad guys while they're on the run."

"What about the political side of this? Where are we at with the new government?"

"The embassy is coordinating with the moderate Afghan opposition—Atal Popal's crew—helping them consolidate power. The diplomats tell me that while these kinds of negotiations are always delicate, Popal is pretty much pushing on an open door. Everyone's so sick of the last president—and the Islamic State. They're talking to the Taliban moderates, and even the factions in the north are on board—anything to be rid of the Islamic State. Everything went relatively smoothly. There were a couple hiccups, of course, and we still have a long way to go before we're done here."

"Did we lose anybody?"

"There were three casualties, one fatal."

I felt nauseous.

Royle noticed. "That's what happens. We're lucky we didn't lose more people. All in all, this operation has been pretty successful...."

"I can sense there's a 'but' coming...."

Royle sighed as he nodded. "I've been working with the Brits. You remember Colin? He's here. He's got pretty good networks out here. And now that we've combed the sites and coordinated with British intelligence, we're thinking that the Islamic State wasn't really behind the terror attacks."

"What?" I took a deep breath as my stomach dropped. "But they took credit. And we verified that they were coordinated by the Islamic State of Khorasan."

"They executed the attacks, definitely. But someone else was behind it all, pulling the strings."

"Sure, but we always knew that they couldn't have pulled this off without external support. Someone had to fund them—from Saudi, or Syria...."

"There's a difference between external support and direct orders. We picked up some hard drives at one of the sites near Kandahar—our computer-forensics guys found evidence that the Islamic State guys were *paid* to declare jihad. To make it look like they were responsible. They were happy to do the job because it made them look like the biggest, baddest assholes in the neighborhood instead of al Qaeda. But it looks like someone outside the country orchestrated it."

"Who?" The room seemed smaller, stuffier, as if someone were pushing the walls closer to me. My lungs seemed to stop functioning properly, as if they couldn't take in enough air, somehow.

"That's the kicker. We don't know. Not yet."

"Oh my god." I felt bile leave my stomach as I thought about the soldier who fell; about the family who would be missing him or her. I swallowed it back down. "I was wrong about this war, wasn't I?"

Royle paused, collecting his thoughts.

"We went to war, and we accomplished our mission, at least so far. But it's true, you were half-right. We came in here for the wrong reasons. We've tackled the symptom, not the cause of this problem."

Blood drained from my face as a sense of vertigo overcame me.

"None of this means that *you* were wrong, though," he continued.

"*What?* How do you figure that?"

"The Islamic State signed their death warrants when they agreed to the plan. If we didn't strike back, and strike hard, there's a lot of other folks who might be more tempted to screw with us."

"But—"

"Heather, some people just need to be killed. That's the way this works. Now we have to manage the consequences."

"You mean, because we've broken Afghanistan again, we've bought it?"

"Yes. But we can't let ourselves get too bogged down. We have to keep our eyes on the bigger game that's being played."

"Whatever that game might be," I said.

Royle nodded. "This information is too sensitive to put on email, and we're worried that the VTC system is bugged. So the ambassador and I need you to go back to Washington and report this back to the building. I'll feed you more information as I gather it, but if what we dig up is as sensitive as what we've already seen, you'll probably have to come back soon."

"So you need me to be a glorified carrier pigeon?"

Royle let a small laugh escape. "A *mission-essential* carrier pigeon."

"I'll jump on the next flight home. Which is…when?"

"Twelve hours from now."

Forty-five minutes later, I was finally clean, having washed away the grime from travel and the dust of Kabul. I lay on the bottom bunk in my converted shipping container, which the military liked to call a "containerized housing unit." The embassy compound was full of these makeshift cabins, each with its own shower and a TV that played reruns of "The Big Bang Theory" in between awkward military commercials about physical fitness. As I lay there, holding Jon's medal of honor over my head and letting it swing back and forth like a pendulum, I guessed that most of the "housing units" had probably been empty since the U.S. withdrew its forces from Afghanistan in 2014. I doubted that would be the case for much longer.

The thought made me feel sick, again. It was hard to shake the unsettling, unnerving snake of doubt that wound its coils around my heart and my stomach. I was *wrong* about this war. A man lost his life. Others would, too. *What if Ryan was right? Did I betray Jon?*

A knock startled my thoughts. I opened the door to see Royle waiting at the bottom of the makeshift steps to my quarters.

"I thought I'd show you to where you can get some chow," he said. "Is now a good time?"

"Yes, thanks."

The two of us walked in silence in the dimming evening sunlight, past the main embassy building and toward a swimming pool that, like so many other things that day, seemed out of place. We skirted the pool, walking toward a door that I presumed led to the cafeteria, passing picnic tables as we went.

We'd turned another corner and just about reached the door when I saw a waist-high tent of canvas shielding candles from the wind. I stooped down to take a closer look at the makeshift shrine. Flowers and pictures surrounded the candles; images of the children that had fallen in the recent terrorist attacks stared back at me.

They lost their lives before their flowers had a chance to bloom. My heart broke for them, again.

"A lot of their parents were stationed here at the embassy not too long ago," Royle said. "Their parents worked hard to help Afghanistan be a better place. It's been pretty devastating to the folks out here."

I picked up one of the photos. A smiling little girl with shining brown hair. A card was attached to the back—*"You'll always be loved, Maisie. We miss you more than you could know."* I thought about her family. The loss they felt. And how there were Islamic State sonsofbitches out there who agreed to stamp out their lives for some money and a public-relations victory. The doubt that had nestled in my stomach earlier turned to a resolve. In the game that was being played, we'd just taken some critical pawns off the board. Now it was time to find—and take out—the queen.

Somehow, Royle knew what I was thinking.

"You're a brilliant strategist, Heather. We need you to help us put the pieces together."

I sighed as I stood, wiping a tear before it could fall down my cheek.

"I'm not sure you'd say that if you knew how wrong I'd been about things."

"You mean, about the Islamic State?"

"About that. About many things, including you, Royle."

"Me?"

"I pretty much thought you hated me and were out to get me."

"Yeah, you made that pretty clear at the Australian Embassy."

"But now I realize that I need to thank you."

"For what?"

"For everything. For looking after Amanda. For saving me when I was on the trip with the Secretary. And for helping me get the job in Policy in the first place."

Royle looked to the ground, sheepish. "It was no problem."

"Of course it was. You bent over backwards for me. And I was rude. You didn't deserve it," I sat down at a nearby picnic table; he sat across from me. "I was wrong about you. On so many levels."

"What did you mean?"

"I had no idea about your connection to Jon. Or to Amanda. If you can believe it, I even thought you were a womanizer," I admitted. "It's so stupid. I'm sorry."

"A *womanizer*?"

I cringed. "Yeah. I thought you were dating Amanda, and that you were cheating on your girlfriend with her."

"Girlfriend?"

"Yeah. The one you were with at Sine's that night?"

Royle's laugh erupted from deep within his belly. Eventually, between breaths, he was able to muster a couple words.

"Heather, that's my sister."

"Your sister?"

"Yes. My sister."

"Oh," I said, unable to think of anything else.

"Heather, do you remember when we met?"

"My first day in the Pentagon. When Fletcher was tearing me a new one."

Royle couldn't help but let out a small grin.

"I suspected you thought as much. But no, that's not when we met."

"Okay, then. When?"

"It was at the Congressional Medal of Honor ceremony for Jon. You had this look on your face, it was mostly blank, as if you couldn't quite process what was going on. A tear fell down your cheek, and at that moment I swore that I'd find a way to make it up to you someday."

Royle ran his fingers through his hair before putting his elbows on his knees and resting his head on his hands.

"And now you're here," Royle said, his face a portrait of mixed emotions.

"Did you know Jon?"

"A little. We were stuck on the same little base in Helmand for a while. Before…." Royle's voice trailed off.

"He loved the Army," I said.

Royle smiled. "He was a smart guy. Always had a book in the side pocket of his uniform so he could read whenever he had a couple minutes' down time." Royle chuckled, softly. "I remember him pulling me aside, and asking me what I thought about Special Forces. Whether he could hack it. He said he had a kid sister who was getting her PhD. That he wasn't as smart as you, so the next best he could do was to try and be the best in the Army."

I nodded as I smiled. "That sounds like Jon."

"He was just so proud of you. He loved to brag about you. And Amanda." Royle paused, absorbed in his memories.

"I just hope I haven't made things worse by helping you out," he finally continued, quietly.

"Made things worse?"

"I'm not sure Jon would be thrilled that I helped his sister get to a war zone."

"That decision—that's on me," I said, forcefully.

"Right," Royle said. He seemed skeptical.

We sat in silence for a moment. Royle stared at his feet, I looked at the roses.

"Why did you throw me under the bus with Fletcher?" I eventually asked.

"Excuse me?"

"When you were still our Chief of Staff? Remember Fletcher telling me you thought I should take the easy assignments? And then you gave me taskers that were just about impossible to accomplish."

"I thought I was helping you get to know the building before you got thrown in the deep end."

"Well, you managed to throw me in the deep end anyway."

"Yeah, I heard about that. Sorry."

"Apology accepted."

Royle sighed. "And I accept yours. Look, I know I'm not always the easiest person to get along with."

"That's kind of an understatement."

Royle chuckled and nodded. "I'm glad we're clearing the air. But none of this takes away from the fact that you've consistently proven yourself the best analyst in the room."

I looked at him with wide eyes. "I don't know about that. There's a lot of candlepower in the Pentagon—"

"Trust me," Royle interrupted. "Sure, there's a lot of brainiacs in the building trying to show everyone they're the smartest kid in town. You've proven yourself their equal, if not better, any number of times. But that's not what I'm talking about. You *care*, Heather. You get what all this means in a way that most people can't even comprehend. That's why I've been pushing so hard for you. Don't forget that."

"Thank you," I said, feeling both honored and humbled at the same time.

Royle set his hand down on the table and his fingers accidentally brushed against mine. Maybe it was because my nerves were raw with the shadows of Jon's memory. Or perhaps because I'd just parted ways with Ryan. Or maybe it was the nervous energy of being in a war zone. Whatever the reason, though the gesture was small, I was suddenly awake, alive, on fire. Royle's eyes widened in a pleasant kind of shock before he looked to the ground and tried to compose himself.

"Screw it," he finally said, almost to himself. "Carpe diem."

I looked at him, puzzled.

"Look, I helped you out at first because of Jon. And Amanda. But as I got to know you…. I didn't help you for them. I did it for you. Because you're pretty amazing, Heather. I guess—I hope that's not too weird."

I didn't know that it was possible to smile as widely as I did at that very minute.

"It's very much okay."

Despite his weariness, I could see Royle's face light up as he cracked a small, surprised smile.

"Okay, then. Great." He looked at his phone. "Nothing's on fire in my inbox. Not at the moment, at any rate." He hesitated. "Would you, uh, mind if I joined you for dinner?"

Despite the craziness surrounding us, the thought of spending a few brief hours with Royle filled me with a kind of peaceful, yet excited, warmth. It would be a couple moments of normalcy—a reprieve from the chaos that would soon engulf my life again.

"I'd be delighted, Royle."

Taking my hand, he helped me from the table and escorted me to the cafeteria. As we ate our lightly wilted lettuce salads and fried chicken, I noticed that somehow our hands were never more than a couple inches apart for the rest of the evening.

The next morning, as the plane rose above the clouds that were scattered around the dusty, snow-kissed mountains of the Hindu Kush, I thought about what I would say to Fletcher. How we would go about finding out who was behind the attacks, which was apparently only the first opening move in a much bigger game, and whether Royle and Voight and I would be able to navigate a war that was rapidly unfolding. I wondered what Amanda's next steps would be, and whether Voight would win back his wife.

I wondered whether Royle and I would explore our newfound connection. And if we did, whether it would survive the gale-force winds that he and I would face, both separately and together.

Only one thing was certain: Even though I found myself squarely in the middle of a geopolitical storm, I felt ready. I looked down at the small mud-brick villages dotting the countryside thousands of feet below; they seemed different than the day before—or was it a lifetime ago? For a fleeting moment, I felt Jon's warmth inside and out.

He's proud of me, I realized, and smiled.

ACKNOWLEDGMENTS

FIRST OF ALL, I WOULD LIKE TO THANK JIM AND SHARON, MY WONDERFUL PARENTS, WHOSE TOTAL, UNWAVERING SUPPORT OVER THE YEARS MADE THIS NOVEL POSSIBLE. You are amazing. Of course, it takes a village to raise a child, and it takes an unbelievably kick-ass modern-day "village" of friends and family to raise an aspiring novelist. You all have my eternal gratitude for the love and advice you've freely shared over the years as I've navigated government service and all its craziness, its ups and downs, successes and failures, and victories and defeats.

Lots of friends helped me along the way: George Rivera, Al Pessin, Jacob Haddon, Alana Querze, Chris Hewlett, Jenna Lane, Angie Tutt, Mike Williams, Britt Roh, Alison Garfield, Heather Williams, Zach Wolfraim, Jon Freeman, Maggie Sadowska, Jen Taylor, Theo Farrell, John Clark, Nick Peters, and Jessy Hassay.

Of course, I would be remiss if I didn't thank some of my stellar DOD colleagues: Ned Seip, Mike Vogl, Tom Cooper, Mark Jones, David Sedney, Dan Fata, Matt Duncan, Jim Townsend, Dan Chiu, Gunner Sepp, Tony Aldwell, Mike Waltz, and those of you who wish to remain nameless. Without you guys, I wouldn't have survived the Pentagon.

My colleagues and friends at the Congressional Research Service are truly some of the most incredible people I've ever had the privilege of working with. Mary Beth Nikitin, Catherine Theohary, Ian Fergusson, Carla Humud, Andy Feickert, JJ Gertler, Marty Weiss and Nate Lucas: Thank you for welcoming me into such a special place.

The Atlantic Council has also been wonderful to work with. Thanks to Magnus Nordenmann, Barry Pavel, and the team there for making me part of your (extended) team. Ryan Evans allowed me to explore some of my wacky ideas at his site *War on the Rocks,* for which I will be forever grateful.

I also want to thank Michele Flournoy, Christine Wormuth, Xenia Dormandy, Kori Schake, Janine Davidson, Aiko Lane, LeeAnn Borman, Tressa Guenov, Leslie Hunter, Rachel Ellehuus, Nina Wagner, Kitty Harvey, Heather Peterson, Monica Bachelor, Loren Dejonge Schulman, Jessica Kehl, and the many other women making a major impact within the Department of Defense and making our nation a safer place.

Among other things, Mike Flanagan helped me understand how hard it is to get a creative project off the ground. Thank you.

Jen Pooley brought her magic, amazing empathy, and extraordinary insights to multiple drafts of this book. Thank you for being such an exceptional editor. Caroline Fletcher also read multiple drafts and gave me great edits, encouraging feedback, and truffle mac 'n' cheese.

It goes without saying that Adriann Ranta Zurhellen and Rachel Miller are simply incredible agents. Thank you for believing in me, and in this project. I am extraordinarily grateful for the time and care you've taken to encourage and support me as we brought this novel to life. The Post Hill Press team has also been amazing: thanks to Ethan Blackbird for his fantastic edits, to Billie Brownell and Maddie Sturgeon for keeping the trains running on time, and to Anthony Ziccardi for giving *The Heart of War* a home.

And to Krysten Park—my dearest and oldest friend—and Irene—her amazing mother: My mom and I think it's high time for another vino evening. Don't you agree?

ABOUT THE AUTHOR

KATHLEEN J. MCINNIS is an international security policy specialist who has worked in the Pentagon, the UK Parliament, and in think tanks on both sides of the Atlantic. She currently analyzes international security and defense issues for the United States Congress. Kathleen lives in Annapolis, Maryland.